KILLED AT THE
WHIM OF A HAT

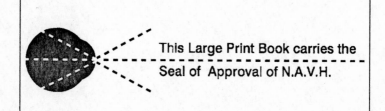

KILLED AT THE WHIM OF A HAT

COLIN COTTERILL

THORNDIKE PRESS
A part of Gale, Cengage Learning

GALE
CENGAGE Learning·

Detroit • New York • San Francisco • New Haven, Conn • Waterville, Maine • London

GALE
CENGAGE Learning™

LIBRARY OF CONGRESS CATALOGING-IN-PUBLICATION DATA

Cotterill, Colin.
   Killed at the whim of a hat / by Colin Cotterill.
     p. cm. — (Thorndike Press large print reviewers' choice)
   ISBN-13: 978-1-4104-4127-0 (hardcover)
   ISBN-10: 1-4104-4127-X (hardcover)
   1. Women journalists—Thailand—Fiction. 2. Hippies—Crimes against—Thailand. 3. Buddhist monks—Crimes against—Thailand. 4. Reporters and reporting—Fiction. 5. Murder—Investigation—Fiction. 6. Large type books. I. Title.
PR6053.O778K55 2011b
823'.914—dc22
                             2011031059

Published in 2011 by arrangement with St. Martin's Press, LLC.

Printed in Mexico
1 2 3 4 5 6 7 15 14 13 12 11

In loving memory of Joan

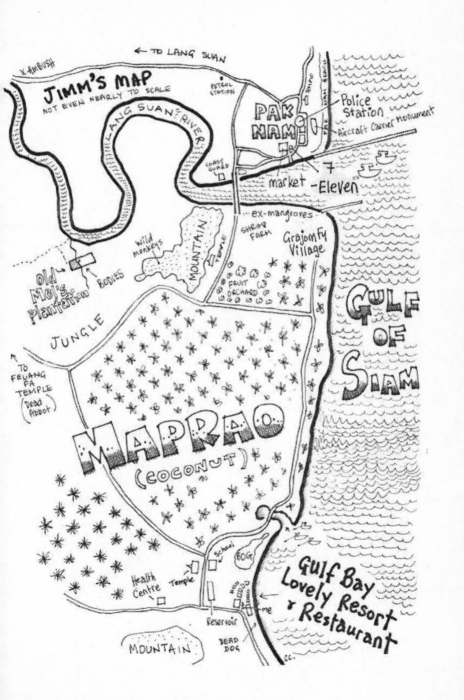

"Families is where our nation finds hope, where wings take dream."
— GEORGE W. BUSH,
LACROSSE, WISCONSIN, 18 OCTOBER, 2000

Old Mel hired one of Da's nephews — the slow-witted one with the dent in his forehead — to sink a well in his back acre. The irrigation trenches his family had dug between the rows of oil palms didn't extend to the rear fence and the new fronds were browning even before they fanned open. It hadn't rained for a month. Mel had been lugging watering cans out there for two weeks and his back bones were starting to clack like mah-jong tiles. So, a well, a cheap Chinese pump, half a dozen sprinklers, and all he'd need to do was flick a switch. Oil palms took care of themselves if you watered them often and gave them manure treats once every three months. Twenty palms

9

saved without crippling his spine. Cheap at twice the price.

So, on Saturday last, Old Mel sat on the top rung of the back fence and watched the young man work. The nephew's skull indentation made Mel wonder if he'd been hit by a metal petanque ball thrown at high speed. Such was the concavity. But he decided it was better not to ask. He knew the response would be long and slobbered. He knew the nephew would stop work to reply because he couldn't perform two functions simultaneously. So Mel merely sat and watched him dig. He could have chipped in with some labor to make the job easier but Old Mel was a firm believer in not hiring a goat and bleating himself.

The tried-and-tested southern Thai method of sinking a well would undoubtedly not have been acceptable in any Western country where concepts such as "quality" and "safety standards" were firmly in place. Four one-meter concrete pipe segments lay on the ground to one side. The nephew would dig a hole broad and deep enough to insert one of the segments. He would then jump into the hole and continue to burrow downward, scooping out earth from beneath the concrete pipe. The latter would sink into the ground like a very slow elevator. Once its top lip was level with the surface of the field, the second pipe segment would be placed on top of it and the excavation would continue. The earth in Old Mel's field was a mixture of dirt and sand and once you got below the knotty pissweed, it was not terribly hard to dig. The problems would begin — if you were lucky — when the third section was inserted and the water started to rise, turning the hole into a mudbath spa. Before the fourth segment was level with the ground, the unfortunate young man could be spending half his time submerged in murky brown water.

But on this arid Saturday morning the well would not allow itself to be sunk. At no more than waist depth below the surface, the nephew's hoe clanged against something solid. A loud metallic gong scattered the wimpy drongos from the trees. Lizards scampered from beneath rocks. The nephew was obviously enchanted by the percussion because he struck three more times before Mel could convince him to cease. The old man climbed down from his perch, hooked his toes into his sandals, and ambled over to the hole. He stopped at the concrete rim and stared down at his laborer's feet which, against all the odds, stood astride a small island of rust.

"It can't be much," Mel said. "Probably a barrel lid. Sink your hoe off to the edges. You can work your way below it and pry it up."

Easily said. The nephew prodded and poked but every foray produced the same tinny clunk. There was no way around it. For all anyone knew, the obstruction might have extended from the Gulf all the way across to the Andaman Sea and been connected to one of the earth's plates. All Mel could think about was that this sheet of metal stood defiantly between him and lower-back-pain relief. He wasn't about to give in without a fight whether it unbalanced the earth or not. He walked to the fence, grabbed a solid black crowbar and held it out to the lad.

"Here, use this," he said. "Smash your way through it."

Da's nephew stared forlornly at the tool. It was obvious some laborious mechanical process was taking place in his mind. The crowbar was getting heavy in Mel's hand.

"I'm just paid for digging," said the nephew, at last. "Nobody said nothing about smashing. That's a job for specialists, smashing is. I'm just a digger."

"Go on, boy. Look at it. It's rusted to hell.

You could sneeze a hole in it."

"I don't know, Old Mel. Wear and tear on the tools. All that added time . . ."

This was a lesson learned for Mel. A brain dent did not necessarily affect a young man's ability to extort.

"All right, look. I'm not going to pay you to start a new well somewhere else, so why don't we just say . . . what? Fifty *baht* extra? How's that?"

There was no further discussion. The nephew began jabbing the crowbar into the metal plate with renewed enthusiasm. With the fifty *baht* incentive, the young man performed like a large, enthusiastic can opener. He stood at the center of the hole and gouged through the metal around him. Like Mel, he'd probably expected to be able to lift out a perfect circle of rusted metal and continue his dig south uninterrupted. He would have anticipated a firm grounding of earth beneath the metal. He probably didn't expect in his wildest and most troubling dreams to hear that teeth-grinding creak, or to have the metal upon which he stood drop like a theatrical trapdoor. He seemed to hover in midair for a split second before plummeting into the dark void beneath him.

The silence that followed stretched into

the hot early morning like warm noodle dough. Crickets and songbirds held their breaths. A solitary wispy cloud hung overhead. Mel stood leaning forward slightly to look into the hole but all he could see was blackness. He didn't recall the lad's name so he couldn't call it out.

"You all right there?" he said. Then, realizing the newly opened shaft might be vastly deep he shouted the same question. "YOU ALL RIGHT?"

There was no reply.

A number of lands around the globe have what they refer to as a southern temperament. Thailand is no exception. Old Mel could surely have gone running off screaming for help. He might have beaten a pestle against the old tin tub that hung from his balcony or trekked those two kilometers to the nearest payphone. But he was a southerner. He broke off a stem of sweet grass to chew while he sat on the concrete segment and gazed into the abyss. There was a good deal to consider. Perhaps this had been a blessing in disguise. He wondered whether they'd chanced on an old well shaft. Saved themselves time. But there'd been no splash. It was probably dry. Bad luck, that.

"Young fellow?" he called again, half-heartedly.

There was still no response.

Mel wondered just how long was a suitable period of time before he should get anxious. He was in the middle of a plan. Go back to the shed. Get a rope. Tie it to the fence. Lower it into the hole, and . . . but there was his back problem. That wouldn't work. He'd have to call his neighbor, Gai, to —

"Old Mel."

The voice was odd, echoey, like that of a lone sardine in a tin can.

"Old Mel. You there?"

"What are you playing at down there?" Mel asked. "You stuck?"

"No, no. I had the wind knocked out of me, that's all, but I chanced lucky. I'm on . . . a bed."

"That's what they call concussion, boy. You need a —"

"No. I'm on a bed. Really I am."

"What makes you think so?"

"I can feel the springs."

"Plant roots, boy. Easily mistaken for bedsprings."

Mel realized that in the nephew's case, concussion wouldn't have made a lot of difference.

"All right, look, I need to fetch somebody," he said.

15

"You know, I can probably get myself out, Old Mel. I'm not so far from the hole. I'm looking up at it."

"You injured?"

"No, but my shirt's snagged on one of the springs. You should come down and have a look. This is odd, Old Mel. The more my eyes get used to the dark, the odder it is."

"What can you see, boy?"

"Windows."

Old Mel chuckled. "You're on a bed and you've got windows round you? Sounds to me like you've found yourself an underground bedroom. What are the odds of that?"

He was wondering where the nearest psychiatric care unit might be. Whether analysis was included under the government thirty-*baht* universal health initiative.

"And there's . . ." the nephew began.

"A bedside lamp?"

"Oh, no. Old Mel. Old Mel."

There was a real panicky timbre to his voice.

"What? What is it?"

"There's skeletons down here."

Mel was hoping he wouldn't have to be responsible in some way for the young fellow's rehabilitation. Whether he'd be obliged to employ him in some menial position in which his affliction wouldn't be too much of a disadvantage. Scarecrow, perhaps? Maybe he could find a witness who'd swear the boy was already eight points brain-dead before he fell down the old well shaft. You had to be careful these days with so many unemployed lawyers around. Mean buggers, those lawyers.

"They animal bones, boy?" he asked, just to humor the lad.

"No, Old Mel. They're people all right."

"How can you tell?"

"One's wearing a hat."

That was as far as I managed to get with the fertile prose version. It takes it out of you, writing with heart. And it was just for me really. Sort of a confirmation to myself that my inner diva can still make love to the keyboard when she's in the mood. I have to keep her roped and gagged when I'm writing for the newspapers. They don't like her at all. They don't want love. They want a quick tryst in a motel room that's forgotten in a few hours. They want dates and times and figures and facts and stats. They want the names and ages of the victims and the perpetrators, the ranks of every police officer vaguely involved with the case, the verbatim quotes from experts, and the ungrammatical misinformation from eyewitnesses. They don't care what I think. I'm just that peculiar woman on the crime desk or, at least, I used to be. I'd try to sneak in the odd metaphor from time to time but the *Mail* would set their editorial medusa on me until my piece looked like a lexicon of criminal terminology and place names. This is what hit the newspaper shops on Sunday morning.

TWO DEAD BODIES IN BURIED VEHICLE

Chumphon province. Two unidentified bodies were found yesterday in a Volkswagen Kombi Type 2 camper van, registration number Or Por 243, from Surat Thani province, buried at the rear of a palm oil plantation in Bang Ka subdistrict, Lang Suan district, Chumphon province. Police Major General Suvit Pamaluang of the Lang Suan municipality announced that the bodies were discovered at 0800 hours on the morning of Saturday 23 August by Mr. Mel Phumihan, the owner of the land. So far, the victims have not been identified and there have been no clues found as to how the vehicle became buried there.

At 1000 hours, constable Ma Yai and constable Ma Lek from the Pak Nam sub-regional municipality police station in Lang Suan sub-district were dispatched to Bang Ka following a call logged at 0923 hours. Upon their arrival at Mr. Mel's palm plantation they were met by Mr. Mel (68 years old) and his day laborer, Mr. Anuphong Wiset (22). The two men had been digging a well and had encountered an unexpected obstacle beneath the ground in the form of a complete 1972 model Volkswagen Camper van popularly known in the West as a Kombi with traces of red and cream trimming. The description of the vehicle was wired to the Surat police station and officers are still attempting to trace any missing vehicles answering this description. Desk Sergeant Monluk Pradibat at the central motor registry in Bangkok informed this newspaper that, "This vehicle will be particularly difficult to trace as computer records of missing vehicles date back only as far as 1994. Any records before that would be filed on paper forms at our central warehouse."

As to the identity of the bodies, Police Major Mana Sachawacharapong, the head of the Pak Nam police station, in whose jurisdiction the discovery was made, told our reporter, "The identities of the dead bodies and the causes of death are still being investigated. But I can tell you that this was either an accident, murder or an act of nature." The captain was not, however, prepared to rule out suicide.

They always did that, Thai police. Cover all the bases. Shot four times in the face over a period of twenty minutes? Don't rule out suicide. They'd recently found a head in a plastic bag suspended on a rope from a bridge in Bangkok and they hadn't dismissed the possibility of suicide. It gave those self-promoting senior policemen something to talk about to the press. Made them sound more important. Rather than admit "We haven't got the foggiest idea," the ranking officer of the day would go down the list of bloody obvious possibilities even if he hadn't visited the site of the crime. As long as you spelled his name correctly he'd talk to you the whole day. Perhaps you can see I have a certain dark feeling toward our gentlemen in khaki.

But the good news is, I was back. All right, I didn't get a by-line, the Thai dailies don't encourage reporter egoism, but word would get out that I'd risen from the dead. I might be living in the buttock end of the world but I could still sniff out a story. After nine months of highway traffic pile-up reports and coconut yield statistics, I'd been thrilled when I heard they'd discovered the bodies. Please let them be murder victims, I prayed. Don't get me wrong, I'm not a bloodthirsty person. I just needed reassuring that man hadn't stopped displaying inhumanity to man. I'd begun to doubt it.

I'd been sitting in one of our grass-roofed huts overlooking the bay, gutting mackerel when I heard the news of old Mel's VW. Unless we get a few sea bass or a tasty anchovy, mackerel gutting's usually the highlight of the week in our cul-de-sac of a village. Kow, the squid-boat captain, stopped by on his Honda Dream with its fishball-dispensing sidecar. He's our local Paul Revere. You don't need a cell phone or Internet connection if you have someone like Captain Kow in the vicinity. I've no idea how he hears it all but I'd wager he's a good hour ahead of the BBC on most news.

"You hear?" he yelled. Of course I hadn't heard. I never hear anything. "They found a car with dead bodies in it under Old Mel's back lot."

He smiled. He's got a sort of mail slot where his front teeth ought to be. It makes you want to doubt him but he's invariably right. His southern accent's so thick I needed a few seconds to decipher his words.

"Who's Old Mel?" I asked.

"Got twenty hectares out off the Bang Ka road just before Bang Ga."

I was elated. This was the first burst of excitement I'd felt all year. I had to get over there. My little brother, Arnon, playfully known as Arny, was out somewhere with the truck and Granddad Jah had the motorcycle. I didn't have any choice but to use Mair's old auntie bicycle with the metal basket on the front. I shouted to my mother that I was taking it and heard a faint "Make sure you put petrol in it" from deep inside our shop. Right, Mair.

Apart from the bridge over the Lang Suan river the roads are mostly flat around here, all palm and coconut plantations. Pleasant enough if you like green — I don't. There are limestone cliffs sticking up here and there, making the place look untidy, but not much in the way of hills. Old Mel's place was a good ten kilometers away and exercise wasn't one of my strong points. But you know how it is when you get the scent of blood in your nostrils. My little legs pumped away at the pedals and the adrenaline coursed through my veins and, in a sudden bubbly rush of clarity, my mind became filled with all my glory moments. The marvelous crimes I'd reported; the numerous bodies I'd stepped over — being careful not to tread in the blood — the castrated cuckolds, the jimmied ATMs, the druggies, the lesbian high-rise suicides, the motorcycle hit squads, the truck smugglers, the mysterious backpacker mutilations, the high-speed school-bus-race crashes, philandering fake fortune tellers, gangsters I'd exposed (albeit anonymously), stabbings, stranglings, garrotings . . . Oh, I could go on.

What a career I had ahead of me. My name, Jimm Juree, was synonymous with accurate crime reporting all over Thailand. Not even the simple dim fare left after the medusa had feasted on me could detract from my obvious affinity for my job. I was respected. I was one seat away from the senior crime reporter's leather chair. Saeng Thip rum had left little of the incumbent and everyone knew his health was shot and his days were numbered. They gave him six months. Then I'd be in. I'd all but been given the nod. The first female senior crime reporter in *Chiang Mai Mail* history. Only the second in the entire country. Me. Flying high.

And then, one hot early evening in August last year, my rice-paper balloon burst into flames and crashed to the ground. I obviously didn't pay enough tea money to the right people in a previous life. Our mother, Mair, despite her red-handed involvement in the affair, would continue to say it was fate. Karma, she called it, but I don't think it was any coincidence that she'd rediscovered Buddhism at roughly the same time the dementia started to kick in.

That evening, almost exactly a year ago, will be forever burned into the DVD of my soul. It plays over and over even when I'm not switched on. I see the scene. Hear the soundtrack. I know exactly which frame's going to freeze with the look of horror plastered over my face.

I'd had a great day, which made it all the worse. I mean, a great day. An old-timer in Maerim had been found shot through the temple with a pen gun. The police had arrested the teenager next door who had a history of trouble and a tattoo of a kitten impaled on a lance on his shoulder. I'd had dealings with him before. He had the devil in him, I knew, but I doubted he had the stomach for a killing. That takes an altogether different type of villain.

His grandparents had raised him, albeit badly, for the past thirteen years, ever since his bar-girl mother had dumped him and vanished without a trace. They obviously hadn't been able to do the job any better with him than they had with their daughter. I went to interview the grandparents. The police case file was officially closed and the boy was at the start of a long murky tunnel that would eventually spew him out in an adult prison for murder. He'd threatened the old-timer in front of witnesses and the police had found the murder weapon under his bedroll. They weren't looking any further. Dirt-poor family. No money for a lawyer. A nice neat victory for this month's statistics chart. Granny was distraught — unavailable for comment. But there was something edgy about Granddad. He'd been the old-timer's drinking buddy. They'd been friends since primary school. I could have marked his grunted responses and lack of eye contact down to angina or the fact he was missing his best friend, but I felt there was something else. He was a man who wanted to talk.

I went to the corner drink stand and returned with a half bottle of Mekhong whiskey. I suggested a toast to the deceased

25

— wish him well on his way through nirvana to the next incarnation. Let's hope he does better there. Granddad poured the drinks without saying a word. There was a slight shake to his hand as he passed me my glass. He raised his drink to his lips but it paused there. He snorted the fumes and looked down into the glassy brown liquor as if he could see his conscience.

"We were drunk that night," he said, more to the whiskey than to me. I put down my own glass to listen. "We often got drunk but that night was more foolish than most. He'd just come back from Fang with half a dozen bottles of hooch and that sodding amulet. He'd bought it from some Akha hill tribesman, he said. It was magic, he said. He swore to me before he'd paid for it he'd seen the Akha stare down a rifle and not even flinch when his missus fired it at him. Bullet just bounced off him . . . he said."

That was the start of the confession and neither of us touched the Mekhong whiskey the whole time. But I considered it eighty-two *baht* well spent. It turned out the old-timer had been convinced the amulet made him bulletproof and as the evening wore on and they got drunker and drunker, the neighbor goaded his friend. "Go on! Shoot me. Shoot me if you don't believe me."

26

"At first I ignored him," Granddad said. "But he wouldn't shut up about it. I knew the boy had a pen gun. I'd seen it. I fetched it more for a threat than anything else. Just to bluff him. Shut him up. You know? But it got him even more excited when he saw the gun. 'Go on,' he said. 'I know you don't believe me. Go on you coward, do it.' "

"And you did it," I said.

"Yeah."

The boy was released and the old man was charged with accidental homicide. The *Mail* let me write it up as a personal account. The medusa didn't like that. She took out all my adjectives and dumbed the piece down but it was still my story: How I solved a case the police had closed. There's no way to describe how that feels. It should have been the happiest day of the week. I bought a five-liter cask of Mont Clair red to celebrate and two packets of Tim Tam biscuits. I imagined we'd all sit around the kitchen table getting pickled, laughing at Mair who turned into a completely different person just from getting her lips wet with booze.

We had a small shop right beside the campus of Chiang Mai University. Most nights you could hear the high-pitched squeals of practicing cheerleaders — some of them female — and the late night drunken revelers careening their motor-cycles into flower beds. Serious scholars retired to Starbucks for peace and chocolate croissants. Education had changed since I studied there. Our shop didn't sell much: packet noodles, rice crackers, mosquito coils, shampoo, beer, that type of thing. We were a sort of rustic 7-Eleven. Mair had put in a few washing machines for the students to leave off their laundry and they'd invariably pick up a snack and a drink at the same time. And we were right beside a condo-minium full of *farang,* the type of white-meat foreigners who couldn't imagine a night of cable TV without half a dozen Singha beers. That was our customer base. We wouldn't make it into *Forbes* but we did all right. The bungalow we grew up in, the only home we'd ever known, was at the back.

I'd taken a shortcut through the university, always an iffy move because the guards often left early to avoid traffic. It wasn't yet four fifty but the side gates were shut. The padlocked chain was loosely wrapped. Lean Thai students could squeeze through the gap; overweight large-boned rapists could not. The girls could sleep easy in their dorms. I parked my motorcycle beside the guard post and inserted myself between the gates. A few more pizza dinners and I'd have to start driving the long way round.

I knew something was wrong when I saw my granddad Jah sitting on the curbstones in front of our shop. He was wearing his undervest and shorts and had his bare feet in the gutter. Neither the attire nor the setting were unusual. He liked to sit beside the road. Over the past few years, his reason for living had become the scrutiny of every vehicle that passed in front of our shop: study the number plate, look at the condition of the bodywork and glare threateningly at the driver. It was evening rush hour, his favorite time, but his head was bowed now and he was missing some fascinating evening traffic.

I asked if he was all right but he shrugged and pointed his thumb back over his shoulder. Granddad Jah wasn't a great communicator and I had no idea what the gesture meant. He might have been telling me about the two customers waiting in the shop with nobody there to serve them. Heaven forbid he'd get up off his haunches and do a bit of work for a change. No. Too many passing cars to observe for that. I called out to Mair but nobody came so I served the customers myself and went through the concrete yard to our kitchen. I

29

walked in on a scene reminiscent of a military court-martial.

At one end of the kitchen table sat my sister, Sissi, who at one time had been my elder brother, Somkiet. Filling up the space at the other end of the table was my current brother, Arny. He was what they referred to as a bodybuilder and this evening his T-shirt was so tightly strained across his muscles it looked as if it had been inked on. He had a wad of tissues scrunched in his right hand and it was clear he'd been crying.

Between these two sat our mother, Mair. She was dressed in a very formal black suit she generally reserved for sad occasions. She'd put on a little make-up, her hair in a Lao bun, and she looked like an elegant, middle-aged funeral director, more beautiful than I'd seen her in many a month. I did notice that the white blouse she wore beneath her jacket was buttoned wrongly. It might have been a fashion statement but I knew better. I couldn't stand the silence.

"Somebody dead?" I asked.

"Us," said Sissi, staring pointedly at the joists inside the roof. The temperature had reached 34 degrees centigrade that day but, as usual, she was wearing sunglasses and a thick silk scarf because she insisted her saggy neck skin made her look like a turkey.

It did no such thing; her neck was fine. There really was nothing sorrier than an aging transsexual ex-beauty queen. At least I used to think so.

"Does anybody want to tell me what's happened here?" I pleaded. Evidently not. Nobody spoke. The ceiling lizards were taking up their positions around the as-yet-unlit, fluorescent lamp above our heads and they were ticking with anticipation of a big night ahead. But my family was silent.

"She's sold us out."

The voice came from behind me. I hadn't noticed Granddad Jah follow me in but he now stood in the open doorway with his arms folded. It had been such a long time since I'd heard him speak I'd forgotten what his voice sounded like. The family was complete now but unstuck. I raised my eyebrows at Mair. The most wonderful if sometimes the creepiest, of my mother's traits was that she never seemed to be fazed by anything. She would greet even the most horrific moments, tragedies and accidents alike, with the same sliver-lipped smile. Her pretty eyes would sparkle and there'd be a barely perceptible shake of the head. I'd often imagined her going down with the *Titanic,* Leo DiCaprio splashing and spluttering beside her, and Mair's enigmatic

31

smile sliding slowly beneath the surface of the icy water. She was wearing her *Titanic* smile there at our kitchen table and I knew it masked something terrible.

"Mair, what have you done?" I asked.

"I . . ."

"She's sold it all," Sissi blurted out. "The house, the shop, everything."

It couldn't be true, of course.

"Mair?" Again I looked at her. She raised one eyebrow fractionally. No denial. It felt as if the floorboards had been pulled out from under me. I plonked down on one of the spare chairs.

"We're going to have a better life," Mair said. "I decided it's time to move."

"Please note the high level of consultation," Sissi hissed.

"How could you make a decision like that without talking to us?" I asked. "This is our home. We all grew up here."

"We should all die here," added Grand-dad.

"A change is as good as a holiday," said Mair. "I'm thinking of you all. You'll thank me for it."

"Is it too late to unsell?" I asked Sissi. She was our contract person, our unpaid clerk and accountant. I was sure she'd have checked the paperwork. She pulled a wad of documents from her Louis Vuitton local rip-off handbag and dropped them onto the table.

"The deed is signed, witnessed and incontestable," she said. A shuddering sigh erupted from the Arny end of the table. Granddad was seething in the doorway. We all knew the land documents should still have been in his name but he'd listened to Granny on her deathbed. Listened to her for the first time in his life.

"Sign them over to the girl," she'd said. "You could keel over any second, then the bastards at City Hall will suck all the taxes and rates out of it. There'll be nothing left. Sign it over to the girl."

So, that's what he'd done, a final promise to a woman he'd never really honored or obeyed. The one time he'd done what she asked him, and look where it got us all. As the sole owner, his daughter had no legal obligation to involve them in her decision. No *legal* obligation.

I took some time to think.

"All right," I said. "Look. Perhaps this isn't such a bad thing."

"It isn't?" Sissi was sizzling like pork in deep fat.

"No."

Of course I was lying. I was as upset as

any of them but I had to put some temporary repair work into my family.

"No. Look, we all know this house needs a lot of work," I said with a knowing look on my uncertain face. "The roof leaks even when it isn't raining and we've got a world of termites. We could use the money from the sale of this place to find somewhere better . . ." Out of the corner of my eye I could see Arny shaking his head. I thought if I ignored him the gesture would go away. "Perhaps a little out of town, a short commute. We could even have a little yard with —"

Sissi let forth with that haughty laugh she'd learned from her TV soap.

"Oh ho. But you haven't yet heard the best part," she said. "There's more to it. The move is already taken care of, little sister."

"I don't get it," I admitted.

"The money I got from selling this old place I've invested in a lovely resort hotel in the south." Mair beamed with pride. "We'll all have such a lovely time. It really is a dream come true."

It was the type of dream you have after eating spicy *hor mook* and sticky rice directly before you go to bed. I could feel the knot. The south? They were blowing each other up in the south. Everyone was fleeing north and we were supposed to go south?

"How far south?" I asked.

"Quite far," she said.

"I know the human being and fish can coexist peacefully."

— GEORGE W. BUSH,
SAGINAW, MICHIGAN, SEPTEMBER 29, 2000

The new owners were building a tall skinny condominium on our home so we had exactly two months to dislodge ourselves from our heritage. Thirty-four years of my junk and memories packed into cardboard boxes. And it was a journey into the unknown. All Mair had to go on was a computer-generated artist's impression of the Gulf Bay Lovely Resort and Restaurant at Maprao in Chumphon province. I had to look it up. It's one of those Thai provinces nobody ever goes to. You have a rough idea where it is but you couldn't pinpoint it on a map. If it was a country it would be Liberia.

We had family powwows in that first month, each of us stating our case as to why we couldn't possibly leave Chiang Mai. Sissi had her computer business and was certain they didn't even have electricity in the south. Arny was in training for the Northern Adonis 2008 Bodybuilding competition. Twice he'd been a flick of a pectoral from making it to the nationals and we were all convinced this would be his year. He needed access to a weight room and steroids. Granddad Jah cited the fact there were more homicides in Nakhon Sri Thamarat than any other province in the country. (Not terribly relevant as Chumphon was two provinces removed.) And me? Damn. I was a heart attack away from my leather chair. I loved my job. I would no sooner voluntarily leave Chiang Mai than I would spend the night in a bath of weasel mucus. I couldn't go. I wouldn't.

Mair didn't seem to care. Her mind had already left the smoggy northern city and was sipping iced water on a balcony over-looking the gently lapping Gulf surf.

"Don't you all fret." She smiled. "Your Mair's big and ugly enough to look after herself. You all go off and have a nice time. Don't worry about me. I can always hire staff."

I don't think she was being sardonic. I

37

think she really believed she could do it all alone.

"It's only a small resort," she said. "Just the five rooms. No harder than bringing up four lively children."

Unless there was something she hadn't told us, there were only the three of us, but numbers were getting a little complicated for our Mair. In fact a lot about life was starting to confuse her. So, that's why there we were, two months later, middle of the monsoons, victims of filial obligation, hanging on desperately to the end of the earth; Mair, me, Arny and Granddad Jah. Sissi moved into a studio apartment in Chiang Mai with her computers and her scrapbooks. She has issues, you see. One of those issues involves not being seen in public, a bit like what's-her-name in *Sunset Boulevard*. And "public" especially applies to sweaty rural fishing communities. She was torn between familial duty and life. This wasn't the first time she'd been torn so she knew how to handle it.

Arny and I resiliently dedicated our deeds to looking after Mair and our words to bitching about everything wrong with our lives. We'd moved to a village surrounded by coconut groves called Maprao. That means "coconut." We're in the middle of a bay called Glang Ow, which means "middle of the bay" and our nearest small town is at the mouth of a river. It's called Pak Nam. I probably don't need to translate that one for you. Pak Nam sits at the mouth of the Lang Suan river which runs through Lang Suan district from Lang Suan town. Lang Suan means "behind the garden," so we can only assume that the river once flowed through someone's backyard.

There are twenty-eight villages called Maprao down here, thirty Thai Bays, thirty-four Middle Bays, and thirty-nine River Mouths. In the south 1,276 villages are named after fruit and vegetables. Exactly 2,567 bear the name of a person who used to live there. It is precisely this absence of imagination that epitomizes the south for me. I doubt anyone down here would even care enough to sit in front of a computer screen and work it out. If southern Thais had colonized Australia I imagine the year 2000 would have seen the opening ceremony of the Big Harbor Olympics.

The computer-generated Gulf Bay Lovely Resort and Restaurant was terminally flattering. The actual place was a dump: girded with mosquito-ridden bogs, bombarded by monsoons three months a year, miles from the nearest tourist route, and . . . depressing. Each storm season the sea claimed a little more of the beach so when we arrived everything was lined up along a crest of sand with the potential to drop into the next high tide. As if ignorant of the place's failings, Mair worked in the sparsely stocked resort shop and sang a lot. Arny managed the accommodation, and I drew the short straw and ran the kitchen. And, for almost ten months, I had tolerated, withstood, and suffered, not exactly in silence, until that wonderful day when Captain Kow rode into town on his Honda and announced that two bodies had been found buried in a VW Kombi.

After asking directions for ten minutes and not really understanding the replies, I had somehow managed to stumble upon Old Mel's plantation. None of the palm fields are fenced down here. Anyone could pull up in a semi-trailer and make off with forty trees if they so wished. But they never did. I was sweaty and wobbly from the ride and I wheeled Mair's bike up the sand track. There were dogs. I'm not a big dog fan and these two weren't going out of their way to convert me. They snarled and salivated at my ankles all the way to the rear of the plot. There was a police truck parked up ahead and a gaggle of onlookers beyond it. In the U.S. you might have found a police cordon with a sentry but Pak Nam's finest were posing for photographs in front of a rapidly expanding pit. All the neighbors had brought along a hoe or a pick and were slowly digging out the VW as if it were some long-interred dinosaur.

They'd concentrated on the front end and the driver and his companion were staring out through a surprisingly clear windscreen. I could appreciate the fact they were skeletons at this stage but they had all the appearances of a perfectly calm couple out for a weekend drive. The driver clutched the wheel, and although his seat belt buckle and his beard had long since dropped onto his lap, his plastic John Lennon cap continued to hold his long hair in place. His date hadn't been so fortunate. She was as bald as a cue ball and only her stature and a thick lei of glass and plastic beads around her neck gave away her gender.

The diggers and posing policemen ignored me at first and I had a feeling I could have clambered all over the half-buried vehicle and taken any picture I wished. There obviously wasn't a great deal of crime scene investigation going on. It was a situation crying out for order so I decided it was worth a try. I marched up to the policemen, stood between them and the clicking cameras, and said, "Officers, my name is Jimm Juree, deputy crime editor at the *Chiang Mai Mail* (I deliberately omitted tense) and I'm here to report on this case."

There was a palpable hush from the photo takers and the diggers hoisted their weapons. I doubted the two young men had heard of the *Mail* or, for that matter, ever read a newspaper, but I held my ground and allowed my hand to hover like a gunslinger's over the camera hanging from my shoulder. After several seconds I was starting to wonder whether they were mute, but the younger of the two finally spoke up.

"I've got a cousin in Chiang Mai," he said. "Kovit."

I was afraid he might ask me if I knew him but instead he surprised me by telling me his cousin was the deputy director of the zoological gardens who had turned down lucrative offers from Europe and opted to stay in Chiang Mai where they were attempting to mate pandas. He meant with one another . . . I think. The constable's partner added the little known fact that pandas live for twenty years and the females only have a three-year window when they're fertile enough to get pregnant. He added that they weren't very fond of sex and the females decided when and where to "do it."

It was all very fascinating and obviously a matter they'd discussed at great length, but would it get me an exclusive on the subterranean VW? The answer arrived in a second brown and cream truck from which stepped Police Major Mana, head of the Pak Nam station. He was a middle-aged man whose dark face seemed as polished as his shoulder badges. He was short and walked as one would imagine a panda in a very tight uniform would walk. I wondered if the two constables had the same thought.

Also stepping from the truck was a skinny young officer with an old-fashioned film camera that seemed to weigh more than he could carry. Major Mana spent several minutes putting on his hat and checking it in the side mirror, then walked past me and the constables to the dig site. He stood back and glared at the stalled excavation. The cameraman stepped up, adjusted his lenses and took what would probably be a fine photograph of his major surveying a crime scene — if it came out, if it wasn't over- or under-exposed or the film hadn't melted in the camera. Digital may not be for the connoisseur but at least you don't have to wait a day to see what a cock-up you've made.

His duty obviously done, Major Mana removed his hat, dabbed his brow with a cloth and headed back to his truck. One of the two constables stepped forward and saluted as he passed.

"Major, sir," he said. "This is *Nong* Jimm from the press in Chiang Mai."

I hated it when they called me "little sibling." It's as if, just because you're short and not wrinkled, you can't possibly be as old as they are. It might have been because of the heat or a sincere respect for the fourth estate, but the major was suddenly overcome with charm. He was in such a hurry to throw his hands together in an undeserved response to my *wai* that he dropped his nice hat.

"*Nong* Jimm," he said, stepping aside for the two constables to retrieve his hat and dust it off. "Welcome to our province. If there's anything I can do to make your stay more comfortable you just have to ask."

I knew his type only too well: slick as a snake in engine oil. I decided to take advantage of his misapprehension before he learned I lived a thirty-minute bicycle ride away.

"Once I've looked around here I'd be grateful for a few words with you," I said. I was dazzled by the sunlight off his teeth.

44

"Then let me take you for a working lunch," he said. "When you're done here, of course."

It suited me. It was in my interest to know my local law enforcers and perhaps I'd get something to eat that couldn't swim, for once. A nice piece of roast pork would make the day for me. A cut of ham. A few slices of venison. I'd suffer an hour of posturing gladly in exchange for a plate of anything that, a few days earlier, had been frolicking around a field. I was losing my carnivorous *je ne sais quoi.*

It surprised me how much I enjoyed my morning at the VW excavation site. In my year in Chumphon, for some reason I'd not had the pleasure of hanging out with a large group of local, apparently unemployed, men. Several were around Granddad Jah's age but they swung those picks with the strength of men who'd carried wounded cattle across their shoulders. And everything was funny to them. Digging was a complete hoot. The repartee and laughter bounced back and forth but I would have needed a northern Thai/southern Thai simultaneous translation to appreciate the half of it. By far the funniest thing that morning was the forensic disaster.

I'd taken a number of instant digital

45

pictures of the skeletal couple that I doubted papers like the *Mail* would use. But I was sure I could sell them to *191,* the ghoul magazine in Bangkok. Nothing was too gory for them. I was wondering how to spice up the photos somehow when Uncle Ly, the dig's own stand-up comic, climbed down into the van through the hole in the roof and posed between the skeletons. His nephew took a picture with his cell phone and I was just lining up to do the same when the inevitable happened.

I suppose somebody should have asked why two skeletons could remain intact despite the absence of those physiological nuts and bolts that hold us all together. Whatever the answer, it was a poor glue, because as soon as Uncle Ly made his V sign over the shoulder of the driver, the latter collapsed like a stack of coins. We all fell silent. Then, as if they'd been joined by some unseen thread, the passenger — and I wasn't the only one to see this — tilted her head slightly to the right and nodded before joining her beau on the floor of the cab like a faithful spouse. In sickness and in health and in pieces.

It was the sight of a thoroughly embarrassed Uncle Ly attempting to put the two bodies back together that had us in stitches.

Constable Ma Yai and Constable Ma Lek came rushing over to the dig site and for a moment I was afraid they'd reprimand us for laughing at destroyed evidence, arrest us even. But first one, then the other officer made comments that merely stoked the hilarity of the onlookers and further flustered poor Ly. When it was clear the skeletons would never be the same again, the two young officers made a very good call. It was the vibration of the digging that had caused the couple to go to pieces, they decided. Everyone agreed. It seemed thoroughly unsociable not to. On my ride home I was mystified at how easily I'd become complicit in an act of deception. It must have been something in the air.

I arrived back at the resort at eleven fifty, which left me half an hour before my lunch date. As I'd deserted the mackerel half-gutted that morning, I broke the news to the family that this would have to be a Mama instant noodle day. I'd planned to have a shower after riding under a big-bellied sun for half an hour but the little god of electrical supply chose that exact moment to dig his trident into the celestial fuse box and the whole area was plunged back to the Ayuthaya period. This happened so often in our little dark corner of heaven that

I'd long since stopped swearing under my breath. My choices were: a dip in the sea that would leave me itching through lunch, or a plastic dipper from the giant jar out back that was breeding more cultures than the natural history museum. I chose the sea.

Major Mana was as amenable as a Venus flytrap. I sat opposite him squirming in my seat as the salt dried on my skin. In my bag I had the bulk of my report written at the scene. After lunch I would make a few phone calls, type it up on my laptop and send it off from the computer game shop. Being a Saturday I could be sure of a skirmish with the teenagers but I had my first real story in a year and a few bruised children was a small price to pay. All I needed from the major were the compulsory names and ranks of all the officers involved and a quote that would instill faith in the community that the police were firmly in control. In Chiang Mai we had a stock of such quotations for the ranking officers to choose from because they were often stuck for relevant grammatical phrases. I didn't have my list with me so I had to let Mana baffle readers with the murder/disaster/accident/suicide theory. The business side of our lunch had been concluded in ten minutes and I was eager to be away from there and send off my story. But as I was a visitor to the south from Chiang Mai, the major had ordered delicious local mackerel and sea bass and watched for my reaction as I consumed my meal. I managed a smile.

He had, as expected, presumed to have a bottle of "Hinnisy" brandy placed on the table for our arrival as if it were a normal service of the restaurant. I knew from a report we'd done for the *Mail* that some of these fake rural liquors could cause deformities in the newborn and rot the teeth clean out of your mouth by the third glass. But Major Mana's superglossed teeth gave me confidence and I matched him swig for swig through the meal. I can drink. I have no idea where my constitution comes from. My mother has to merely sniff a mosquito coil and she's singing old Bird Thongchai McIntyre ballads. So it has to be down to the genes of my mysterious missing father. Perhaps he was an alcoholic. Mair is ever mute on the subject. I have no recollection of him at all. Sissi, the eldest, remembers a handsome, funny man who came and went and came . . . and went. That's all we have of "Dad." No photos. No fond reminiscences from Mair. Just genes that don't seem to match.

So, anyway, we were at the fruit plate and

well down the Hinnisy and Major Mana was slurring and his volume had risen. With a wink to the restaurant owner he'd slid his chair around so he could whisper secrets into my ear. As he talked about himself the entire meal, I didn't have to lie about where I lived. He insisted on mixing our drinks from the rack of ingredients standing beside his chair. Without exception he'd put twice as much brandy in my glass and, without exception, I'd wait till he was distracted and switch glasses on him. Twice, he'd told me that he'd booked a motel room in case I wanted to rest after lunch. All the class of a dollop of lizard dung — I mean, really. Perhaps he'd never before had a lunch date who didn't sport fur or scales.

At one stage he failed to return from the toilet. Given the time it had taken for him to find the outhouse in the first place, I wasn't terribly surprised. A penis is a lot smaller than a toilet. I gave him five minutes, poured the remainder of my drink into the ice bucket and walked down to the main road where I'd parked my motorcycle.

"Did you have a nice Sunday?" Mair asked.
   "Yes, thanks."
But it was Saturday.
I still hadn't forgiven her for what she'd

50

done to us and I'd planned a full year of social disobedience, but as always it occurred to me that my acidity didn't get through her leaden mother casing. Most of the time she was Mair: sweet, happy to listen to our problems, unintentionally funny, just normal Mair. But there were times she frightened us. Her slide had started with little things. You'd see a trail of ants leading to a cupboard and you'd find an open caramel pudding in there.

"Mair, why isn't the caramel pudding in the fridge?"

"It isn't?" She'd shake her head. "That's funny. That's where I put it, child. I can't think who'd have moved it." Then there were times she'd try to change TV channels with her cell phone or to get the local radio station on the microwave. It was probably a good thing that we'd moved to southern Thailand rather than southern Chicago. Mair would pull down the shutter and go to bed and leave fifty bags of rice outside the shop for the night. I can't think why nobody ever helped themselves.

Since we moved down here, Mair had also started to develop inappropriate relationships. To understand this Thailand of ours you have to realize that some things are endemic. A politician, for example, cannot,

51

by the very definition of a politician, be entirely honest. Honest politicians have no influential friends to help them over the first hurdle — vote buying. Then there's the business community. Businessmen and women have no social obligations. The whole point of being in business is to screw — politely if possible but not compulsorily — the next guy. Which brings us to dogs. Millions are born every day. In human terms, the vast majority will not make it past their nursery school graduation. Only the fit survive which means teenaged dogs are already mean and nasty and thoroughly unlovable. Helping an infant doggy, therefore, is tantamount to defying the laws of the jungle.

But something happened in the heart of Mair when we moved south. It was as if Mother Teresa had possessed her soul. In Chiang Mai, she'd been perfectly content to chase away strays with a broom. But here she suddenly couldn't pass a crippled animal without bursting into tears. She'd stop and talk to them. I mean, words. The type of googoo language you use to confuse newborn babies. Normally a stray would flee in panic at the sight of a person but there was obviously the scent of marrow about my mother.

The first sack of bones she brought home had elbows all over. The mutt had so little meat on her she could have been the Kombi driver's family pet. Mair fed her and nursed her to health and named her John. Within the month, John was strutting around like Bambi, not quite coordinated but with that unmistakable swagger of hope. For the next six months the dog had nothing to worry about other than how quickly she could grow into her enormous feet and how many people she could charm with her damp dog smile. She didn't fool me. She wasn't tethered or caged but she stayed. I tried to explain the concept of Stockholm syndrome to my mother but she insisted that the dog remained with us because she loved us.

Buoyed by this miracle of life, Mair then picked up a naked and squeaking grub-like creature from beside the road one day. If not at death's doorstep, it was, at least, in the front garden. She recognized a potential that none of us could see and took the bundle to Dr. Somboon, the livestock specialist. Dr. Somboon had set up his after-hours veterinary clinic, not because he was fond of domestic animals, in fact he found them most unpleasant, but because very few people took their ailing cows to a clinic in the evenings. And, of course, there was much more money to be made from pets. He'd put on rubber gloves before deigning to touch Mair's latest find. He obviously recognized the angel of death hovering over the pup because all he could prescribe was euthanasia. But Mair wasn't having any of it. She ordered a cocktail of drugs for a menu of ailments and spent two weeks nursing the skin bag back to health. She kept it there in a basket under the counter of her shop repelling the few customers who chanced by. When chocolaty hair began to sprout, Mair named her Gogo: Thai pronunciation for Cocoa. Gogo had a stomach complaint that prevented her digesting her food. She ate more than me and shat like a buffalo. Her condition made her permanently menopausal. For reasons I could totally understand, she didn't like me. I didn't like her back.

So, by the eighth month of our southern incarceration, Mair had already launched a new generation of offspring which she regaled with the same love she'd afforded her children. Me and Arny were starting to hope that our services would no longer be needed. Our rival siblings were sitting either side of Mair in front of her shop when I returned from the Internet café. Gogo turned her back when I arrived but it didn't faze me. I was in a good mood. I'd sent my story to three newspapers and the photos had been snapped up by *191*. *Thai Rat* and the *Mail* wanted follow-up stories as soon as possible. I could see an end to the dark tunnel of selling empty bottles and used newspapers to the recycling truck. It was humiliating having to queue up there with our garbage. It was just one of the growing number of things I didn't like about our life. I didn't want to sound ungrateful for the opportunity to move to the backwoods marshes of Maprao but, purely for my own entertainment, I'd put together a list of my top unfavorite things about my new home.

1. Power cuts
2. The constant smell of drying squid
3. Neighbors with nothing intelligent to discuss
4. The thud of coconuts falling from trees in search of a head
5. A shallow sea so warm it breeds Jurassic life-forms
6. The drone of passing fishing boats at three a.m.
7. The close proximity of reptiles
8. No telephone line so no Internet
9. No nightlife (no daylife either)

10. Garbage from all the so-called high-class resorts being washed up on our beach.

The original list ran to sixty items but I didn't want to look like a bitch so I parsed it down.

My household duties were laid out on a roster. The seafood invariably came to me, caught by neighbors along the bay upon which we lived. For vegetables, until I could convince the chickens to lay off my vegetable garden, I had to go to Pak Nam. Pak Nam, our nearest "town" (sorry, I chuckled then), is ten kilometers from us over the Lang Suan river bridge. It's such a dinky place it's like driving a Humvee through LEGO-land. One-man footpaths crowd in on you from both sides. Blind people on motor-cycles and bicycles pop out of unseen side streets like computer game antagonists forc-ing you to swerve out of their way. Vendors push carts in front of you just for the fun of it. And Burmese, more Burmese than you can shake a cheroot at, all walking in the road as if they don't have pavements in Burma: girls with ghostly powder-caked faces and boys with long checked tablecloths hanging from their waists. At last count there were two million of them loose in our country, all probably powdered and table-clothed and walking in the road.

The heart of this annoying hamlet is the 7-Eleven. It's a bustling hub of Slurpee buying, exotic magazine browsing and self-watching in the CCTV screen above the counter. Local teenagers hang out in front on their motorcycles until seven p.m., sometimes eight p.m., largely because it's one of the few places still lit after dark. If the 7-Eleven is too exciting for you, there's always the post office. The concept of queuing, introduced to the rest of Thailand in the mid-1980s, has yet to make it to the Pak Nam P.O. Elderly ladies in floppy sun hats assume you're standing behind another customer because you're fascinated by the curvature of their shoulder blades. They smile at you, these old biddies, and step up to the counter in front of you. And they get served. But even at its busiest you will see no more than six customers jockeying for position. Our P.O. box is number two, which shows you how much correspondence passes in and out of Pak Nam. I imagine they merely lost the key to number one.

Along the street there is a small photocopy shop which specializes in gray, fluffy versions of your original. The manager puts on her shoes whenever a customer enters the shop. Next to that is a Chinese pharmacy which allows you to sample medications right there in the shop. They'll give you a cup of iced tea if a pill needs to be washed down, and privacy if you need to apply cream to a delicate spot. There's a hairdresser's with a photograph in the window that gives the false impression that Julia Roberts is a patron, and no fewer than four traditional barbershops. As this is Thailand, there are numerous food stalls and seven restaurants which all have the belief that unpainted gray wood, Happy New Year banners and glamor calendars are an acceptable style of decoration in the food and beverage industry. Despite two small establishments masquerading as coffee shops, you can't get a decent cup of coffee or an edible cake in Pak Nam. Not that you could park anywhere long enough to eat one. The spaces not taken by motorcycles and bicycles and handcarts are occupied by trucks delivering exciting goods you never actually see on sale in the shops. On very special days in Pak Nam, the intriguing odor from the fish factories squats on the town like an unwashed swabbing mop. This, is our nearest town. Have I made my point yet?

I often complained that I had the raw end of the sausage at our place as, apart from regular shopping trips into this metropolis, I was obviously the only one doing any work. Mair was in charge of the shop, which largely entailed standing at the cash drawer gazing out at the quiet road and chatting with the two or three customers who came in to buy something they probably didn't need. I suspect they felt sorry for Mair. Everything in stock was in cans, packets, boxes or bottles and some of the labels were written in languages they hadn't used since King Taksin ruled the country two-hundred-odd years ago. We had nothing fresh, exotic or home-made and, more importantly, nothing you couldn't buy from Yai Yem's much bigger shop half a kilometer along the road.

As the resort manager, Arny was in charge of the five budget bungalows that faced a largely uneventful body of water and the five thatch-roofed tables we playfully called a restaurant. Including the hectic Songkran holiday rush in April, that year we'd averaged two overnight guests and eight diners a week. Currently, our cash cow — no offense to her — was an ornithologist from Khon Kaen University who'd booked our end room for the week. She was studying the migration of hawks on a grant and was attracted to us, not for our five-star service or our luxurious rooms, but because we were so close to a bog which, evidently, the hawks were particularly fond of. I suppose I should be berated for having a fixed image of an ornithologist in my mind. There was nothing pasty, shortsighted, spidery or matronly about our own bird fancier. She was a Thai Indiana Jones type with tight-fitting safari shorts, muscled legs, luscious thick hair and a certain attitude that I admired. I have no idea where she ate or how she spent her day as she was out of her room before sunrise and back after dark. She'd paid in advance and was the nearest thing to an income our resort had experienced since we'd moved in.

With guests like this to manage, Arny found himself with a lot of free time, so he'd set up a flotsam gym on the beach. He'd improvised with old oil drums and car tires, bamboo poles and rocks. He'd chase crabs and swim till the jellyfish forced him from the water. It was all very sad to watch him roll half coconut trees from one end of the beach to the other because we both knew he wouldn't be attending any bodybuilding galas for some time, if ever again. After school, teenagers, both boys and girls would sit in clumps at the extremities of the beach where he turned around. They'd smile and be friendly and exchange small talk but it's hard to know what to say to someone like Arny. I got the feeling my brother was more of an exhibit than a celebrity.

Granddad Jah was responsible for sitting on the bamboo platform opposite and overseeing our desperate resort. He may have been distracted now and then by passing trucks and motorcycles and other old men who nodded as they passed and whom he ignored. But mainly he sat for hours beneath the banana leaf canopy, wearing one of his wardrobe of coral-white undervests . . . and he oversaw us. If he was formulating a grand plan for our improvement he never did share it.

"It's a time of sorrow and sadness when we lose a loss of life."

— GEORGE W. BUSH,
WASHINGTON, D.C., DECEMBER 21, 2004

A day after the discovery of the VW they had the entire vehicle uncovered and they'd ferried the bones to the army hospital in Prajuab. There was talk of the case being taken over by the main station in Lang Suan, the nearest "city" (sorry, I chuckled again). It was only twenty kilometers away but I couldn't let that happen. This was my case and I wanted it to stay local, within cycling distance. I'd phoned the Pak Nam station four times since that Saturday afternoon, only to be told there'd been no developments in the case and that I should be patient. My patience had expired. I demonstrated good manners and warned

62

them I was coming in to see them on Sunday.

I arrived at the Pak Nam police station at ten a.m. The building was the usual white, two-story concrete affair with a wide forecourt surrounded by token displays in flower beds: either a humble psychological ploy to calm violent criminals or a sign of the lack of anything else to do. The elderly man at the desk — Sergeant Phoom, he said his name was — beamed with sincere joy when I told him who I was. He was a soft, happy-uncle type with cropped white hair and teeth like rectangles of tapped rubber drying on a line.

"Constables Ma Yai and Ma Lek told me all about you," he said. "You met 'em at the dig site. Remember? They're around here somewhere. *Thai Rat* newspaper, isn't it? My word, you must have lived an exciting life for someone so young, mixing with all those celebrities and political nobs."

I couldn't hold back a laugh.

"I was . . . am on the crime desk," I told him. "I mix with exactly the same lowlifes that you do here: criminals, murderers . . ."

"Here?" He looked surprised. "We haven't had any serious crime here since they put the Burmese fishermen on a curfew in 2005. One murderer in the past three years and he was so drunk he couldn't find his way from the crime scene. He was there waiting for us sleeping like a baby. We get the odd domestic dispute, kids smoking ganja and chewing on buzzy *bai gratom* leaves. That's pretty much it."

My heart sank.

"Otherwise, it's community policing," he continued. "A lot of meetings, traffic control, the young people's club, football. But this VW thing, I tell you, this is the one we'll all be talking about for years to come. Plus you being here, of course." (I felt a lump of embarrassment.) "I'm afraid the major's not around today. It's supposed to be his day off but he was dragged away to Lang Suan for some emergency or other. I'm sure he would have liked to see you."

I wasn't so sure, but I was relieved to see he'd made it out of the toilet.

"So you'd be here on some type of update, I'd imagine." Sergeant Phoom was a man who liked to talk. "We ran out and got some Pepsi when we heard you were coming. Hope you're thirsty. We weren't sure what you liked so we got Coke, too. Never can be too careful. Diet Coke, I think it is, just in case you're on one. But I can see you have no need to be."

In all my years in Chiang Mai police stations I'd never been welcomed so warmly as a member of the press. The sergeant offered to take me up to the briefing room but he looked uneasy about leaving the desk unattended so I told him I'd find it. Most stations have a standard, unimaginative floor plan: open reception downstairs with bus station seats in front of the desk, interview rooms leading off to the right and the left, fines paid to a cashier behind reception, offices upstairs, briefing room at the end, couple of small cells out the back. It was one more example of the lack of individuality that typified Thai policing, in my mind. Where was the splash of color, the gay idiosyncrasy? The answer to that question I found at the end of the hall.

The sign, BREIFING ROOM, over the door was so small you'd hardly notice the spelling mistake. The door was open and inside the room sat Constable Ma Yai and another officer with the stripes of a police lieutenant but the mannerisms of a fairy. He stood and clapped his hands delicately.

"Our angel has arrived," he said.

I'd met gay policemen before. When Sissi was in her prime as a cabaret star she introduced me to a lot of her boyfriends. She had a thing for uniforms. She'd started with postmen, then worked her way up through the police ranks until reaching her ultimate high: an air force fighter pilot called Bin. But, excluding the postal workers, I'd never met a man in uniform who didn't overcompensate on the side of male testosterone when he was on the job. This officer put up no such pretense. He introduced himself as Police Lieutenant Chompu and gave me a deep *wai* just short of a curtsy. I loved him instantly. I had no idea how Lieutenant Chompu had passed his medical and his oral exam and why he still remained active in a police force that rejected applicants for the most insignificant reasons, but at that moment I could only smile with admiration at a man clearly unembarrassed by his femininity. His posh central-Thai accent suggested to me that Chompu was at the end of the line, shunted further and further away from mainline stations until he could regress no further. Here he was at the Pak Nam siding with nowhere to go.

We exchanged pleasantries and funny comments and sat down at the large Formica-topped table where upturned glasses, bottled water, small cellophane-covered packets of sweets, jumbo Pepsis and Cokes, and an island of artificial poinsettias waited for our meeting.

66

"Constable Yai is our briefing person," said Chompu. "He has a super speaking voice. Our lady typist almost melts when she hears it. So gravelly."

The constable blushed but he seemed to enjoy the compliment. He had a rather undernourished file in front of him. In fact, when he opened it, there appeared to be just the two sheets of paper inside.

"You have to realize," he said, "that once the case is taken up by any of the central police agencies like the CSD's Archive Registry in Bangkok, they aren't obliged to keep us abreast of their ongoing investigations. What we have here is the result of our own inquiries and bits we've picked up locally, word of mouth, so to speak."

I knew the Archive Registry. It was the elephant graveyard where old cases went to die. I'd done a piece on them for the *Mail*. Went down to Bangkok on the train and met up with the director. When any evidence of historical malfeasance came to light, they'd read the file and do a cursory cross-check through their computer banks. Unless a flag went up that it was connected to any ongoing inquiry, they'd bury it in an indexed grave and go on to the next. Don't forget, they can't even get the ongoing cases right. Who was going to care about thirty-year-old skeletons? The medusa had decided to trash that CSD piece, by the way, because it presented the police in a poor light. I didn't bother to point out that most police lights were dim anyway.

I knew the two sheets that Constable Ma Yai held in front of him were all we'd have to go on.

"First," he said, "the vehicle. Nothing."

"Nothing?" said I.

"The registration plate is from 1972. The Surat motor registry department didn't start to computerize their records until ninety-four. Everything before that was on card."

"Doesn't he speak well?" said Chompu. "Wasted. Wasted as a constable. He should be on the radio."

I had to smile. I'd grown up with such out-of-order asides. I missed them.

"Where are the cards?" I asked.

"Well, you have to look at it like this. We're in the south. Those cards have been through, what? Thirty monsoon seasons? Stuffed in sweaty old rusting file cabinets."

"They're destroyed?"

"Not by man, I'd say. By nature itself. Those that are still legible might be stored somewhere in boxes, but I'm not even sure where you'd look."

"The Surat motor registry department

didn't know?"

"Said all their surviving card files were sent to Bangkok ten years ago."

"I suppose it's possible some poor little secretary's there copying old registration records onto a database," said Chompu. "They probably pay her a pittance and treat her badly. Whip her, I shouldn't wonder."

I suppose I shouldn't have been surprised. There was a Stephen King short story about the edge of time where the past just crumbled away one step behind you. In Thailand, everything before computerization had joined the rot. There wasn't a great deal of motivation to go wading back through all that musty, mildewed smelly paper. Anew. Afresh. Forget the mistakes of the past and let's start making our brand-new mistakes for the future. But where did that leave us and our VW?

"Do you have the engine and chassis numbers?" I asked.

The two policemen exchanged a condescending look of admiration. You learned to live with it. Yai copied the two numbers from his sheet and handed the slip of paper to me.

"Have you contacted VW Thailand?" I asked.

"They're in Bangkok," said the constable,

as if that were reason enough not to try. Long-distance phone calls. Funny accents. Reports to fill out. Hassle. They might as well have been contacting Rio de Janeiro. I told them I'd see if I could get through.

"And that brings us to the bodies," said the constable, flipping to his second sheet. "As there were no organs to examine, no flesh, no brain matter or stomach contents, the army pathologist in Prajuab could only say with any certainty that these were one male and one female. He wasn't even sure how old they were. There were no visible traumas and, therefore, there was no obvious cause of death. But the head of the national forensic pathology institute is due down there in a few days and she might have a look." He closed the file.

"That's it?" I asked.

"Don't you think it's fascinating that they can tell the difference between male and female just from the bones?" Lieutenant Chompu said. "And they weren't even connected."

"You don't watch a lot of television, do you?" I suggested.

"Lots. Why?" he replied. "How would that help?"

Right. The countryside. All Thai soap operas and game shows. Deprived of those rich satellite helpings of crime scene investigations. These people didn't realize you could tell a man's age, nationality, religion, belt size and sexual orientation from the bar of soap he washed with that morning. We had two complete skeletons and we couldn't tell squat. Where was Kathy Reichs when you needed her?

"There was a label found among the surviving shreds of clothing," said Yai, hopefully. "It said, 'Made in India.' "

I remembered a suicide case in Chiang Rai a couple of years earlier when a foreigner was identified as Italian because he had his name in his shirt: *Signore* Armani.

"Labels can be misleading," I said.

"Of course, you're right," said the lieutenant. "Has any of this been any help to you at all?"

"No."

"Would you like to come and see the van now it's uncovered?" he asked. "I could drive you."

I had follow-ups to do for three newspapers and I had nothing to tell them. I held little hope that the fully excavated VW would offer up anywhere near enough insights to fill a column. Newspapers recognized fluff when they saw it and, as a country reporter, my offerings would be scrutinized very closely by the evil editors. I'd barely make it off the inside back page. I was dead again.

Lieutenant Chompu stopped off in the little officer's room to freshen up and I was just about to walk out into the car park when I heard the booming voice of Major Mana. I ducked back behind a pillar.

"I wasn't expecting you back today, sir," said Sergeant Phoom in his usual jolly tone.

"Here is the last place I want to be, given what's just happened," said the major.

"Something serious, sir?"

From my nook between the pillars with a cardboard SAFE DRIVING accident cut-out blocking most of me, I was able to see the major walk to the desk, lean close to the sergeant, and whisper something. I couldn't hear what he said but I noticed the sergeant reel backward as if he'd been slapped. This was a secret I wanted to know. I waited for the major to race up the stairs three at a time and I strolled over to the desk.

"Have you heard?" I asked.

"Heard what?" asked Sergeant Phoom, still pale from receiving the news.

"Oh, sorry. I thought the major would have told you by now."

"Well . . . that depends."

"Look, it doesn't matter. I don't think I'm

allowed to share it with you if Major Mana hasn't said anything."

I turned and headed for the car park but I could hear his mind ticking over behind me.

"This wouldn't have anything to do with" — and he lowered his voice — "the abbot?"

"See? You do know." I smiled. "You're just playing with me." I walked back to his desk.

"Terrible thing, isn't it?" he said.

"I was shocked. Shocked, I tell you."

"We go three years with barely a punch on the nose and then, bang, two cases in the one day."

My heart turned a little but I had to be careful now. I didn't want to alienate one of my new friends at my local station but I had some fishing to do.

"What do you think happened?" I asked, leaning across his desk.

"Now, wait," he said. "How do you know about it?"

"Sergeant Phoom," I said, with my most sincere face attached, "I'm a reporter for national newspapers."

"But there's supposed to be a news blackout."

"Never underestimate the power of the press. Come on, what's your theory?"

I could hear Chompu speaking upstairs. My time was running out.

"Well, I don't have many facts," he confessed.

"But?"

I seemed to hover there for an inordinately long time before:

"But the stabbing to death of an abbot suggests a personal conflict to me."

An abbot got stabbed? Holy mackerel. I was suddenly in the crime capital of the Eastern Seaboard. I was so excited I wanted to pee. Look out Pulitzer prize. I made a mental *wai* to the abbot for my disrespect. One last cast of the net.

"But wait, it's out of your jurisdiction, isn't it?" I tried.

"Not at all. *Wat* Feuang Fa is just on our side of road four-three-six. That's the border. Anything on the other side is handled by Lang Suan."

Chompu came tripping down the stairs and I pulled in my net. I had everything I needed. The lieutenant was shaking his hands in front of him. I took him for the type who didn't trust communal hand towels.

"Ready?" he asked.

The VW visit had lost a certain amount of piquancy for me in the past few minutes but it would have been suspicious for me to cry off.

"And willing," I said.

Old Mel was sitting on the back fence of his plantation wondering where all the peace and quiet had gone. He was admiring the water spraying from the heads of a dozen sprinklers. The blue PVC pipe upon which they perched snaked between the palms until it reached a sturdy Chinese pump. This in turn drew water from a newly dug pond at the center of which stood a rusty but surprisingly intact VW Kombi van.

"Good morning, Mel," said Lieutenant Chompu.

"Morning," said Mel.

The old man remembered me from the previous day's dig. He briefly slapped his hands together in response to my *wai*. I imagine he'd read my news report that morning, which largely ignored the thirty-minute interview he'd given me on Saturday.

"Your well is surely the envy of the province." Chompu smiled. "Such an attractive centerpiece."

"Right," laughed Mel. "Until the rust kills all my palms."

"Nonsense," said the policeman. "All that iron. They'll flourish. You watch."

The old man had been in a hurry to get

his sprinklers working. I looked around at the plantation. Deep ditches ran between the rows of palms all the way from the road to about twenty meters from the back fence. Each contained a shallow trough of water. It was a confusing layout. One that didn't make sense.

"*Koon* Mel," I said (selecting the polite "Mr." over the less-than-polite "Old"), "can you tell me why the ditches don't extend all the way to the rear fence?"

"Ah," said Mel. "We dug the ditches fifteen years ago. I was a lot fitter then. Me and my brothers dug them by hand. None of that mechanized backhoe stuff. Everyone was still planting coconut palms back then. Only a few of us had the foresight to see the future of palm oil. Now everyone's cutting down their coconut trees and planting palms. We were the pathfinders."

"So, why . . . ?" I pushed.

"Oh, right. Well, back then the ditches did go all the way to the back fence. But about seven years ago the owner of the land out there came by and asked if I'd like to buy another three hectares to extend our plantation. He said they had properties to develop and needed to sell off some of his scrubland in a hurry to grab some good building real estate in Phuket. He needed cash in hand so he was selling cheap. We had money in the bank so I said yes."

I walked to the pit and looked at the rusty VW.

"So, this vehicle was actually buried on your neighbor's land," I said.

"Yeah."

From the truck, Lieutenant Chompu had removed a large Government Savings Bank umbrella which he now held over us to keep off the sun. He remained silent as I continued my questioning.

"And what do you know about your neighbor?" I asked.

"Chinese."

I'd heard the word "Chinese" on numerous occasions down here, not used as a description of ethnicity but more to explain a multitude of ills. In a lot of South-East Asian countries there were us — the natives — and them — the Chinese business community. Old Mel had decided that "Chinese" gave me all the information I needed about his neighbor. The land beyond the fence was twenty-odd hectares of overgrown grass and shrub land. People parked their cattle there year-round to graze for free.

"Did your neighbor offer to sell you the whole lot?" I asked.

"No." Mel shook his head. "I asked, but

he wasn't interested."

"Just the three hectares?"

"Yeah."

Just the strip of land that incidentally happened to contain two dead bodies in a VW. Some coincidence. I decided it might not be a bad idea to locate the owner and have a little chat.

"Fancy a paddle?" Chompu asked, nodding in the direction of the van.

I couldn't say I was fond of the idea but that was the reason the nice lieutenant had brought us here. I doubted the investigators had left too many stones unturned but I kicked off my sandals, rolled up the legs of my jeans to my knees and lowered myself into the warm, stewy pond. The water only came to my shins but the gunk below it was so soft I sank to my thighs. Jeans probably ruined. To his credit, the lieutenant was right there beside me. We waded one cursory circuit of the old van. Things were slithering around my feet. I wanted to go home. I half expected a Transformer moment where the old VW reared up on its hind wheels and snapped at us but, of course, it didn't.

I reached the side where the sliding door had once been. It now lay beneath my feet, giving me some solid base upon which to stand and examine just how ruined my jeans were. I climbed into the belly of the beast and sat on one of the two stubs that had once been front seats. In no time, the salt air would consume this museum piece but today it stood defiant. The steering wheel poked out gamely before me. I grabbed it, half expecting it to crumble like the driver but it was surprisingly solid. A testament to German engineering. The seat, too, felt secure. The back had wilted but the square of springs beneath my bottom still squeaked when I moved. My feet were submerged in water still but I imagined that the water had only risen once the pit was dug; otherwise I doubted all this metal could have survived. The windscreen in front of me was intact. The view was a wall of dirt, but I had an active imagination: a hippy driver and his companion.

"You happy, babe?"

"Blissful."

"Glad you came?"

"Yeah. You OK to drive?"

"Sure. Not much traffic. Floating really."

"Want another smoke?"

"Why not, sweet baby? Why not?"

Mair had told me about the hippies, the cheap foreigners who came on her treks. They didn't come for the nature or the culture. They came for the opium and the mushrooms. She didn't say she'd joined in. That's one of the gaps I had to fill in myself. But Mair was something special. She'd been a lot of things. I'm guessing she was a communist for a while — spent time hiding out in the jungle during the military dictatorships. I remember hearing she'd spent time as a karaoke lounge waitress. Then she grew pomelos out in Kanchanaburi and raised, I think it was, pigs. But what I remember most warmly is her time as a tour guide. That's where most of her stories came from. Granny Noi was still alive then. She ran the shop in those days. Granddad Jah was with the police. They'd look after us when Mair was away on her tours. Her homecomings were like someone turning on a tree swathed in fairy lights. She'd have stories to tell us about exotic and weird places and even weirder people. She'd bring bags full of sweets and souvenirs, hand-crafted cloths that she'd sat and watched being woven, shells from the islands, animals crafted from straw and beautiful colored stones. I had a collection of dirt from every province in Thailand. It was New Year's every time Mair came back. Then, one time, she came home and she didn't go away again and, one by one, the fairy lights went out.

But one thing I'll never forget is Mair

laughing about the resolve with which the stingy, locally labeled "bird shit," foreigners hung on to their weed. Ganja was growing all around but in their drug-induced bouts of paranoia they'd protect their own personal stash with their lives. It was very Granddad Jah of me to assume that everyone in the seventies smoked dope. But the combination of Kombi, long hair and beads made me think I could get away with being prejudiced just this once. And I wondered where our VW couple kept their stash.

"Who did the search of the van?" I asked Chompu, who was tugging the sliding door out of the mud.

"The boss sent Senior Sergeant Major Tort to go over it."

"And he's a forensics expert?"

"No. He keeps our books in order."

"So, nobody's really . . ."

"Nope."

"And who's in charge of the case?"

"Me."

"So why haven't you . . . ?"

"Because I was just bequeathed it by Major Mana in front of the toilet door in the upstairs corridor of the police station half an hour ago. He doesn't want it anymore. Something else came up."

It certainly did. But the fact that nobody

had really looked at the VW gave me new hope. The stash. The glovebox was a gaping hole. What was left of the mattress and all the trace evidence it contained was probably in a skip behind the police station. I didn't have too many places to look. I felt under the seat and wished I hadn't. It occurred to me later that this was where all the body fluids and loose parts would have found their way over the years. I wasn't about to dive into the murky water and feel around. I was on the verge of giving up when I remembered the Web site. I'd had to look up the make of the VW before I could send my report. The site had photos of a renovation and there behind the driver's seat was a mound — some toolbox or the like — but it had stuck in my mind. It would have been directly under the mattress. A perfect hiding place. I clambered behind the seats and reached down into the shallow water.

"You look inspired," said Chompu.

I found a latch of some description and some rusty knobs.

"Have you got any tools in that truck of yours, Lieutenant?" I asked. "I think we might have something here."

"Arny, Arny, not now."

My brother was about to set off along the beach in the midday heat rolling his log. It was starting to irk me. It was up there with self-flagellation and cross-carrying. He stopped, sighed and walked over to me along the light brown sand. My brother was a creation, the answer to a problem. He'd been bullied at school due to his sensitive nature and the fact that his brother, four years his senior, wore lipstick to class. Arny spent more time playing with girls than boys so it had been relatively simple for bullies to single him out from the herd. If she'd been around more, my mother would have taught him to negotiate his way out of trouble, taught him the value of a well-placed joke. But he was left to the one-track male logic of Granddad Jah to sort him out. Toughen him up. Teach him to fight. Of course, he didn't ever learn how to fight but he did bulk up. The deeper his frustration, the harder he hit the weights. He couldn't punish the boys that were making fun of him so he punished himself. Every barb put another disk on the barbell. And soon the weight room became his sanctuary and his body his barricade.

And here he was, a mini–Mr. Universe. And the type of people who wanted to meet him saw an incredible hulk of a man. They assumed he ate pigs whole and smashed bricks with his forehead. Men wanted him as a friend because he was incredibly cool to be seen with. And women? Forget it. Once his love emotions were unscrewed there was nothing holding him together at all. Women assumed he was all animal, but in reality Arny was delicate. He was a sort of Grand Palace made of potato crisps. From a distance you saw invulnerability but you just had to lean on him slightly and he crumbled. It took a special kind of person to befriend a contradiction like that.

Arny and I were close. We'd been insepa-rable — now we were just close. Since we'd followed Mair down to nonevent world we'd been oddly distant. We'd both been too busy locked up in our respective moods.

"What is it, *pee?*" It was nice to hear him call me "older sister."

"Can you drive me somewhere?"

"OK."

That's the way it was with Arny. He'd always do what anyone asked whether he was busy or not. He'd never ask why. He'd always assume you had a good reason, otherwise you wouldn't have asked. In fact I didn't have a reason at all, not one I could explain. I just felt having Arny around on this trip might provide a distraction. Sometimes you have to follow your instincts. He was reversing the truck out of the carport when Mair came running out of the shop and stood directly behind us. Arny stamped on the brake.

"Now, what do you two think you're up to?" she asked, her hands on her waist, John between her feet.

"Going for a drive," I said. "Won't be long."

"I suppose you know how old you have to be before you can drive a vehicle on the main road," she asked.

"Mair, I'm thirty-two," Arny told her.

There was a pause, a brief awakening, then, "Well, then that's all right, I suppose."

She smiled and returned to the shop. We'd been on the road for five minutes when Arny turned to me.

"That wasn't a joke, was it?"

"No."

We turned our heads to admire a hedge of glaring yellow golden trumpet. It probably caused a lot of accidents.

"Do you think she'll get worse?" he asked.

"No, not at all," I lied. "All this fresh air and nature and healthy macrobiotic food and calcium. It's big city pollution that eats away at people's sanity. There are ninety-year-olds down here who can recall what they had for breakfast on their sixteenth birthday."

Arny drove, focusing on the white lines.

"That's because they've had the same breakfasts for the past ninety years," he said.

I laughed. "You're right."

"We did the right thing."

I knew he was talking about following Mair south.

"Yes, we did. She'll get better. She just needs something to occupy her mind."

"Yeah."

We turned at an intersection where towering casuarina trees stood sentry on either side of us. I called it Christmas corner. I was always surprised that evergreen conifers could find it so easy to grow in the tropics. Didn't they know where they were? I wondered if they had dreams of snow. They looked as out-of-place as us but they thrived. Perhaps we weren't trying hard enough.

"We stopped being brother and sister," Arny said.

"We've been angry."

"I think it's time to let it go."

"You're right."

"It's good here."

"I know."

I doubt whether a more unconvincing

exchange had ever taken place on planet Earth. Both of us desperately wanted to believe it but didn't have the acting skills to make it sound real. Before yesterday I doubt I would have even bothered to make the effort. But since then I'd been introduced to two dead hippies who were now giving up clues, and a dead abbot that nobody was allowed to talk about. I'd checked the wire services, the Web sites, even phoned the Thai Reporters' Club information line. There was no news of a stabbed abbot. Either Major Mana had tossed out a red herring (a good source of vitamin D) or there really was a press blackout. But the only way to be certain was to go and see for myself. Nowhere in our electoral district was more than fifteen minutes away by truck when Arny was at the wheel.

"Do you think we'll ever make any close friends down here?" he asked.

"I don't know. I met some nice policemen today." He looked sideways at me and laughed. "All right. I know that didn't sound like me but it's true."

"Stop it, *pee.* I can't drive and laugh at the same time."

"Really, I . . . OK, never mind."

It was nice to hear him laugh.

Feuang Fa temple was at the top of an

incline with one of our rare hills as a backdrop. From the road it didn't look like anything special but when you got to the top of the dirt track you could clearly see that it really was nothing special. There was a standard, rather dowdy prayer hall to the right, a cramped ordination hall, a gazebo and a stupa. None of these were worth investing adjectives on. The highlight of the place was a spectacular bank of bougainvilleas on the crest of the hill to the left that followed a path toward the monks' quarters at the rear. There had been little rain for several months and the plants were ablaze with color. Like Scotch whiskies, bougainvilleas were at their happiest without water.

We were only halfway up the hill when a middle-aged man in a slate gray safari suit and flip-flops stepped out from behind a large pregnant water urn with his hands up. He seemed to be some kind of low-budget sentry.

"Nothing for you here," he shouted.

Arny braked and we stared at the scrawny man through the windscreen.

"Arny," I said. "Remain calm. Don't get into one of your flaps. If it helps, you can put your hands over your ears."

I rolled down my window and gestured for the man to come to me. His footwear suggested he wasn't police. I took a gamble.

"We're here to collect our father," I said.

"There's nobody here," said the man. His voice and his teeth were great adverts for not smoking. "He's probably left already."

"Oh, I doubt that," I said.

He squared his shoulders at me.

"If I tell you there's nobody here, there's nobody here. Just turn around and leave."

Arny fumbled for reverse gear but I put my hand on his.

"I'm not leaving without my father," I told him.

"I've told y— What does he look like?"

"About thirty centimeters high and silver."

"What?"

"They cremated him yesterday. If we don't take what's left of him home, our Mair will give us no peace."

The man hesitated. Fortunately he didn't notice Arny's look of shock. The sentry gazed once toward the temple, then back at us, then he stepped away and waved us through.

"Be quick," he said as we passed.

"Thank you," I replied, *wai*'d and wound up the window. "That's weird, don't you think? Closing a temple?"

"That wasn't nice, *pee*."

"What wasn't?"

"Saying our dad's dead."

"You mean he's not? Damn. Why didn't you tell me?"

"It's just . . ."

"I know. Not respectful. Can't help but respect a creep who dumps a wife with three little babes."

"He probably had his reasons."

"Can't you hate anyone, little brother? Can't you just find it in your heart to sprinkle a handful of animosity here and there? This is the first time in thirty-two years our father's been of any value to you. I think he'd be pleased to hear he'd contributed something, don't you? Stop right here!"

"I . . . where?"

"Here. By the handcart."

Arny pulled over and I opened the door.

"Where are you going?" he asked.

"Attacking from the rear."

I climbed out.

"What do you want me to do?"

"Pull up noisily in front of the prayer hall, go inside . . . and pray."

"What for?"

If this had been a Catholic church he could have asked for our normal service to be resumed: careers, social lives, respect, access to decent cheese, but Buddhist temples didn't do wish lists.

"Just fake it."

I closed the door quietly and ran behind a bush. From there I could see him pull away with a confused look on his face. I watched him drive over to the prayer hall and park the truck. Four laymen and two monks immediately stepped out of the side office and walked hurriedly toward him. They surrounded my brother like housecats round a rat. I have no idea what he said but I saw the truck door open, the men stand back, and Arny walk, shoulders hunched, into the prayer hall. A second later he reappeared, kicked off his sandals and went back in. Religion. It's been a while.

Most temples down here have their resident nun. Nuns in Thailand don't get nearly the same respect as monks. They cook for and feed the dogs, clean, look after the garden . . . Wait. This all sounds familiar. No wonder they look so sallow, the lot of them. But it's that unspoken animosity that makes them more likely to give up top secret information.

I found my nun whitewashing a wall, half her head and one arm.

"Would you like me to just pour the can over you? It'd be quicker," I said.

My nun smiled. She was in her sixties, I

imagined, and she'd probably been a heart-breaker when she was younger. She wasn't much taller than me but unless she had some spare brushes stuffed down her shirt she'd been much more generously endowed. An old monk draped in a robe was sitting on a step with his back to her. There were barely breathing dog carcasses littered all around like casualties of a major canine battle.

"Some can whitewash," she said. "Some can repair cars. Of the two, whitewashing is my strongest hand so I suggest you don't let me anywhere near your engine."

I liked her. I suppose I could have thrashed around in the small-talk undergrowth for ten minutes and crept up on the subject, or I could just attack. I read her as more of the direct type.

"I heard your abbot got killed," I said.

"You did?"

She let the fat brush drop to her side where it put another coat on her already white sarong.

"Yup."

She seemed to be waiting for something.

"So, did he?" I asked.

"Get killed?"

"Yes."

"Should we ask him?"

"I . . . ?"

The pretty nun turned to the old monk sitting on the step. He appeared to be composing a psalm in the air with his long fingers.

"*Jow a wat,*" she said, the formal address. "This young lady was wondering whether you'd been killed."

My facts were undoubtedly less than accurate. The abbot wheeled around to look at me. He was weather-beaten like the wreck of a small canoe. His ribcage was an old Chinese abacus whose beads had been long lost, his face a clumsily sketched grid of experiences with pockmarks. Life had apparently had a go at him but he seemed comfortable in his ravaged body.

"No." He smiled.

"Well, you can't win them all," I said.

"Hoping for a dead abbot, were you?" my nun asked, still smiling.

"In a way, yes," I confessed. "But I'm also very pleased to see that the good father is alive and well."

"And how would a death improve your quality of life, young lady?" asked the nun. "I watched you breach the security post and jump from a car and sneak up on us. So, I have to assume the news of a killing was important to you in some way."

You know they're often characters with shady pasts of their own, no more free from sin than you or I, but there's something about a figure wrapped in saffron or virgin white that makes you want to tell the truth. So we sat, the three of us, and I gave them the blog version of the saga of my current life. They smiled and nodded along the entire journey, apparently fascinated by my decline. And I arrived at the juncture at which I now stood. And there was an exchange between them. If I'd been distracted by a hornet I might have missed it. And I agree I might very well be wrong, because monks and nuns and imams and Catholic priests are nothing more than little green space aliens in my mind. I'd been far too hip a teenager and too cynical a young thing to be snared by team religion. But I sensed there was a history between these two. I visualized it as a deep crimson pool in which they'd swum together somewhere in their past lives. I believe that brief unspoken look said:

"You tell her."

"No, you tell her."

There was a pause during which I heard our truck start, reverse and drive away, but I was too close here to give up and chase after it. The abbot coughed and spoke.

"Two of the men you saw walk out of my office are detectives from Bangkok. One other is a local detective from Lang Suan CID. Then there's the head of our local council. The monks are attached to the Buddhist *Sangha* Supreme Council, a branch called the *Pra Vinyathikum.* If we were police it would be known as Internal Affairs. The reason I am not down there with them, even though this is my temple — my *wat* — is that I am being investigated. In fact it would appear I am the chief suspect in a murder inquiry."

Good line.

In fact it was several seconds before I realized my jaw had dropped.

"Whose murder?" I asked.

The nun had taken up a curled, feline pose on the step beneath ours. It made me feel uncomfortable but I wasn't about to get involved in stage direction. The abbot continued.

"The monks from the *Pra Vinyathikum* arrived here two days ago with an abbot. His name was *Tan* Winai. In fact I'd met him many years before. We'd developed a friendship then but had gone our separate ways. But he had been sent here by the council to investigate a complaint — about me. Before he left Bangkok we had spoken on the telephone so I knew he'd be coming. I told him he was welcome. They have the power to disrobe monks, but there is nothing they can do to an abbot apart from put in a report to the RAD: the Religious Affairs Department. The RAD would then conduct an inquiry of its own. So, this was a very initial investigation and none of us thought too seriously about it."

"So the visiting abbot gave you details of the complaint against you?" I asked.

"He was very open. We discussed the matter at great length."

"But you weren't able to talk him out of pursuing the complaint."

"It was an interesting debate. A very contentious area. One that is not clearly laid out in the Buddhist doctrines. In many respects I could see his side of the matter. I was keen to hear all of the arguments and make my own."

"And you would have abided by his decision?"

"Of course."

"What was the complaint?"

Both the abbot and the nun smiled.

"You speak your mind," the nun said. She got to her feet and put her hand on my arm. It was my signal to walk with her. "You could very well be a southerner."

That didn't automatically register as a compliment and I was unhappy about being steered away before my question was answered. But I'd always been uncomfortably aware of rituals and unwritten rites in temples. I seemed to be the only one who didn't know all the secrets. As children, Mair had hurried us in and out of ceremonies as if some spell might infect us if we lingered too long. Consequently I always felt like a foreigner with only a basic grasp of the language.

"So?" I pushed.

We were behind the half-painted wall. The nun's voice dropped to a hush no louder than the swish of her robe.

"Abbot Kem here was accused by one of his flock of fornication," she said.

I looked at her and took a stab.

"With you?"

"Yes."

Nuns and monks and fornication. Is it any wonder I avoided it all? When I was at primary school we learned the golden rules by rote. None of them came to mind right now but . . . abbots sleeping with nuns didn't seem to be OK.

"And did you?" I asked. "Did he?"

"No."

"But you used to have . . . something."

"We have known each other for many years," said the nun. "We cared for each other. Before all this, before religion overwhelmed us, we had the most beautiful and pure friendship two people could ever know. We were, and remain, as close as any two creatures on this earth. We saw through one another's eyes, breathed the same breaths."

Perhaps I was being a bit dumb here and this probably wasn't the right time to ask about sex, but it was all relevant.

"So even with all that eye sharing and co-breathing, it was still platonic?"

"Yes."

"And you had this really nice connection but nothing came of it and you went your own ways and found religion?" I hoped I wasn't being cynical.

"Yes."

"And by chance, even though there are forty thousand *wat*s in Thailand, by some quirk of fate, you ended up here together."

She smiled again. "Of course not. We have always been in touch: letters, phone calls. We are like family. We have a connection. I think we always knew that we'd end up at the same place. Abbot Kem told me about the simple beauty of this region and I decided to move from the northeast."

OK, the millionaire question. No friends

to phone. No help from the audience.

"Are you still in love?" I asked.

The nun sighed deeply, then switched over to profound mode. She sandwiched her hands together in front of her lap and spoke to her toes. It felt rehearsed.

"When you understand the dharma," she said, "all love and hate is absorbed into a greater appreciation of the universe. Personal likes and dislikes are irrelevant. You are no longer an individual. You are a part of the whole."

Good speech. I didn't believe her. I was annoyed not to have the abbot's view of events. I needed to look into his eyes and see what his slant on all this was. For all I knew, this could all have been the nun's personal fantasy. But somehow I doubted it.

"So, you don't love each other anymore?" I asked.

I was probably sinning like hell by forcing a nun to answer personal questions about her love life, but I had a murder inquiry on my hands — at last. Thank God I wasn't shackled by any of those guilt trips that are such a lovely feature of organized religion.

"My love encompasses all," she said.

All right. Technically I'm a Buddhist. It's written there on my ID card. But I was brought up as a sort of warped realist. My mother threw me into this modern world where I was supposed to make friends with technology and alien cultures. And although part of me believes there's a higher plane where jogging and *Big Brother Thailand* and Bon Jovi aren't important, I find it really hard to believe skinny old Abbot Kem had ever stopped loving the warmest nun on the planet. But was she worth killing the IA abbot for? I'd like to see Raymond Chandler get his chops around that one.

With the detectives and the IA monks back in the office detecting and my brother and his truck nowhere to be seen, I took the opportunity to visit the scene of the crime. The live abbot, Kem, was confined to the temple grounds but not to his quarters so he walked with me along the concrete path to the spot where the dead abbot, Winai, was found. A lethargic procession of temple dogs trailed along behind us. I attempted to push him on the relationship issue but he was mute on the subject. Not surprisingly, the body was no longer ahead of us on the path, but a large section of concrete had been stained a chewed-tobacco brown.

"Lot of blood," I said.

"He was stabbed several times in the

stomach," Abbot Kem said.

I looked around. It wasn't a secluded spot at all. I could see the road clearly down the hill with our truck pulled up beside it. To the north, anyone visiting the prayer hall, the monks, the nun, all of them had a clear view of where we now stood. And at our backs, the bright bank of bougainvilleas in full bloom reared up like an advertising hoarding declaring: MURDER OF THE DAY.

"Who found the body?" I asked.

"I did."

"What time?"

"Just after three yesterday afternoon."

"What made you come up here?"

"The dogs. There was a lot of commotion. They're normally asleep around that time when the air's at its driest. I was afraid they'd come across a cobra. When I got here I found the abbot dead on the path."

"You came all this way because of a snake? Are you a snake charmer, Abbot?"

"Most of the snakes up here are harmless but we lose a lot of the dogs to cobra bites. The snakes only bite in self-defense so it's often merely a question of refereeing. I have a cane basket. I get between the dogs and plonk it upside down on top of the snake and sit on it. When the dogs get bored and go home, I release the snake."

"So, in fact, you're rescuing the snake?"

"In a way, yes."

I'd heard some wild witness statements in my time but that was a good one. However, unless any of the snakes were prepared to give evidence, it didn't do a thing for Abbot Kem. I thanked him and watched him stroll back along the path, stopping here to pick up broken branches, there to pluck a dead leaf from a plant. As I walked down to the truck, I considered the variables. One resounding question that stuck in my mind was: Would a man who valued life enough to step between a pack of dogs and a cobra be able to kill another human being? But, I'd seen stranger things.

"How did you manage to talk your way past all those policemen?" I asked Arny as I climbed into the truck.

"I didn't have to."

"You must have said som— Oh, you were anxious, weren't you?" He nodded. "And when you're anxious your eyes water." He nodded again. "And they thought you were crying and in desperate need to pray."

"It was stressful," he confessed.

I could picture the scene. Arny steps out of the truck. He's surrounded. He panics. The detectives decide the only reason a one-hundred-kilogram brick barn would burst into tears is if he's in desperate need of salvation. See? I knew there was a reason to bring Arny along. I climbed up his left side and gave him a kiss on the cheek. He liked it.

"Information is moving. You know, nightly news is one way, of course, but it's also moving through the blogosphere and through the Internets."

— GEORGE W. BUSH,
WASHINGTON, D.C., MAY 2, 2007

Two or three nights a week I'd phone Sissi in Chiang Mai or she'd phone me. We're probably as close as two siblings who have nothing in common can be. I love her but I keep expecting that phone call where she says, "Jimm, I've decided you're only pretending to like me so I don't want to talk to you anymore." That would bring her close-friend count down to exactly zero. To explain her temperament I'd need to go back a ways with this story.

When I was growing up it took me a while to realize that boys and girls were different. I'm not talking anatomically here, I mean, my brother Somkiet and I were one creature, and it was decidedly pink. We co-wore all my clothes but never his. We giggled and slapped a great deal. We had dolls and we spent an awfully long time looking at me in the shower. Mair started off angry. "You take off that nightie at once, mister, and clean your football boots." Granddad Jah bought him boxing gloves and enrolled him in the local gym. But over the years I felt a gradual decline in their resolve to divert Somkiet from the flowery path he skipped along. In fact it was Mair who gave him the final push.

At sixteen, Somkiet was at that crossroads we hear so much about and was in desperate need of good advice, preferably from a father figure. But all he got at home was Granny preparing herself for nirvana, Granddad Jah moping about his lack of advancement through the ranks of the police force, and me, hopelessly in love with Liu De Hua, the Hong Kong TV star. Nothing seemed as important to me as Liu. Even I had abandoned Somkiet. Once she'd given up her happy life, Mair waded through several years of depression. She lived like Aung San Suu Kyi under house arrest. Her world started at the pavement in front of our shop and ended at the spirit house at the back fence. We weren't much of a support group for a girl in a boy's skin.

Somkiet's two years at high school were probably miserable. He loved to study. He was smart and could have turned his hand to anything. But he was one of a small gaggle of what they call *grateuys* at his school, whose hobby was to mince around the yard, squeal loudly and do their nails during maths. There were no escape clauses, no crossovers. You had to be either one or the other: a serious student or a fairy. If peer pressure hadn't been so great, and faculty expectations so meager, Somkiet could have found his way into any university in the country. But those were confusing times. Boys who wanted to be girls had nothing to offer society beyond prostitution and lip-sync cabarets, so the latter was the road he traveled.

Before his high school graduation, Somkiet ran away from home. Actually, Mair packed him lunch and gave him a brown paper bag full of money. She no longer knew how to reason with him so she became an ally. I think at the back of her mind she believed her son would "get over it" and become one of us again. Somkiet changed his name to Sissi and worked his way up through the transvestite cabaret ranks: pot man, waiter, back-row male lip-sync chorus, male dancer, back-row female lip-sync chorus, front-row dancer, specialist dancer, and, at last, every young boy's dream — specialist lip-sync female lead. And it was there that the glamor began to wrap itself around his/her life. The regulars flashing their eyebrows and their wallets in the front row. The busy secretaries passing on the name cards of their businessmen bosses who'd like a fling — fee not negotiable.

But still Sissi's star continued to soar. Now began the beauty pageants: Miss David's Cabaret, Miss Transworld Bangkok, Miss Tran Pan Asia, all the way to Miss San Francisco Pride, all expenses paid, first runner-up. From this to spreads in straight magazines and fashion shows and advertising contracts, even a brief appearance on a television drama. Serious offers from government officials and military officers and film stars to be set up as a minor wife in her own luxury condominium. She was a sex symbol and everyone wanted her.

And then, at last, love.

An architect. A German called Walter. He courted her, followed her around, not stalking exactly, more romantic perseverance. And, most important of all in Sissi's mind, he wasn't gay. He didn't want her as a man in a dress. He wanted her as a woman and he had an unlimited budget to make it happen. No more weird sex tourists and perverts for Sissi. This was a "normal" relationship.

I remember the day Sissi arrived at the shop looking like Marilyn Monroe with her hair permed into a platinum bouffant and heels as tall as oil platforms. She had a real diamond on her ring finger. A Benz with a driver was parked opposite on our small street, blocking traffic and not caring. I ran to meet my new sister, stubby me with my Bermuda shorts and unruly hair and sleepy dust still caked around my eyes. We hugged until the rhinestones on her jacket started to gouge into my bra-less chest.

"I've come directly from the hospital," she told me.

"Are you sick?" I asked.

"No. I'm one of you now."

For a wedding present, Walter had bought Sissi the gender she'd dreamed of. I screamed with delight and we danced around the shop and she air-kissed Mair who'd remained smiling behind the counter, and she went back to her limo and was gone. I wondered why Mair had taken it all so calmly but learned soon after that she and Sissi had engaged in numerous telephone consultations leading up to the big snip. It takes a special mother to talk her son through the stratagem involved in becoming a woman.

That day was significant for me too. Once Sissi had pulled away I went back to my room, her old room, and I looked at myself in the full-length mirror and I phoned Yot and told him I'd changed my mind and I'd marry him after all.

Yot was a friend who was desperate to be married to anyone, which wasn't a great premise for a life together. Marriage to him was those paint advertisements. The dopily smiling couple in chinos and matching Lacoste. Two slightly overweight but comatose children, all sitting together on the overstuffed white leather couch. Iggy the lovable pedigree golden retriever holding back his drool for the photograph. A genuine Navajo throw rug made in Phuket. A large pot that real children and a real dog would have destroyed in seconds. Spring sunrise and clotted-cream walls inside a house that looked exactly like the one on the front of the brochure. A neighborhood of well-adjusted couples who wave and say good morning and never fart or vomit gin cocktails into the trash can at three in the afternoon because they were too drunk to make it to the bathroom.

I didn't even have any keepsakes at the end of my 3.7-year marriage to Yot the Siam Commercial Bank teller. We made no kiddies, entranced or otherwise, because I didn't want any. Who'd risk children when there are strangers with soundproof cellars driving around in panel vans? He thought he'd talk me out of that one but it wasn't open for negotiation. He thought he'd talk me out of work, too, and have me standing beside his cooked dinner in my pinafore when he came home from a hard day of bare-handling the banknotes of people with skin diseases and disgusting habits. He thought he'd coax me into feminine dresses and long tong-curled hairstyles. Call me slow, but it took me a while to realize he'd married the wrong person. He'd had her in his mind all along and he believed it was just a question of breaking me in, getting me used to the nip of her high-heeled shoes.

Once he realized his blunder I suppose he didn't have any choice but to re-advertise the post. He lied about the affairs. There were four that I knew of. I was disappointed about the first affair and for perhaps three months into the second. Then it occurred to me that I wasn't thrown into a whirlpool of misery and I didn't really care. I had a nice house to come home to and cable TV and a washing machine and dryer. What did I need a husband for? All I had to do was pretend to myself that I was living alone. I loved my job. I had my family to visit. I needed Yot to come home one day and say, "Jimm, I'm leaving you for a long-haired girl who wears dresses." Then it would have been perfect. But he didn't ever say it and he continued to share my house. I got tired of having him in my life. When I walked out I wasn't making a stand, it wasn't a statement; I'd just burrowed down to my threshold. He didn't put up much of a fight to keep me.

How did this get around to me?

We didn't hear from Sissi again until eight years ago when she turned up on the doorstep of Mair's shop and asked if she could have her old room back. I was shocked at the difference time had made. She was looking every bit the twenty-eight-year-old ex-beauty queen. Her baggy clothes couldn't disguise the fact she'd put on a lot of baggage and not even cement-thick make-up could tighten up the droop in her face. She'd let herself go and gave no impression she'd be chasing after herself any time soon. She also had no intention of telling anybody what had happened to her life.

I was still tinkering with my marriage at the time and living in my husband's home so her old room was free. She moved into it with her overnight bag and her computer and there began her self-imposed exile. The only consolation was that you can't have two recluses in the same house, there's a regulation or something, so Mair broke out of her cocoon and started to breathe again. It was a great load off her mind and I often wonder whether that escaping load might just have contained fragments of her sanity.

It was at this time that Sissi began putting down the first few bricks of her Internet empire. She purloined the wireless Internet signal from the condominium next door and began a sedentary career at the low end of the World Wide Web pecking order. Apart from teaching herself the mechanics of this awesome network she started to pick up odd jobs: marketing, translating, editing. And eight years later she was already the George Soros of dodgy Internet business. Cyber-fiddles had made her a lot of money. I tried not to ask too many details because I didn't like the idea of lying in court. What I didn't know couldn't hurt me. But I'd picked up hints about scams she was particularly proud of. For example, she had a knack for hijacking other people's porn sites and making them her own for a month or two. That was a big earner. I think she might have dabbled in Nigerian bank scams for a while and, of course, who hasn't been involved in identity theft? I believe it was hacking that gave her the most pleasure. She could break into a site, clear it out in seconds and use the information to commit audacious crimes even before the site owner was out of bed the next morning.

There were days when I asked myself how I could dedicate my life to solving crimes and apprehending villains yet do nothing to bring Sissi to justice. And the answer came to me one evening when I was playing Grand Theft Auto III with her. Why, I wondered, was I getting so much joy from blasting innocent old ladies with a sawn-off shotgun? Of course it was obvious: because it wasn't real. The world in which Sissi perpetrated her crimes didn't exist. The online banks she robbed had no bricks or mortar or pens on strings; the charities she made up were never there to begin with. Even the identities she stole were fictitious. Nobody was born with a name or address or Social Security number. They were all artificial add-ons. So, who cared if someone borrowed them? It was like kidnapping

Winnie the Pooh off the street, locking him in a cold, wet cellar, slicing off little bits of him and sending them in manila envelopes to the police. You know what? They wouldn't care. He's fiction. "Go for it," they'd say.

That's how I justify Sissi's career to myself. Her success in the cyberworld meant she had no need whatsoever for the actual, tree-dotted world beyond her walls. After dark she might have squeezed through the gate of the university and done a little power walking but she was too ashamed of her looks to go out in public in daylight. Her looks, I might add, were far from frightening. Once she'd abandoned the demon drink and started to eat Mair's nutritious but tasteless food, her old ruddy complexion began to break through the crust. Granddad Jah set her up a little exercise station in the backyard with a stationary bicycle and a fold-up yoga mat. She was looking better and starting to feel good about herself. She'd done one or two heavily disguised forays to Tops supermarket and even attempted a daylight stroll around the campus. And I think that's why Mair's act of treachery hit her so hard.

She was back in her shell now, a small dark condominium bedsit shell. She ordered in meals, had a young girl assistant who ran errands for her, and she disappeared completely inside her computer. I was one of her few links to reality so you can imagine how disappointing my regular reports from the bush had been to her so far.

"Hey, Sissi."

"Wassup?"

Oh, I forgot to mention, Sissi and I throw large helpings of English into our conversations. If we were more confident we'd probably forgo Thai completely. This stew is our sort of private language. English is what they speak inside her computer screen and I get the feeling she doesn't trust the Thai language anymore, or anyone who speaks it. The staff at her condominium think she's a Filipina. I, on the other hand, speak English because I had an overseas bridging year between high school and university. I wanted to go to an English-speaking country but they were all full so they sent me to Australia. By the time I'd worked out what they were saying it was time to come home. Mass Communication was my undergraduate major and English my minor. I was halfway through my M.A. in English when Mair sprang her little surprise on me. I speak English with the sort of Thai accent that makes words sound as if they don't have endings but Sissi understands me perfectly well.

"Nothing much. How's the Net?" I asked.

"Rocking."

"How's Leather?"

Leather was her current online Lothario. They had a stormy frantic sexual monsoon of a relationship on the Internet. In his photos he was a sort of George Clooney in bondage gear. Sissi's online persona was — Sissi, eighteen years earlier and knee-wobble gorgeous. In her mind that's how she still was.

"He's getting a six-inch screw in his scrotum," she said.

"Impressive."

"Yeah. How's the chicken ranch?"

"Two new cocks just started last weekend. They're on probation. If they haven't performed by Friday they're out."

"How hard can it be?"

"Exactly."

"Mair?"

"She's . . . I think it's good for her down here. She's crazy about her dogs and we've got the ocean right here and . . . you know."

"Yeah."

"Sissi?"

"Yeah?"

"I've got people dying down here."

"Boredom?"

"No. Murder. Do you think you can help?"

"Bloody oath."

I'd taught her that. It's Australian. It means "yes." It was one of the few things I learned down under. I talked Sissi through the VW situation right up to the last visit.

"And I found something, Sissi. This van had a shallow tool chest attached behind the driver's seat. The tools were still in there. But I found a stash of grass wrapped in plastic. It was taped to keep it dry."

"Did you smoke it?"

"Forty years on? I don't think ganja improves with age, Sis."

"It's worth a try."

"OK, but the point is, the water hadn't got in. There was paper in there, two sheets torn into quarters. I imagine they were using them as papers to smoke the ganja. And they were torn from advertising flyers I'd have to assume were from the company they rented the van from. It was a Thai travel agency called Blissy Travel located in Surat Thani."

"Phone number?"

"Yeah, but it wasn't long enough. They only had six digits back then. There's no Blissy Travel in the book now and the post office in Surat told me the address is now a

Honda service center. So I'm stuck."

"I'll see what I can do."

"Thanks. And while you're at it, can you check out a family called Chainawat? They're the ones who sold the sliver of land to Old Mel. It strikes me as more than a coincidence they'd want to off-load a plot of land with dead bodies on it."

"Any idea how they got the van in the ground?"

"The police are assuming it was a pit. Dig a big hole. Push the van in. Cover it up."

"But you don't agree."

"No, but only because it doesn't make sense. I saw the bodies as soon as they were dug out. The skeletons were seated like — all right, they were skeletons — but it was as if they were sitting there enjoying the drive. They weren't tied or gagged. If you're about to be dumped into a pit you panic, right? You try to fight your way out. You don't just sit there and stare out the windscreen clutching the wheel. The girl had her hand on the driver's thigh, damn it."

"That's really poignant."

"So you get my point?"

"Absolutely. It's weird. They'd have to die calmly, drugs or gas or something. Probably dead when they were put in the van. Sounds like a very considerate killer."

"Or a psychopath."

"Do you know whether they're foreigners or local?"

"The forensic people didn't want to hazard a guess. They said their stature was small but they're waiting for the boss from Bangkok instead of making any wild predictions. Do you think it makes a difference?"

"Sure. If they were Californian they might have just insisted on being buried with their favorite vehicle. They do stuff like that over there. I assume you don't know how old they were?"

"No, and I imagine we're out of the loop down here. I don't think anyone at the forensic lab would tell Pak Nam even if they did find that out."

"Where there's a Web there's a way."

"You won't do anything too illegal, will you?"

"If people are foolish enough to wander through darkest cyberspace with their pockets full, they deserve to get mugged. It's a lawless wasteland out here."

"And you're the queen of bandits."

"You're too kind. Anything else I can do for you?"

"I'm not sure. You got time for another story?"

I told her about the abbot and his nun

problem. The more I told her, the more I realized I didn't have enough background on any of the main characters. I'd have to make another trip over there. I gave her what little information I had and she promised to help. I was hoping she'd be able to tell me why there was a press blackout on the case. I also ordered a copy of the *Vinaya Pitaka,* the Discipline Basket containing the 227 rules for monks. It outlined the rules and regulations that governed the dharma in Thailand. I didn't want to have to compete for the printer with the game fiends at our local Internet shop so I asked if Sissi could get her Girl Friday to post it to me.

"No problem," she said.

"Has your PA actually seen you or do you conduct all your business seated behind a red curtain?"

"Now, now. No sarcasm. Kin and I have long chats."

"And she isn't repulsed by the horror of you?"

"She's Burmese."

Burmese weren't easily repulsed. They needed the money. I was glad my ex-brother had someone to talk to but it worried me that she no longer needed to get any air, polluted or otherwise.

"We all miss you," I said. "Why don't you

come down and stay with us?"

"Right. Pol Pot's blog from hell. 'It's great. Wish you were here. We could all shovel burning excrement together.' "

I took that as a no.

Mair always insisted, once I'd fed the dogs, I had to take them for a walk along the beach. These are unchained, unfenced feral animals. I tried to argue with her that if they wanted an after-meal stroll to aid digestion, they'd do it with or without me. But she did the eyebrow thing and our morning and evening constitutionals became part of my routine. Me tramping through the soft sand with John throwing herself in front of me expecting constant tummy rubs, and Gogo twenty meters behind pretending she just happened to be walking in that direction anyway. It was a good time for putting ideas together. But on the Monday morning, John didn't join us.

Arny was rolling his log and I was up in the resort kitchen making breakfast. We both looked up to see Ba Nok, the noodle lady, walking along the sand toward us. In her arms was the body of John draped limp like a long linked chain. Around John's mouth was foam as if she'd been inter- rupted cleaning her teeth but, of course, she hadn't. She was dead. Ba Nok handed over the corpse to me because Arny hadn't stepped forward to volunteer. She said that she'd found the dog in front of her noodle stand that morning. She said she'd seen our mother sitting with the dogs often so she recognized it. She thought we might like to . . .

I asked her if she knew who'd poisoned our dog and she said no too quickly. I knew she was lying. I thanked her and turned toward the shop. Mair was standing out the front with her arms folded and her *Titanic* smile already pasted across her face.

"Mair, I . . ."

She laughed a little and came to take the body from me.

"There are any number of ways a dog can meet its Master down here," she said, wiping away the foam with her hand. "A scorpion bite, a falling coconut, drowning, not to mention all sorts of diseases and insect infestations." I didn't hear "murder" on her list. "It's good that she had six months of happiness she hadn't expected. So, if you'll excuse us."

She carried John very respectfully to the rear of the shop and we decided not to follow her. I squeezed Arny's big hand and left him there with his damp eyes. We hadn't had breakfast but I got the feeling nobody would be hungry on that morning of mourning so I went for my walk by myself. I almost made it to the far copse of coconut trees before an astounding grief exploded in me. Although I was sitting on a washed up raft of old bamboo it felt as if I was being thrown to the ground, thrashed around in the mouth of a crocodile. I couldn't understand it. The tears wouldn't stop. They just wouldn't. I was pleased for once to be in this desolate place where nobody would pat me on the back and tell me it'll be all right. I'd cried plenty of times since I was ripped from my twenty-first century but all that water had been for me. Sorrow for me. Pity for me. Poor, poor me. But this was the first time I'd shed tears for somebody else — something else — and I felt ashamed for all the selfish tears I'd wasted. I looked up and sitting a few meters in front of me was Gogo. Time for her walk. Life went on.

When I arrived at Feuang Fa temple on my bicycle I expected the security man to leap out from behind the water urn but he wasn't there. I'd had to push the bike up the steep incline because the last time I was fit was in 1997: a brief three months of volleyball training I soon came to regret. I took the trail to the left that joined the concrete walkway and noticed that large chunks of the bougainvillea bushes had been ripped out in an apparent act of extreme gardening. I passed the semi-whitewashed wall and came to the nuns' quarters. My nun was sitting on her front step watching the twenty or so temple dogs. They were politely jostling for places at the large tin tray of rice and sardines she'd laid out for them. I stood back to watch. I saw not one skirmish, heard not one growl. Not one fight to the death over the last fish bone. And I thought of John.

I thought nuns were the types who'd run to a crying girl and offer her a handkerchief and a hug but this lady just sat and pretended not to notice I was bawling my eyes out. It was several minutes before I could find my voice and tell her what had happened. She tried to convince me it was John's karma, fob me off with the likelihood she'd find a better life that would erase the tragedy of this one. I hadn't really been thinking that far into the future. Someone had murdered our dog. I asked if revenge was still an option in this life. Predictably, she told me the killer would get his comeuppance in some later incarnation but it didn't make me feel any better. I wanted him to get it here and now so I could watch.

I realized I was giving off too many bad vibrations for a temple and reminded myself why I was there. I inquired as to whether I'd be able to ask the *jow a wat* a few followup questions. She surprised me with,

"He's at the central police station in Lang Suan."

"Whatever for?"

I couldn't see the old fellow as a flight risk.

"There was an incident last night."

"What happened?"

"The local hooligan they'd recruited to stand guard over the temple — you met him yesterday — he was attacked."

"Is he dead?"

I tried to temper my enthusiasm.

"No, but he was knocked unconscious. He's in the hospital."

"Do they know who did it?"

"The detectives are pointing their fingers at Abbot Kem. They reasoned he was trying to escape."

I looked around. There was no wall, no perimeter fence. Anyone wanting to escape could set off in any direction.

"That's ridiculous."

"Exactly, but they were clearly not in control of the situation here and decided it would be better for all concerned — meaning them — to have the abbot under lock and key."

"So, who jumped the guard? Was anything stolen?"

"Nothing I could see. But, as you probably noticed on your way up, the flower bed has been vandalized."

"What did Bangkok's finest have to say about that?"

"That it was probably the dogs trying to dig up a lizard. They didn't seem to think it was important."

"I think I should take a closer look."

I reached down for my sandals and found just the one. The partner was nowhere to be seen. The nun laughed.

"That would be Sticky Rice," she said.

"What would?"

"He's one of our pack. He's the youngest and the naughtiest. He's also a kleptomaniac."

She collected her own sandals and walked around to the rear of her hut. I hopped behind her. There, looking smug, was a pudding-shaped pup with the markings of a Jersey cow, one eye black. He did look like a handful of glutinous rice. He had my shoe between his teeth. He yielded it reluctantly with a few yelps, then allowed the nun to squeeze his ear.

"He looks well fed," I said.

"He eats absolutely everything: tree bark, insects, dirt, Styrofoam, plus a few unmentionables. I have no idea how he digests it all. We didn't get to your sandal a minute too soon."

We walked together to the vandalized hedge with the dogs trailing behind. The greenery was only disturbed in the area around the bloodstained path. The dirt wasn't dug so I didn't see how anyone could blame the mutts. Someone had just ripped out chunks of bush. The nun was standing over me with an enormous white umbrella that kept the sun off both of us. I was about to stand up when I noticed a cheap transparent plastic cigarette lighter lying in the gully beside the path. It was out of fluid. It probably meant nothing. Junk. A patron at a funeral takes a cigarette break and walks along the path. He runs out of fluid and chucks away the lighter. But it was either some country and western singer or Sherlock Holmes who'd said, "Nothing means nothing." It's been my mantra throughout my career so you'd think I'd know who said it. I rescued a black plastic seedling pouch from the flower bed opposite and scooped the lighter into it.

We walked back to my bicycle, the nun and I squashed together beneath the umbrella, her arm around me. An unannounced intimacy had crept up on us.

"Abbot Kem said he'd gone up to the path on Saturday because the dogs were acting up," I said. "He told me he was afraid they'd come across a cobra."

"There are a lot around here."

I looked back at the funereal procession behind us. Only Sticky Rice with a coconut husk in his mouth seemed oblivious to the cross he bore as one of the doomed dogs of the apocalypse.

"This crowd doesn't strike me as the excitable type," I confessed.

"It's hot," she replied. "None of us has much energy this time of year."

"So, what would spark a riot?"

The nun smiled and reminded me of Mair for a second. She reached up and lowered the umbrella. She folded it and handed it to me.

"Wait a few seconds, then walk after me," she said and headed off down the path.

It seemed like a weird request but I did as I was told. First one, then another of the dogs at our feet looked at me with the umbrella in my hand. Then at the nun's back. Then at me again. And suddenly I was in an alligator pit. Fangs and drool and frenzied howls and a sort of group ire that frightened the daylights out of me. I wanted to throw the umbrella down and run but the nun turned and walked to me and took back the weapon. The dogs tucked away their frenzy like cowboys holstering their guns and returned to their languid march.

"They're very protective of us," she said.

"I know how hard it is for you to put food on your family."
— GEORGE W. BUSH, GREATER NASHUA, NH, CHAMBER OF COMMERCE, JANUARY 27, 2000

"It was Monday the seventeenth of June, 1978," Mair began. "The second time I lost my virginity."

Arny and I looked up from our squid fried rice, our spoons in midair. Granddad Jah continued to eat, either because he'd heard it all before, or he hadn't heard it this time. I wasn't sure I wanted Mair to continue, not over dinner.

"I was at the temple again today," I said. It was the first thing that entered my head. I hadn't planned on sharing news of my discreet investigation but this seemed like a good time.

"His name was Krit," Mair pressed on.

"Why didn't you say?" Arny asked. "I

130

could have given you a ride."

"Because I thought arriving on a bicycle wouldn't alert anyone. And look at me, I'm already a kilo lighter and I've only been riding for a week. A month of this and I'll be modeling bikinis."

"He was very good looking," Mair said.

When we were younger we'd let go of the leash and allow Mair to run wild with her stories. We'd travel with her through her confusing history. Her accounts often fizzled and died without a punchline or a point but we'd encourage her in hope that one day she might mention our father. But she never did.

"Mair, I'm telling a true story here," I said. "Give me a minute."

I hoped I'd be able to distract her long enough to forget her second virginity anecdote. I told them about the attack on the guard and the abbot's arrest and the dogs and the cigarette lighter. Arny listened spellbound as he always had to my stories. Mair waited patiently for a gap. Then, to my surprise, Granddad Jah drank a swallow of water and stared at me, eye to eye like he was about to put a curse on me. Then he said:

"He was looking for something."

Granddad Jah had spent forty years in the

Royal Thai police force and never made it beyond police corporal, traffic division. I'd often considered there were those who were natural policemen, who climbed the ranks and passed exams and landed on a perch that was just a flutter above their ability. Then there were those who had money and could buy their promotions all the way to the top. Then there were people like Grand-dad Jah who just didn't have a clue. Like, I really needed advice from a traffic cop.

"Who was?" I asked, just for the rare experience of engaging my grandfather in conversation.

"Abbot Winai's killer," he said.

Of course I'd considered this possibility. If this were a crime novel, every reader, even the educationally challenged ones, would have shouted, "HE WAS LOOKING FOR SOMETHING." Thank you, Granddad.

"Well, if he found what he was looking for we'll never know what it was," I said. End of story.

"Maybe they had CCTV cameras," said Arny, never the most astute of the litter. He had visions of a world where every street, every house, every tree was covered by closed circuit cameras. Every crime could be solved by replaying the tapes — something like England.

"Arny, little brother, I —"

"He didn't."

Granddad was getting annoying.

"Didn't what, Granddad?"

"He didn't find what he was looking for."

"What makes you think that?"

"There was a thick cloud cover last night. No moon to see by. He didn't dare use a torch 'cause it would have been seen for miles. All he had was his cigarette lighter and he used that till he ran out of fluid. He didn't find what he was looking for."

"Granddad Jah" — I tried to filter out the condescension — "the lighter could be anybody's. It could have been dropped there a month ago."

"Ha," said Granddad. "You don't spend much time in temples, obviously. The novices are out at first light with their long straw brooms and their litter spikes. Then all the widows come with their food donations and they're on their hands and knees picking up rubbish. And then, just two days ago the place is crawling with detectives looking at a murder scene. Even the idiots they have in the CSD these days would have spotted a lighter. No, girl, the lighter arrived after all that. It was dropped there last night. It belonged to the killer and he'll be back."

He took his plate and dropped it in the washing up bowl and left. I was astounded that Granddad knew so many words. That was the most we'd heard him say since before Granny died. And, I'll give him credit, it wasn't such a bad point, either.

"Can I finish my story now?" Mair asked.

"Go ahead, Mair," I said. "But I warn you, Granddad's was a tough act to follow."

"His name was Krit," she said.

"Was that before Dad?" I asked.

"He was very good looking but he was a bastard. He was a lecturer at the university. He got one of his students pregnant and pretended he knew nothing about it. Don't forget those were the days before DMZ."

"DNA, Mair."

"Before any of that. So, there was no evidence. No proof. But I knew the girl and believed her. Krit used to come into our shop and I cornered him one day. I told him I was a virgin and I wanted my first time to be with a real man, not one of the boys on campus. I wanted a man who knew what girls expected."

There's something squalid about sitting around the dinner table listening to your mother telling sex stories, but she had a way of making the dirtiest anecdote sound like a fairy tale. Arny and I were twelve again. We

134

smiled at each other and nodded for her to continue.

"I was a little older than his usual taste but I was petite enough to get away with it, particularly in my borrowed CMU uniform. I arranged to meet him late one night at the Little Duck Hotel just in front of campus. I even booked a room. I was already inside when he arrived. I asked him to go and take a shower. By the time he came out I'd turned off the light. He could just see me under the sheet by the light from the bathroom. I told him to turn that off as well. I think he liked the dominant type. I told him I was completely naked and asked him to remove his towel and I heard it drop to the floor. That's when I screamed. The door flew open, the light came on and three students from the campus photographic club rushed in with their flash cameras and took pictures of me and him running around in our birthday suits in a state of panic. It was such fun.

"For a month, photographs of Professor Krit appeared on telegraph poles and trees all around the campus. Only his head was missing. I have to say that once the raid had taken place, the poor man shriveled to almost nothing, so the photographs were terribly embarrassing. We'd written captions such us, 'Do you know who this little fellow belongs to?' and 'Who is the little boy lecturer chasing this time?' Of course you only saw parts of me in the photos. I had a very pleasant body back then but that didn't mean I wanted everyone to see it, did it? As the month progressed, the photos showed more and more of Krit until it was obvious it wouldn't be long before everyone on campus got to see his face. As we expected, the pregnant student was approached by a third party who agreed that everything would be 'taken care of,' including a tidy sum in compensation. Once the taking care of was taken care of and the money safely deposited, I could see no reason to play the game anymore."

"You stopped putting up the photographs?" Arny guessed.

"Goodness, no. I stopped cutting off the head. It had been a mystery for several weeks, you see? You can't leave people dangling in midair, can you?"

We didn't care whether it was true or not. Like most of Mair's stories, we just appreciated it for the piece of art that it was. I was at the sink washing dishes and Mair came up behind me and put her arms round my waist. I loved the feel of her so close. I had to keep reminding myself she was in my bad books.

"That was a very good dinner, child," she said. "I don't know where you get all your skills from. Not from me, that's sure."

"With fresh produce you can make anything taste good."

I sounded like an infomercial, but it was true. One of the few good things about living far from civilization was that you got to sample foodstuff before the chemistry lab laid hands on it. A few hours earlier, our dinner had been swimming blissful circles in a largely unpolluted sea, and chillies grew everywhere like weeds. The eggs were still warm from . . . well, you know where eggs come from. And you'd just reach out the window and grab a papaya. I had a small tented garden that might one day produce vegetables. Once you became self-sufficient you could say with authority where everything on your plate came from. Which couldn't be said for the plastic container I'd come across in the freezer.

"Mair, what was that stew-like substance I found in the fridge?"

"I'm not sure what you mean," she said, and gave me an "oh oh" moment.

"That murky gray-green melted ice-cream-looking stuff."

137

"Don't touch that," she said, and released me from her motherly embrace. "It's a broth the woman at the petrol pump gave me to try."

"We could have it for dinner tomorrow."

"No. No, we won't. She's an awful cook. I took it just to be polite."

And with that she left me to do the dishes by myself. Once everything was clean and stowed, I walked down to the beach. Gogo tagged along twenty meters behind me. If the moon was full as the calendar would have it, the clouds were so thick you'd never know it. Granddad Jah was right. The squid-boat lamps formed a sparkling chain along the sea line. It was like looking at the far bank of a wide river. I walked along the sinking sand until I reached one of Arny's coconut tree logs. I sat with my back against it admiring the green and white cat's eyes that blinked at me from the horizon. Gogo strolled past me, turned two circles, then lay on the sand with her back to me. She was about two meters away. As usual, she pretended I wasn't there. I'm not sure which of us was more surprised when I clambered across to her and patted her — twice. There was no reaction. It didn't matter. I only did it in case she turned up with froth in her mouth the following morning.

At least then she'd have sampled a brief moment of intimacy with my name on it.

It had occurred to me very early in my incarceration in this colorless circus that I was slowly becoming a traditional Thai woman: regressing, slipping back through time to an age before cable and cappuccino. I looked myself up in one of those old "Understanding Thailand" books for foreigners. Why was it, I wondered, that these books were always written by Western men, usually British, who professed to know us better than we knew ourselves?

I didn't know the people in those books. I've never looked like any of the charming women in the photographs. Last year I wouldn't have found mention of myself in them at all. I was born into an era that is rapidly freeze-drying and shrinkwrapping our culture, distorting it through Western and Eastern influences. I grew up dressing like Winona Ryder and listening to Bon Jovi. My mother was a Beatles fan. My second cousin's girl is fourteen. She has dyed light-brown hair that stands up like a cartoon look of surprise, and she wears her jeans well below the belly button. All her heroes are Korean. So tell me, what is a typical Thai woman in 2008?

She'd be around 120–130 centimeters

(I'm a palm print short of that range). She certainly wouldn't wear flip-flops to go shopping, eschew the positive effects of cosmetics or consider dark skin to be more attractive than that of the cadaver-white actresses on television. She'd have a collection of cute e-mail emoticons larger than her spoken vocabulary but still have dreams to go to live in a foreign land. If the polls are to be believed, she would have experimented with booze, drugs and/or sex before she reached fifteen. She'd wear her hair long because men preferred long hair and, heaven knows, our only purpose for being on the planet is to flutter our tail feathers and snare us a mate. Sissi might argue that I'm only talking about modern gals in big cities but I know for a fact the mentality goes all the way down the food chain to the smallest village.

So where do I fit exactly? I'm thirty-four. I have the type of face that looked adorable on a twelve-year-old but that will pucker like an old peach by the time I reach fifty. I wear my hair short. I have small but whimsical breasts and a little pot belly that makes me look four months pregnant when I sit at the computer. I'm moody for long periods either side of that inconvenient time of the month — two weeks on either side. In fact,

I've never seen what it is in me that attracts, not a deluge to be true, but a steady drizzle of male interest. Perhaps the boys' mothers taught them what a nice homely girl should look like. "Get a housewife in the kitchen, then go find yourself something sexy, son."

But suddenly there are shadows of me between the pages of the Thai Female chapter. I'm slowly becoming charming, heaven help me. Since we moved south, I've been forced into a state of politeness, returning smiles from people I don't know and making conversation. In Chiang Mai I could walk around in a non-seeing social trance. I'd never find time to cook, shop, garden or feed livestock, but suddenly that's my life. And here, although I dread to say it, I feel inferior to men. They can all cut down trees and drag heavy nets full of fish and dig wells and tap rubber and build. And all I can do is gut fish, and I learned how to do that on YouTube.

This had been one interesting day. It had begun with a death and ended with a tale of revenge. It concerned me that Mair should choose that particular night to tell that particular story. If she'd been capable of humiliating a professor when her mind was still in reasonable working order, I wondered what her unfastened self might think suitable for a dog killer. It was time for me to keep a close eye on my mother.

I was woken early the next morning by the steel drum version of "Mamma Mia" on my mobile phone. We were five kilometers from the nearest landline but some communications billionaire had acupunctured our country with cell phone towers. I could see the nearest from my window, its regal rust-orange beauty marred only by the unsightly mountain view behind it. The call was from my former colleague, Dtor. She was breathless to tell me that our Government House had been invaded by old yuppies in yellow shirts overnight. Politics used to be a lot more complicated before the recent introduction of the English Premiership system of colored shirts which helped no end to know who was who. The yellows, headed by a media magnate and backed discreetly by the military, were locked in battle with the red shirts, mostly from the north, backed by an ex-football-club owner, ex-prime-minister, ex-telecommunications czar, ex-policeman currently in exile. It was a matter of time before we got the black and white stripe and the large pink polka dot factions. I kept thinking, "If you could just give them a ball . . ."

According to Dtor, during the night, the yellow shirts had strolled through police lines, staged a bloodless take-over of our seat of power and changed the curtains. The Bangkok middle classes had revolted. It might help to think of it like the Richard Branson party staging a sit-in at the Houses of Parliament in Westminster. Couldn't happen, right? That's what I'd thought. But there they were. Thai politics. I'd had the opportunity to switch to the political desk. They'd told me crime wasn't safe for a wee girl. I fought them out of the idea. The point was, in Thailand, murder and theft and violence were tangible. Politics was all smoke and mirrors and, basically, silly.

What worried me about the situation in Bangkok, apart from the fact we'd be a laughingstock in the world press, was that important things like police inquiries and monk murders and autopsies would no longer be getting any attention. All the policemen would be lined up around Government House in their macho black riot gear. And nobody knew who was in charge. The incumbent prime minister and well-respected television chef was being ousted for cooking on prime time while the country fried around him. Police chiefs were being replaced and dispatched to inactive posts with such regularity that there were more inactive police generals than active ones. So it seemed to me we'd be on our own in Pak Nam for quite some time.

Oh, and one more thing Dtor told me; the head in the plastic bag at the end of a rope? It was a suicide.

My second call of the morning was from Sissi. We had a bit of a chuckle about politics but finally moved on to something serious. The Chinese family, Chainawat, who had sold the land to Old Mel was based in Ranong on the Andaman coast. She gave me an address and several phone numbers for Chainawat Inc. and the personal number for Vicha, the current CEO. The family had, at one time, been involved in a variety of small businesses and investments but had recently amalgamated all their efforts into the fishing and real estate industries. They had some fourteen thousand hectares of land held in speculation in the south and operated a fleet of deep-sea beam trawlers that dragged enormous nets across the seabed and devastated the corals. Good for profits, sorry about the environment. Sissi hadn't been able to find any other dirt about the company's holdings but she was still digging.

Blissy Travel, the company mentioned in

the ganja papers, was dissolved in the late seventies when the expected tourist boom in the south didn't happen. Blissy had been set up by a local Surat businessman called Somjit Boondet. He seemed to have vanished after that for twenty-odd years until, in the year 2002, a Somjit Boondej arrived on the business registry as the district manager of the Surat branch of the Home Art Building Accessories Mega Store.

"I see this a lot," Sissi told me. "These slight inconsistencies in spelling. It could be a legitimate clerical error — happens all the time — but if you're an old cynic like me you're more likely to suspect foul play and less likely to be disappointed. I know from experience how easy it is to lose your old ID card and apply for a new one. You slip the typist a thousand *baht* and her finger skids on the keyboard and, voilà, you're somebody else. Nothing from your past appears on a computer security check. So, I ran a background search using the old spelling, and what do you think I found?"

"Jail?"

"You're good at this. Songkla Correctional Facility, 1979 to 2002."

"Ooh, that sounds serious."

"Manslaughter. Negligent homicide. And do you know why he'd had to serve the complete term? No pardon, no early release for good behavior? Because he killed a tourist couple."

"What? That's great. I mean, not for them, but, you know."

"I knew you'd be pleased."

"It evidently wasn't serious enough to get him a criminal murder rap."

"The prosecutor was certain. He pushed for life."

"Sissi, you're . . ."

"I know."

The day couldn't have started any better. Two leads and I hadn't even started breakfast. I showered and dressed and stepped on Gogo on my way out of the hut. She shrugged as if being stepped on was her lot in life, and fell in behind. I wanted to know why she was sleeping in front of my room but, well, she's a dog and I didn't know how to find out. Apart from our five "luxury seaside cabanas" (small conjoined concrete boxes with no refrigerators or ambiance) there were four less luxurious huts off the beach where our family lived. One apiece. According to Kow the squid-boat captain, the way the monsoons were chomping at the coastline every year, it wouldn't be long before our back cabins were beachside and our cabanas were floating somewhere off the coast of Vietnam.

I didn't see any movement in the other three huts. I was usually the first one up in the morning but that day Mair was in the shop working on what she called a display. It involved piling sardine cans into pyramids and putting a ribbon on the top. I pointed out that customers were less likely to buy the sardines because they'd be afraid of disturbing the ribbon. She told me that was nonsense.

"Ed came by again," she said.

"Do I know Ed?"

"He's the tall man who does the grass."

He sprang to mind immediately: lanky with big untrustworthy eyes and a mustache that looked stuck on. Far too young.

"And?"

"He was asking about you."

"Asking what?"

"You know. If you're single."

"But you told him, right?"

"Told him . . . ?"

"What I told you to tell any man who starts to ask personal questions."

"Well, I . . ."

"You didn't, did you?"

"I can't, child. It's not nice. And you aren't."

"Mair, it doesn't matter whether I am or

147

not. It's what they believe that counts. Men are worms, maggoty worms. They'll keep on chewing away on you unless you put a bad taste in their mouths."

Sometimes metaphors let me down when I need them most.

"He's a nice boy."

"I'm sure he is . . . a boy."

"It's not right, child. You're still young. You should be having fun with men. A bit of a kiss and a cuddle would cheer you up."

"Mair, do you really want to get into the 'You need a man' routine? Because I can play that as well, you know? So, did you tell him or not?"

"I might have said that you weren't particularly interested in men at the moment."

"Great. That's not really the same as saying I'm a lesbian, is it now?"

"All right. I'll try."

"Thank you."

"He has his own palm field."

"Every man and his cow has a palm field. I wouldn't call it financial security. You need ten hectares just to make enough money to pay the men to come and cut down the berries."

Mair did her *Titanic* smile.

"What?" said I.

"It's nice to see you developing an interest in the local markets," she said.

I walked behind her, turning over all the tins she'd placed upside down.

"Come on, Mair. We aren't catering to bats, you know."

She stopped.

"Your father kept a pet bat."

Hallelujah. My father, at last. I couldn't believe he'd snuck in. How was I to react? What should I say not to nudge her off the track?

"What kind of bat?"

"Oh, you know. The usual ugly, hairy little bastard. It used to scare the daylights out of me. He let it stay in the bedroom."

"What was his name?"

"Oh, I don't think you need to know that."

"I meant the bat."

"Thanom, you know? Like the Field Marshall. Same eyes."

I leaned on the bat story as heavily as I could. Her memory was intact when it came to Thanom but she skipped around my father with alacrity. I didn't pursue it. I had my key word now. It was like the trigger hypnotists use to put someone in a trance. I felt I could return to that time and place with Dad just by asking her about bats. Patience. It had taken thirty-four years to get this far.

"I've hired a man," Mair said.

"To do what?"

"He's a private detective."

"You hired a . . . ?"

I was astounded. Not so much that Mair had need of one but that in a place like this she'd been able to find one. And when?

"You didn't say anything last night," I said.

"I hadn't hired one then."

"Mair, I saw you go to bed. How and where did you find yourself a private detective between then and now?"

"Ed the grass man knew somebody."

"And you've contacted him already?"

"Ed stopped by his house on his way home. You'd be surprised how much is going on in Maprao early in the morning. We should all get up earlier."

"Are you telling me there's a private detective in Maprao?"

"Meng."

I dredged through the names I'd heard. It shouldn't have been that difficult. According to the official register there were five thousand residents in our district but I got the feeling that figure included everyone who'd ever died here. I was sure I'd seen every face there was to see. A couple of hundred at the most.

"Not Meng the plastic awnings man?"

"That's him."

"Mair" — I sat on the little stool at my feet — "he's the plastic awnings man. He attaches plastic awnings. That's his job."

"And window shades."

"Same difference. Tell me, where does he find time in his busy awning schedule to squeeze in private detecting?"

"There isn't a lot of detective work here."

"Of course not." I lowered my voice. "Of course there isn't a lot of work for a private detective who puts up plastic awnings. Who's going to hire him?"

"Ed did."

"Ed the grass man hired Meng the awnings man as a private detective?"

"He said he's very good."

I suppose a day that started like this one only had one direction to go.

"What, Mair, did Ed hire a detective to do?"

"To find his wife."

"Oh, super. Super. You're trying to fix me up with a married grass man."

"He's not married anymore."

"Why not?"

"Because Meng found his wife. She was living with a glazier in Lang Suan. Meng took photographs. They're divorced now."

I was exhausted.

"You found this all out this morning?"

"I think we should get up with the sun-rise."

"How much does this private detective awning man charge?"

"He said it's up to me. I can pay what I like. Whatever I think the information's worth."

"Well, that's a relief. And what information are you looking for, exactly?"

"Just local gossip."

She was so transparent I could see the sardine tins behind her.

"Mair?"

"Basic information, that kind of thing. Who lives where? What do they do for a living? If they have a boat or a truck. Where you can get hold of basic goods and materials like bricks or manure or cement . . ."

"Mair?"

". . . or rat poison."

"I am a person who recognizes the fallacy of humans."

— GEORGE W. BUSH,
OPRAH, SEPTEMBER 19, 2000

Lieutenant Chompu and I were driving across the skinniest part of the country. If you looked at the map of Thailand we were at the very squeezed waist. Since the seventeenth century they'd talked about digging a canal from the Gulf to the west coast but to lift such a long-term project off the ground it probably would have helped to have an administration in power for longer than five months. If they ever did get around to it, this would be the perfect place. There was so much pretty nature to churn up. In an air-conditioned police truck with Mai Charouenpura on the CD player and a little strawberry-shaped bottle of air freshener on the dash, the journey from one coast to the other would take us forty-five minutes. Chompu drove like a beast.

Involving the Pak Nam constabulary in my inquiry had been a calculated risk. If we stayed here, I mean if my family didn't move away or if we weren't all arrested for complicity in Mair's revenge killing, I knew I'd need friends at the local police station. I decided to share my information about the Chainawat family, and invite the lieutenant along on the interview. It couldn't hurt to have a policeman beside me. As he was now officially in charge of the VW investigation he decided it would be a lovely day for a drive and we both agreed it was such a picturesque route. He talked about the weather and the lack of excitement in Pak Nam and the joy of being in one of the last places on the planet where men all wore mustaches.

I took a chance and asked him about the progress in the Feuang Fa temple slaying. He turned his head to me with his mouth wide open and almost ran off the road.

"How could you possibly . . . ?"

"I find things out," I told him. "It's my job."

"But it's ultra top secret."

"I know."

"I shall have to watch my mouth."

154

"So . . . ?"

"Off the record?"

"Of course, unless it's really interesting."

"It's not. Believe me. Feuang Fa temple is slap in the middle of our jurisdiction. All right, perhaps not slap, but it's certainly more ours than those crustaceans at Lang Suan. My word, they wouldn't know what to do with a murder if it crept up their trouser legs and bit them on the you-know-what."

"So Pak Nam should be running that inquiry too?"

"Yes. But what do you know? Bangkok, that cauldron of anarchy and fashion disasters, decides this is too high profile for us to handle. They send down a few plain-clothes super-detectives, put a media blackout on the whole thing, set up Lang Suan as their center of operations, and pretend we don't exist. Rude, if you ask me."

"So they don't give you any feedback?"

"Not a whimper. Major Mana goes into Lang Suan every day because, technically, we're all supposed to be coordinating our efforts, sharing information. And we all know how that works, I don't think. They treat him like a motorcycle messenger. It's all take and take and no give. It's our officers doing the legwork, the interviews, the paperwork, providing the local color, but they don't tell us a monkey's back end."

"So why do you think they've blacked it out? Isn't it just 'Abbot gets killed in rural temple.' 'Another monk goes bad.' Page two of the *Daily News*. End of public interest?"

"What do I think?"

"Yes."

"Well, I'll tell you what I think. I think somebody is somebody."

A statement like that probably wouldn't have meant much to a non-Thai. But we lived in a country where being somebody, or being related to somebody, was far more relevant than what you did or how you did it. Sissi hadn't got around to discovering what had caused the news blackout but the "connection" angle was a likely one. During this great period of foolishness that pervaded in the capital, I could see a nod from a senior politician to a senior policeman suggesting, "We really don't need any more bad press right now." If either abbot was somebody's brother or a member of a certain dynasty, there were those who'd exploit the connection for political gain. It would never work as a Hollywood movie plot device because nobody in the West would believe it, but it was one of the many cancerous growths in our culture and we'd come to expect it.

"Does your major tell you what snippets he's picked up from Lang Suan?" I asked, ignoring the "somebody" track for the time being.

"Well, like I say, they don't give very much away, but Major Mana is livid. He thinks this case should be his career buster. He bitches about the whole thing. Before Bangkok came in and trampled all over us he'd handled all the initial statements, the crime scene photos, evidence searches, the lot."

"You took photos?"

"Of course."

"Can I see them sometime?"

"No."

"Don't be nasty."

"No, I mean you can't see them because they're all gone, swept up in the great CSD evidence plunder. They even emptied our computer files and took our discs."

"This sounds deep."

"Doesn't it."

"Did you see the photos?"

"I'm afraid I did. I could never forget them. Blood's never been my strong point."

"Could you describe the scene to me?"

"Do I have to?"

"It might help." Chompu pulled the truck

over to the side of the road.

"What are we stopping for?"

"I need to use my hands."

"To describe a crime scene."

"It makes it more dramatic."

"OK."

"Well, he . . . the deceased, was lying facedown on the concrete path, feet pointing . . . it must have been east. His head was almost in the flower bed, blood puddled under him half a meter to either side."

"What was his expression?"

"Couldn't see it. His whole face was masked by his hat."

"And his robes?"

"Normal enough. No wounds, no blood at the back. The major said he'd been stabbed at least a dozen times in the stomach."

Chompu stabbed into the air in front of him.

"That sounds extreme."

"We discussed that in the station once we were excluded from the loop. The frenzied stabbing ruled out a lot of small-time crimes. Unlikely to be a mugging, not that he'd have a lot of money on him. Unlikely the perpetrator was caught red-handed doing something he shouldn't. Even a hired hit seemed unlikely. This was more a . . . a grievance. It was a hate killing, either of Abbot Winai personally or of what he represented."

"Someone with a grievance against Buddhism?"

"It's happened before."

"What's to hate about Buddhism? It's the most nonviolent, forgiving religion there is."

"You never can tell. A novice abused by a monk when he was young. Someone who believed his grandma was cremated before she was dead. An old feud. Land deeds. And, don't forget, the temple's quick to welcome ex-thises and thats into its fold without background checks. There are a lot of gangsters in saffron."

"Was there anything in the evidence they took that might have pointed to a motive?"

"Nothing at all."

"And that was the last you heard from Lang Suan?"

"Yes . . . well, no."

"No?"

"There was a call asking if we'd picked up a piece of equipment they'd misplaced at the crime scene."

"What type?"

"A camera."

I had to laugh at that.

"That's rich. Someone stole the police

camera? Nobody's safe. It's a good job you took your own crime scene photos."

"I imagine they're accusing us of stealing it. We are just country policemen, you know."

I stared out of the window and a landscape of thoughts panned in front of my mind. Mai was singing "I don't want you to know."

"When did they call?"

"Who's that?"

"The people who lost their camera."

"Oh, it must have been . . . Sunday."

Perfect timing.

"Are you sure it was Lang Suan?"

"Why?"

That seemed like a fitting time to tell him about the attack on the guard at Feuang Fa temple on Sunday night. Given all he'd said about the lack of feedback, I wasn't surprised he hadn't heard. I reached into my shoulder bag and handed him a black plastic pouch containing an empty cigarette lighter. I told him where I'd found it and what my granddad had said about the likelihood of it being dropped by the attacker.

"Are you suggesting it was the killer who phoned to see if we'd found a camera?"

"It's a theory."

"And once he found out we didn't have it . . ."

"He went back to the temple to look for it. He tore half the hedge down."

"And, if your granddad's right, his lighter ran out of fluid before he could find it."

"Either that or he found it just as the lighter was running out, or after a fumble in the dark, in which case we'll never know. But at the very least you might have the killer's fingerprint on that lighter."

"But if we didn't find the camera, and he didn't find it, that could mean someone else did."

"The plot thickens. What are you going to do?"

"As soon as I get a moment I'll call this in to the major. The first thing we need to do is confirm whether it was Lang Suan who phoned. Then we'll see."

We drove through the rich green hills of Phato, passed Pak Song in a blur and reached the west coast with hunger in our bellies. Before heading into Ranong we stopped off at the main intersection with highway 4 and ordered yellow rice and chicken and green curry soup and, although the lieutenant was on duty, I indulged in a small Chang beer. To my surprise it arrived so cold it poured like sleet from the bottle. The first sip froze my brain and loosened my tongue.

"Exactly how did you get into the force in the first place?" I asked him.

"How do you mean?" He smiled.

"I've seen the recruitment process. I've read the protocols. If you'd been this camp at the interview there's no way they'd have let you in."

I thought I'd overstepped. It wouldn't have been the first time. I got the feeling he was angry and I was about to apologize, but . . .

"I acted," he said. "I'd debated making an issue of it, you know? Inviting the TV stations to come. Getting someone on camera to explain why people with my characteristics wouldn't be suitable for the police force. Nobody had ever attempted it. Of course there are lots of gays in uniform but they're all in their respective closets, not daring to poke their heads out. But when it came down to the wire, I chickened out. I was afraid they'd pretend I had some other fault which was the reason I'd been rejected and embarrass me with that instead. I was afraid I'd make my point and lose my opportunity. So I took the job over the principle."

"And spent your career being transferred to nowhere places like Pak Nam."

"What makes you think I didn't request this?"

"You're a waste of talent, Lieutenant."
"You're too sweet."

The Chainawat building was a modest two-story slab of bricks not far from the bustling dockland of Ranong. There were a number of places with the same lack of style in the dusty side street. The southern Chinese went for simple practicality in their workplaces until they'd made as much money as they possibly could, then built gaudy, furniture-filled homes to retire to. Then they found they still spent most of their time in the workplace because, actually, you can never make too much money. In Thailand it was the Chinese who'd developed the south. Without them, the native southerners would still be lying in their hammocks sipping coconut water. Well, no. Come to think of it the natives still were. But the Chinese liked to work. It was tin that attracted them in the seventeenth century. Once they'd exhausted that they put in the southern train line to transport rubber to the capital. Despite what Old Mel would have us believe, it was the Chinese who introduced the oil palm, closely followed by drugs, gambling and prostitution. And with all that revenue, legal and otherwise, it was only fitting for the Siamese court to send out

Chinese accountants to count the money. A lot of them became so rich counting it that they dug in as governors. Money and power became inextricably tied. You won't find too many prime ministers over the past two hundred years without some decantation of Chinese blood in their veins.

But for those of southern stock, refugees from Malaysia and India, there's always been that dilemma — that unanswered question: "Why would you want to work eighteen hours a day just to make money when you could lie back and watch the terns skim across the surface of the water, when you could marvel at the height of a coconut palm or put mind bets on the layers of cloud that raced at different speeds overhead?"

Small fat children on bicycles played in front of the Chainawat building, watched by an elderly lady so white and crinkly she appeared to have been carved out of polystyrene with a box cutter. She glared at us. This street, like the whole of Ranong, smelled of fish. We walked into a large reception space with nothing but an island of clunky wooden benches arranged into a square around an unmatching glass coffee table. A small child played with letter bricks on the tiled floor. A cat rolled over and exposed her nipples at us when we walked past. The middle-aged man who appeared from a side room seemed not at all pleased to see a strange uniformed officer in his midst. Companies had their regular police to pay off and didn't appreciate interlopers.

"Yeah?" he said. He looked like Jackie Chan's accident-prone brother. We'd decided to let Chompu do the talking.

"We're looking for Vicha Chainawat."

"Yeah."

It wasn't clear whether we'd found him or if he'd merely understood the question.

"Are you Vicha Chainawat?"

"No," he said, and headed off toward a rear office. We assumed we were supposed to trot after him. This was a busy place with peopled desks and tables and computer banks and, seen through the French windows, Burmese women in long sarongs packing dried fish into plastic bags. There really was nowhere in the south where you didn't trip over our disadvantaged neighbors. Our escort abandoned us in the midst of all this. We stood there like hat stands until, a minute later, Jackie's brother returned with an old lady and an absolutely gorgeous man. Memories of my incomplete love affair with Liu De Hua came flooding back into my underused heart. He wore a shirt so white and with such precisely ironed

165

seams he looked like a wing of the Sydney Opera House in sunlight.

"Can I help you?" he asked.

Oh, yes, I thought.

Chompu stepped in and introduced himself and gave his rank and offered up my name without any explanation. Vicha led us back to the wooden benches and the coffee table which had miraculously sprouted glasses of red fizzy Fanta, a plate of rambutan and several little peanut biscuits wrapped in greaseproof paper. Once we had sipped our drinks and ignored the rest, Chompu described our case to Vicha and the old lady. He told them about the VW and the fact that it had probably been buried at the time when the Chainawat family still owned the land. Throughout, the gorgeous man provided a simultaneous translation in Chinese for the woman who, it transpired, was his mother, the matriarch of the Chainawat clan. She was even paler than the polystyrene woman out front. She gave no sign that she was listening to her son or remotely interested in the story. It wasn't till the description and the translation were exhausted that she came alive. Her cackled speech began like dry branches crackling on a fire. Then, one by one, someone threw fireworks into the flames. It was surprising that such a colorless woman could bang and whoosh and kerplonk with such splendor. We were all exhausted when she finished, and enjoyed the brief silence.

"My mother said our family had owned all the land in that area since back in the early nineteenth century. It was, of course, a land development investment because most crops planted so close to the sea would be inferior. As our family became more successful and better land became available, we started to sell off tracts around Pak Nam."

"Does your mother recall the plot she sold to Mel?" Chompu asked.

"She remembers it," said the son. "She has a very good memory."

"Your family first sold seventeen hectares of land to Mel for a palm plantation but kept hold of the neighboring twenty-six hectares. Then, seven years ago, out of the blue, you asked Mel if he'd be interested in buying a small tract of land, just the three hectares attached to his field. Originally, it was included in the land deed of your plot but you'd gone to the trouble of separating your land into two deeds: one for three hectares and one for twenty-three. Why did your mother do that?"

Chompu had been doing his homework. Good boy. Vicha asked his mother and we ducked as the rockets flew.

"She says we needed cash in a hurry for another investment."

"All right. Then why didn't she just divide the land in half: two thirteen-hectare plots? Surely they'd be more salable. And Mel was interested in buying more."

The reply was worthy of Chinese New Year celebrations, but the old lady was mostly bangers and crackers by now. She spat and fizzled and her eyes flicked angrily from mine to Chompu's. Junior interrupted to clarify some points before translating.

"My mother didn't think anyone would want to buy a plot of land that was hemmed in by other owners. She wanted to wait till one of the other neighboring land owners made an offer. She only offered a small plot to *Koon* Mel because she knew he wasn't a wealthy man and she could help him by offering it cheap."

My turn.

"That's very neighborly of you," I said. All eyes around the table were on me now. "You don't happen to recall an open pit at the end of your land, a fish pond or reservoir?"

I'd looked straight at her when I asked my question. I'd begun to notice her hostility toward me from the moment she'd first set eyes on my running shoes, so I didn't think I could work on the female bonding angle. She cackled a question.

"My mother would like to know who you are, exactly."

"I am exactly —" I began.

"*Koon* Jimm is my investigative assistant," Chompu cut in.

The question "What's her rank?" was channeled through Vicha.

My lieutenant surprised me by sliding either into or out of character. He squinted and dropped his voice several octaves.

"*Koon* Vicha," he said. "Please tell your mother we haven't come to be interviewed. We are investigating two suspicious deaths on land that once belonged to you. Right now, she is our chief suspect. If she'd prefer, we can come back with two clerical assistants and go through every one of your deed records. Failing that, answer the question."

He gave me goose bumps. The old lady sneered at the translation, then spluttered her answer.

"My mother says that our family never actually occupied the land. It was purely an investment. Nothing was planted there. The land was neither filled nor excavated. If any work was done there — or any funny busi-

ness — it was done so without the knowledge or permission of the family." The
mother and son huddled again. "My mother
says this interrogation has tired her out and
wonders whether your lady friend here has
any more questions before she goes to lie
down."

We were driving back across the picturesque
hills of Phato. This had been the driest
August on record but still the vegetation
was lush and the roadside trees hung out
their blossoms of lilac and yellow and
orange like risqué underwear on drying day.
Spirit houses were wrapped in gaudy colored cloth. A bus stop was tied to a power
pole with plastic string. Children not old
enough to smoke were driving motorcycles.
Unpainted concrete houses. Mountains of
coconut husks. Royal Umbrella rice and
eggs of different natural hues for sale in
bamboo shops the size of cupboards. Things
you only notice when you take the trouble
to.

"She was lying," I said.

Chompu turned down the screaming of
Mariah Carey and discontinued his ac-
companiment.

"Now, how would you know a thing like
that?"

"Because little old Chinese ladies always lie."

"Ah, a sound investigative premise."

"They do. They have a code. If they feel they're in a corner they give you whatever answer they think you want to hear."

"At what point did she begin to leave you in doubt as to her veracity, lady friend?"

"From the moment she started speaking. Don't you think it odd that the company owns fourteen thousand hectares of land but she can recall the details of one little plot in the boondocks? And all that horse manure about helping out a neighbor. Did she give you the impression she was the caring type? No, she had a reason to remember that land. It meant something to her."

"You're a suspicious lady."

"Crime reporters can't afford to believe everything they hear."

"Crime reporters aren't that trustworthy themselves. Oh, there goes my mouth again."

"Did you have any particular crime reporter in mind with that statement?"

"No, really, I shouldn't."

"It's too late to turn back."

"All right, let's start with a charming reporter from the *Chiang Mai Mail* who flew down to pursue a case in the south."

Busted.

"I didn't actually use those words."

"And you didn't actually use the words 'I quit my job and moved down to live in a rundown resort in Maprao,' either."

"People hear what they want to hear irrespective of what I actually tell them. Their mistake."

I cast a sideways glance at the lieutenant who was smiling serenely at the scenery.

"How long have you known?" I asked.

"Since the day of your romantic lunch with the boss."

"You checked up on me?"

"Call me nosy."

"Do the others . . . ?"

"Not sure about the major. He's been hard to tie down lately. Can't even get him on the phone. The constables? Well, they're locals. Nothing happens down here that doesn't spread like water hyacinths on a warm pond. Everyone knew about you the day you stepped over the provincial border."

I pouted. I hated to get found out on a lie.

"You aren't exactly lieutenant open-and-aboveboard yourself."

"How dare you. I'm as honest as a mountain spring. Not that I actually know how honest mountain springs are. I imagine they're quite unsullied, however."

"Really? This morning? My phone call telling you I'd found the previous owners of Old Mel's land? 'Oh, can I come along?' he says. 'You're so resourceful,' he says."

"So?"

"So we arrive in Ranong and you drive straight to the company. I hadn't told you the address."

"Oops. You hadn't?"

"No."

"Lucky guess?"

"You're a man to watch, Lieutenant Chompu."

He blushed.

"And talking about men to watch . . ." he said.

"Hmm. Lovely smile. And I bet he ironed his own shirt."

"Too bad he's his mother's pet."

"Reminded me of Liu De Hua."

"Ah, scream. I had a crush on him for years."

"Me too." We slapped palms and the truck swerved dangerously onto the hard shoulder. "And there I was thinking I'd never have anything in common with the police."

The family ate dinner that evening at the table nearest to Mair's shop so she could keep her eyes open for a sudden unexpected rush. Arny watched over the two cabanas occupied that night: one by our largely absent ornithologist, another by a young couple who had arrived with no luggage on an old motorcycle. The television in the room was old and clunky and, frankly, not worth stealing, so Arny had taken cash in advance and didn't bother to fill out the Tourism Authority of Thailand registration form. He considered it an unfriendly intrusion into the guests' private lives. It was in Arny's nature to trust everyone he met. I suspected his oversensitivity was a result of the constant beatings he'd taken from the gloves of disappointment. He never learned.

The last of the evening light was reflecting off the slimy backs of beached jellyfish: hundreds of them like macrobiotic UFOs forced into shallower and shallower waters by the over-fishing of the Gulf. Overnight they'd be cannibalized by our nascent community of tiny crabs that lived in pinprick holes in the sand. Once I'd seen what they could do to a jelly the size of a bin lid, I was loath to sit on the beach for longer than five minutes at a time. To a shortsighted crab, my expanding backside could very well have been mistaken for some washed up sea urchin.

"Anyone got any news or should we just sit here and eat in silence?" I asked, breaking Mair's dinner rule by surreptitiously letting a prawn tail drop through a crack between the floorboards to where Gogo waited on the sand.

"I found a gym," said Arny. "I mean, a sort of gym."

"Good news, little brother," I said insincerely. I knew a gym would drag him further away from his duties and leave more for me to do.

"Where is it, child?" Mair asked.

"Bang Ga. Just two villages away. It's not exactly California Fitness. They've got weights and a Nautilus, but it's better than rolling logs along a beach. Some old fellow donated money to the temple there and the locals couldn't think of what else they needed. So, someone suggested investing in health rather than death. He figured everyone would be in better shape for the trip to the afterlife."

"That someone sounds like a football coach," I offered.

"Muay Thai boxing. I met him today. He asked if I'd be interested in joining his squad."

Some hope of that. First kick in the ear and my little brother would be squealing.

He wasn't the fisticuffs type. It always surprised me that bodybuilding was classified as a sport. It had its own categories in the national games. All the strutting and posing. I would have put it in the same category as hairdressing. I wouldn't dare mention that to Arny, though.

"And what did you tell him?" I asked.

"Said I'd think about it."

"Good for you. Don't make any rash decisions. How about you, Granddad Jah? What have you been doing today?"

I hoped we'd be able to build on the previous day's uninterrupted flow of speech but I guess he'd exhausted himself. He looked up from his rice and grunted. He needed inspiration.

"Fine," I said. "Then it's my turn."

I didn't dwell on the visit to Ranong, if only because it wasn't that interesting. Instead I described the crime scene at Feuang Fa temple as recounted to me by Lieutenant Chompu. There's nothing like a murder scene description to keep the family engrossed during a meal. At one point, Granddad Jah looked up and I thought he was about to make a comment. But he had second thoughts and continued to shovel food into the hatch of his mouth. Granddad Jah had good solid bones but you could see most of them, so I had no idea where all that food went to.

"And Mair," I asked, "how was your day?"

"Ed stopped by again," she said. I wished I hadn't asked. "He was on his way to put up a roof."

"I thought he cut grass."

"He's a carpenter, too. He asked after you again."

"I hope you told him . . . you know what."

"It was against my principles, but, yes I did."

"Good Mair."

Granddad Jah grunted and pointed his fork. We followed the direction of the prongs. Someone was outside the shop waiting. Mair put down her utensils and went to attend to the customer.

"Business is booming," said Arny. He collected the plates from the table and carried them to the kitchen. It was his turn to wash up. Granddad Jah refused to give up his bowl and spoon. He was apparently attempting to scrape the pattern off the ceramic. I wondered if he had the same worms as Gogo.

"There are two avenues," he said, unexpectedly. Again I was surprised to hear his voice. "One," he continued, "is when you go to a crime scene and look for what isn't there, what's been stolen: knives missing from drawers, computer discs removed. You've seen those scenes."

Right. Now he was telling me how to look at a crime scene. The only crime scene he'd ever worked involved bent bumpers and squashed truck drivers. I'd attended more crime scenes than he ever would. All right. Respect for the elderly. Humor him.

"You follow the victim around and make a list of all the things that should be there but aren't," he continued. "Then there's the second avenue. You go to a crime scene and you look for things that are there, but shouldn't be: footprints would be one example, cigarettes in an ashtray, a forgotten umbrella, that kind of thing. And sometimes, what shouldn't be there is so obvious you don't see it."

I didn't know whether this was a general lecture or whether he had something specific in mind.

"Was there something the police didn't see at *Wat* Feuang Fa, Granddad?"

"There was, Jimm. There was."

"And what was that?"

"A hat."

"A hat?"

"You said Abbot Winai was wearing a hat. It obscured his face."

"That's the way the lieutenant described it to me."

"And how many monks have you seen wearing hats?"

I had to think about it. In the north there were some.

"The monks wear little woolly beanies all the time up in the mountains," I said.

"That's true. There are those that get away with it. But it's more for survival. Better than freezing to death. But it's still against the regulations. You won't see any monks down here wearing a hat in the daytime, especially not a high ranking abbot."

"It was hot, Granddad. And he was old."

"It's hot everywhere, and most abbots are getting on in years. But you don't see it. And that's because it's clearly laid out in the Monastic Code that you can't wear a hat. You can put up a saffron umbrella, even pull your robe over your head, but a senior abbot who'd reached that level of responsibility would never dream of breaking the rules. There's no way he'd wear a hat."

Granddad took up his bowl and spoon and went off to the kitchen.

"Thanks, Granddad."

I sat on the rattan seat on my veranda, the seat that always creaked rudely as if I weighed eighty kilograms, and I slapped mosquitoes against my bare arms. I told myself a story. "An abbot's about to go for a walk in the afternoon heat. The sun burning down on him. There happens to be a nice straw hat on a hook so he grabs it. Nobody watching. No harm done. And he strolls off to enjoy the blossoms." Why complicate something so simple? Mair was a born-again Buddhist; I decided to ask her.

I walked to the shop. Mair was sitting at the round concrete table out front talking to someone. I could only see the shadow of his back against the shop lights. He was slightly built and wore a cap. Mair saw me coming and said something that made her guest rise quickly and head off along the road into darkness.

"Who was that?" I asked.

"A customer," she said.

"Mair, you did a three-week intensive meditation course at *Wat* Ongdoi to make yourself a better Buddhist, and I know for sure that on the door of your cabin, number four on the Top Hot Precepts list, if I remember rightly, was, 'Abstain from False Speech.' "

"I'm not lying. It was a customer."

"It was Meng the plastic awnings man. Maprao's own private dick."

"He bought a box of matches."

"Distortion is just a breed of lying. What did he have to tell you?"

"Nothing."

"Mair?"

"Really. He said most people have poison of some type or another. It's too broad a field. We need to narrow it down."

"Mair, you're trying to find out who it was that killed John. What good will that do you? You aren't going to bring her back to life. And forgiveness is a blessing, or something, isn't it?"

"I can forgive. I just need to know who it is I should be forgiving. I think the perpetrator needs that release from guilt."

"You want to know who poisoned John so you can tell him John forgives him?"

"Yes, exactly."

I felt one of those Maprao migraines coming on.

"It's late, Mair. We should shut up shop."

I scooped an embarrassingly small sum of money from the takings drawer, turned off the light and helped Mair pull down the shutter. We walked down to the water's edge, found a spot with no jellyfish and sat on the sand. Crabs eyed us hungrily. I started the timer on my watch. Mair was smiling at the moon as it slipped in and out of the clouds. She really could find beauty anywhere. I told her about Granddad Jah and his new-found detecting aspirations. I expected her to laugh along with me, but instead she took my hand.

"Your Granddad Jah didn't get beyond the rank of corporal . . ."

"I know. That's why I was so shocked he —"

". . . because in all the forty years he was with the police, he refused to take bribes."

"He . . . ?"

"He passed his exams but no stations wanted him because of his reputation. He had a philosophy, a moral code. He vowed never to break it. If something was against the law it was against the law no matter who the perpetrator was. It wasn't affected by interference from influential figures or pressure from senior police officers. Eighty-seven percent honest was dishonest in his book. He'd been one of the brightest recruits of his year and would have been fast-tracked for the higher ranks if only . . . But all a clean policeman succeeds in doing is showing all the others just how dirty they are. Nobody trusted him. Your granny tried to convince him to take the odd bribe, just to fit in, but he wasn't having any of it. So, for forty years he blew his whistle and directed traffic."

I could feel tiny claws nipping at my rump. It was long past the safe period for beach sitting. Mair had left me to my thoughts and gone to bed. It was just me and the back end of Gogo and the crabs. A longtail boat was passing slowly. The crewman was thumping the calm water with a heavy plunger to scare the sandfish out of the holes and into the nets. The steady rhythm was like a buffalo's heartbeat. My own pulse had quieted some. There really was never a dull moment in our household. Why had Mair or Granny or Granddad Jah himself never told us about his moral code? Did they think we'd laugh at him because of it? Was honesty such an embarrassment? Why, I wondered, were we such a family of secrets?

"First, let me make it very clear, poor people aren't necessarily killers. Just because you happen to be not rich doesn't mean you're willing to kill."

— GEORGE W. BUSH, WASHINGTON, D.C., MAY 19, 2003

I was awoken early the next morning by the sound of someone banging on my cabin door. I opened it to find Arny dressed in only a towel.

"They've gone," he said.

"What?"

"The guests in room two."

"They paid in advance, didn't they?"

"Yes, but . . ."

Constable Ma Dum was the poor man assigned to investigate the loss of our television. He was honest in his appraisal that, as we didn't ask for personal details of the couple in room two, nor did we insist on holding on to their motorcycle license until they checked out, we shouldn't become too excited about the possibility of recovering the stolen TV. True, there may have been witnesses who saw a couple on a black'n'rust Suzuki fleeing with a large television, but as the sheets, towels and curtains were also missing, one could assume that the television was disguised in some way. People piled their motorcycles with all kinds of junk in these parts.

So, our TV was as good as fenced. A very small crime. Room — two-hundred *baht*. Sale of secondhand TV — five hundred *baht* maximum. Profit, about the cost of a Starbucks mocha supreme and a vanilla slice. When I'd phoned Pak Nam to report it, Sergeant Phoom had instantly recognized my voice. My name found itself on a report card which was checked by Major Mana. He turned up at our place at ten a.m. in his shiny truck. He was extremely uppity.

"So," he sniffed, walking around with his hands behind his back like a very confident bullfighter. "Flew to the south for the VW case, decided you liked it so much you convinced your family to move down here permanently, uh? Swift move."

"I didn't actually say —"

"Deceiving a police officer."

"Which isn't a criminal offense unless I'm a witness or a suspect," I told him and immediately bit my tongue. "As I'm sure you know."

"Of course. And I'm willing to forgive you."

That didn't make sense but I'd take it.

"Thank you."

"After all, you did spell my name correctly in three major newspapers."

I knew it. I bet he went out and bought all the dailies the morning after our interview.

"Spelling's one of my strong cards," I told him.

"And I see this as a beginning, rather than an end. It certainly can't hurt to have a reporter with such lofty connections just ten minutes down the road. I can see us forming quite a formidable alliance. A little bit of information here, a mention in a report there."

"I was hoping for exactly the same."

"But . . ."

I'd been waiting for a "but." He was leading me toward the beach with one hand gently annoying the small of my back.

". . . you did me a great disservice."

"I did?"

"My favorite restaurant. Staff who know and respect me. A regular customer taken ill in the bathroom and his female acquaintance flees the scene. Not at all good for a senior policeman's reputation."

"I assumed you'd been called away on a case. I waited twenty minutes."

"I was disturbed to find you gone."

"I'm sorry."

"There's only one way to make up for it." Surely not.

"I know," I said. "You should come and have lunch here someday."

"Wouldn't work, *Nong* Jimm. That wouldn't clear my besmirched name at my favorite restaurant, would it now?"

I suppose I did owe him.

"All right. I'll just have to clear it with Ed."

"Ed?"

"My fiancé."

His hand didn't leave my back but it stopped massaging.

"Very sudden."

"Not really. Ed was the reason I . . . we all moved down here."

It was a ploy that usually worked but Mana was a slimy one.

"Very well," he said. "Clear it with Ed. I'm at Lang Suan tomorrow so we should make it the weekend. I'll call you re the place and time."

He was bulletproof. He hadn't even met Ed and he'd already dismissed him as small fry. He didn't even know the man cut grass for a living. Arrogant. But wait . . . Lang Suan?

"Actually, *Thai Rat* have asked me to look into the *Wat* Feuang Fa murder," I said, as casually as I was able. He was a dark-skinned man who was suddenly flushed vanilla.

"You? They what?"

"Abbot Winai's killing."

"How could you possibly . . . ?"

"Lofty connections."

"The press knows about it?"

"Just us at the moment. But we have plenty to run with when I'm ready."

"When you're ready?"

The guilty hand fled from my back and rejoined its colleague behind his.

"You know. Right place right time. Just ten minutes down the road. I think it would be a very good idea for us to swap notes over lunch. There's so much I need to know."

I could see the word "leak" spill out of his brain one letter at a time. I knew he'd been warned not to have anything to do with the press on this case. And here I was, his pet reporter. Where else would I be getting my information from?

"Ah, look," he said. "We should certainly liaise on this in the future. But perhaps now isn't such a good time. As I hear of developments I'll pass them on to you, of course. In the meantime it would probably help both of us if you sent me your notes on the case. Then I can fill in the gaps for you. I'm playing a key role in the proceedings."

"Really?"

"Absolutely."

"My source tells me Pak Nam isn't in the loop anymore. Something about not being trusted. I heard you even lost one of the Lang Suan crime-scene cameras."

"That is not true. I have no idea where that rumor began and I can refute it categorically. I've talked to the forensic department at headquarters. I went there in person. It's a very small department. One man, in fact. Not only did he not lose a camera at the crime scene, he was off getting rabies shots that day and didn't even visit the site."

"Interesting."

"So I would appreciate it if that rumor did not find its way into the newspapers."

"I'll see what I can do." I was alpha now

and snarling. "Are they still holding the Abbot Kem in Lang Suan?" I asked.

"No," he said. "He's back at the *wat*. They have him under house arrest there."

"How's it looking for him?"

"Not good," Mana confessed.

"Murder weapon?"

"Not so far, but there are any number of places to toss a weapon over there."

"Any other suspects?"

"No. Look, I really can't . . ."

"Car, motorcycle sightings around the time of the killing? Strangers in town?"

"No."

"Anyone with a grudge against the Bangkok abbot? I mean, his job was to investigate wayward monks and make recommendations for them to be disrobed. There may be a cause for revenge there."

"We haven't found anything. That is to say, no comment."

So much for our new open relationship. Either the Bangkok detectives had shut him out, or there really were no other suspects or motives, or he was lying to me. I didn't like people lying to me. He leaned too close to me and smiled.

"I could arrange for you to interview Abbot Kem," he said.

"I already have," I said, haughtily.

He looked at me with awe. The press had climbed several rungs in the power rankings of his admiration and I knew there'd be no more hanky-panky lunches with the good major. He doffed his cap, vowed to recover our lost TV, and even waved at me as he climbed into his truck.

Abbot Kem was back home and living in his stilted hut at the rear of *Wat* Feuang Fa. Two uniformed constables from Lang Suan had been assigned to watch him, but when I cycled past them in my disguise — baggy flower-patterned shorts way past my knees, Red Bull T-shirt under a long-sleeved gingham shirt, flip-flops and straw hat — they barely looked up from their comics. I was so obviously nobody to admire or fear that I depressed myself.

I found the abbot alone. He was sitting on the same front step drawing patterns in the hot air in front of him. The dogs sat at his feet watching his fingers sculpt.

"Good morning," I said.

He turned to me and smiled. There was no evidence on his face that the murder inquiry was causing him any grief at all. But I guess that's what it's all about. When you get to warp-factor gamma three on the self-discovery orbit, worldly worries bounce off

191

your defense shield. I envied him. I could use a little karma when the handlers brought their monkeys to collect coconuts and the wicked beasts deliberately threw them down onto my vegetable nursery. I wish I had the patience to take it all seriously, this religion thing. But I have sacrilegious ideas rushing through my mind all the time like a continuous, graffitiladen subway train passing through a station. There's no way I can eviscerate the troubling thoughts and leave myself with purity. I'd implode.

"So, they let you out, I see," I said.

"Yes."

"Did they treat you well?"

I was mired in clichés, too. I needed a good clean out.

"Yes."

"I'm assuming they didn't actually charge you with anything."

"No."

"Can I ask you some more questions about that day? The day you found the body?"

I hoped I could come up with a question or two that evoked more than one word answers.

"Yes."

"Did you notice anything odd about Abbot Winai when you found him lying there on the path?"

"Odd?"

"Incongruous, illogical, downright weird."

"Are you talking about the hat?"

Bingo.

"I am."

"I mentioned it to the detectives. It's been on my mind since that afternoon. The officers dismissed it. They said it was a hot day — late afternoon glare of the sun. The abbot could be forgiven for slipping on a hat, they said."

"But you don't agree."

"I know how strictly my friend followed the regulations. That's why he was elected to conduct inquiries on behalf of the *Sangka*. It's clearly stipulated in the Disciplines, book five, regulation four, that a monk cannot wear a hat."

This was starting to feel rather silly.

"So what do you think would possess him to break with tradition and put on a hat?"

"That's just it. He didn't. We had been debating my prickly situation with regard to the precepts . . ."

"Arguing?"

"More like a philosophical discussion. We'd been mulling over points for two days already. It was his habit to walk and digest his thoughts, then return with more questions. He was a very logical and fair man. He stood and stretched and told me he would be back soon and began to walk along the concrete path. As soon as he stepped out of the shade of the fig tree he readjusted his robes and covered his head with one flap of material. He wasn't wearing a hat, of course."

"Perhaps one of the gardeners left it there? He could have picked it up on the way?"

"What for?"

Good question. I had no idea.

"So, when you reached him, that was the first time you'd seen the hat?"

"Yes."

"What kind of hat was it?"

"It was very bright orange with a red flower."

If I'd been wearing glasses, I would have looked down them at him.

"Orange?"

"Bright orange. Like the traffic cones."

"And the police didn't see anything odd about that?"

"Again, they assumed he'd grabbed the first thing he could find to go on his walk."

"But you told them . . . ?"

"I am a suspect. They were more interested in the abbot's investigation of me."

"Do you want to talk about that?"

"There is nothing to talk about."

"But you were engaged in long philosophical discussions with a man who was killed. It's all relevant."

"Philosophy has no personal investment. We discussed theory."

"The theory of a relationship between a monk and a nun."

He smiled. That was always a bad sign with an abbot. I could see he was rearranging his sandals with his feet for a quick getaway. I was about to lose him.

"There is nothing there of relevance," he said, and stood.

"One last question, then," I said.

"You must be heavy with answers by now."

"I can squeeze in one more dessert. Do you remember seeing a camera?"

"Where?"

"At the crime scene."

"No, but I was far away."

"You didn't approach the body?"

"No."

"You didn't kneel down? Feel his pulse?"

"No."

"Then how did you know he was dead?"

He smiled as he started away from me.

"Of course, I knew," he said.

He walked so evenly across the dirt ground it was as if he had little hover jets on the soles of his sandals. If only I'd paid more attention in Religious Instruction. Of course he knew? Why? Because he'd killed him? Because he'd witnessed his girlfriend kill him? How do you know a man's dead without touching him? I could see why the detectives still had their doubts.

Abbot Kem was gone and the nun was nowhere to be seen and I decided there was nothing more to be learned from *Wat* Feuang Fa. I had things to do elsewhere, starting with a lunch to cook. A peculiar family to feed. It was time to get back on my bicycle and head off home. It would be another long cycle but I was starting to enjoy the rides. I could feel tone in muscle that I'd long since given up on. I was sleeping whole nights rather than segments. Exercise had its place. I was starting to see myself as this Maprao-based Agatha Christie character pedaling off to solve crimes on her two-gear shopping bicycle and modeling in her spare time. I reached down for my flip-flops and found just the one. I looked around at the frogs-wouldn't-melt-in-my-mouth expressions of the half-dozen dogs that hadn't left with the abbot. They were all as ugly as sin, Fellini dog extras: silvery eyes bulging, sores gleaming, this or that limb missing. These were the dogs who came to temples to see out their final days. But, as is always the case, the most innocent-looking suspect is invariably the culprit. And Sticky Rice sat at the corner of the hut with an obviously fake expression of innocence on his face. He was sitting on my flip-flop as if it was a surfboard and he wasn't about to give up his ride. When I reached for it he tore off, my sandal between his teeth.

I hopped after him to the rear of the nuns' quarters and homed in on the back of a hut I knew to be one of his stash houses. There was no sign of cute but fat Sticky R. and I really wasn't in the mood to play. I considered leaving my flip-flop behind and riding home without it but it was the principle of the thing. I'd watched *The Dog Whisperer* on Animal Planet once when there was nothing else on. If dogs think you're weak they'll take control of your world. I had horror visions of them walking through police lines and taking over Government House. I needed to stop the revolution right here. I lowered myself into a push-up and stared into the forty-centimeter gap below the hut. The shadows were dark but, sure enough, one black eye like that of a rogue panda stared out at me from the gloom. The pup let out an unconvincing juvenile growl

197

which failed to terrorize me. I growled back. I edged forward on my belly and he retreated with my sandal. Edge, retreat. Edge, retreat. The farther in I crawled the darker it became so I took my cell phone out of my back pocket and turned it on. A warm blue glow emanated from the screen.

In this swimming pool light I could make out Sticky Rice backed into a corner. He was trembling. It made me feel like a terrible bully. I was sure if he kept up his current regimen of eating everything he saw, he'd soon outweigh me, but at that moment he was still a little fellow. Life hadn't been kind to him. Barely six months on the planet and he was already in the dog house. An inmate of the mutt penitentiary where all bad street dogs came to die a slow death. I decided I wouldn't thump him with my shoe once I'd retrieved it. He'd suffered enough. But he was still a meter from my grasp. Luckily I was wearing clothes I could throw away when I got home because I had to crawl through grime to get to him. I emitted those clicking sounds that are supposed to make dogs feel at ease but I positively refused to engage him in a Mair-type conversation. I knew if I could just reach out and touch his ear like the nun had done he'd regain some self-esteem. I was now close enough to my shoe but the fat kid refused to give it up. I walked my fingers to it and he snapped at them. I growled again and he trembled. Mexican stand-off.

That's when I was distracted by the sight of a small black shape off to my left side. I moved my cell phone to get a better look. Eureka and bejabers! It was a camera. Half the Nikon label was visible although it had been almost completely chewed off. The whole thing looked as if it had been attacked by sharks. It seemed a little upmarket for the usual Pak Nam crowd: a fancy lens and dials and what have you. Would it have been too much to hope that I'd found the elusive crime-scene camera? Was it likely that an overweight pup would have the energy to drag it all the way back here from the concrete path? Sticky answered that himself. He abandoned my shoe and leaped to defend his camera. He bit into what was left of the strap and started to drag his booty away from me. But that little prize was mine and, puppy or no puppy, I was prepared to fight him for it.

"I don't know. It's jammed or something."
"You should have given it to the police."
I swore that if Arny said that one more

time I'd push him out of the truck and drive myself.

"I will," I said again. "Just as soon as I've seen what's on it."

"No, I mean, you should have given it to the police as soon as you found it."

If ever my mother retired from mothering, I knew I'd always have brother Arny to take her place. How could three siblings come from such different planets? We were on Highway 41 heading into Surat. It was a monotonously straight stretch of road and it was only the surprise arrival of holes or lumps that kept you awake at all, which is probably why they were never repaired.

"Arny, listen," I said. He was driving, so he had no choice. "Do the police know I found the camera? No. Has anyone actually reported it missing? No. If I handed it over tomorrow, would they have any way of knowing I hadn't just that very minute discovered it? No. Is the fat pup going to fess up? I don't think so. So, relax."

"We know. Our consciences know."

Honestly, if Lieutenant Chompu had been available, I would have asked him to drive me. It was his case, after all. But he'd gone to Prajuab to the army base where they'd taken our bodies. He wouldn't be back until late. I needed back-up so Arny was my only choice and on long-distance drives he could be like one of those self-help tapes stuck in the player on a loop.

I had the camera in a transparent plastic bag and I'd tried everything I could to play back any photos it contained. But somewhere between the dropping and the dragging and the chewing, and probably a good helping of saliva, the temperamental piece of equipment had lost its ability to display. The only markings I could make out between the scars were the letters DSLR and the beginning of a code, D3555. It looked like a very expensive camera, sturdy but not too heavy. It wasn't the type of thing a regular tourist would carry around. Our photographer at the *Mail* had a Canon that looked similar. I'd get Sissi to look it up. But, right now, I wanted to see pictures. I took my laptop out of its case and switched it on. I couldn't get into the camera but I could take out its memory chip and display it on my computer.

"Arny," I said.

"Mmm?"

"The laptop." It was open on my lap and dead as a jellyfish.

"I don't know anything," he lied. Only my mother lies with less conviction than my brother.

"Yesterday, this was fully charged."

"Really?"

"Really."

He folded like a deckchair.

"I just took it down to the beach for a few minutes."

"I hope you had a very good reason." My teeth were grinding together.

"I listened to music."

"You have an iPod."

"Yeah, but the laptop's got that program with the psychedelic animations that move in time to the music. It's very restful."

I counted backward from a hundred in Portuguese.

"And the sink unit was cracked?"

"Right down the middle."

"Well, you see? In such a situation, the customer would normally bring back the damaged unit for us to determine whether the crack was structural or whether excessive force was used on it."

"What excessive force can you exert on a sink unit?" I asked.

He smiled at Arny with a slight rise in his right eyebrow. He was old school. His jacket was a little too large and his choice of tie made you think he didn't have a wife at home, at least not a fully sighted one. He had ebony-dyed and moussed-back hair that curled up into a gutter at his collar and the look was rounded off with a pencil mustache, HB light.

"I'm sure I don't need to tell you and your wife what happens on the spur of the moment in bathrooms." He winked. Arny looked blank.

"I think you do," I said, dumbly.

We'd arrived in *Koon* Boondej's office at the Home Art Building Accessories Mega Store with our sink complaint as an excuse to get past the Service desk. We'd hoped to have the ex-con, ex-manager of Blissy Travel to ourselves, but the Quality Manageress had accompanied us and she was hovering. The realization seemed to loom above the manager that nobody was going to play along with his sex on the sink unit fantasy.

"We actually have people standing on the sink to paint the ceiling" was his escape. Not terribly convincing.

"So, how can you tell we didn't stand on the sink?"

"We have experts who can determine that." He smiled and looked at the quality woman. I guessed he meant her. I thought it was time to shake her off.

"So you have investigators?" I asked.

"In a way, yes," he said.

"Are they the same people who check the qualifications of prospective staff members? People applying for administrative positions, that type of thing?"

His smile melted at the edges and his dark skin blushed mauve.

"Are . . . are you applying for a job?" he asked.

"It's tempting," I said. "Convincing newlyweds to buy taps has always been a dream career for me."

"Then I think I can handle this myself," he told the woman.

"What about the sink?" she asked.

"We'll wipe off the footprints and bring it in for you to look at," I said.

She walked out with a sideways frown at her boss. She wanted his job. I'd used that same frown myself. Once the door was shut the manager seemed to develop a nervous tic that unmoussed his hair one strand at a time.

"What do you want?" he asked.

"I was concerned about the background of the management here at Home Art."

"I don't know what you mean."

A column of hair fell over one eye, leaving behind a slash of bald.

"Well, let's just say that somewhere along the line someone by the name of Boondet with a 't' gets muddled up with someone else by the name of, ooh, say, Boondej with a 'j'?"

I paused for effect. All the features on his face seemed to be attempting to change position. I was in.

"I mean, could we, with a clear conscience, buy a Jacuzzi jet bathtub from a convicted murderer?" I continued.

He stood and walked to the door, looked out, twitched, put his hands in his jacket pockets.

"How much do you want?"

"I beg your pardon?"

I noticed Arny looking pale.

"I know what this is," said the manager.

"What is it?"

"Blackmail."

I considered the concept.

"In a way, yes, you're right," I said.

"I . . . I know people," he said.

I knew what he was getting at but gangland figures didn't take salaried positions at Home Art.

"No, you don't," I said. "Don't let your imagination run away with you. We just need information. You tell us what we need to know and your life and your career are secure. You lie to us and I'm not so sure I'll be able to keep Fang here on his leash. I'm sure you know what I mean."

Arny's hands were shaking on his lap. I suppose it could have been interpreted as pent-up aggression.

"Who are you?" Boondej asked.

"Fair-weather friends," I said.

I couldn't remember the name of the movie I'd lifted that from but it worked just fine.

"What do you want to know?" asked the manager. He was still at the door. I wondered whether he planned to bolt for it.

"Blissy Travel," I said.

He looked surprised.

"What about it?"

"You tell me."

He obviously didn't know what to say. Didn't work. New track.

"You were the manager."

"Yeah. So?"

"Couples would stop by to sign up for tours?"

"Couples, singles, groups. That's normal, isn't it?"

"I don't know. Is it?"

"Yes."

On TV it was always a lot easier. They'd answer a question with a question and the suspect would tie himself up in knots. Soon he'd be singing like a caged dove. Arny had a pale green tint to his cheeks. I didn't know how long I had before he threw up behind the manager's desk. So I got to the point.

"Exactly how many couples did you kill, *Koon* Boondej?"

"Just the one."

I admired, but was taken aback by, his honesty.

"Look, I've done my time," he said. "I'm setting out on a new life here. I'm not a threat to society. Can't you just . . ." He looked at Arny. "Is he all right?"

"The thought of extreme violence moves him," I said.

I pushed the wastepaper bin in front of my brother and he took himself and the bin off to the executive bathroom.

"All right," I said. I was suddenly feeling vulnerable but I spoke calmly to make the man think I was just as dangerous as Fang. "Just you and me now. I want to hear the whole story."

"You're press, aren't you?" he said.

Busted again.

"Yes."

"Oh, shit."

"But you aren't my story. If you can point me in the right direction, your name doesn't have to be mentioned at all."

So he told me about the couple he'd

207

killed. After Blissy Travel collapsed, he'd run a boat trip out to the islands. One of the most popular cruises was to the caves of the *nok nang an,* the birds that built nests from their own spit. The trips were boozy and most of the tourists were sloshed by the time they arrived back at the dock. Boondej often missed the pier entirely. One day they went out to the cave, anchored a few hundred feet from the island in shallow water. The guests waded in to the caves, took pictures, waded back out and continued with the serious task of getting plastered. Boondej was a little more pickled than usual that day and he miscounted. One couple had gone deep into the cave and he left them there. The tide rose and they drowned. Culpable negligence. The husband was the son of a Scandinavian diplomat so Boondej served the whole eight-point-two-three meters.

Actually I'd been hoping for something more fiendish. The Home Art Mega Store manager didn't sound like the serial killing type. So I brought up the topic of VW vans.

"I had two," he said with pride. "I went down to Malaysia and got them second-hand. Hardly used. They were the only ones of their kind around then. I did a lot of business with them. They were all the go with backpackers in Europe. So when the hippies came over to Thailand they'd take the bus from Bangkok on their way to Ko Samui and pass right in front of my shop."

Arny, a few shades lighter, re-entered the room. He replaced the waste bin and lowered himself slowly into the seat.

"Go on," I said.

"They, I mean the VWs, were on the road most of the time. They'd come back and, poof, the next day there'd be a new customer. I charged rental by the day. The customers paid for petrol. They'd invariably trip up one coast, then back down the other. Stop off in Chumphon and Ranong and Phuket, down to Krabi. I included a recommended itinerary in the cost of the rental with the names of guesthouses and resorts. But there were mattresses in the back of both vans so they could save money on accommodation if they liked. I tell you, if I'd been able to hang on to those vans I'd be a rich man today."

"What happened to them?"

"Vanished."

"Beg your pardon?"

"Disappeared, both of them. Within the space of a week."

"You reported them missing?"

"Of course I did. They were my cash cows.

I'd always hang on to the passports and ID cards of the customers and take a security deposit. Once the vans vanished I showed the IDs to the police. You know what they told me? Fakes. Fakes, all of them. Thais, I tell you. Can't trust 'em. I should have stuck with foreign backpackers."

"The vans were rented by Thais?"

"The police told me there was a car theft gang sweeping through the south, renting cars and motorcycles on false IDs and reselling them. I'm not sure if they ever caught up with the gang but I know I didn't get my vans back. That's what killed off the rental business for me."

"So, do you have any idea why one of your vans might have been found buried under two meters of dirt in a field in Chumphon?"

Boondej attempted to replace the lock of hair that had been annoying me all this time. He had a look of genuine surprise on his face.

"Shit. Is that what this is all about?"

"Yes."

"You came here just to ask me why one of my vans was buried in a field?"

"Yes. Well, there was also the fact that there were two bodies buried with it."

That upset him.

"Damn. Do the police know about me?"

"Not yet."

"They'd put two and two . . ."

"Afraid they would."

"Just like you."

"Yes."

"I couldn't take any more of that. I'm not a criminal, but once you've got a record they pull you in for anything."

"Then we should try to solve this before they get to you. I don't suppose you remember the people who rented your vans?"

"I'll never forget them. Two couples they were, both ripped from the same cloth. I'd seen their type before, young Thai kids pretending to be Western hippies. Long hair. Fluffy excuses for beards. Dressing like bums so people would think they were artists or musicians. Stench of musk. They walked in off the street looking so straggly I thought they were about to ask me for the cost of a cup of sweet tea. Then they handed over a wad of money to rent the van. Those musicians, you never could tell. So you had to be nice to all the bums just in case they were rich. I should have been suspicious that the two couples were so alike."

"And why weren't you?"

"I assumed the first pair had told their friends. Either that or there was some hippy music festival on somewhere. It was just a

211

few days between the two rentings. Of course, it's easy to be logical after the damage is done. No. I was just greedy. I'd rent the vans out to anyone with the money to pay for them."

"And the IDs they left you?"

"Like I say, they were fake. The photos were a lot more respectable than the kids but there was a likeness."

"Did you keep them?"

"No. I had to hand them over to the police."

"Did the kids have any distinguishing marks?"

"Not really. Beards. Hairy armpits on the girls. Nothing soap and a razor couldn't fix."

"All right. I might have more questions but, if I do, I'll phone you."

"And you aren't going to . . . ?"

"*Koon* Boondej, in my line of work you meet liars with varying degrees of skill. You have to recognize the signs. You strike me as a man forced into dishonesty by the system. So, no, I'm not going to tell anyone about you."

"I appreciate it. There's nothing else?"

"Well, yes. There is one more thing. I need five minutes with your computer without you in the room."

"I —"

"I'm not going through your files. I just need to open some photos. But they're personal."

The manager turned on the computer for me and left quite placidly. I clicked out the memory card from the camera and worked it to the rim of the plastic bag so I wouldn't have to touch it directly with my fingers. I slotted it into the Home Art computer and waited for the machine to find it. I looked over at Arny. He was sulking but the color had returned to his cheeks.

The computer found the external link and asked me what I wanted to do. I didn't want to save the photos on the computer so I opened them in ACDSee just to have a look. I clicked.

"Holy . . ."

It felt as if the office had sucked all the air out of me. My stomach was up somewhere around the fluorescent lights. Until I saw those pictures I'd always believed there couldn't be a great deal of difference between your basic, six command, non-rechargeable digital camera and anything at the top of the line. Digital was digital. But, I tell you, I was wrong. I was in those pictures between the 3D layers, feeling every horror as if I were the victim. I swear I could hear the flies buzzing and smell the blood. I was mesmerized and horrified all at once by the awful clarity of the photography.

"Arny," I said, "normally I wouldn't show you pictures like these but, just in case anything goes wrong, I need you as a witness here. But I warn you, you aren't going to like them."

"Free societies are hopeful societies. And free societies will be allies against these hateful few who have no conscience, who kill at the whim of a hat."
— GEORGE W. BUSH,
WASHINGTON, D.C., SEPTEMBER 17, 2004

Of course they'd affected me. How could they not have? All the way back in the truck Arny kept coming back to the fact I had no heart, no normal senses. That my work for the newspaper had turned me into a zombie.

"How could you sit there and look at those pictures without your heart being torn out?" he'd asked.

"It's work," I told him

That's what I always told myself. It's work. People get mugged. People get caught. People die. They hadn't touched your life before the crime. They don't touch it after. They weren't friends. You had no investment in them. Perhaps a little grief might leak through when you're interviewing the loved ones of the deceased. You might shed a tear of sympathy even. But it was the worst day of someone else's life, not yours. You write up your report in dull, unemotional language. Novelists cry into their keyboards. Reporters count words and watch the clock.

When I first looked at the photos on that previously untainted Home Art computer monitor, I'd been shocked, of course. Here was a murder in progress. A monk poses reluctantly for a photograph. Even by the second snap his hand is raised as if to say "enough." His robes and his pale skin contrast elegantly with the tall bank of bougainvilleas behind him. In the third picture he looks down curiously at a hat that's being offered to him, presumably by the cameraman. It's an orange straw hat. A woman's hat. In the fourth picture he has it in his hands, holding it like an alms bowl in front of him. His expression is one of amused suspicion. The camera is clicking continuously now and the hand of the cameraman is back in the shot. It appears to be gloved in a bright oven-mitt, shocking pink. But held firmly in its grasp is a knife. The blade is slasher-movie long. In some shots the afternoon sun glints off the blade and changes the quality of the photographs. As we step forward with the cameraman we are urging the monk to put on the hat. At first he smiles his incredulity, but as the blade touches his shoulder, he relents. We step back. There is one shot of the hat perched uncomfortably on the monk's head. Ridiculous. But it's as if this one shot has been sculpted in color. It's a frightening but artistic photograph, one which resonates with dread. Time had been taken over it.

And then the knife and the oven mitt re-enter the frames: one, two, three as we approach the abbot. And then the butchery begins. The cameraman and murderer are one and the same. The abbot falls to his knees, stares once at the unseen murderer, turns away as if attempting to crawl through the flower beds, then he is supine across the concrete path. The puddle of blood spreads beneath him and then, as if from out of nowhere, a dog enters the frame. Its eyes are red with rage. Then it's a blur, halfway out of the picture and there's a second dog with teeth bared. It fills the frame. It's about to consume the camera. Then there's sky. The blur of movement. Then . . . nothing.

Altogether there were forty-six photos documenting the brutal murder of a peaceful man.

Just work.

The moon was almost full that cloudless night and the squid boats had all stayed home. Those romantic squid were drawn like mindless lovers to the glow of the moon rather than to the deceptive lights of the boats that lured them into their nets and onto their hooks. The moon made the beachscape glow pale gray but clear as day. Despite the absence of color around me, I couldn't get the damned photographs out of my head. They were still vivid and loud in my mind. Neither could I free myself of the stupid theory that a senior monk had died at the whim of a hat.

I think I mentioned I was halfway through my M.A. at Chiang Mai University when THIS LIFE IS UNAVAILABLE flashed up on my screen. Half an M.A. isn't really anything, you know? Who'd give you a job on the strength of just an M? The course was one of those money-making schemes the Education Ministry had become so fond of. Learning for rich people. Knowledge by the cubic centimeter. "Need a top-up on that degree, madam?" I didn't think it would be that long before they had slots you'd have to continuously feed with ten *baht* coins to keep the lecturer talking.

But, anyway, our course was a weekender. Two days of classes and homework for the weekdays. Most of us were working Monday to Friday so you had twenty mature (said with a straight face) students like me with no social lives getting together at weekends to read out our essays on magical bloody realism in English and being critiqued by our peers. After three years of that, assuming you continued to pay your fees and could fight your way through a final dissertation that neither you nor the lecturers really understood, you ended up with a Master of Arts in Critical English. Stay with me. There is a point to this sidetrack.

One course was called Public Oration and Oral Improvisation. We called it Pooi for short. It was taught by an old ex-playboy Englishman who still thought he had what it took. He flirted a lot and held in his gut for an hour and a half. It must have been a relief for him to get home and breathe normally. At the beginning of the course he allotted everyone a case study. This came in the form of a famous person who gave a lot of speeches. The point was to select one of his or her speeches, or excerpts from several, and analyze the techniques following a style analysis chart handed out by the lecturer. I was envious of my friend, Ning, because she got Bill Gates and he kept his speeches simple to the point of sometimes dropping his audience into a coma. I was lumbered with George W. Bush. I tried to trade him for Condoleezza Rice. I'd always thought if an ethnic girl with the surname Rice could pull herself out of anonymity, we all could. But nobody wanted George, so for six months I studied the oratory skills of the President of the United States of America. And I hadn't thought it was possible but Condoleezza was way down the if-this-one-can-make-it . . . inspiration table compared to George W. The poor man really wasn't a public speaker and I wondered whether he could make real sentences in his private life. But George was a hit and I got an A for that course.

Now, that was a very long way around explaining where I'd heard the phrase "killed at the whim of a hat." George was in Washington, D.C., and he'd fallen off the edge of the teleprompter again and he was caught somewhere between "on a whim" and "at the drop of a hat" and ended up with terrorists killing one another "at the whim of a hat." I'd spent a fortnight trying to work out what it meant. But it was the first phrase that came to mind when I heard about the abbot's orange hat. For some reason, weird as it may seem, I knew that hat had a bearing on the case.

Every log and shell and homicidal crab was picked out by the big full spotlight in front of me. I sat on the grassy lip where the sea had left off its sand supper last monsoon season. Gogo was beside me, absentmindedly munching at the hair on her haunches. I always got the feeling dogs had seen cats do it and thought it was cool without really grasping the concept. Dogs were all male when it came to cleanliness. It was midnight. I'd considered breaking open one of the wine bottles I'd brought with me from Chiang Mai but while I'd searched through the unopened packing cases for the missing corkscrew the question "Why should I?" began to flash in front of me like a low-battery warning. Was I celebrating the comeback of crime journalist, Jimm Juree, or mourning the demise of my short-lived innocence? Would I be toasting the return of my hard-arsed self or bemoaning her arrival? Or perhaps I was hoping that, wine-drunk on a grayscale beach, I would no longer see those forty-six photographs in color. I thought that big, almost-full saucer in the sky — just a chip off the underside — might help me to think, to have something to tell Arny the next morning. Something more satisfying than:

"It's work."

But it just hung there and drained me of all my excuses and, for the second time in three days, I cried my eyes out in front of a dog.

I handed over the camera to Major Mana the next morning. I'd exchanged greetings with Sergeant Phoom at the desk and he'd waved me up. Mana was in his office talking on his cell phone. It was something personal judging from how he put his hand over the phone and turned to the window when I appeared in his doorway. He didn't seem terribly pleased to see me. He finished his conversation and nodded for me to come in. I put the camera in its plastic bag on his desk.

"What's that?" he asked.

"Me, scratching your back," I said. "I think this might be the camera nobody lost."

I told him how and where I'd found it earlier that morning and that I wouldn't mind at all if he took credit for its discovery. I expounded my theory that the mystery person who'd called asking if anyone had retrieved a forensic camera from the crime scene, might, in fact, have been the killer himself trying to find a camera dropped during the attack. I could only hint that the dogs may have frightened the killer away as I obviously couldn't tell him I'd already looked at the photos.

Major Mana looked decidedly unenthusiastic about my theory. He thanked me for bringing in the camera and gave me a brief lecture on the importance of not touching evidence, as if the plastic bag had been a stroke of luck on my part.

"Should we take a look?" I asked. I felt that a journalist who'd recovered a camera should be excited about what was on it.

"At what?" he said.

"The pictures on the camera. They might be important."

"Ah, no. We need to process the camera first."

"Process it?"

"Check it for fingerprints and trace elements, you know . . . blood, fluids. We don't have those facilities so we'd need to send it to Lang Suan who in turn would take it to Chumphon."

"Aren't you just a little bit curious to see what's on it?" I asked. "You know, once you send it to Lang Suan they won't share their findings with you."

"Of course they will."

"All you'd have to do is turn it on and take a look. You'd be perfectly justified."

"There's certain . . . protocol."

"Really?"

"I promise, as soon as Lang Suan reveals the contents of this camera I shall pass the information on to you. I haven't forgotten our deal."

That pretty much confirmed that I wouldn't be getting any useful inside information from my major. I thanked him for his cooperation and *wai*'d as I reversed out of the room and walked along the corridor to Chompu's room. He was enjoying a morning *pla tong go* dough puff and coffee whose color confirmed its instantaneousness. He looked up and smiled.

"My journalist. I've missed you. Doughnut?"

I sat opposite him and broke off a limb of dough.

"I wasn't expecting you all to be in so early," I confessed.

"Are you joking? Two murder inquiries? The province has sent us oil tankers full of overtime money. We're supposed to be on call. If Lang Suan needs a manicure or a change of light bulbs, we'll be there. You watch."

"I just stopped off at the major's office.

He didn't seem pleased to see me."

"You probably interrupted his Amway dealings. Direct sales of unwanted products for the discerning housewife."

"He sells Amway?"

"Not a lot of income from bribes down here. He has to make his money in other dishonest ways."

"How was the crime lab?"

"Useless and marvelous. How was Surat?"

The creep. How could he possibly know I went to Surat?

"If you've fitted a GPS device to the bottom of our truck I'll —"

"Tsk, tsk, little scribe. I've had a requisition for staples in the system for three months. How long do you think it would take me to produce a tracking device? You really should stop watching all that televised American junk. It's all made up, you know?"

"Then how do you know I went to Surat? You're starting to give me the willies, Lieutenant."

"It's all very simple. Imagine a world where there are no strangers, where everybody is either related or acquainted."

I resisted aristocracy jokes.

"It sounds unhealthy," I told him.

"But it exists. My mother has a girl who does the garden. The garden girl's husband drives fish from Lang Suan to Surat. The owner of one of the restaurants he delivers to has a daughter who works on the Dairy Queen stand in front of Home Art Mega Store. I've had her observe the manager for me. Collect gossip from staff, that sort of thing."

"That doesn't sound particularly ethical."

"Everybody wants to be police. I'm just letting them live out their fantasy. And my Dairy Queen police lady reported to me this morning that she'd observed a woman with a bad haircut accompanied by the Incredible Hulk go into the manager's office yesterday afternoon and stay there for a very long time. She even took a picture on her cell phone. Technology continues to astound and frighten . . . You're looking particularly depressed. Can I help?"

"She said I have a bad haircut?"

"Surat isn't ready for the accidental-razor-attack look. It's really you. Don't let it ruin your life. She works in Dairy Queen, God bless her."

"But how the hell did you find out about the manager?" My voice had climbed into the soprano loft.

"I'm a policeman," he said with a straight face, and there was no evidence to the contrary. Lieutenant Chompu really was a policeman. You couldn't let those minute traces of nail polish fool you. He knew his job. We made a deal. I'd tell him all about our interview with *Koon* Boondej and he'd share his findings from the lab in Prajuab. I decided not to tell him about the camera, out of spite, I suppose. I wanted to hold something back or there'd be no lollipops for negotiation. It was a mistake but I'm not immune from stupidity. I finished my tale first. He drained the last coagulants from the bottom of his coffee cup.

"Well done," he said. "No, really. Very well done."

"You understand it does rely on my instincts," I told him.

"No problem. Your instincts are super. But that does leave us at a nasty dead end as far as our VW goes."

"Not really. At least we know the couple in the VW weren't just innocent tourists. They were involved in a criminal act. I wouldn't be surprised if they did something to piss off old Auntie Chainawat and she got revenge on them."

"I don't th—"

"In fact, it wouldn't surprise me if she wasn't masterminding the whole carnapping caper and I bet she had a whole network of poor but dishonest couples out

227

scamming rental companies. They'd drive the stolen vehicles to her place and she'd traffic them on to Malaysia or over to Cambodia or she'd break them down for parts."

"But presumably not bury them underground."

"What? All right. That doesn't make sense, but —"

"I'm losing faith in your instincts."

"No, keep listening. One couple screws her out of some money so she makes an example of them. Lets all the other gang members know that insubordination won't be tolerated. She gathers her people around her at the fish pond, slowly lowers the VW into the water. The doors taped shut. Everybody gets the point. She values loyalty. They walk away like relatives after a funeral."

"One or two bubbles rise from the pond," said Chompu, dramatically, "then it is still. A lone white tern takes off and we follow it out to sea. It would make a stunning final scene for the movie version. I see Meryl Streep as the Godmother. They can do wonders with make-up now."

"It's a hypothesis. You have to start with a hypothesis."

"What did that poor little old lady do to you?"

"She glared at my running shoes disrespectfully."

"Oh, well. That's it then. Send in the SWAT team."

"OK, your turn."

"Do I have to?"

"It's a deal."

"Very well. The lab at the barracks in Prajuab is stiflingly hot and showed distinct lack of artistic input in the decoration. The lighting was abysmal. They had our two skeletons side by side on one trestle table. It was quite sweet. I wanted to interlock their fingers but I was watched all the time. I wasn't convinced they'd got the puzzle exactly right. We'd sent the couple mingled so I wouldn't have been surprised if they'd just thrown them together, first come first served. One of the technicians kept referring to a textbook, for goodness' sake. He was pretending to educate me as to this or that phenomenon but I got the feeling he was checking his own work. They couldn't tell me a thing about the cause of demise apart from the fact that they weren't chainsawed, axed or machine-gunned to death. Nor were there any arrows or spears sticking out of them. Nor were they the victims of explosions or bone-eating diseases. But, in fairness, they were certain these two hadn't died of old age. The textbook con-firmed for me that they were quite young, early twenties."

"So, in summary, it was a complete waste of a drive."

"Not at all."

"How so?"

"I was on my way out through security and this swarthy, top-heavy army captain came running after me. I assumed he was taken by my good looks and wanted my telephone number, but he had a large manila folder in his hand and he asked me, 'Are you the lieutenant from Lang Suan' My reputation had preceded me. I smiled and said 'Yes.' Then he handed me the envelope and asked me to drop it off to Major General Suvit. I did my terribly formal salute for him and he didn't know whether to nod or wag his tail so he saluted back and turned on his heel and fled. Not for the first time in my life, I didn't realize exactly what a prize I held in my hand. I as-sumed it wasn't terribly important because it wasn't sealed, just tied with one of those string thingies."

"But even with the pressure of such a temptation, you didn't take a peek?"

"Of course I did. I mean, he didn't make me swear not to look, did he? And it didn't say, 'For the eyes of Major General Suvit only.' And, knowing the military, it might have contained something illicit. It was my duty to look. And what do you think it contained?"

"I give up."

"I'll give you a clue or two: knife, blood, abbot . . . Oh, come on, you must have it by now."

"I thought they'd sent the body to Bangkok."

"It appears the legal system in the capital is busy at the moment so they rerouted Abbot Winai to Prajuab."

I scraped my chair close and he winced at the noise.

"All right. What did they find?" I whispered.

"I'm not sure I can tell you."

"You'd sooner face the embarrassment of being beaten up by a girl?"

"That was threatening behavior toward a police officer. I could arrest you for that."

"Chompu?"

"All right, but this really is not for publication. Thirteen stab wounds, no less. Seven were postmortem."

"No!"

"All stomach and groin. Long, very sharp knife. Blade about thirty centimeters." I knew that. I'd seen it. "Perpetrator probably shorter than the victim, left handed, no defense wounds so the abbot was, no doubt, taken by surprise." I knew that, too. Shock, more like it. Completely bemused, but, as I recalled it then, not fearful. Just a look of resignation. And I doubted the killer was left handed. He just needed his right hand free to take pictures. "Victim otherwise in good shape. Died from exsanguination. No other marks on the body."

"What do you make of it?" I asked him.

"From what little I know of the case I'd say the killer wanted to make a point. The first two wounds would have done the job so this was a statement. 'Look what I've done.' There was something bottled up inside the killer that needed to be let out. There's madness there."

"Do you think another abbot could have done it?"

"No."

His answer was crisp and definite.

"Then why do you think the head of *Wat* Feuang Fa is still a suspect?"

"If he is, and I'd have to take your word for it because nobody tells me anything, it's because A, he has a motive, or B, he's the only suspect they have."

That was a bull's-eye on both.

232

"I don't believe he did it but all they'd need is a murder weapon," he said, "and your Abbot Kem is well and truly defrocked."

"I understand small business growth. I was one."

— GEORGE W. BUSH,
NEW YORK *DAILY NEWS,* FEBRUARY 19, 2000

I arrived home just in time to start preparing lunch. I wondered whether my family might just happily starve to death if I didn't bother to come home again. The nearest pizza restaurant that delivered was four and a half hours away. I'd even checked how far they'd be prepared to go. I tell you, I don't make long-distant calls just to get laughed at. That was the last hint of business they'd see from me. I was exhausted. I thought of all the male crime reporters around the country returning home about now to those wives in Understanding Thailand who greeted them with a smile and a table of food. Why didn't I have a wife like that?

I would start on the mackerel. I was sure

they'd missed me, whereas Arny walked past and ignored me completely. I'd had the truck all morning, preventing him from going to his gym. I knew he'd be mad. Mair was in the shop slicing huge banana bunches into smaller banana bunches and writing the price, 5 *baht*, on the skins. Everybody in Maprao had banana trees so I couldn't think who'd buy any. Across the road, Granddad Jah was sitting under the banana leaf roof on the bamboo platform watching traffic.

I had nobody to tell about my morning. I'd been a busy investigator. There were four hotels and seven resorts in or around Lang Suan, eight if you included ours, but I can't think why you would. After leaving the police station at Pak Nam I visited every one of them. I could have flashed my press card with my finger over the expiration date and gone that route, but I was sure the police would have been there already and told them to get in touch if anyone came nosing around. Someone would always call if they were approached by the press.

So, I made up a story. I told them my family had taken over a resort and we didn't really know what the hell we were doing. All right, perhaps I didn't make it up, but I did say we were having trouble with registration. I had the stolen TV as a ready anecdote and I wondered how other places registered their guests to avoid such a dilemma. I started off general, was very friendly, laughed a lot, then got on to the subject of the guest register itself. Every one of them let me take a look. In fact they were all so forthcoming and amiable it was almost embarrassing to be deceiving them. I was looking for guests who'd arrived the day of, or the day before, the killing, then checked out after the attack on the guard. This was merely my attempt to eliminate out-of-towners from the list of suspects. Lang Suan wasn't the kind of place you could spend a night in your car without being noticed so I thought I'd start with hotel guests: someone who'd registered with a car or a truck. The victim was from Bangkok and had only been scheduled to stay here for three days during his investigation. It was conceivable that the killer followed him here.

Either way, it was easier to start at this end of the investigation rather than knock on doors in ever-increasing circles around the temple. As it turned out, elimination was a lot simpler than I'd expected. Room occupancy everywhere was down to fifteen percent. Apart from the fact that nobody really wanted to come here in the first place, the downturn in the economy, the cost of petrol, and tourism killed off by the silly unrest in the capital, would have left the majority of the rooms empty anyway. Most of those who'd spent the night had been driving along the main highway, been overcome with fatigue, and pulled into the first place they could find. They'd invariably continued on their journeys early the next morning.

From the hotels I ended up with a sketchy list of two: a salesman called Apirat who was booked into the Radree for the week and someone called Adul who was staying at the Uaynoi Grand and had put his occupation down as "tourist." He had no definite departure date. He was traveling on a very large motorcycle. Nobody with a car or truck matched, or got anywhere close to, the dates I was interested in.

The resorts were even worse. Even the high-end places were virtually empty during the week when very few Thais would consider staying there. I found just the two at the 69 Resort, a short ride from Pak Nam. One was a middle-aged man who'd signed in as Dr. Jiradet, and the other a teenaged girl called *Nong* Pui on the far side of the compound. They told me the doctor was an adviser for the Pak Nam hospital. There were two foreigners. One was an elderly Korean lady who smiled at everyone, which appeared to be her only method of communication. She'd chosen a room by the busy road rather than the beachfront which made the staff think she might be deaf or demented. Then there was a German man who sat drinking beer on the balcony of his room most of the day. The receptionist had no idea when either was due to check out. I nodded at the German who invited me to join him, I assumed in a little more than a drink, and I quickly exhausted my three words of Korean on the lady.

At five other resorts there were no guests at all, although I was assured there was a good deal of "night traffic" at all of them. I knew what that meant. But the Tiwa Resort, my last port of call, was my best bet of all. A middle-aged Japanese backpacking couple stayed in one of the cheapest rooms and were, according to the staff, living on instant noodles. They'd been their only customers for three days. But then a mysterious Thai guest in room seven had arrived in a very expensive black Benz the day before the killing. He'd retired immediately to the room and ordered room service from their restaurant. My interest had been piqued when the receptionist described him as a hit-man type. It was a fact in Thailand that criminals often went out of their way to dress and look like criminals. It made the job of identification a lot easier. He'd registered as *Ny* Wirapon and left all the other boxes in the form empty. He hadn't yet checked out. I drove slowly past his room. There was somebody inside but the Benz was nowhere to be seen. The only thing that made him an unlikely suspect was the fact he was still there. Why stick around once you've made your kill?

The most significant outcome of my inquiries had been an overall feeling of doom for the tourist industry and the Gulf Bay Lovely Resort and Restaurant in particular. If the places of quality couldn't attract guests, what hope in hell did we have? I took my scaling and gutting buckets and sat beside Granddad Jah. He ignored me, pretending to be more interested in a meter-long monitor lizard ambling along the grass verge. I read that they can grow up to fourteen feet. I'm assured they only eat insects and small rodents but it seems to me, if you're as big as a truck, you can eat anything you damned well please.

I was on my third mackerel before I spoke.

"I could use some help on another case," I said, as if into thin air.

"Ask the police," he said.

"I did. They're lost."

"That's a state they should feel familiar with."

I mentioned to the hot midday breeze that I'd had a chance to visit the excavation of a VW camper van and went on to describe everything that had resulted from that discovery. By the last fish, I'd arrived at the tail end of the story. He didn't speak for a very long time and the mackerel was starting to sing off-key in the heat. I was wondering whether the old man had heard me at all. I stood.

"Sit down," he said.

I sat down.

"You'd need to find the original detective," he said. "The one that investigated the case of the car hire scam."

"I've got his name," I told him. "It's Waew. He was a captain. He's retired now."

He turned to look at me as if perhaps there was some sliver of hope for me in this world.

"So, find him," he said.

"I did."

"And?"

"He won't talk to me."

"Get your police on it."

"He won't talk to them, either. I believe

he said something like, 'You bunch are just corrupt, evil bastards.' Then he hung up."

I wouldn't have put my life savings on it but Granddad Jah might just have cracked a smile about then. If only I'd had my camera with me.

"He sounds all right," he said.

"I thought you'd like him. Do you want his address?"

"All right."

"Lunch in half an hour."

"Mair. Have we found the sinner in our midst?" I asked. "He that shall be forgiven?"

"Not yet," she said.

I was in her cabin and we were hand writing brand-new menus for the restaurant. Our resort was officially empty again following the flight, that afternoon, of our bird lady.

"You will tell me when you do, won't you?" I said. "I'm really interested to know . . . who it is we aren't going to do anything vindictive to."

"I'll tell you," she said, absently.

I watched her stick fish transfers on the corners of the menus. My mother. At high school I'd gone through periods of not liking her. But whereas my classmates were not liking their mothers because they were

241

too much of a presence in their lives, I resented mine because of her absences. When she was home it was as if you were plugged into the world. When she was away you'd sit staring at the empty socket: Granny Noi sitting counting and recounting the banknotes in the shop till, Granddad Jah with his vocabulary of grunts.

It was probably because of Mair's absences that I studied so hard. I wasn't trying to impress her. I was trying to earn whatever qualification it took for me to be out there with her, her personal assistant carrying her bag of tricks like a wise caddy. By the time I was sixteen I knew what I wanted to be. What better way of reaching the horizon than as a journalist? I read all the newspapers, Thai and English, that we sold in the shop. It was the perfect start. I didn't have to pay for any. I saw myself interviewing my mother, exploring the mysterious depths of her life. Mair, a special feature. My mother, exposed. And I broke into a metaphorical trot to get through those cumbersome study years so I could be the person outside that I already was inside. And I was running so fast that I almost missed the middle-aged lady I passed ambling in the other direction.

"Mair, is that you?"

She'd run her race. Done her dash. Her bag of tricks was upended and she had no more passion. Even her stories became gray, as if she could no longer see her life in the Technicolor it once was. I was flying out of the missile hatch just as she was docking. Overnight we changed places and once more we'd become unfamiliar. I missed my exciting mother but I learned to love her as a different person. But then, three years ago, she'd started to put her handbag in the washing machine, to walk into my bedroom thinking it was hers, to give customers four five-hundred-*baht* notes as change for a five-hundred-*baht* note. Those cracks were few but through them I saw the light of somebody I recalled. She began to surprise us with stories, blurt them out with no rhyme or reason. And her voice would crackle with joy as she recalled a place or an event. There would be gaps like a dream remembered upon waking but it made the stories even more mysterious.

When they'd first begun I'd thrilled at those moments and urged her on. But slowly, far too slowly, I came to realize that this was my mother traveling backward on a mechanical walkway, passing through time, past huge placards advertising moments from her life. And I began to fear that one day she'd be so far along that escalator she'd no longer recall where it was she climbed on or who was there to see her off. Now, three years on, the condition was no worse, suspended as if the walkway had broken down and a team of men in blue overalls was underneath trying to get it going. So, sometimes, ever so gently, I dared to nudge her along to another placard. There was one I desperately wanted to see.

"We had another bat fly into the bulb on my porch two nights ago," I said. "Smashed it completely. But that bat just shook off the glass shards, walked around in confusion, then flew on out of there. It didn't panic at all. It was like a pet. It made me think of . . . Thanom."

Mair smiled. I'd pressed the secret code button and was ready to enter that hidden room where she and my father kept a pet bat.

"How do you know?" she asked.

"You told me. You said you and —"

"No, I mean, how do you know it walked around in confusion? If it smashed the light it would have been dark. It was cloudy two nights ago."

"I heard its footsteps in the broken glass."

"Bats never were ones for walking, you know?"

See what I mean? When my mother wasn't out of it, she was completely in it. Saner than all of us. The pet bat story would have to come in its own sweet time. I stood to leave.

"On your way out can you remember to put water in John's bowl?" she said, without looking up. "She'll be thirsty."

I phoned Sissi later.

"Sis?"

"Nong."

"How's Leather?" I always liked to ask how Leather was because, in his own weird, probably nonexistent way, he was a bench-mark of stability in Sissi's life.

"He's gone."

"Gone?"

"I deleted him."

"What did he do?"

"He announced he was coming here on holiday."

"Oh, that's terrible. Is it terrible?"

"Of course it is. I don't want to see what they're really like."

"He might have been nice."

"He calls himself Leather and whips women online. He's either a factory worker or a bus driver."

I felt sad. Really. I'd like to see her settle

down with a bus driver.

"So, who's next?" I asked.

"I'm giving up on men for a while."

This sounded a lot like me in Pak Nam. I told her about Ed and my temporary dip into gaiety.

"Have you ever considered . . . ?" I began.

"Women? No, don't even joke about it," she said. "Who would stoop so low. No, little sister, I'm going to be an auntie."

I had to think about that.

"Wouldn't that involve either Arny or me doing the business?"

"Ha! I should live so long."

"Thanks for the vote of confidence."

"No, I'm going to be an auntie to thousands, perhaps millions. Do the words Cyber Idol mean anything to you?"

"I . . ."

"No, of course they don't. It's a very Asian thing. Started in Korea. It's now even bigger in Japan and it's slipping south."

"Does it involve singing and being humiliated by impresarios with limited talent of their own?"

"Not even. This is the ultimate self-makeover site. You have young girls who look like, say . . . you, and you set up your homepage with photos of what you actually look like. And the site has make-up and hair and — get this — Photoshop advice to do whatever it takes to make you look absolutely stunning online. There are no rules. You can pull any trick in the book to make yourself look like a babe. Then you enter online beauty competitions and the Web audience votes for their favorite and it doesn't matter that everyone knows you're a dog underneath. It's all about what you can do to give the impression that you're glamorous. And they have the same thing for men: the hair, the zit removal, the corsets and the airbrushing and you end up with these darling Barbies and Kens dating each other on the Web."

"It sounds sad."

"It's wonderful."

"It's not real."

"It's better than real. It's totally honest. They all know they're unattractive but they can live these lives as beautiful people."

It didn't sound honest at all.

"How do you fit into this?" I asked.

"I know the geniuses who set up the site. They want me to be their style guru. I'll be giving advice on how to dress, how to move, how to present themselves on Webcams."

"Are they paying you?"

"You know how I've always wanted to give to charity but I could never find the right one? Well, this is it. I'll be doing it pro bono."

"A very worthy cause."

And an appropriate choice of guru. Auntie Sissi encouraging an entire generation of empty people to pretend to be something they weren't. The thought of it depressed me. After another twenty minutes I was able to wrestle the subject around to crime.

"Sissi, do you have any moral objections to hacking into the DRA computer banks?

"That's the Drug . . . Rehab . . . ?"

"Department of Religious Affairs."

"Oh, absolutely not."

I gave her an update of the *Wat* Feuang Fa case and told her what I needed to find out.

"Any chance of getting back to me by tomorrow night?" I asked.

"I tell you from experience, religious sites are so easy to hack I know monkeys that could get into their inner sanctums. They all believe they don't need security 'cause they're protected by a Higher firewall. So, it's all an agnostic's playground. You want me to leave any mystic symbols to screw their minds up?"

"No, just a simple smash and grab will be fine. Thanks."

When I hung up it was ten thirty, half an hour after my bedtime. I was just about to step into the shower, then stare forlornly at myself in the full-length mirror when my cell phone rang again. I'd forgotten to turn it off.

"Hello?"

"Little scribe? Are you awake?"

"Chompu? What's up? Are you lonely?"

"Hardly. I'm surrounded by men in uniform."

"Are you fantasizing?"

"Er, no. I'm on speaker phone. We were wondering if you could pop down to the station."

"What? Now?"

"There's been an incident."

"... the storm clouds on the horizon were getting nearly directly overhead."
— GEORGE W. BUSH,
WASHINGTON, D.C., MAY 11, 2001

Arny and I arrived at Pak Nam police station at ten fifty. We had a long-standing arrangement whereby if ever I had to leave home after dark for anything that wasn't a date (three in the past three years) he'd come with me. He pretends it's because he's worried about the truck getting stolen but I know if he didn't come he'd stay awake all night worrying about me. Mair succeeded in making us all weird in our own ways but she also gave us a deep sense of loyalty. We walked up to reception and a sergeant, slightly crooked like a bamboo root, was sitting on a stool behind the counter. I'd never seen him before. He looked nervous.

"I'm —" I began, but he waved us through

without saying anything.

There were police everywhere that I didn't recognize and I was starting to think the place had changed hands in a coup, but then I saw Constable Ma Dum hurry out of the meeting room. I called to him.

"In there," he said, looking twice at my bodyguard.

We walked into a room that was crowded but not active. It was like half-time at a sporting event when the team was being thrashed to within an inch of its life. A few mumbled conversations ceased and all heads turned to look in our direction. I recognized the two detectives we'd seen at *Wat* Feuang Fa. Major Mana was there and Chompu and a dozen men in uniform, most of whom I didn't know.

"Well, this is an interesting turn of events," said the taller of the two detectives. His hair was stiff and spiked like the bristles of a bottlebrush and his face looked as moistureless as the skin of a longan fruit. His partner was in poor shape but thought he could also get away with wearing tight jeans and a black T-shirt tucked into his belt. He couldn't. Both men homed in on Arny who cowered beside the door.

"Manage to pray your way through your loss, did you?" said the paunchy cop.

Of course, they remembered him from the day we'd first visited the temple, but neither of them had seen me that afternoon.

"What brings you here, big man?" asked longan skin.

"He's with me," I said, stepping up to the two detectives and offering them my most subservient *wai.* Neither man bothered to return it.

"This is the reporter," Mana told them. Chompu stood behind him with his eyes fixed on my brother.

"Interesting," said the detective. "And what a coincidence. Titan here turns up at *Wat* Feuang Fa the day after a killing to cry over some imaginary bereavement, and his girlfriend just happens to be interfering in a case that no other reporter in the country knows anything about."

"Fishy," said the paunch. "I'd like to hear how you both wound up at the temple in the first place."

"Very well." I nodded my head. "Then let's all get comfortable, shall we?"

I walked through the throng of visitors to the bosom of the local team. It was one of those "think on your feet" moments. I needed time to come up with a story that didn't damage the already fragile reputation of Pak Nam police but one that didn't push me and Arny into the front chorus of suspects. I sat on the low window ledge and folded my arms.

"The reason we were at Feuang Fa temple," I said, "was because I'd received a telephone call telling me there'd been a killing out there."

"Who from?" asked longan skin.

"I'm afraid I'm not at liberty to divulge my sources."

"So, you're saying that someone just happened to have your number, knew you lived around here and randomly chose you to pass the information on to?"

"No, nothing random about it. I moved down here nine months ago at which time I traveled hither and thither passing around my name card and telling everyone I'd pay for information on serious criminal activity in the district. This was the first seedling to poke up its head following that early sowing. With regard to my . . . our visit to the temple, my boyfriend, who is actually my brother, agreed to drive me there that afternoon, despite the fact that he was still grieving over his beloved dog, John, who had been poisoned that morning. Arny is a very sensitive man and the journey proved to be too much for him. His need for solace was quite genuine. I, on the other hand, was devious. I opted to sneak out of the truck in search of witnesses. As there was no crime scene marked off I was perfectly within my rights to do so."

I was grateful that the expense and the lost weekends of my M.A. course hadn't been totally in vain. If nothing else, my analysis of George W.'s oratory style had taught me that a sincere countenance and a confident stance were sufficient to distract your audience from the fact that you were talking rubbish.

"Which brings me to the camera," I said. "This may be harder to believe, but there was a small dog called Sticky Rice who was in the habit —"

"All right," said longan skin, "we know the dog story. What we need to know is whether you made a copy of the photographs."

"How dare you?" I said, with heapings of indignation in my voice. I was ashamed at how quickly the deceit had sped from my mouth. In the background I could see Arny's eyeballs roll.

"I confess, when I found the camera I did attempt to turn it on," I said. "I mean, it could have belonged to someone at the temple. But it had experienced serious damage at the paws of the dog and I couldn't operate the 'play' mode."

"You didn't think to take out the memory card?" asked the paunch.

"Cameras have memory cards?" I gasped. "I thought that was just computers. What-ever will they think of next? Why are you asking? Haven't you been able to open it?"

I hadn't seen so many heads exchange guilty glances since our secondary school chemistry teacher asked us who was responsible for exploding a stink bomb in the staff room. There was a geometric web of eye contact around me. At last the tall detective nodded to Mana.

"First of all," said the major, "nothing you've heard over the past week, nor things you'll hear tonight, are for publication. You print anything before we're ready to release it and I'll have you arrested." He paused but I didn't react at all. "The reason we called you in, is that . . . the camera's lost."

"Lost?"

"Stolen."

The police were always good for a laugh.

"From a police station?"

"No," he said, grimly. "This afternoon I had Sergeant Phoom run it over to the Lang Suan station on his motorcycle. There was an accident."

"That was no accident," said Chompu.

255

"Lieutenant! Quiet! We don't know for certain. It could have been an accident."

"Is the sergeant all right?" I asked.

"He's in Pak Nam hospital," said Chompu. "He was run off the road by a car. He lost a lot of skin and was knocked out. A passerby phoned an ambulance and the hospital called us. When we got there, the passerby was gone and so was the camera."

"Technically, it could have been highway robbery," said longan skin. "But it's unlikely. There are much safer targets than a police officer in uniform. That's why we need to know who you've told about the camera."

"Who I . . . ?"

I had to think about it. If they asked Arny he'd tell them without even a suggestion of thumbscrews.

"Just me and my brother knew," I told them.

"You didn't tell anyone at the temple?"

"I didn't see anyone, apart from Abbot Kem."

"You told him?"

"Er, no."

"Are you sure?"

"Yes, I'm sure. I said goodbye to him, went to get my shoes, then followed the dogs to the back of the hut."

"What about the nun?"

"She wasn't there."

"But she could have seen you. She could have been somewhere else."

I looked around the room. Some of the men turned away in embarrassment.

"Is the nun . . . ?" I began.

"That's nothing for you to worry about," said Mana. I could see he was perturbed at being outgunned in his own station. He'd been relegated to crowd control. I didn't want to think about the nun being a suspect. I swung the subject back to the accident.

"Is anyone with Sergeant Phoom?" I asked.

"We've got a man there," Chompu said.

"Were there any other witnesses apart from the person who phoned it in?" I asked.

"It happened at a point on the way to Lang Suan where the road curves around the river," Chompu told me. "There are no houses there and the road's very quiet after midday."

It was the perfect location at the perfect time.

"All right, then assuming I'm not lying, and I really didn't tell anyone," I said, "how could the perpetrator know that Phoom had the camera? Did the sergeant have any idea?"

"He's still unconscious," said Mana. "But

we didn't actually invite you here to conduct an interview. We just want you to answer our questions and leave the inquiry to us."

"And there I was thinking I'd been helpful," I said.

"You have," said the paunch. "Did you happen to note down the make of the camera?"

"Yes."

He produced a piece of paper from his folder.

"Do you remember if it was a Nikon DSLR D3555?"

There was something going on between Bangkok and our Major Mana. They glared icicles back and forth across the room. I wondered why the police needed to ask me about the make of the camera. I have a good memory for little facts with numbers and letters in them.

"That's the make that I wrote down," I told them.

"Are you sure?"

I wished he'd stop asking me if I was sure. If I wasn't sure I wouldn't say anything, would I now?

"Yes. Why?"

"Because, according to our detective friends from Bangkok, here" — Mana smiled — "the camera details that both you and I wrote down are wrong."

"We didn't say they were wrong," said longan skin. "All we said was there was no such camera listed in the Nikon catalog. We'd have to contact the company and have them run a check on it. It may be a discontinued line."

"And you're sure you didn't make a copy of the film?" asked the paunch.

If only I'd had a machete on me . . .

"Sir," I said, earnestly, "not all reporters are rebels. I worked for a responsible newspaper and they taught us ethics. My grandfather was a member of the Royal Thai Police force for over forty years. He taught me the difference between legal and illegal." I noticed Arny duck out of the room. "My mother is a religious woman. She taught us all the difference between right and wrong. Please don't insult me by suggesting I'd do anything underhanded."

See? I didn't exactly say, no.

"Then that'll be all," he said. "We may have to contact you again."

I was dismissed. The meeting broke up. The detectives and city cops retired to Lang Suan and I heard Major Mana's souped-up truck growl out of the car park. I didn't know where Arny was. He was probably in the temple opposite, sulking. Lies weighed heavily upon him even if they belonged to somebody else. My lieutenant had told me to meet him in his office in five minutes and I was sitting on his side of the desk enjoying its neatness when he arrived. He was carrying two suspiciously non-steaming mugs and put one down in front of me. I gazed into it and saw the stain on the bottom.

"Water?" I asked.

"Vodka tonic."

"They've got tonic down here?"

"Tesco. They've got everything at Tesco."

My entire family had gone to the opening of Tesco Lotus out on the highway. It was the biggest thing to happen to the province since . . . no. It was the biggest thing to happen to the province. Our own superstore and the first possibility to find cream cheese and wine and made-in-Vietnam Chez Guevara T-shirts for forty *baht.* They had palm oil made from our own local palms via Bangkok on special at twenty *baht* a bottle, cheaper than we could make it ourselves. They had chocolates from Switzerland and skin whiteners from Malaysia. Except we hadn't been able to get in that day because there'd been so many people nobody could move in or out. We got to within four meters of the door and Arny lifted me onto his shoulders and I could see a lake of heads spread out before me. But it was a stagnant lake and I doubt any of those people made it out of there before the week was out.

But, meanwhile, back at the police station,

"Should we really be drinking vodka tonic on duty?" I asked.

"It's almost midnight and they called me in from a very promising soiree. They owe me. So?"

"So?"

We sipped our drinks. The tonic barely troubled the vodka.

"Brother?" he said.

"Oh, ho. Don't. Don't even . . ."

"He doesn't look straight."

"He's no shape at all."

"He's gorgeous."

"Forget it."

"I'll take your word for it but I may involve him in fantasy moments if you think he wouldn't mind."

"Go for it."

We sipped again.

"You and I need to make an appointment," he said.

"What for?"

"To view the you-know-what."

"No, I don't know what."

"Certainly you do. You wouldn't want me

to say it out loud, would you?"

"Weren't you listening before?"

"The *Chiang Mai Mail* taught you ethics, Granddad taught you the law and Mummy taught you morals. How's that?"

"And why didn't it register?"

"Your granddad was in traffic for forty years. Your mother did a three-week Buddhism refresher course, and newspaper ethics . . . ?"

This man was starting to make me feel uneasy.

"Do you have a remote camera in my bathroom too? You know nothing, trust me."

"I know you made a copy of what was on that camera memory card."

"And how would you know that?"

"Because it's exactly what I would have done. And you and I have a lot in common."

"We're both girls deep down?"

He lingered before his next sip. I wondered if my knee had landed a blow.

"We're both more capable than people around us give us credit for," he said.

He'd dusted off my powder-puff attack without a flinch.

"If you don't want your career to flush completely down the cesspit," he continued, "you need someone here at your local police station providing information. I need your back-up to make me more than just a pretty face around here. It's a simple professional trade-off on friendly terms."

I knocked back the remainder of the drink. My mouth was too small to take it all but I was determined not to choke in front of him.

"You presumably know where we live," I said.

He smiled.

"Ten a.m.," he said.

I spent what sleep time was left of that morning in a nightmare of graphically epic proportions. The colors were so loud I couldn't hear any dialogue. There were nuns and monks in there and noisy bougainvilleas. Yuppies in yellow shirts were vacuuming. Purple heads in plastic bags were swaying at the ends of ropes. Chompu was dancing. John the dead dog was bleeding in B-movie red everywhere. It was the kind of dream you needed ski goggles to get through or else you'd wake up blinded. I came around at six, more exhausted than I'd gone to bed. The sunrise was shocking pink.

I was apparently still seeing life through the lens of that very expensive camera when I arrived at Pak Nam's mini hospital. The outpatients area was ablaze with color: the dull yellow of hepatitis, the scarlets and crimsons of recent motorcycle accidents, the mauve of football injuries, the pale greens of food poisoning, and the various shades of pink from pregnancy right through the color chart to the weak pallor of anemia. I sat with my hand shading my eyes waiting for the nurse to take me to Sergeant Phoom and I thought about logistics. If it really had been the killer who ran the sergeant off the road and stolen the camera, he had what he wanted now and had no reason to stick around. There would have been a sudden departure. I took out my cell phone and called the hotels I'd visited a few days earlier. My suspects in Lang Suan hadn't checked out. So I tried the resorts. Nobody picked up the phone at the Tiwa Resort. I talked to the receptionist at the 69 who told me only the Korean lady had left the previous day. A group of Korean electricians had moved in and had spent their lunchtime drinking in the restaurant so there might have been some conflict. It was anyone's guess. Dr. Jiradet was scheduled to check out that morning and the receptionist also hinted that she thought the teenager might have moved in with the German.

Sergeant Phoom was in a small ward with four beds. The other beds were occupied by people who looked like there was absolutely nothing wrong with them. They were chatting with seven or eight village types who were sitting cross-legged on the floor eating. Only the sergeant seemed poorly and I wondered whether I should suggest the revelers keep the noise down. A young constable I didn't know sat beside him reading an illustrated brochure on kidney diseases. He looked up when I walked to the bed.

"How is he?" I asked.

I had a bag of mangosteens that I placed on the bedside table. Phoom wouldn't be in any state to peel away the thick skins for some time to come. Both his eyes were purple and bloated and a shaved section of hair framed a nine-centimeter millipede of stitching. His mouth was closed and bloody. His arms and legs were wrapped in bandages like a cartoon explosion victim.

"He's fine," said the constable.

He was a pretty boy, not rugged enough to grow into a gnarled old detective.

"Really?"

"He was awake a little while ago."

"Did he say anything?"

"Nothing coherent. Um, who are you?"

I was about to dive straight into a lie just in case they'd told him not to allow in the press, but in this little corner of Utopia, that would always come back to bite me.

"My name's Jimm Juree. I —"

"You're the journalist."

"I know the sergeant. I just —"

"I always wanted to write."

Nine months earlier, my reaction to such a straight line would have been "You should have paid more attention at nursery school" or "Lucky the police entrance exam is all pictures." I doubt I would have voiced those smarmy comments although I would certainly have imagined them. But something was happening to my sarcasm skills and I didn't like it. I found myself feeling disappointment on his behalf, sad that he'd become a policeman and missed out on the chance to be nominated for an S.E.A. Write Award.

"It's never too late to start," I said.

Sergeant Phoom coughed and the constable held a small bottle of Red Bull to the older man's bloody lips.

"Is that prescribed?" I asked.

"He swears by it."

Whatever works, I thought. Why not a placebo of sucrose and glucose and caffeine? The sergeant turned his bruised and bloody head slowly to my side of the bed. It was like watching a piglet turn on a rotisserie.

"*Nong* Jimm," he said. I had to strain to hear him.

"Isn't this ward a bit noisy for you?" I asked.

"It's like this all the time," he said.

I looked to the constable for an explanation.

"His family," he said, nodding at the floor party. A couple of them waved at me. I waved back. I pulled across a chair and sat close to the sergeant.

"Did you see the car that hit you?" I asked.

"I've asked all that," said the constable.

"Poor man's hit his head," I reminded him. "It always pays to ask twice just to confirm the answer's the same. Sergeant?"

"I got a brief glimpse of it in the mirror," he said. "It was right on top of me then. Black Benz. New one."

I got that bat in the belly flutter and looked up at the constable.

"That's what he said before." He nodded.

"Have you got your radio with you?" I asked. He patted the back of his belt. "All right. Call the station. Ask them if anyone's been to the Tiwa Resort. If not, tell them there's a guest from out of town staying there in room seven. He's got a black Benz."

The young man looked uncertain.

"Go ahead," said the sergeant.

267

The constable called through and passed on the message. There was silence as he listened. I listened. The three patients and the family on the floor listened. The policeman nodded when the reply came through and he switched off the radio.

"They'll send some men out there right away," he said.

That didn't result in a cheer exactly, more a group "Hmm." There really is no way to describe that feeling you get when you believe you've contributed to the solving of a crime. I might have even joined the police force but for the fact I'd be cleaning toilets and making tea for the rest of my career. Gender equality hasn't found a home in the police force. At least as a journalist I was allowed to ask questions. I leaned back down to the sergeant.

"Did you see the driver?" I asked.

"The glass was smoked," he said. All I got was a shadow. Little fellow. It all happened in a flash. I hit the ground. I was woozy for a second. I looked around and then I was out of it."

Something troubled me.

"Were you riding without your helmet on?" I asked him.

He laughed and the scent of a dentist's

268

office, blood and antiseptic, puffed into my face.

"More than my career's worth, that would be," he said. "You just have to sit on the saddle, parked, without your helmet and they'll have your stripes these days."

"And it was fastened?"

"Strapped tight."

"So, how did you get that crack on your skull?"

He reached up slowly and painfully and caressed his head.

"I was wondering about that myself," he said.

I found the office of the hospital director, Dr. Fahlap. He was a small man of Chinese stock in his late fifties. He had the most forgettable face I'd ever seen. In fact if you asked me now to describe him, I wouldn't be able to. I asked him whether the injury to Sergeant Phoom's head could have been a result of him hitting his head on the road. Fahlap was the type of man who gave thought to questions and you could see the replies forming in his eyes.

"No," he said at last. "It was a blow from a blunt object. Perhaps a tire lever."

That's what I'd been afraid of. On a quiet stretch of road, the killer had removed the sergeant's helmet and smashed him over the head. He wanted the policeman dead. Perhaps he was afraid he'd been seen and could be identified. So why was the sergeant still alive? Why just the one blow? Of course. The killer was interrupted. That had to be it. We needed to find who phoned in the accident. I bet that person had seen the killer.

I was just about to thank the doctor and get back home when I had another thought.

"Doctor, do you know anything about a hospital adviser staying at the 69 Resort?"

A pause.

"What hospital is he advising at?"

"Yours," I said.

"Do you have his name?"

"Dr. Jiradet."

"I've never heard of him."

I arrived home at ten fifteen. Sitting at the concrete table out front of the shop were my Lieutenant Chompu and Ed the grass man. They seemed to be getting along famously. It had a strange effect on me. It wasn't jealousy exactly. Neither of them belonged to me or ever would. It was more like an annoyance that they should form an alliance so quickly. I ignored them both as I stepped down from the truck and walked into the shop.

"*Nong* Jimm," Chompu called. "Are you

not talking to me?"

"I don't want to interrupt," I said, deliberately not looking at Ed the grass man.

"When's showtime?" the policeman asked.

"Give me five minutes."

I walked in through the open shop front. There was no sign of Mair. I looked in the storeroom and peered out into the back garden. There were chickens aplenty but no mothers. I was on my way back when I noticed two bare feet sticking out from under the counter. By edging sideways I was able to take in the entire vista of my mother's backside.

"Mair?"

"Shhh."

I went to the counter and knelt down.

"Mair, why are you under the counter?"

"There's a policeman out there."

"I know."

"It's all over. The game's up."

I had the strongest urge to laugh but I felt there was some method to this particular madness.

"Mair, what have you done?"

My mother was shaking like a rat at a lab interview. I reached under the counter and hugged as much of her as I could.

"Mair, the policeman's here to see me. He's a friend of mine. We're working on a case together. There's nothing to worry about."

One by one the shakes subsided and I heard a couple of recovering breaths, then a rapping sound. She was tapping on the underside of the counter with her knuckles.

"I'll have to get Ed in," she said.

"What?"

She reversed past me and climbed stiffly to her feet. She started to knock now on the top of the counter.

"Everywhere, they are. Little bastards."

"Who?"

"Termites."

I really had to laugh then.

"Mair, that down there had nothing to do with termites."

"Don't be silly, child. What else would I be doing on the floor?"

"Hiding out?"

"Such an imagination. You should be writing novels, girl, not reporting on other people's failings."

I watched her banging her fist on the plastic countertop and knew it was the time for me to go and have a talk with the awning detective. But, first things first. I walked outside and collected my lieutenant and had intended to ignore Ed, but the beanstalk called out to me,

"*Koon* Jimm?"

I was afraid he'd shout something embarrassing so I left Chompu tapdancing on the gravel in the driveway and walked casually back.

"Yes?"

"I need to speak with you," he said. He stood up and towered over me like a palm tree.

"I don't need any grass cutting," I said. I mentally took a long run up and kicked myself in the backside. There had been no need for rudeness, but it was said so I couldn't take it back.

"It's not about grass."

"As you can see, I'm rather busy."

His hands were in front of him holding his cap like some farmhand talking to the wife of the prime minister. I looked up at his face glaring at me, tangled in the rays of the sun. It was the first time I'd looked him in the eye. His mustache didn't suit him and his hair was either uncombed or uncombable. But his eyes were molten dark chocolate. I wished I hadn't looked into his eyes.

"I can wait till you're free," he said.

"It might be a while."

"I can wait."

"Don't you have some important weeding

273

to do, or something?"

I already had welts on the cheeks of my mental bottom.

"The weeds will still be there tomorrow," he said, and he smiled. If the eyes hadn't been bad enough, the smile . . .

"Suit yourself," I said. "I'll be finished when I'm finished."

I left him standing there. He really was far too tall to be taken seriously and annoyingly persistent. I collected Chompu and we went to my hut. Unless there'd been another power failure — daily now; a concerted education project provided by the Electricity Generating Authority of Thailand to show us what life was like in the Stone Age — my laptop should have been fully charged. Just in case it wasn't, Chompu had brought his own. A darling little Dell in puce. We sat on the veranda with the laptop on my cane table and us on the rattan chairs that squeaked and creaked like mouse S&M. I offered him a can of beer from my bar fridge but he said he was watching his weight and settled for an iced water.

As we waited for the computer to come to the boil, I told him about my visit to the hospital and the Benz. It didn't surprise me at all that he'd already heard. He'd been following events on his truck radio and he'd passed by the hospital in my wake. The driver of the Benz had long since departed and the police were following up on both the name he'd registered under and the license plate of the car. He said he'd pass on the theories about Sergeant Phoom's injuries.

I plugged in my USB onto which I'd copied the photos from the computer at Home Art. When the "select file" message popped up, I hesitated to click. The pictures were still heavy in my otherwise lightweight heart.

"This isn't family viewing," I told him

"I imagine I've seen worse," he said.

I doubted it. I clicked, and one by gruesome one the slides appeared on the screen. He watched the entire show with his hand over his mouth but the pupils of his eyes active, darting from point to point on the screen. I'd had my fill of that. I'd been through it all, zooming, highlighting, sharpening, redefining and all I'd found was the brutal assassination of an abbot.

"Again," said Chompu.

He dragged his chair closer to the screen so his nose was barely a sniff away from the carnage. He watched the entire performance one more time from beginning to end. When the skinny dog sang in the final frame, Chompu stood and unclicked the hinges in his neck before walking inside my hut and getting himself a beer.

"Damn," he said, "that was beautiful."

That was the scariest moment of the morning by far.

"Beautiful?" I said. "Beautiful? How sick are you to see anything beautiful in that?"

He took a very masculine swig of his beer and dabbed his lips with a tissue.

"What do you want me to say?" he asked. "That it was awful and bloody and premeditated and sick?"

"Yes."

"Well, of course, 'yes.' It was all of those things. Nobody in his or her or its right mind would think otherwise. But didn't you see it? Didn't you see the composition? The scenery? It was staged. It was a final operatic montage. It was a *tour de force* of color and spectacle."

If I'd been a police officer at that moment and he'd been a run-down resort manager, I would have asked him about his whereabouts on that Saturday afternoon. I even felt uneasy sitting there beside him.

"What do you think?" he asked.

"I think it's lucky you didn't watch the show beside Major Mana and the Bangkok detectives. You'd be in a cell by now."

"But that's why it's so much more fun to watch it with you. They'd just have seen it as the documentation of a murder. You and I see it as so much more."

"We do?"

"Of course we do. It's not just a killing. It's a climax. It's a loud, 'Look what I've done, world! See how poetic this murder has been.' "

"Poetic justice?"

"Exactly. It all had to be recorded because it's an artistic image that's been germinating in the killer's mind. The cameraman or -woman just needed to match the actual slaughter to the vision. That's why getting back the camera was so important. It was confirmation that justice had been done according to the divine ordinance."

"Man or woman?"

"What?"

"You said, 'cameraman or -woman just needed to match . . .' "

"Hmm. Did I?"

"You know you did. What did you see in those pictures that suggested the killer might be a woman?"

"Not that it precluded a man, more that it included a woman. The glove."

"It was an oven mitt. I assumed he'd worn it to add to the color."

"Whereas I assumed it was worn as a disguise. A tight glove or none at all would have immediately given away the size of the hand, the length of the fingers."

"That's all?"

"I don't know. If it had been a video recording I would have felt more confident to pass on my gut feeling. There was just something about the grip on the knife, the way the blade was poked rather than thrust, the forensic report that said the wounds had all been comparatively shallow. It all suggests a lack of strength."

"Ergo, a woman. Huh! And I thought you were one of us."

"And I thought you had to be gay to be prickly."

"You do. But once you open up the possibility of the killer being a woman, you're down to the one suspect. I don't like that."

"The nun? And you like her."

"I don't know her well enough to like her. But I want to believe that all this time in the bush hasn't completely erased my instincts."

"Don't underestimate the power of love."

"Oh, shut up. I suppose I'm going to have to pay another visit to the nun lady. You won't arrest her just yet, will you?"

"Based on what? We haven't seen anything

to suggest the killer could have been a woman because we haven't seen anything. Right?"

"Right."

"And that's another problem."

"What is?"

"I have to find a way to introduce these pictures into the case without committing you to a three-year jail term for tampering with evidence in a murder inquiry."

"Come on. It wasn't even evidence when I tampered with it."

"Even so, you did lie to, ooh, how many was it? Twelve police officers?"

"Play back the tape. I said nothing of the sort. I just intimated."

"Of course you did. You're basically a very honest person. That's why I knew you were lying through your teeth. But I doubt Mana will remember it like that, nor the Bangkok detectives."

"Who'd ever have thought they'd lose the damned camera? So how do you propose we do this?"

"Do you have a printer?"

"Yes."

"Is it traceable to you?"

With every encounter, Chompu climbed higher and higher in my esteem and lower on the table of people I'd trust, which was a very short table to begin with. I left him to watch the painfully slow color printer and made my way to the kitchen to prepare lunch. I'd invited the lieutenant to eat with us. Something minuscule in the far back left-hand closet of my mind wondered whether Ed was still waiting at the concrete table for me, but before I could get that far I heard a grunt from behind. I looked around to see Granddad Jah sitting at one of our grass-roofed tables. He was dressed, which surprised me. He wore a dark blue Mao shirt and gray slacks.

"So, you weren't planning on asking me anything?" he said, gruffly.

"I haven't seen you," I told him. "How could I — ?"

"I travel halfway down the country for you and you don't even say thank you."

"You've been to Surat already?"

I must have been impressed because I'd squealed my question. He definitely smiled this time. I sat and squeezed his hand and he enjoyed that for a few seconds before pulling his coralesque fingers away.

"No big deal," he said.

"And you saw Captain Waew?"

"Of course."

"Brilliant." We'd all tried. Me, the major, the lieutenant. He wouldn't give us the time of day. "How did you do it?"

"I'll tell you someday."

I knew he wouldn't. It was starting to look as if lunch would have to cook itself.

"All right. I'm all ears," I told him.

He cleared his throat and produced a small notepad from his back pocket. He barely referred to it.

"An influential person . . ." he began (always a bad start to a story), "headed a gang that was involved in various nefarious operations. Waew, who was a lieutenant colonel at the time, had been approached by an aide to this gangster who brazenly offered Waew a very reasonable monthly stipend if he would keep his eyes averted from the gang's activities. Waew being, at that time, one of the very rare Thai police officers with a conscience, told the representative that he was on board, but also informed his superior officer of the offer. Thereafter followed a very in-depth investigation of the gang's comings and goings. Even though this said villain had his finger in a number of pies, the police decided to focus on just the one activity in order to build a cast-iron case against him."

I noticed then as I looked across the table, that there wasn't actually anything written in Granddad Jah's notebook but he gave the appearance of reading from it like a report. Impressive. I was sure if ever I made it to seventy-four I'd not even remember which end of the toothbrush to hold on to.

"As Waew had received three complaints of automobile theft from car rental companies," he continued, "and as the detective knew from the aide that this was one of the figure's most lucrative operations, he decided —"

I put up my hand.

"What?"

"Why take cars from rental companies? Why go to all the trouble of counterfeiting IDs and investing in deposits when you could just break into a parked car and hot-wire it and drive it off?"

It was a dumb question but I thought Granddad Jah would enjoy it.

"A good point," he said. That was probably the first compliment I'd received from him since grade six when I won the new-year greetings card design competition at Guides. "But use your brain, why don't you?" (deflation) "You rent a car for, what? A week? Two? That gives you two weeks to change the plates, forge the paperwork, and drive the vehicle across a border. If you steal someone's car, you have the police out after you from day one."

I smiled to acknowledge the point. Where was this granddad during the early days of my career? Watching traffic. I could have used him.

"Should I continue or would you like to interrupt again?" he asked.

"Please."

"It was clear that the influential figure was recruiting hippies to do his dirty work. There were a lot of backpackers hanging around the islands, living cheap, smoking marijuana. Of course, most of them were foreigners. But there were the dregs of the communist movement, Thais who'd fled to the jungles to escape the junta, and they'd never been able to fit back in to society. Some of them set up communes that attracted younger kids. Most of them were just anti-establishment; others were playing at being flower children. There were a couple of farms down here in the south.

"Blissy Travel was the sixth tour company to be hit by the gang. Then there was a similar establishment down in Songkla. Hiring out cars without drivers was a relatively new phenomenon here, so it wasn't hard to chart all the establishments that offered rentals. It wasn't possible to stake out all of them so Waew had to take a chance. Blissy Travel had reported a van of theirs hadn't been returned on the agreed date. Their second van had been rented out two days earlier, also by what the owner called "a hippy couple." Waew put out the registration information and got lucky. The second VW had been pulled over in Tha Chana the day after it was rented. The driver and his passenger had been charged with indecent exposure. They'd been found sleeping naked in the back of the van early that morning.

"Waew went to meet the arresting officer and talk to the hippy couple. They made a deal. They would implicate the influential figure and give evidence against him in return for charges being dropped against them. Waew arranged a place for them to stay, what we would now refer to as a safe house, and they arrested the figure. Waew had his case, open and shut. They just awaited the trial date. Then, two days before the trial, the witnesses disappeared."

"They got cold feet?"

"Not according to Waew. He said there were signs of a struggle and there were personal belongings and money left behind. All the things they would have taken if they'd just done a runner."

"Who knew about the safe house?"

"Waew and his boss."

"Ahh. So do we assume the influential

figure found an ally at the police department after all?"

"No question about it. The case was
dropped. Waew was demoted to captain,
and the major general started driving round
in a brand-new Saab."

"And our hippies?"

"Nobody saw hide nor hair of them
again."

"So there's every possibility the couple we
found under Old Mel's land were the missing witnesses. They buried the hippies and
the evidence in one foul swoop."

"Sounds logical."

"I don't suppose there's any way we'd be
able to catch up with the influential figure?"

"That wouldn't be any problem at all."

"It wouldn't? Why not?"

"Does the name Sugit Suttirat mean
anything to you?" It didn't. "He was briefly
the Minister for the Environment and then
Rural Affairs in two, just as brief, govern-
ments in the late eighties. Long enough to
make his fortune. He's now the national
chairman of the Awuso Foundation. He's
got a big house and an office right there in
Lang Suan."

After Granddad Jah had left I sat and
watched the sea for a while. It was silver

285

and languid like a lake of snot. There was a wall of weather on the horizon, a dark blue line like ranks of special effect orcs about to invade our Minas Tirith. It didn't do a thing to assuage my feeling that it was me against them. The last archer on the battlement. It was all there embedded in the system: get rich whatever way you can, use the money to get power, get richer. And there were no public outcryings because your average man in the paddy envied them their success. Those middle class yellow-shirted idealists playing ping-pong in our assembly building weren't going to change anything apart from the flower arrangements around the fountain.

I sat on a stool in front of Maprao Awnings, the shop belonging to the private detective, Meng. It was humiliating. He had a client. His wife had placed the stool in shadow and given me a cool pack of 30 percent fruit juice but I was still visible from the road. I'd been in a funk since Granddad Jah's story. I'd completely forgotten to make lunch so Chompu had driven back to Pak Nam and the family had been forced to make do with *dom yam*-flavored instant noodles with a side plate of dried squid. I couldn't eat. I sat and watched them and wondered why I'd been so keen to beam myself back into the ugly twenty-first century. Once I could no longer stand watching them tuck into the fast food with the same relish they attacked my meals, I jumped on the auntie bike and set off for the plastic awning shop. I could have walked. It was only three hundred meters. But I felt I needed to be traveling at speed to get past Ed who was still there at the concrete table.

"*Koon* Jimm . . . ?" I heard over my shoulder.

"Not now, Ed."

What kind of man, I ask you, given the current economic turndown, would have two and a half hours to waste in the middle of the day? An unemployed loser, that's who.

But now I wish I'd walked because a stroll in the midday heat would have been preferable to being eyed by every motorcycle and truck that passed along our village's one road. At last I heard voices emerging from the shop, and Auntie Summorn, the mother of Maprao's only known villain, Daeng, was thanking the detective and walking with him to the roadside.

"That makes me feel much more comfortable," I heard her say, and I didn't get the feeling she was talking about awnings. A truck that was neither a taxi nor the vehicle of an abductor of elderly people stopped beside her and swept her off. That happens a lot down here. You go for a stroll and everyone stops to give you a ride. Annoying in a lovable kind of way, I suppose. The detective turned to me. If you already have an image of a private detective in your mind, you'll need to delete it and start again. *Koon* Meng was about my height but skinny as an ink line. I was surprised he could stand up under the weight of his clothes. I assumed it was the pen in his shirt front pocket that gave him his stoop. He had a five hair mustache and long gray hair tied in a ponytail.

"Sorry to have kept you," he said. "It's getting to the stage that I could use a waiting room."

He laughed with only his bottom teeth which I thought was impossible.

"Nice to see the detecting business is doing so well," I said with a thick smattering of irony I didn't expect him to get.

We walked to his office which was merely the front room of his single-story house with a desk off to one side. I sat. He sat.

"How can I help you?" he asked.

"I want to know what service you're performing for my mother and how much you intend to charge her for it," I said.

I hoped he wouldn't ask me if I'd posed

this question to Mair because then I'd have to admit I hadn't, not directly, which would make it look like I didn't communicate with my own mother. And then, as I'd been sitting on his humiliating little stool I'd wondered how I might react if he cited the problem of detective–client confidentiality, at which juncture I'd point out that he was a plastic awnings installer and, as far as I knew, there was nothing in the Awnings Code of Honor that covered such ethical dilemmas. But he didn't give me a chance to use any of my smart-arsed retorts.

"I'm chasing up some poison for her," he said.

All right. I gave him points for honesty.

"And how would you go about that?"

"Take a sample to the lab in Chumphon."

"A sample of what?"

"Stomach contents. From your poisoned dog."

"And where did you . . . ? Oh, yuck."

The plastic container in the freezer flashed into my mind. Surely she didn't . . . She couldn't have. I shook the thought from my head like a dog shaking off a bath.

"And what did you discover?"

"Lannate 90."

"And that is?"

"A common pest control. It was considered too toxic for use as an insecticide but it's still available. A nasty way to go, I'd imagine. A lot of restaurants and resorts use it to keep down the stray dog population. They don't like dogs worrying customers. They mix it with scraps and leave it out front overnight."

"And this poison has the ability to distinguish between stray dogs and dogs in collars with their telephone number printed on them?"

"No. Kills 'em all."

"But the only resort or restaurant for five kilometers is ours."

"Right."

"And we didn't . . ."

"Right."

"So, was that the end of your involvement in this case?"

"No."

"What else are you doing?"

"Your mother wanted to know the strength and effects of Lannate 90 and who'd have access to it. I told her anyone can buy it but most people with plantations or orchards would have it handy. But that's most of the population of Maprao."

"And that was it?"

"Almost."

"Almost?"

He twirled a plastic curtain ring around his little finger. I glared.

"She asked me to buy some for her."

"What? How much, exactly?"

"Twenty bags."

I decided not to ride back home right away. I needed a break from intrigue. My mind was out of practice. The nearest thing to a crime I'd experienced since we dropped down here was the kidnapping of our brand-new red garbage bin from the front of the shop one night in April. The case hadn't even made it as far as the police station. The neighborhood council had been so devastated that they'd set up a vigilante team. Bless them, they'd found the bin at a small peripatetic fishing community of northeasterners who were using it to ice their catches. The head of our council fined them in lieu of arrest, our bin was returned and we had free squid for a month. It had been an impressive display of local support but hardly front page *Thai Rat* news.

Now, my out-of-shape intellect was having to juggle buried hippies and stabbed abbots and battered policemen, and grand television larceny . . . and crazy, revenge-seeking mothers. All this on top of my cooking, gardening, and chicken feeding duties.

I parked the bicycle out of view from the road under a sprawling deer's ears tree and sat on a block of polystyrene. In the monsoons, the Gulf spewed up so much of the stuff, some mornings the beach looked like the frozen coastline of Alaska. But we can all rest assured that, thanks to man's inventiveness, that same indestructible polystyrene will be washed up on other beaches for many decades to come. Why did I always get distracted by issues when there was a life to live here?

I needed that moment. I'd seen it often in the cinema. The weathered old cop, mired in a case of unspeakable horror, drops everything and takes his rifle and his case files off to a cabin deep in the woods where nature has lain unchanged for thousands of years. And after emerging from a week-long affair with a case of rye, the answer comes to him. "It was the twin brother suffering from amnesia that done it." That was the moment of clarity I craved. I called to the trees, to the ferns, to the god of polystyrene for an answer. The cell phone in my back pocket rang. I was impressed. Mother nature had gone high tech. I pressed the green phone icon.

"Jimm speaking."

"Hello, little sister."

"Sissi?"

"Wachadoin?"

"I'm in a jungle retreat cut off from all forms of communication."

"All right then. I won't keep you long. I've been reading the personal e-mails of a number of senior members of the *Sangka*."

"Do you feel okay about that?"

"I checked. There's nothing about hacking in the precepts. It doesn't count as a sin."

"Then tell me all."

"Your abbot, the live one, he's got a relative in high places."

"Well, that might explain the media blackout. Would this relative be a leading light in the current board games in Bangkok by any chance?"

"Right up there between the bishop and the rook."

"OK. So it would be very helpful if this relative in saffron wasn't accused of stabbing another monk to death at this particular time."

"Any other time and nobody would say a thing."

"I get it."

"It would be very, very convenient if the investigators could produce another suspect in a hurry."

"Would a nun do?"

"Ah, so your mind's already there. There's been some research commissioned on your nun. An agency was hired to dig for dirt."

"I'm not sure I really want to hear this."

"She was a singer."

Lot of implications there.

"Nightclub?"

"No. *Molum.* Thai country. Quite a following, evidently. Then one day she shook off the spotlights and announced she was leaving the profession. The record people tried to sue her, but she was outta there."

"Did she give a reason?"

"Nope. And six months later she was hairless and didn't have to worry about the colors running in her washing machine anymore."

"When was that?"

"Thirty-two years ago."

"She's been a nun for thirty-two years?"

"In fourteen different provinces."

"Ooh, that's a lot of walking."

"It is. But, at this point, let me take you back to a time when Sister Bia was just flatchested *Nong* Bia, a high-school student in a little village in Burirum. In her class was a young fellow called Kem."

"Abbot Kem?"

"Don't spoil the story."

"They're about the same age? I don't believe it. He looks twenty years older."

"It appears he picked up the odd skin-ravaging disease during a prolonged stay in the jungle. But you're pushing me ahead of myself. Kem wasn't the most handsome boy in the class even before the leprosy. But he was sincere and honest. He obviously had something the other boys didn't have because Bia spent a lot of time with him. There were those who speculated that these two might even get married. But on the final graduation night, when all the other couples were rushing off into the bushes to celebrate their arrival at adulthood, Kem announced that he was entering Thamathiraram temple and would be ordained as a monk.

"Imagine her surprise. She continues to sing with her family troupe and soon makes a name for herself. But, whenever she's in Burirum, she visits her old flame at the temple. She becomes famous for a love song she wrote herself called, 'My Love Is Draped in Saffron.' "

"You're kidding? I've heard it. It's beautiful."

"I'm sure. It thrust her into the serious ranks of *molum* celebrities."

"Did she wear a hat?"

"What sort of hat?"

"An orange one. A sort of a prop, like Michael Jackson?"

"I didn't see one. I downloaded pictures of her on stage. I didn't notice a hat, but I tell you, she was something. You'd have to be one serious monk to turn your back on a babe like that. There were quotes from her manager. He said she was a difficult client because she insisted on regular returns to Burirum in her itinerary. And, on one fateful trip to the temple, Kem's no longer there. He's gone on a pilgrimage. For years nobody knows where he is. Bia's career plummets. She lacks the confidence and motivation to continue and so she makes the astonishing announcement. In her late twenties she becomes a nun and begins her trek from province to province."

"In search of Kem."

"Isn't it sickly?"

I would never have admitted to the tears in my eyes just then and I knew Sissi would keep her mouth shut about hers.

"So, when did they get back together?" I asked with a sniff.

"Four months ago she arrived at *Wat* Feuang Fa."

"Any record of them getting together in those interim years?"

"None."

"Then finally she finds him and refuses to leave and he accepts her as a nun in his temple until the *Sangka* IA bangs down the door."

"Ironic, isn't it?"

"But she said they'd been in touch, letters, phone calls . . ."

"No evidence of it."

"And what did the council make of the murder and all?"

"That the Bangkok monk arrived in Maprao and told the nun she'd have to leave. That she'd been searching for her love for over thirty years and she wasn't going to go without a fight."

"So she hacks him to death with a carving knife?"

"That's the way they're seeing it."

"It's all wrong."

"It may be but that's the version they'll be passing along to the police."

I'd looked at the photographs. I didn't see it as the work of a broken-hearted woman. It was premeditated, cool, not hot blooded. It was no crime of passion.

"Sissi, there's something wrong here."

"Perhaps, but don't you think it would make a fabulous movie?"

I thought about it.

"Yes," I agreed.

"I could play the lead."

"The abbot?"

A silence gushed out of the end of the phone in a scolding blast. I sometimes forgot how hairy was the trigger upon which her finger rested. You'd never know what might cause it to twitch.

"That was a joke," I said.

Ever-increasing silence. I expected to hear a click and the groan of a dead line.

"Come on, Sis. Laugh!"

"Not funny."

"I know. I'm sorry. But to make this movie work for Clint . . ." We both had a burning admiration for Mr. Eastwood — we'd seen all his stuff on pirated DVDs. All right, perhaps we didn't admire him enough to contribute to his royalties but we did like him. "We can't send Sister Bia to the chair."

"It'd be lethal injection."

"So, what do you want me to do?"

"I'm not sure."

For the next ten minutes, until my cell battery ran dry, I told my sister about the incident with the camera and described the photographs. I think she got most of it. When I stood up, the polystyrene stuck to my backside like a saddle. I don't know whether it was as a result of the heat I exude down there or some natural latex dripping from the tree but it took me five minutes to disengage myself. It wouldn't have been fitting for me to go and visit a former Minister for the Environment with a block of foam stuck to my rear end.

The plaque stating that this was the Awuso Foundation National Headquarters was screwed to a solid concrete post beside a fancy fretwork iron gate that towered above me. The two-story house beyond was an iced wedding cake with Roman pillars and strawberry trimming. I dabbed at the gate with a damp finger in case it was electrified. The glass shards topping the four-meter wall had alerted me to the possibility, but my finger wasn't shriveled to a sausage stub. I put more effort into the gate and discovered that the big fancy beast rolled effortlessly on rubber wheels. It was so well oiled, in fact, that it didn't stop rolling and I had to run to catch up with it before it crashed into an ornate flower bed.

By then I was aware of eyes. At first count I made out six belonging to camouflaged gardeners in army surplus, armed with hoses and hoes but merely standing around like extras. Two more eyes were looking at me from an upstairs balcony. These, I assumed, belonged to the man I'd come to see, Sugit Suttirat. They were set deep in a piggy little head on top of a beefy body. It was like looking up at the underbelly of a turtle except this particular turtle was wearing a Kim Il Sung special safari suit and a baseball cap. I didn't know whether he'd come to the balcony specifically to meet me or whether he'd been there all day practicing his false-teethy smile and his air-calculator finger wave. I'd phoned ahead, of course. "Freelance journalist doing follow-up stories on memorable politicians." I couldn't have been accepted any more warmly if I'd arrived naked on a mattress of thousand-*baht* notes.

"*Nong* Jimm?" he called.

Nong was designed to rub you up the wrong way if you weren't an actual younger relative. You used it on waiters and cleaners and street children so it really put you in a place you didn't want to be. But to a man of his standing it meant nothing at all.

"*Tan* Sugit," I squealed.

Tan was top-end suck-up. As far from *nong* as Klong Toey slum was from the Ginza. Once I'd jumped through all those superfluous honorific hoops and clambered over the ice-breaking debris, I was beside him on a vast brown leather couch in his living room. From this close I could see that *Tan* Sugit had been worked over by a plastic surgeon or two. He was able to move his mouth but, north of his neck, that was pretty much it. His beady eyes didn't blink and his cheeks didn't billow when he smiled. He was in a sort of facial truss.

My old faithful tape recorder sat between us. I could have gone the digital route but I enjoyed watching the tape rotate. I tested it; "One-two, one two," in English to establish my international credentials, then launched into the interview. My intention was not to head straight into the "Did you murder two hippies and bury them because they threatened to expose your criminal activities?" question. That could come later. This was more a get-to-know-you session. As an almost award-winning journalist I had to remain impartial and talk to him as if he'd been born of human parents rather than eels. As a member of the press you remained passive and talked to your interviewee without allowing yourself to imagine feeding the tail of his navy blue safari suit into the jaws of the ice crusher at the fish factory. You are a professional.

Throughout the interview, as I studied him, the question "How does a short and overweight person, obviously incapable of looking after himself with his fists, get to be an influential figure?" kept arising. The answer, as always, was "money." He stank of it. My brief run through his early years had arrived in Surat in 1978. I looked pointedly at my clipboard.

"I believe at the end of the nineteen seventies you were involved in the rental car business," I said. It was just another in my list of questions and I didn't put a great deal of emphasis into it. His smile stretched to its limit. I was afraid it might crack a seam all the way up the sides of his face and across his bald head. I'd be a witness to his face falling off. But it held.

"I don't know where you heard that one," he said. "I was involved in a number of ground-breaking ventures back then but car hire wasn't one of them."

An overweight woman in her fifties with short cropped hair dyed crimson arrived with coffee on a tray. She was dressed all in white like a late-starting Judo student with no belt to her name. He ignored her so I knew she was either a maid or a mistress. A wife he'd be obliged to introduce.

"Really?" I asked.

"I think I should know."

I flipped back to the previous page of my clip file.

"It says here that there was a disturbing

incident in nineteen seventy-eight when allegations were made that your . . . company had been accused of stealing rental cars. My records tell me you spent some time in prison."

He laughed again, or, at least, his mouth did. As there were no tics or flickers to be found on his face I couldn't look for indications of guilt.

"Nong," he said in his deep baritone, "with a man of my standing, it's only to be expected there'll be envious individuals trying to pull you down. There's a lot at stake. When you have an honest man at the helm, the criminal classes see him as a threat to their well-being. A man who cannot be corrupted or bribed is always going to be a target."

"So you weren't ever arrested?"

"Of course not."

Ooh, he was smooth. The lie was so deft I felt certain a polygraph needle wouldn't have flickered through the whole performance. A politician if ever I saw one. He glanced at his watch and I could tell he was becoming irritated by the direction in which the interview had headed. So, I fed him a few more scraps of ego fodder to get him back on track. He was chuffing along nicely again with all the aplomb of an elected official, so I chanced throwing another metal bar across the rails.

"So, we come to your relationship with the Chainawat family in Ranong," I said casually.

Of course, I had no idea whether there was such a relationship but it was worth a try.

"Where are you getting all this background information from, exactly?" he asked sternly.

"Oh, you know, public records, old news archives, the Internet. I was even discussing you with the provincial governor on the telephone a few weeks ago. He was the one who suggested I write a feature on you. You're really a local celebrity so it's thrilling for me to be here in person. I actually went to see the Chainawats on another matter and even they mentioned you."

"They did, did they?"

I had him. His teeth had been exposed to the air for too long and they'd stuck to the inside of his lips. My tentative dig had hit a pipe and caused a sudden charisma leak. There was something. I was prepared to leave it at that and go on to a different topic but he'd switched to slow advance.

"What exactly did she say?" he asked.

"Who?"

305

"The . . . Madame Chainawat."

"Well, actually, we were discussing land. There's a plot in Ny Kow that my family's interested in procuring. We have a number of projects on the drawing board, hotels, you know, study camps for university students, cattle ranches, erm . . ."

I was struggling. I needed a few seconds to think of why on earth wicked old lady Chainawat might have mentioned the eel to me.

". . . paintball courses, that kind of thing," I continued. "Mrs. Chainawat said if I needed to know anything about land in that area, *Nong* Sugit was the man to ask."

Whew! I thought the *Nong* was a nice touch.

"That's how she put it?"

"Pretty close."

"*Nong* Jimm," he said, after a sip from a coffee cup long empty, "there are a large number of good, respectable Chinese families such as that of my ancestors: families who only have the future of our great kingdom in their hearts. Then, there are people like the Chainawats. Be very wary about doing any business with their sort and certainly don't believe anything they tell you."

With that, we were suddenly at the end of

our interview. The ex-minister was on his feet and hustling me to the door.

"Would you mind if I scheduled another session with you?" I asked. "I'd like to get on to your years in government and perhaps take a few pictures. *Matichon Weekly* news magazine wants to make it a two-page spread."

"Of course, of course," he said, still prodding me onward. "Only too pleased to speak with the press."

"When can . . . ?"

But he'd turned and was back in the shadows of his house, leaving me in the sunshine of the front step surrounded by three or perhaps four camouflaged gardeners.

"We must all hear the universal call to like your neighbor just like you like to be liked yourself."
— GEORGE W. BUSH, AS QUOTED IN THE
FINANCIAL TIMES, JANUARY 14, 2000

You know how it is when the chicken manure man comes by with his truck and, instead of placing the dung in an orderly fashion twenty centimeters around the trunk of the palms as is *de rigueur,* he dumps it all on top of your best watermelon and drives off? One great mountain of dung. And all the chickens in the yard are looking at this pile and wondering why you'd pay for it when they could have produced it for nothing, eventually — not a mountain exactly but certainly a creditable amount. "Aren't you pleased with our work?" they'd say.

You don't know how it is? Well then you

wouldn't know how I was feeling when I finally got back to the resort that evening realizing I still had dinner to cook. I was like that watermelon, feeling claustrophobic and damp and dungy. I needed time to spread some of the manure around. A little bit of breathing space. But Mair, in one of her billion customer-free moments, strolled over to me in the kitchen.

"Ed . . ." she began.

"Mair, can we not talk about Ed for once?"

"All right. He said he'd be back at eight and he has something to say."

"Thanks. Look, Mair. I'm running a bit late. Can you peel the carrots for me?"

"Oh, child. If only I could. But somebody has to watch the shop."

I felt my cool pop like a tendon.

"You get three-point-seven customers a day," I said. "They spend, on average, twenty-seven *baht*. Our biggest sales are bottled water, ice, individual cigarettes and garlic. At this rate, in twenty-three years we can afford a wind chime to hang in front of the shop. We're surviving on what's left of the sale of our place in Chiang Mai, and at the speed with which we're spending, that should all be gone by the new year. Watching the shop isn't going to put a meal on the table. Peeling carrots just might."

She did her *Titanic* smile and I knew I'd got through to her. She picked up a carrot and started to eat it.

"The skin of a carrot contains most of its goodness, you know?" she said.

I upended the bowl of unpeeled carrots into the pot of boiling water and probably deserved the scalding splash on my cheek.

"There," I said. "Goodness."

"Did I mention that Ed would be stopping by at eight?" she asked.

"No, you didn't."

"He will."

She turned and headed back to the shop.

It was seven thirty. Ed, if he actually came, would be here in half an hour. I had to admire his persistence. He was a nice young lad, obviously enthralled by the exotic nature of our family. It had nothing to do with romance. Not really. He'd heard about us city girls and how loose our morals were. He was jumbling love and lust in his country boy mind. It wouldn't take long to frighten him off. I'd suggest we become friends. He'd agree but soon tire of that sort of relationship and head off to the Pepsi karaoke beyond the bridge and work it all out of his system.

I imagined the fellows down here would prefer a more traditional mate than someone like me. It's evident from the almost completely flat back tires of motorcycles I see passing that they like their women meaty. Wide and solid as boulders. I'd put my life savings on a Maprao ladies tug-of-war team. So, although my broad hip line shouldn't be a hindrance for me, I'd be hard pressed to find anything in common with a local man. Yes I like spicy food but I prefer a good slice of pizza. What good would pillow talk be with half the night spent with your nose in the dictionary? And what kind of southern wife would I be if I couldn't fix nets or trim palm trees with one of those chisel thingies? No, Ed the grass man, aka Ed the carpenter, would be very disappointed if I ever gave him the opportunity to get to know me.

I'd showered and put on my most matronly white blouse even though it did leave my shoulders bare. I'd compensated for this inadvertent titillation by putting on a full-length batik sarong with fish pictures on it. It didn't even provide a glimpse of ankle. I'd gelled my hair back but only because there was a stray breeze from the Gulf and my untidy locks had been blowing in my eyes. The red lipgloss was in lieu of the lip salve which I hadn't been able to find.

I sat on a deckchair on the sand with Gogo at my feet and a glass of Romanian red on my lap. We'd bought twelve cases, ten bottles in each, from Chiang Mai but hadn't found anyone with the sophistication to sample them. It wasn't any kind of a brew to write home about but I doubt brand identity was the reason the bottles remained untouched on the top shelf. We weren't living in Paris. Since we'd arrived, I'd taken it upon myself to work my way through the stock to clear up that shelf for sardines. I had one case to go. The bottle and one spare glass sat beneath my seat. I mean, it would have been rude to drink alone and not offer. He'd accept, of course, sip at his drink, say it was delicious, and leave nine-tenths of it behind.

I heard footsteps along the sand and stared moodily at the shimmering boat lamps strung out across the horizon.

"First sign of alcoholism."

I turned my head to see Granddad Jah standing black against the light from the kitchen with his hands on his waist. He looked like a bulimic superhero.

"It's late, Granddad. You should be in bed."

"It's half past seven."

"You can never have too much sleep."

"You do know I drove the motorcycle all the way to Surat for you this morning?"

"Yes. You want me to reimburse you for the petrol?"

"No, I want you to have the decency to keep me informed of ongoing inquiries."

"What makes you think I'm not?"

"I saw you."

"Saw me do what?"

"Go into that place."

"What pla— ? The foundation? You were in Lang Suan?"

"I was passing."

"Passing? I had the truck. Arny had the motorcycle all afternoon. Lang Suan's twenty kilometers away. How did you happen to be just passing?"

"There are motorcycle taxis. There are buses. I'm not completely senile, you know? I have been getting around for seventy-odd years without the benefit of an escort."

I laughed.

"You were doing surveillance," I said.

"I was not. I was just . . . interested. After all I'd heard that morning from Captain Waew I wanted to see for myself. It was curiosity. But I saw you waltz in there as calm as you like, and I tell you . . ."

I waited a long while but he didn't finish

the sentence. As time was pressing and I had a young man to let down gently, I ran through the content of the interview with Sugit as succinctly as I was able. Granddad Jah didn't nod or make comments. He merely squatted on the sand in that rural toilet pose I'd always failed to get comfortable in. When the story was told, he stood without creaking and said:

"All right. I might have some free time this week if you need . . ."

He turned to walk away.

"Granddad?"

"Yeah?"

"I think I'm going to need a lot of help on this one."

He looked back. Even with the moon masked by clouds I could see the glint of his false teeth by the lamps of the fishing boats. He grunted and walked back toward the lights of the huts.

According to my luminous pocket alarm clock it was seven fifty-five when my second visitor arrived. Punctuality wasn't a word that found its way into the vocabulary of too many of my fellow countrymen so I was impressed.

"*Koon* Jimm," I heard and paused to study one or two more boats before looking back over my shoulder. Ed was standing behind

314

me. He was wearing a white silk shirt, local style, and shiny black fisherman's trousers. There was something heroic about the way he looked. Missing only a scabbard in his belt, I thought. Even his mustache fitted the costume.

"Ed, isn't it?" I said.

"Yes."

He walked down the sand and stood beside my deckchair, breathing in the salt on the sea breeze with one healthy gulp. From where I sat he seemed every bit as tall as the coconut palms, every bit as upright and resilient.

"How did you know where to find me?" I asked.

"Looks like someone turned one of the table lights to face this direction," he said. "I could see you a hundred meters away."

"Well, that was a bit of luck, wasn't it?" I said. "I usually sit here in the dark of an evening and disappear into my thoughts. I'm having a glass of wine. Would you like one?"

"Thank you," he said. "I don't drink."

"Good for you. I have a glass rarely. It stimulates my imagination. Please sit down."

There was only the sand but he found a spot two meters from my seat and folded himself down onto it. To my utter surprise,

Gogo got to her feet and waddled over to him as if they'd been wagging buddies for years. He caressed her with one of his big hands and she rolled over to show him her belly. Her underside had always been taboo. Not even Mair got to touch it, but there was the grass man fondling her nipples with impunity.

"She's skinny," he said.

"She has a condition. She can't digest her food. It passes right through her."

"Has she been done yet?"

"Done?"

"Her tubes tied."

"Oh, no."

"She's about five, six months old. She could come on heat any time soon. In the condition she's in, one rooting from the local studs could kill her. I'd get her to the vet sooner rather than later. Get her tubes tied and it might help to settle her insides down too. Somboon's a cow specialist but he's good when it comes to de-sexing."

That was quite a recommendation. Not once had he looked at me. His gaze alternated between the boats and Gogo's belly. I surreptitiously emptied my wine out onto the sand beside the chair and stowed the glass.

"You seem to know a lot about dogs," I said.

"We've had I don't know how many over the years. You get to know what works for them."

Enough about them.

"Anyway, what can I do for you, Ed?"

There was a long pause. Long enough for Thai Airways flight TG250 from Surat to Bangkok to pass overhead with its taillight flickering.

"I was talking to your mother," he said.

"Oh, yes?"

"Asking about you. I'm sorry to be so nosy."

"That's all right."

I think the wine had given me a little heart flutter. They say it's a result of kick-starting a heart that's already working just fine.

"Mine's a small family," he said, apparently trying to pick out stars in the moonlit sky. "Just me, my mother, and my sister. My mother's doing all right. She's got sixteen hectares of land with coconut and oil palm. Lots of fruit trees. Yeah, she's doing all right."

"That's nice."

Probably what they'd refer to down here as "a comfortable dowry."

"My sister had a man for a while," he

continued. "What they'd call an arranged marriage. Don't think that ever works. So she came back to live with us last year. She's not . . . you know, her mind isn't really here. She knows she's different. She doesn't really fit in. She'd probably be better suited for the city but she's shy."

It was quaint of him to tell me about his family. They seemed very normal, probably some girl's dream relatives. I doubt anyone in their right mind would say the same about our family. I almost envied the simplicity of his life. I decided I owed it to him to perhaps go out for a meal with him so he could tell me about the grass business and how he'd learned roofing from Uncle Wit the builder.

"But she's very attractive," he was still going on. "Men are around all the time. I have to beat them back with sticks."

I watched him smile. It was a lovely smile, warming like good whiskey.

"I was wondering if you'd like to meet her," he said.

"Well, of course. That would be very nice. Sometime."

"She heard about you and she's seen you around. She saw you on the bicycle one day. It was all she could talk about over dinner that night. I've never heard her talk so much. The Chiang Mai girl with her trousers rolled up to her knees."

We both laughed and then . . . I suppose there are times when you can't see the rain for all the water that's falling out of the sky. That was one of those times. I was already soaked before I knew what had hit me. I don't know how it had gone so far without me getting the point. I'm usually a lot brighter than that. I felt sick, not wobbly sick, sick like I could happily throw up my entire day's food intake right there on the beach. I was stupid. So very, very stupid. I couldn't get away from there soon enough.

"OK, that'll be fine," I said without thinking. "I have to . . . cook dinner. Bye, Ed. Thank you."

I left the chair and him and my wine and half my face there on the beach and clambered up through the soft sand to the resort. I lost one flip-flop but couldn't even imagine going back for it. My hand shook as I reached for the handle of my unlocked hut and I threw myself onto the bed without turning on the light. Lucky the bed was in the same place as always. It wasn't yet eight thirty. I wasn't yet tired. The only thought in my wide-awake head was Ed the grass man trying to fix me up with his sister. I rolled onto my back and crossed my arms against my chest and willed myself to die.

I woke up at three a.m., four fifteen, five ten and five seventeen before I finally admitted I probably didn't need ten hours sleep. I heard the grunt of returning squid boats in the distance and the pre-dawn rehearsal of the cocks. I turned on the bedside lamp and looked in the mirror. I was still stupid. I had a shower, dressed, and went to make an early start with breakfast. It was still dark and I was using a crack of shimmering gray at the bottom of the sky to see by. I was about to turn on the light in the kitchen when I saw a dark figure walking along the beach toward the resort. It was wearing baggy dark trousers and a black windcheater with the hood up. The lower face was obscured by a mask. There was something ominous in its heavy footfall across the sand. I took a step back behind the customer toilets, hoping I hadn't been seen.

I could hear the crunch of footsteps on the gravel and there was no mistake they were heading directly toward me. I ducked inside the toilet block and hunted desperately for a weapon by the glow of the little red nightlight. Bathrooms are notoriously poor arsenals. There was a toilet brush, a plunger and a bunch of aromatic plastic tulips. None of these instilled in me the confidence to step outside and confront our invader. Then I found my weapon. Leaning against the far wall was a meter section of PVC piping. It was solid enough to bang an intruder over the head but light enough not to bring me up on a murder charge.

I took one step outside with my pipe raised and there, facing me like a mirror image, was the dark ninja with a block of beach bamboo hoisted. I screamed. She screamed.

"Mair?" I said.

"Jimm?"

We dropped our weapons and embraced, mainly to bring our respective shakes under control.

"Child, what on earth are you doing hanging around the public toilets at this time of the morning?"

"I woke up earl— No, wait. Never mind me. What are you doing creeping along the beach dressed like a *bunraku* puppet master?"

She pulled down her mask, lowered her hood and looked down at her costume.

"Oh," she said.

"Yes."

"I got dressed in the dark. I had no idea I was wearing black. And besides, these trousers are navy blue. You'll see when the

321

sun comes up. And this?" She pulled the surgical mask up over her head. "Chicken flu."

"Chicken flu?"

"From the poultry manure. Very high incidence of chicken flu from dung. It's airborne."

"Where exactly do they sell black face masks?" I took it from her.

"There are so many viruses around you can buy almost any color. It's become a fashion statement."

"Mair, this is a regular surgical face mask colored in with a black felt pen."

"Really?"

"All right. Enough."

I led her by the arm to the nearest table and sat her down. A puddle of pink was leaking out through the gap at the bottom of the night. The sun was rising somewhere beyond the Philippines and our sky was rushing through the dark tones in an effort to find something suitable to wear for the new day.

"Mair, what have you done?" I asked, staring her straight in the eyes. She stared back and slipped on an entirely different skin.

"Nothing to be ashamed of," she said. "And I'm your mother. And I remind you that I am the breadwinner of this family and the day you go out and earn a salary, then, and only then, will you have the right to criticize your mother. Do I make myself perfectly clear?"

She stood and huffed away from the table with an indignant gait. She walked toward the shop but realized that wasn't where she'd intended to go and retraced her steps toward her hut. I watched her march. I knew that walk and that speech well. All of us did. Eight-year-old Jimm had heard it a thousand times. On every occasion Jimm junior complained about having to clean her room or do her chores she'd had to sit through that same rant. Mair was in a dangerous altered state and wherever she'd been that morning I needed to know before the police found out.

"They misunderestimated me."
— GEORGE W. BUSH,
BENTONVILLE, ARKANSAS, NOVEMBER 6, 2000

Granddad Jah and I had arranged to meet Lieutenant Chompu at the Northeastern Seaside Restaurant overlooking the concrete battleship. Arny had wanted to take the truck to his gym and he sulked so much when I challenged him that I finally relented. He wouldn't even tell me why he needed it so badly but he was dressed up: long-sleeved shirt, jeans with a crease, real shoes. I tried to joke with him about a date and he turned the color of ripe chili.

That left me with a new problem. I had to use the motorcycle but I had Granddad Jah with me, and he was old-school when it came to sexism. There wasn't a hope in hell that he'd let me drive the motorbike. He even tried to get me to sit sidesaddle as it was more ladylike. I won that tussle, but Granddad Jah on a motorcycle was road safety personified. We spent half an hour digging out the spare helmet from the removal boxes before he'd agree to set off. He rode 100 percent by the book: correct procedure, hand signals, turning protocol, but, as everyone else was ignorant that there *was* a book, they were busy doing everything the wrong way just as their forefathers had done before them. That made us the most dangerous people on the road. And heaven forbid you'd be in a hurry. He practiced what he called "defensive driving" which meant we traveled so slowly we were often overtaken by maimed war veterans on tricycles.

We'd gone first to *Wat* Feuang Fa as I'd wanted to show him the crime scene and, perhaps, get him in conversation with Abbot Kem. It took us so long to get there I could feel myself aging. I wished I'd brought some embroidery to while away the trip but instead I yelled the details of the case through his thick helmet. All I left out was the contents of the camera. I was afraid if I told him, he'd be morally obliged to pass on the information to the police. He was a tough one to read.

At the temple, we were to be disappointed.

All we found there was a young novice whose duty it was to feed the dogs, and a monk so ancient and so covered in religious tattoos that he looked like he'd been excavated from some historical site. He seemed half blind, staring out through misty opal eyes and massaging each shuddering hand with the other. I joined him in the office. Granddad Jah had opted to stay outside. He seemed uninterested.

"We've come to see Abbot Kem," I told him. I half expected his inner workings to be as rusted as his casing but his voice was surprisingly young and his mind bubbled with energy.

"Vanished, poof, into thin air," he said. "Haven't seen a sight of him since they took the girl."

"The girl?"

"The nun. Can't remember her name but we only had the one."

"Who took her?"

"Those scruffy Bangkok detectives, the tall one and his podgy mate."

"Was she formally arrested?" I asked the monk.

"Must have had a warrant, I'd suppose. Not even Bangkok detectives can just kidnap a nun and whisk her off, can they now?"

"Do you think the abbot followed her?"

"You know I do a bit of palm reading on the side but I can't claim my ESP's all that hot. All I know is she's gone and he's gone and I'm left holding the fort. Just hope I can stay alive long enough to welcome him back. Wouldn't want to be running a place this size all by myself."

I thanked the old fellow and went outside to join my granddad. I was surprised to find both sandals there waiting for me although I did spot one black eye peering out from the bushes. We walked up to the crime scene along the concrete path. Granddad stood back for a few seconds and shook his head.

"If ever I saw a murderer who wanted to get caught," he said.

"Open, isn't it."

"Look at it. Top of a slope. Well used road at the bottom. Bright flowering bushes advertising the location. Plain view from the temple. And you say the dogs attacked him?"

"Abbot Kem said he'd been alerted by the sound of the dogs barking."

"Well then, anyone might have looked up once the dogs got going."

"So he was lucky?"

"I'd say so. And where did he run? A man with a pack of dogs after him. He's not going to head downhill into a wide open space. He'd have to go this way."

Granddad Jah pushed his way through the unruly bougainvilleas and, for want of a better plan, I followed him. We emerged on the far side where the temple perimeter posts were lined up alongside a wood. There was no wall. To the left, the posts stretched all the way down to the road. To the right I could make out a small green roof.

"Any idea what that is?" he asked.

"Yes."

He waited.

"Gonna tell me?"

"It's the nun's hut."

"Well then."

I'd suggested the possibility of the nun being implicated in the murder and done my best to make it sound unlikely. The concrete path meandered over the crest of the hill and approached the living quarters from the south. It was a very open track. But looking along the perimeter directly to the hut, I could see a case for someone concealing herself in the bushes and leaping out on an unsuspecting abbot. That's when I decided to tell him about the photographs. Not that I'd downloaded them, but that Arny and I had seen them. We sat in the shade of a particularly tall bush and I hoped that my description of the crime might point the finger away from my sweet, lovestruck nun.

"You still think she did it?" I asked.

"Well, if I was one of those modern, hi-so techno yuppie police superstars from Bangkok, I'd probably put all this information together and say, 'Yes, she's the common denominator,' " he said. "And I'd stop looking. But if I was an old, retired traffic policeman with not a single commendation or service ribbon to his name, I'd probably do this."

And with that he headed off into the overgrown woodland straight ahead of us. He was fit for his age. It was all I could do to keep up with him. The branches he pushed past whipped back into my face and the ground was thick with roots and nasty nettles that bit my ankles. I doubted any other creature had entered this jungle since the dinosaurs. But some thirty meters from the perimeter fence, Granddad Jah and the vegetation stopped dead. I ran into his back. Before us was a red dirt track cut through the undergrowth. It was common enough down here where locals planted cash crops where they could and dug out trails through the jungle for access. The way was heavily rutted with what looked like truck tire and motorcycle tracks. Granddad Jah looked left and right but didn't step out onto the dirt.

"All right," he said. "It's narrow. If, for whatever reason, I was to stop here in a car, I'd know some local farmer might need to get past to plant his palms or collect his berries, so I'd pull over as tight onto the verge as I could. About . . . there."

He was pointing to a grassy area ten meters ahead. We picked our way along the edge of the wood, being careful not to step on the track, and stopped at the rough patch of weeds.

"What if he came on a motorcycle?" I asked.

He contemplated that possibility.

"Then we're buggered," he said. "But let's go with the black Benz theory for now and see where that takes us. Ready?"

"OK. He parks here," I said. "He cuts through the jungle, kills the abbot, for whatever reason, then comes back to . . . Wait! Look at this."

I crouched down to get a better look. A cigarette butt in the grass. It was tipped and imported, not the type of thing Maprao locals would smoke. Granddad Jah knelt beside me and found another, then one more. We didn't touch them.

"Three cigarette ends," he said. "Now that's either totally irrelevant or really significant. If the latter, it changes the theory completely."

"It does?"

"Certainly. It either means our killer was so cool and collected that he felt he could get away with having a leisurely smoke or three, either before or after the murder . . ."

". . . or he had an accomplice waiting in the car," I added.

"Sometimes, Jimm," he said, with one of his almost smiles, "I think you're wasted as a girl."

I held my tongue. In his mind it might have even been a compliment.

"You think that was good?" I said. "How about this? You've got a whacking great Mercedes Benz on a little dirt track and somehow you've got to get it out again. Sooner than reverse all the way back to the road, you keep going till you find some-where to turn around so you're facing the right direction for the getaway."

He really smiled this time and squeezed my hand. I don't remember him touching me since primary school.

"And that," he said confidently, "is where we'll find our perfect car tracks. Good girl."

We hurried along the edge of the trail. There was one break in the tree line but the ditch there would have made it impossible to drive in. Then, around the next bend, we came upon forensic heaven 101. Sand, and one perfect M of tire marks, in and out. Forgetting myself briefly, I raised my hand for Granddad Jah to high-five me. He had no idea what I was doing and glared at me until my hand was back at my side.

That was the morning's work, and now we sat waiting for Lieutenant Chompu at the empty Northeastern Seaside Restaurant. Opposite, local tourists paid thirty *baht* to set off firecrackers in honor of the Prince of Chumphon, father of the Thai navy, part-time magician. This would be followed by a climb up to the deck of a fifty-meter concrete battleship erected in his honor. Pak Nam's most famous landmark, complete with concrete sailors and interlocking dolphins. What can I say?

Chompu arrived on foot. I was surprised. Pak Nam police station was only six hundred meters away, but policemen rarely walked. It made them look too common. I'd been nervous, I confess, about what Granddad Jah's reaction might have been to this flowery policeman. He was hardly in a position to complain, of course. He'd indirectly sired one grandson who was the 1992 Miss Pattaya World, and one more who'd refused point-blank to have sexual relations unless it was a sincere love match, ergo, a thirty-two-year-old virgin. With a record like that, a man would have to have serious doubts about his own gene pool.

To my surprise, Granddad Jah stood and saluted when Chompu arrived. It didn't feel sarcastic. The lieutenant generously returned the salute and removed his hat. We sat under the wooden canopy and Granddad and Chompu briefly exchanged professional backgrounds. I took the female role and ordered an assortment of *Esarn* Lao delicacies and cold beer and Coca-Cola for the lieutenant. Chompu was very respectful and I got the feeling my granddad had warmed to him early on. He told the policeman about the dirt track we'd found beside *Wat* Feuang Fa and I smiled at Granddad's look of awe when the lieutenant immediately took out his cell phone and passed on the information to somebody at the station. He related the story exactly as it had been told to him. He even asked Granddad for his full name so he could be cited as a witness. With the detectives back in Bangkok with their suspect, the local stations were now responsible again for any ongoing developments in the case. When Chompu turned off his phone, both he and Granddad were grinning widely.

"Well, that's one happy major," said Chompu. "If this comes to something, you'll have a friend for life."

He raised his glass and we all clinked.

"Any news from your end?" I asked.

"Afraid there weren't any prints on the cigarette lighter you gave us," said Chompu. "But we've got word back on the camera. It wasn't a make that can be bought."

"You have to steal it?"

"Either that or you have to be a professional photographer. Canon has a policy of asking professionals to trial their prototypes. That brand number was a prototype. They make a hundred or so of each and ask the pros to test them."

"So it should be possible to get a list of the people asked to trial the camera," I said.

"Technically. But it involves contacting Canon offices overseas. That could take some time, given . . ."

"Given all the foolishness going on in Bangkok," I said. "Any news about the Merc driver?"

"None of the mobile units spotted him on the highway heading in either direction," he said. "And, as you both know, I'm not at liberty to divulge information on an ongoing investigation, et cetera, et cetera, blah,

blah, but, between you and me, the daughter of the 69 Resort owner remembered the license number of the car."

"Good for her," I said.

"Even more impressive if you consider she's four."

"So we shouldn't put too much faith in it."

"No. I'm told she's quite a prodigy when it comes to license plates. Anyway, they're running the number. There are also developments on the attack on Phoom that I'm not at liberty to tell you about. The person who phoned in the accident on his cell didn't stick around once the ambulance arrived. That's quite common. Folks wanting to help but not to get involved in reports and interviews."

"Better than not taking the trouble in the first place," said Granddad Jah.

"Couldn't agree more," said Chompu. "But there was something. We had the local radio station, 106.50, ask for witnesses and a lady called in saying she'd passed an accident on the road. There were two vehicles parked already so she hadn't stopped. But she saw a man and a woman leaning over the victim."

"Two vehicles?" I said. "Really? Did she mention what types they were?"

"One pick-up truck and one car was all she remembered. No make or color."

"Is there any way to trace the good Samaritan call to the hospital?" I asked.

"It's not easy. We'd need a warrant from a judge."

"But it can be done."

"I'm assuming the major has already started the paperwork. What's on your mind?"

"Well, suppose the killer bumps Sergeant Phoom's bike, is afraid the sergeant could identify him and decides to stop and finish him off. He's bent over the body with a tire lever when this lady in a truck comes around the bend and stops to help. Our killer pretends he's just come across the accident and is aiding the victim. The woman phones the hospital and our killer flees the scene. The woman, for reasons of her own, also vanishes as soon as she's certain the sergeant's taken care of."

"In which case, the woman would have been in close contact with the killer," said Granddad Jah. "She could identify him."

I hadn't seen Granddad this animated since the great diarrhea onslaught of 2005. I liked him like this — without the diarrhea, naturally.

"Good," said Chompu. "I'll keep prodding the major on the phone records."

"Remind him what a boost it would be to his career chances," I suggested. "The man's a bubbling volcano of ambition."

"There's one other possibility," said Granddad.

"What's that?" I asked.

"The one you're deliberately avoiding," he said. "Somebody might want to call the hospital and ask whether it was a man or a woman who phoned in the accident."

I got it immediately. I didn't want to imagine my nun having a secret life outside the temple with wigs and fast cars and sharp knives. Granddad Jah was right. I really wanted the killer to be a man.

"I'll get onto that first thing this afternoon," said the lieutenant.

"Which brings us to the VW case," I said.

"There's more?" Chompu feigned horror. "Should I cancel my pedicure?"

"You should at least order us a couple more bottles," I told him. "You could be here for some time yet."

Again I left it to Granddad Jah to tell of his visit to demoted Captain Waew of the Surat police force. I kept expecting Chompu to say, "Of course, I knew all that." But it was evident that he didn't. He had his Paddington Bear notepad open on the table and

337

was throwing down a rapid shorthand. Granddad excused himself at one stage to take care of his long-suffering bladder, and it gave me a chance to ask Chompu what he'd done about the photos.

"It's difficult," he admitted. "I considered leaving them at the front desk and running away, but I realized everything would fall back on you as you were the one who found the camera. I can't plant them anywhere and it's a bit late to discover them at the crime scene. So, I admit, I'm boggled. I'm hoping something will come up to make their appearance unnecessary. Meanwhile, they're under my mattress."

"I appreciate you doing this."

"We're partners in crime."

I looked up to see whether Granddad had completed his ablutions.

"Which reminds me," I said in my low, conspiratorial voice, "have you heard of any . . . serious crimes committed today?"

"How serious?"

"Oh, I don't know. A killing?"

He laughed. "You're insatiable."

"So, have you?"

"No."

"No missing persons? Almost fatal injuries? Suspected poisonings?"

"Be patient. All these things will come."

I hoped in my heart that they wouldn't, but it looked as if Mair might have got away with it so far.

"Oh, and I forgot," said the lieutenant. "We traced your Dr. Jiradet the so-called adviser to the Pak Nam hospital. It appears he was there at the resort on a tryst with a juvenile harlot. They checked into separate rooms but nobody was really fooled, particularly his wife. Word has it that when her doctor left town the young lady in question found herself a tourist. You have to admire her opportunism, don't you?"

Two more suspects dust-bitten. I was running out of possibilities. Granddad returned. I'd considered not telling Chompu about my visit to ex-MP Sugit. I supposed there'd be arguments made that I was interfering in police business and unduly alerting a potential suspect in a dual homicide inquiry. In Chiang Mai I would have been arrested for it. But this was Pak Nam, and Chompu and I were already up to our necks in evidence tampering so I figured, what the heck. When I was done, he closed his mouth.

"Unbelievable," he said. "You wouldn't believe how dull life was in Pak Nam before you lot arrived."

I wondered at that moment whether he might be considering us suspects. Odd family turns up in town — bodies everywhere. But I got the impression he wouldn't have minded that either.

"So, you aren't angry?" I asked.

"Angry? I'm throbbing with excitement. Batman and Robin have arrived. Whatever will they do next?"

I wasn't particularly thrilled with the analogy, especially if I was supposed to be Robin. But Granddad Jah continued to glow, both from the beer and the adulation. He rather spoiled the mood once the bill was paid, by informing me that we were both over the alcoholic limit for safe driving and insisting we walk half a kilometer to the 7-Eleven to get motorcycle taxis home. He ignored my pleas that most of the drivers were addicts or imbeciles and we were safer driving drunk. He then wasted another twenty minutes arguing with the freak circus that he wouldn't allow them to go anywhere unless they put on helmets. I hadn't seen a motorcycle helmet in all the nine months we'd been here.

Eventually, we arrived home with doggy bags of *Esarn* food for Mair and Arny and a peopley bag of scraps for Gogo. As we pulled up, I saw Mair in front of the shop talking to the same elderly lady I'd seen at the plastic awning detective agency. This, I remembered, was the mother of Maprao's only known villain: an alliance I felt most uncomfortable about. I paused nearby for a moment but the two women were deep in conversation and seemed not to notice me. I went in search of Arny to give him his lunch but he was nowhere to be found. A family of four, young parents and two toddlers, were sitting in front of one of the cabanas. The door was open but their bags were on the front steps. I'd noticed a Suzuki Caribbean in the car park but I'd assumed its owner was walking on the beach.

"Excuse me, do you work here?" the father called to me.

"Kind of."

"Hope you don't mind," he said, "but we couldn't find anyone to talk to and the door was open."

"Are you staying the night?" I asked.

"Two."

"No problem. I'll find a key for you."

"We could use a meal."

I somehow managed to convince them that our *plat du jour* was delicious spicy northeastern food and went to heat up our takeaways. I ignored the whining from Gogo when I added the scraps and I was quite pleased with the finished meal. The guests didn't complain either.

I called Sissi.

"iFurn executive line," she said. "I'm Dr. Monique Dubois. Can I help you?"

She sometimes used this number for her IKEA II customers. She had a Web company called iFurn. Little i's and e's were really big in online sales evidently. She had an i-Furn Web site with pictures of her exclusive furniture range which was actually cut and pasted from the IKEA site. The only difference was that her prices were three times theirs. Her slogan was *IKEA looks but iFurn quality.* She claimed to be the IKEA top end, the stuff they produced before they started cutting corners and downgrading materials. And people fell for it. When she got an order she'd pocket the remittance, rewrite the invoice, and send it to IKEA, paying the catalog price. IKEA dispatched it directly to the customer. The phone line was back-up in case anyone received their package and noticed the discrepancy in the invoice. It rarely happened, but when it did she'd explain that this was the company's way of reducing the tax and, in turn, lowering the overall cost to the consumer. Her philosophy was that some people desperately wanted to pay too much for what they perceived as quality and were less likely to complain. She'd run this scam for two years. The phone connection was untraceable and the Web site was wired against intrusion. She'd know if anyone tried to shut it down. She was a diva.

"Hello," I said. "I was looking for a card table that collapses as soon as you rest your arm on it."

"Little sister."

"You busy?"

"The world never sleeps."

"Are you getting out to see that world, Sis? Breathing any of that air? Bumping into any of those world citizens on street corners?"

"We have a rooftop garden. It's very airy at three or four a.m."

"Restaurants? Bars? Bank queues? Crowded shopping centers? Society?"

"Are you channeling our mother?"

"I worry about you. What was that movie about the woman who stayed in the house all the time and ate and ate and got bigger and bigger till she filled the room, then she exploded?"

"Yeah. I remember. It was one of Audrey Hepburn's best."

"Sissi. I think Mair's done something bad. I'm frightened."

There was dead air on the iFurn line, then she said, "All right. Let me hear it."

I told her the lot: John, the awning detective, the poison, the early morning ninja show by Mair.

"I have frightening visions of her wiping out anyone in Maprao who bought that particular brand of insect killer. And we're talking hundreds."

"Hmm. Hickville genocide. Have there been any reports of a death?"

"No."

"Then, good luck to her. She's getting away with it. She still has the savvy to cover her tracks, and we always encouraged her to get a hobby."

"You think I'm being paranoid, don't you?"

"No. I think you're a complete idiot. Mair's a little odd. But you don't go from dotty to wiping out half a community with rat poison. What I do think is that you've been down there in oogaboogaland long enough. It's time to come home. I have a spare room and a whole cabinet of movies you haven't seen. We can drink Absolut vodka and watch old *Wagon Train* episodes on Utorrent and stuff ourselves with chocolate."

I sighed. It did sound tempting. Almost a deal. But I had some unfinished business.

"All right," I said. "That's close to being

344

an option. But let me sort out all these murders first. Have you had any thoughts about my abbot slaying?"

"I had a brainwave," she said. "I'm a member of this Web site called Police Beat. It's like Facebook but it's for anyone with police connections. It's mostly old cops, men, retired and active — unattractive police officers trawling for women with uniform fetishes. In fact, that's why I joined. But it gets an interesting mixed clientele as well. Some female officers, public prosecutors, crime writers hoping for scraps, the odd hooker throwing in a discreet ad masked as a chat. But the fascinating thing is, it's international. You get dialogues in bad English discussing law and swapping police techniques. I guess there are a lot of people out there who don't realize what the site's really about.

"My site identity is Elena. I'm a Russian homicide detective who lost a leg in a gang fight. But I'm gorgeous, you see, and all those noble police officers are prepared to ignore my stub. You'd be surprised what information one-legged Elena can elicit. But, anyway, there's this chatroom for discussing cases. So I mentioned our temple killing and the weird thing with the hat and I sent out a plea for any other hate/hat related stories."

"You mean, just in case there's a world-wide serial killer who puts hats on his victims before he stabs them to death? Siss?"

"You asked me to think outside the box."

"Not outside the planet."

"Fine. You don't want my help then I won't . . ."

"I'm sorry. I'm sorry. You're right. I mean, you're absolutely right. So? Any luck?"

"Not yet. I had an alcoholic ex-detective in southern California tell me in great detail about a performance artist who used to put party hats on roadkill and photograph them. She had an exhibition. That's as close as we've come so far. But this is a huge network. It'll take time."

"I trust you."

"You should."

"How's the Web idol job?"

"We have conflict."

"Already?"

"They want me to post my picture — pre-work. Me in the raw."

"Naked?"

"My Webcam would never forgive me for such a thing. No, they want me to show my actual, time-ravaged face. They say it would inspire the youth."

"Do they know your real name?"

"No."

"So, do it."

"Are you mad? What if anyone recognized me?"

"They'd send you an e-mail and ask how you've been, and you'd answer and that's the last you'd hear from them. Internet reunions are fleeting and they tire fast. I'm serious. Do it."

"I'd sooner die."

"When I was coming up, it was a dangerous world, and you knew exactly who they
were. It was us versus them, and it was
clear who them was. Today we are not so
sure who the they are, but we know they're
there."

> — GEORGE W. BUSH,
> IOWA WESTERN COMMUNITY COLLEGE,
> JANUARY 21, 2000

Sugit Suttirat, ex-minister of the environment,
parked his cliché red Corvette opposite the
Olympuss in the space saved for him with two
plastic shower stools. He looked at himself in
the rearview mirror.

"Not bad. Not bad at all."

Some might suggest it was his standing in
society that made him so popular with the
girls, but he knew there were those among
them that found themselves uncontrollably
turned on by his looks. They'd told him so,

even after he'd handed over the money. Women were easy to read. He beeped the central lock and watched as his lights blinked him goodnight. They'd see him again at two or three, drunk as a porpoise on diesel fumes, sexually satisfied and satisfying sexually thanks to Ovariga. Ovariga was produced and packaged in Yunan, China, and every bit as potent as Viagra. He'd wake up the next morning and it would still be there. Sometimes he had to sit through two meetings with his notes covering his lap. Excellent stuff.

He started across the street. The Olympuss lights were beckoning in red and silver. The girls sat out front on a bench, watching traffic, their little skirts climbing up their thighs, their faces . . . well, who really cared if they had faces? He stood on the white line to let a slow-moving Milo chocolate milk van pass by but it slowed even more, then stopped in the middle of the road. He was expecting the driver to wind down the window and ask directions but the glass was dark and he saw no one inside. He cursed and walked behind the van. The left rear door was flung open suddenly and it smashed into his face. He heard his reconstructed nose snap and felt the blood flow over his lips.

"What the . . . ?"

■ ■ ■ ■

I remember that Sunday in a blur, manure flying in every direction as if a ceiling fan had fallen into a tub of chocolate mousse. It began at six a.m. with a call from Sissi.

"Jimm, I've got one," she said.

I was still fuzzy from the Romanian wine. I took my cell phone out to the veranda and squeaked down on one of the rattan chairs.

"Since when did you get up before sunrise?" I asked her.

"Never," she said. "I haven't been to bed. I've had rather a heavy night with the police."

"You in trouble?"

"Not the real police, fool. The Police Beat police. They're really bullies online too, let me tell you. I have bruises."

"I believe you."

I looked down at the beach and saw a shadowy figure trudging along the sand.

"And I found you a hat," she said. "An orange one."

"OK, thanks. Mail it down."

"Look, will you slap yourself in the face or something? You're always educationally challenged when you first wake up. I'm talking about a case. An unsolved murder."

"All right. And it's a stabbing?"

"No."

"Victim have religious connections?"

"No."

The little enthusiasm I'd managed to rouse was on its way back to bed.

"Thailand?"

"Guam."

If you'd handed me a map and offered me a million *baht* I couldn't have told you where Guam was. Neither could I give a lizard's back end.

"So, the connection is an orange hat?"

"Do you think you can downgrade a little of that cynicism? I've been up all night looking for this frigging hat."

I'd unlocked the beast so it was the least I could do to hear her out.

"All right. I'm sorry."

"Toshi."

"Bless you."

"My Japanese detective. A judo black belt. Olympic medal and very fond of Eastern European women."

How sweet. Two nonexistent people had found one another.

"He replied to my search 'unsolved murder — incongruous hat.' His English was crap but he made up for it with his enthusiasm. He said this was the case that had most baffled him. A Japanese engineering firm was in Guam building a two-million-yen hotel."

"Which is about fifty dollars."

"All right, I don't know, two-hundred billion yen — a very expensive hotel, twenty story, designed by a famous architect. One of the Japanese foremen supervising the local workers falls from the top of the almost complete hotel into the empty swimming pool. An accident, they all assume, until the coroner discovers a small-gauge bullet hole in his lower back."

I was growing impatient. The figure on the beach was clearly my mother in her ninja costume.

"Does the incongruous hat arrive soon?" I asked.

"That was the confusing thing. Something nobody could explain. You know the Japs and their look-alike costumes. The firm that undertook the construction had their own very distinct uniforms: luminous green full-body overalls and white hard hats. No fashion statements. No individual touches. They were Japanese and they'd all arrived on the bus together that morning. But when the foreman hit the pool, he was wearing a bright orange hard hat. And do you know why?"

"Rebellion?"

"Somebody had spray painted his hat luminous orange while he was still wearing it."

"He didn't do it himself?"

"The paint was in his eyes, around his neck. There was no sign of a can. Whoever sprayed him took it with them. And they never found the shooter."

It was weird and it was irrelevant and I was distressed to have been woken up so early and forced to listen to it.

"That's great, Siss. Thanks."

"You don't sound very excited."

"No, I am. Tired, that's all. Let's keep pushing on the orange hat thing. Good job. Listen, everyone's growling here for breakfast. I'm going to have to leave you. Talk to you later."

Bad start to the day: hangover, long stupid phone call, mother up to no good. It could only get better.

It didn't.

Sitting in front of the kitchen block was a little man on a very old motorcycle. He weighed so little I imagined it was only his thick gold helmet that stopped him being blown off the saddle as he rode. In his hand he had a brown paper envelope.

"Are you *Koon* Jum?" he asked.

"Jimm."

"That's probably it."

He handed me the envelope and drove off. I hadn't had the presence of mind to ask him where he was from or why he'd ridden out at such an unholy hour to make his delivery. By the time I'd formulated all my questions he was gone. The envelope did indeed have the words "*Koon* Jum, Lovely Resort," written in thick felt tip. I put on the pot to boil water, then ripped open the envelope. It contained a simple black and white election flyer. On the front was a photo of a grinning candidate with a large rosette on his shirt. The flyer was very old, the paper almost separating at the crease. If the name hadn't been written there I would never have recognized the man. It was the decidedly younger and unplasticized face of *Tan* Sugit beside a large, handwritten, number three. It was the type of thing poll delegates would pass on, hand to hand in villages.

"Here's twenty *baht*. This is the number you'll vote for. We'll know if you don't and we'll be back."

The only thing that had changed since those days was the cost of a vote. You could get up to five hundred *baht* for your name on a list these days. I turned over the paper and on the back in scrawled handwriting were the words, "Ask his daughter about the VW." It was written in some watery ink that had dried brown at the edges. I really wasn't in the mood for a mystery.

Breakfast was a simple affair. Our guests had given up on us and driven off early to find somewhere else to eat. We couldn't do that. We were captive. Most families would help themselves as they were coming and going from bed to work: rice porridge, a quick Chinese doughnut, some sort of dried meat, a plastic bag of warm soybean milk for the road. But Mair insisted we all eat breakfast together; sit down at one of our tables and "talk." The policy hadn't been a great success so far. Most mornings we'd just stoop over our plates and fuel up for the day. But, on this awful Sunday, Arny had an announcement to make.

"I've got a girlfriend," he said, a smile sliming across his face. We all looked at him with our spoons and forks on pause, some full on their way up, some empty on their way down, but all static. For many years we'd hoped to hear such a proclamation. We'd encouraged him. I'd introduced him to girls at school. But by the time he'd reached thirty we'd come to the conclusion there was more likelihood of America getting an African American president than of Arny having a girlfriend. We'd all secretly assumed there was something of Sissi in him that he was trying to suppress. I blamed our absent father for his lack of male hormones. We'd all given up.

Mair dropped her spoon, leaped from her seat and threw her arms around her youngest.

"Oh, child," she said, "I'm so pleased for you. Well done. Well done."

I settled for reaching across and squeezing his hand. I was still suspicious. Granddad Jah, looking like death boiled up, stared at him in disbelief.

"Nice one, *nong,*" I said. "Who's the unlucky girl?"

Mair returned to her seat with a damp and shiny face.

"Don't be cruel," she said. "What's your young lady's name, child?"

"Gaew," he said, still beaming with pride.

"And what does she do?"

"She used to be a bodybuilder. I met her at the weight room at Bang Ga. She still does weights but she doesn't compete anymore. Who'd have thought it? A little wooden gym in the countryside and I'd find someone like Gaew. I recognized her right away from her photos."

"What photos, child?" Mair asked.

"In *Body Thai.*"

"She was in a magazine?"

"Not just in it. She had features regularly. International journals too. She was a celebrity."

"And she lives in Bang Ga?" I asked. I hadn't reached the goose-bump stage but I could certainly feel little prickles of foreboding.

"Even celebrities have to be born somewhere," Arny reminded me. "Her family's all there. I went to their house. All the awards. All the photos. It was like a museum. Everything I've ever dreamed of. She told me all her stories at lunch."

"So, you've eaten with her?" Mair asked.

"Twice now. I took her into Lang Suan yesterday. We talked a lot. When we got back to her house there was nobody there. We almost had sex."

Granddad dropped his doughnut. Mair laughed out loud.

"Arny," I said, astonished. "We're eating here. And you weren't going to lose your big V until you found the big L, remember?"

"Oh, Jimm, really. This is it," he said. "The heart freeze and everything. I know it's right. I'm going to ask her to marry me."

"Oh, child," Mair said. "You're a big boy

now but there's really no hurry. Trust me. How long have you known her?"

"Three days."

"Three days, right. Then if it's love after three days, it'll still be love after three months. None of us wants to make commitments on impulse. I'm delighted, really. But passion is an egg. You have to see it grow into a chicken before you decide whether it's a boiler or a roaster."

Mair always had a way with idioms.

"What does Gaew think about all this?" I asked.

"She feels really exactly the same. She said as soon as she saw me it was 'clunk.' That's how it hit me, too. Clunk. She said she hadn't felt that way since she met her first husband. She said it was a rare, almost impossible feeling to reproduce but she had it."

The frame had paused again without us noticing.

"Her first husband?" Mair asked.

"Yeah. He was the one who got her into bodybuilding. He was an icon, too. Dom, Mick's Gym, Purachart. He won the all-Asian title twice. You remember him. I had his poster on my wall when I was just starting out."

"You started out when you were fourteen,"

358

I reminded him.

"Yeah. Really" — Arny nodded — "that was a while ago, wasn't it?"

Ahead of me was a metaphorical field which was peppered with metaphorical landmines. I could have progressed lightly and tiptoed around but I knew we were headed for a messy bang whatever I did.

"Nong?" I asked. "How old's your girl-friend?"

"Fifty-eight."

There was no shame or embarrassment in his voice. He'd said it proudly and loudly. It didn't seem to cross his mind at all what effect such a statement might have on his fifty-seven-year-old mother. Mair hung on to her *Titanic* smile but couldn't bring herself to speak. She wiped her mouth with a tissue, stood, and walked unsteadily in the direction of the shop. Arny watched her go with a real smile on his own face.

"Looks like Mair's as excited about all this as I am," he said.

The silence that followed was interrupted by the beep of a motorcycle horn. Ed rode past and waved. Sitting behind him was an attractive girl about my age. She smiled at me and put her hand to her heart. Not for the first time that day I didn't know how to react, and it was barely seven o'clock.

■ ■ ■ ■

Lieutenant Chompu came by at eight. I'd given him the heads-up about my note. Granddad Jah and I piled into his truck and headed off out of Maprao. Da Endorphine, the slick ballad queen was cooing on the CD player. Of course, I was the girly in the backseat. Chompu read the note and flipped it over to look at the election poster.

"Any idea what year this might have been?" he asked.

"Seventies by the look of his tie and his sideburns," Granddad said. "Probably the man's first attempt at conning his way into public office."

"But why was it delivered to me?" I asked. "Who knows I'm involved in the case?"

"You mean apart from all of Lang Suan, seventy-two percent of the province and approximately half the south of Thailand?" Chompu asked.

"All right, yes," I agreed. "But why send it to me and not you lot?"

"Because nobody trusts the police," said Granddad, matter-of-factly.

"That's the truth," said Chompu, "but I wouldn't be surprised, given the events of last night, if this note isn't part of a . . .

deeper story."

I noticed how Chompu liked to leave dramatic gaps, probably so they could edit in music bites later.

"What happened last night?" I asked.

"Of course, I'm not at liberty to divulge details of an ongoing case, but I can probably, at a pinch, tell you that they found your *Tan* Sugit handcuffed naked to a bench at the Lang Suan train station early this morning."

"Dead?"

"Stop it. They can't all be dead. We have a three-body-per-decade quota. No, he was bruised and woozy from some drug and he had the words *sa som* — 'deserved' — written on his belly in some animal blood. But he was very alive and thoroughly embarrassed. He told Lang Suan police it had been a terrorist attack. That they'd threatened to kill him but he'd been able to play on the sympathy of the kidnappers — a technique he'd learned, he said, from many years of dealing with southern insurgents — and they'd let him go unharmed."

"But chained naked to a train station," I pointed out.

"A symbolic gesture. A small victory."

"What did he say they were after?"

"He hinted he might have been in possession of some sensitive documents on the new government policy for dealing with Muslim separatists."

"Bunch of cow dung," said Granddad.

"But you think it has something to do with my note?"

I asked.

"Coincidences such as this only happen on television."

We'd turned onto the highway and were heading north.

"Do you know anything about Sugit having a daughter?" I asked.

"Yes. I imagine you'd have seen her if you went to the house."

"The fat girl? He treated her more like a maid."

"She's been living with him for several months, I heard. I think it's important that we find out what she knows."

"So, if you think the daughter is a key factor in solving the case, why are we heading away from Lang Suan?"

"All right, I'm not at liberty, et cetera, blah, blah, but I might have committed a slight error yesterday. Following our very pleasant lunch, I decided to follow up on your Sugit's violent reaction to wicked Auntie Chainawat. I was curious to know why he disliked her so much. So I went over to Ranong."

"And you're afraid your visit was the reason for Sugit's kidnapping. You think you've sparked a Chinese mafia war between two of the south's most dangerous clans and that soon the entire region will be a battleground of blood and revenge."

"I wouldn't have put it quite as dramatically but yes, I may have hinted that Sugit had referred to the Chainawat family in less than glowing terms."

"So, we're going there now, as a team, heavy back-up, to accuse them of kidnapping and torture."

"No, you're going there as an innocent young lady and her elderly but very competent grandfather. I'll be parking several blocks away. I can't be seen there again, just in case I'm right about the feud. You just happened to be in the neighborhood and you had such a nice time when last you met them, you thought you'd stop in to say hello. You just need to get a sense of whether you think they had anything to do with last night."

"And why should we do that?"

"Because you're both as curious as I am."

"And what if we're right and they throw us in a cellar and cut us up into little pieces?"

"Then that's proof that they're up to no good. I'll be able to wear my captain's stripes to your funeral and shoot real bullets in the air. Can you believe I've never fired live rounds outside the shooting range? Such a shame. I'm a terribly good shot."

Granddad Jah was grinning like a crocodile in the front seat. He loved all this. It was as if his life had been recharged. Me? I was wondering whether we'd make it to lunchtime.

"My mother wants to know why she should answer any of your questions."

The son's face had become even more enchanting since the last time I'd seen him but he was using his smile less generously. We were sitting at the same coffee table with probably the same uneaten rambutans and peanut snacks in front of us. The old lady's fuse was shorter than ever without a uniformed policeman beside us. It had taken a very long time for her to grant us an audience and I could tell she wouldn't be staying long. The question had been simple, "Do you know *Koon* Sugit Suttirat?"

With thoughts of torture and disembowelings in my mind, I planned to tread a very diplomatic path. But Granddad Jah headed off into the jungle again.

"Because Sugit says your family's as corrupt as a Burmese general," he said. "He told the press you couldn't be trusted, then, a few hours later, he was kidnapped and tortured to within an inch of his life. That puts you way up there on the list of suspects."

It was fascinating. I sort of admired my granddad and wanted to hit him over the head with a blunt machete at the same time. The son started to translate but Granddad interrupted him.

"Enough of that," he said. "The old witch has been in the country forty years. She understands everything that's being said, don't you, dear? Yes. I've seen enough of these fake translation dramas to last me a second lifetime. You aren't fooling anyone. It doesn't make you look or sound like you're somebody. You're just another foreigner, no more or less important than those day laborers you employ out there."

There followed several seconds of chilled silence.

"I more important than Burmese," the old woman spat in clipped Thai. "More important than you, old man. Who are you?"

"None of your business," he said.

That was it. That was when the hands clap and the coolies rush in with knives between their teeth and they bundle us down to the dungeon. Good one, Granddad. I held my breath. But it didn't happen. She glared stiffly at my granddad until a horrid betel nut smile filled her little mouth. There was almost a flirt in her eyes.

"Sugit is bastard," she said. "I happy his face break. I shake hand this kidnap man. Sorry he not dead, old Sugit." A pause to calm her excitement, then: "But is not me."

And, for some peculiar reason, I believed her. I didn't like her. I didn't trust her. But I believed her. Once she'd exhausted her Thai language supply she reverted to speaking through her son although he no longer needed to translate what we said. She understood everything. She had a lot of dark tales of broken land deals and underhanded profiteering. She smiled when she related victories she'd had over Sugit and even spat betel on the floor at one stage as she recounted his dishonesty. I saw it as a turf war between two old Thai Chinese bandit empires. They'd each assumed an air of respectability in modern times but deep down they were all crooks. I didn't favor one camp over the other but neither did I see a connection between this rivalry and the little plot of land at the back of Old Mel's plantation. I dared ask the question again as to why she'd sold that small sliver of land. The answer was different this time and she answered personally.

"People who make connect past and future may know the present," she said.

It sounded like a fortune cookie. I had no idea what she was talking about. It must have been an inscrutable Chinese thing that I could never hope to understand. In the police truck on the way back Granddad Jah and I tried to recall every small detail of our discussion. Did we believe her? Who were we to say? But . . . no, not all, not completely. Did she have Sugit abducted? I didn't think so. Her final riddle stuck with me for some reason and it's just as well it did.

"If you don't stand for anything, you don't stand for anything! If you don't stand for something, you don't stand for anything!"
— GEORGE W. BUSH,
BELLEVUE COMMUNITY COLLEGE,
NOVEMBER 2, 2000

We arrived at Lang Suan at eleven thirty. Meteors had landed, dinosaurs had turned into goldfish, sprouted legs and become presidents, and it wasn't even lunchtime yet. Lieutenant Chompu drove us directly to Sugit's house. The lieutenant assured us that the old politician was in the hospital on a drip, milking all the sympathy and press attention he could get.

"So, why are we here?" I asked.

"We're taking his daughter out for lunch," he said. "I called to make a date while you were off partying with the Chainawats."

Upmarket dining wasn't easy to find in

368

Lang Suan. You could forget French, Japanese and Italian, even American, Vietnamese and German. It was all too fancy for the locals. Even the new KFC had been empty since its launch a month earlier. So, we took the ex-minister's daughter to a tiny place beside the Uaychai Department Store. It was owned by the minor wife of a propane gas tank baron who didn't really care what she cooked as long as she turned a profit. The food was cheap but tasty and eclectic and the service was so slow it gave you plenty of time to chat.

The daughter, Mayuri, was indeed the crimson-haired servant I'd met, but not been introduced to, at the house. She'd come with us without protestation or fuss, just walked out past the camouflaged gardeners and climbed into the truck with a friendly smile. She seemed truly delighted to have an excuse to leave the property. She was funny and as colorful as her hair, but she seemed to be sadly lacking in instincts. She had no apparent fear that we complete strangers might have motives for this lunch other than food, and no sense at all that our questions were leading. It didn't take a great mind to deduce that Mayuri wasn't the brightest squid boat in the sea. I felt no pressing need to be discreet.

"A VW Kombi . . ." I began.

"I read that" — she thrashed into the gap. "Can you believe that? Buried. Unbelievable. Those poor people."

I had no idea where to go from there.

"But you knew what a VW Kombi was before you read about it?" Chompu asked.

"Oh, yes." She grinned. "They were so 'it' back then. They said there were more VW vans criss-crossing the world than there were in the whole of Germany. And that's where they were made. Imagine that. A flock of, like eagles flying out in a fleet of Kombis all round the world. Wow!"

"Did you ever see one?" Chompu asked.

Mayuri was sitting next to him and she leaned close and cupped her hand around her mouth as if she were about to impart a deep secret.

"Not only did I see one," she whispered aloud, "I rode in one. That's why it was so awesome when I saw it in the newspaper."

She had my undivided attention. There weren't that many VW Kombis around.

"When was that?" I asked.

"Nineteen seventy-eight," she said.

She'd hammered the year. Put herself right there.

"How old were you then?" Chompu asked.

"Twenty . . . what? Twenty-two?"

"How did you get to ride in a VW Kombi?" I asked.

She tutted and sipped her Coke.

"The things you do," she said. "The things you do when you're young." She looked around at us all staring at her and decided it was probably no big deal to go on. "The seventies were crazy," she said. "This army coup and commies everywhere, and government spies, everyone suspicious and blaming each other. It was a really hard time to grow up and, you know, believe anything. Some of us headed down to the beaches where the backpackers were. We had these wild times down there. We met this crazy Thai guy who'd been living in the jungle hiding out from the junta, and he had this family land outside Surat. He asked us to live with him there. There was like a group of us. We thought we were flower children but I think we'd been just pretend hippies till he came along. This Thai guy gave us a chance to live a real alternative lifestyle, you know? We set up this, what do you call it? This cooperative farm. He'd lived on something similar in the States, he said. We were trying to do it all without money. We grew most of what we needed, raised animals, cut wood for cooking, you know? It was this very simple, like, beautiful life.

"But there were needs, you see? The bigger our commune got, the more we needed — petrol for the pumps, you know, a truck, a little tractor — but we weren't making anything from the stuff we produced. We were just, you know, surviving. And we needed money. I guess, when I think about it now, that means we weren't very good at being self-sufficient. The whole point was that we . . . Anyway, I had this father, of sorts. I hadn't spoken to him for years but I got in touch and asked him if he could let me have some money. He wasn't into it but he said he had a few odd jobs he could let us do to earn some bread. He told me about this car rental deal. He'd front the rental money and arrange IDs. Two of us would hire a rental car, drive it to this friend of my father up the coast, and leave it there. His friend would take it to Hua Hin and sub-rent it to foreigners at three times the price. Then he'd drive it back."

"What makes you think that's what they did?" Granddad Jah asked.

"What else would they do with them?" she asked.

"Steal them."

"Ooh, do you think so? That sounds a lot more dishonest than just borrowing, doesn't it?"

"You don't think it odd that they didn't have you drive them back to the rental firm?"

"Right. I hadn't thought about that."

"Right," I said. "And how long were you and your friends involved in this rental scam?"

"I don't know. Three months? About that. It was a nice easy income. And we didn't see it as illegal, you see? Just sharing rich people's wealth around. That was our philosophy, our mantra."

"Rob from the rich and give to yourselves?" said Granddad Jah.

Mayuri missed the point.

"We'd have nice cars to drive, look at the scenery, take our time and come back on the bus. And we had money for the commune."

"So, how did the VWs change things?" Chompu asked.

Two of our seven ordered dishes arrived on the table. We didn't know whether to tuck in or wait for the rest. Mayuri solved the dilemma by dipping a spoon into the prawn fried rice and ladling a good helping onto her plate.

"There were two or three couples renting cars, I remember," she said. "They were mostly, you know, Fords and Austins, that kind of thing. Nice cars but nothing excit-ing. Then we were told to go to this com-pany and they had two VW Kombis. They were, like, these chariots of the flower gods. We were awestruck. Dad wanted sedans but we couldn't resist it. We rented one of the two VWs. It was a gas. We were so close to heaven we lost it."

"The van?"

"Our minds. We'd wanted that life. That VW nirvana. Once we were driving around in a Kombi it was better than drugs."

"Which you also had," I threw in.

"Mostly ganja. We grew it in the hills around the commune. It was a sin, of course. But so was beer and swatting flies so we ignored that. Religion was one of those strangling, you know, doctrines we were anti at the time. So we all traveled with a stash of dope for the journey. We found somewhere secure to hide it 'cause the cops were even more Bolshevik then than they are now."

"That's nice to hear," said Chompu.

"My soul partner then, his name was Wee, beautiful man. He said we shouldn't take the van straight up to the dealer guy. He said we should enjoy it a little bit."

"So you didn't make it to Chumphon?" I asked.

She giggled and I saw traces of the wild girl in her eyes. My mother had those same remnants of devil.

"We didn't even make it out of the province," she said. "We were picked up by the highway police the next morning and packed off to the Chaiya police station."

"What for?" I asked. This and the account of the Surat detective, Captain Waew, were beginning to merge.

"Oh, you know. The supernatural magic of the Kombi. We'd driven around, had a little toke. Drove some more, had a little toke. Next thing you know we're heading back into Surat. Going completely the wrong direction. So we found a pretty nature spot and bunked down for the night."

"The police found you naked and stoned in the back of the van," said Granddad Jah. "You weren't twenty meters from the highway."

"We were crazy, uncle. Like I say."

She giggled again and shoveled in some rice; she seemed energized from the memories. Her past was obviously a lot more fun than her present.

"What happened then?" Chompu asked.

"We were using fake IDs. We knew it wouldn't be long before the cops got wise to that, then tied us to the other cars we'd rented. We didn't want to get in trouble. Then this inspector came from Surat and, like, told us he was investigating my dad — except he didn't know he was my dad — and that we could do a deal. He said he'd keep us out of jail if we gave evidence against the old man. Of course, anything's better than being in jail, right? So we agreed."

"To give evidence against your own father?" Granddad Jah asked.

"Yeah. We weren't that close. I don't know. We might not have gone through with it if he'd helped get us out, but he just went quiet. Pretended he didn't know us. I was afraid he was going to let us burn. You know? He was like that. But, anyway, while we were thinking about it, they put us up in this nice little locked-up house with a fridge and a TV. The detective said it was to keep us safe but there wasn't any way to get out. There was this fat constable there at the gate watching over us. It was cool. We were just hanging out, watching TV. It was all so surreal. Then Dad showed up."

"And he helped you stage the kidnapping?" I said.

"Yeah. It wasn't that hard 'cause the constable had vanished and left the doors unlocked. Weird, that."

The last of our food order arrived, passing our hopes on the way which were heading at speed out of the window. The bodies in the VW were obviously not this couple.

"Did you go back to the commune after that?" Chompu asked.

"No. We weren't game. We figured the police would have found out about it and raided the place. Dad told us to get out of town and lie low."

"Where did you go?"

"Just drifted. Smartened ourselves up. Got casual work here and there and the whole love-child thing sort of got old in a hurry. It turned out me and Wee couldn't get along in the normal capitalistic world. We drifted apart."

"Any idea what happened to the VW you'd rented?" I asked.

"No. Last time I saw it, it was in the parking lot behind the Chaiya police station. I imagine they sent it back to the owner."

"No," said Granddad, "he didn't get it back."

"No? Probably got adopted by some kind law enforcement officer, then," said Mayuri, out-eating us two to one despite all the talking. "I'd been thinking perhaps the one they found buried was the one we'd used."

"Any idea who rented the second van?"

377

Chompu asked her.

"No, like I say, we didn't go back."

"Do you know the names of anyone else in the commune?" Granddad Jah asked.

"Yeah, but it wouldn't help. We were all Bread and Steed and Morning Glory. We discarded our decadent labels when we joined the farm. We didn't know anyone's real names. Wee wasn't really Wee, you know? It's English for urine. It's full of nutrients. Indian fakirs drink it like orange juice."

"Nice," said Chompu, putting down his glass. "Where did you drive your stolen . . . I mean, borrowed rental cars to?"

"Tako."

Tako was about thirty kilometers up the coast. There were two routes from Surat. If you took the highway you'd pass through Lang Suan. The quiet back road that avoided police blockades would lead you along the coast almost to Pak Nam. Back then, there wasn't a bridge so the detour would drag you way up-river almost past Old Mel's land. We needed to find out who rented that second van. *Tan* Sugit still wasn't in the clear.

"Mayuri, you still aren't very close to your father, are you?" I said.

"Can't think what gives you that idea.

378

You've only met the old bastard once."

"Oh, just a hunch, I suppose," I continued. "You're implicating him in all kinds of illegal activities. You're calling him names. You aren't sitting by his bedside holding his hand."

She laughed and a noodle slipped out of her mouth.

"He doesn't need his hand held," she said. "There's nothing wrong with him."

"He was kidnapped and tortured," I reminded her.

"He was not."

"Do you know anything about last night's events that you'd like to share with us?" Chompu asked.

"The doctor I phoned said the only evidence of torture they could find was in his imagination. He broke his nose but with all the reconstruction I doubt he felt it. No, I bet he just got downright drunk with his whores and they got carried away in some prank. He doesn't have a clue when he's drunk. The terrorist story was just something to save his face."

"Why are you living with him?" I asked.

"He took me in as an unpaid housekeeper. I was out of work. Out of men. Out of luck. I contacted him and asked him if he had any odd jobs I could do. He asked if I could cook. I'd never actually lived in his house before. Ha, don't look so surprised. I'm child number four of twenty-eight or so. Seven different women. There was only one that he married. I had to remind him who my mother was. There isn't a lot of, what you'd call, paternal affection going on here, although there are nights I have to remind him we're blood relatives, if you know what I mean."

We dropped Mayuri back at her house, and on the way back across town we admitted we'd come full circle with the VW case. Granddad and I sat in the truck while Chompu popped in to see the duty officer at Lang Suan police headquarters.

"Granddad Jah," I asked, "what do you make of it all? I mean, the kidnapping, the note to me?"

"I don't know," he said, shaking his head. "The girl could have been right. It might have been S&M that got out of control."

"Stripped and handcuffed to a bench in the train station?"

"Some of those bar girls can be vindictive, *Nong* Jimm. You dump one and move on to another . . ."

"So, what about the words on his belly, *sa som?*"

"It means 'deserved.' "

"I know what it means, Granddad, but why would bar girls write it on him? Don't you think it sounds like something a bit more sinister? And surely you don't think the note to me was just a coincidence. There has to be a connection."

But I didn't get a chance, then, to hear his response. We were interrupted by the breathless return of Lieutenant Chompu who jumped into the truck and showed us his small but perfect teeth.

"I don't need to tell you," he gasped, "I'm not at liberty to tell you this, but . . . we've got good news and bad news and good news and bad news, and then good news. But it's all better than no news at all. Where should I start?" We both glared at him. "All right. The good news it is. First, the girl child was indeed a genius because the Benz number checked out. They found the car. The bad news is that it's a rental from a company in Phuket, and the fellow that stayed over at the resort was one of their hired drivers. His name's Wirapon, nickname, Keeo."

"That shouldn't rule him out," I said. "Rental car drivers can be murderers, too."

"That's true. But it appears he's more than happy to help the police with their inquiries. They're driving him over from

Phuket along with the details of the customer who hired the car and the daily log."

"Doesn't sound like a criminal to me," said Granddad Jah.

"Me neither. He'll be here by three so we should have some answers then. So, where was I? All right. Good news number two is that the court gave us the go-ahead to trace the number of the person who called in the accident of — aka attack on — Sergeant Phoom. The cell number belongs to the owner of a wheelchair and crutch dealership in Lang Suan. The bad news is that the owner says he wasn't the person who called in. He'd lent his phone to his brother who was visiting from Chonburi that day. He was doing some business down here and had forgotten to bring his phone charger with him. He said his brother was due back to his home the next day and didn't want to hang around here making police reports. The hospital number was on speed dial on the phone."

"Well, if that's true . . ." I said.

". . . and if the second witness was correct about seeing a man and woman at the accident scene," Chompu added, "it means that the other car at the scene was driven by a woman. The police here can't get hold of the brother. He presumably hasn't yet

382

worked out how to charge his cell phone. But the crutch dealer said his brother had mentioned the accident. He'd said something about a Chinese woman in an expensive car who couldn't speak any Thai. She was all aflutter because she was the first at the scene. Once the brother arrived she drove off. He was by himself. He didn't have any choice but to phone for help."

"This is all getting rather complicated," I said.

My head buzzed. There was a road team in there working on my narrow mind. Trying to broaden it. I had to go over all the events of the previous week, deleting a male perpetrator and replacing him with a female. How sexist was I? I hadn't once asked the hotels and resorts about women. I hadn't once considered the possibility of a female being capable of a series of violent acts. Even when they presented me with a female suspect, I balked at the possibility. I was a chauvinist of the worst kind.

"She wasn't necessarily Chinese at all," said Granddad Jah in his annoying unexpressive tone. "She could very easily have been a Thai with a wig."

I laughed.

"Why would she need a wig to convince anyone she was . . . ? Oh." I got it. "You're still with the nun, aren't you?"

"It all fits," he said. "She sets it up to look like someone from outside has done it, puts on a disguise. Car rental. Sneaks in and out of the temple without being seen. Motive. Opportunity. Plus, she's a classic psychopath, following this monk around for two thirds of her life. She takes my bet."

I didn't buy it. It wasn't just because she was a nun who'd spent most of her life in pursuit of true love. It's possible I might have empathized, but a good journalist is able to remove herself from a case. Even if I went along with Granddad's scenario and I arrived at the point where I needed to exterminate Abbot Winai from Internal Affairs so I could be with my lover, it could never have been planned this methodically. I didn't see the murder of the abbot as a mid-play act. This wasn't the bumping off of a threat, the removal of a plot spoiler on the way to the final scene. I'd seen the photos. Abbot Winai was undoubtedly the star of the show and his demise was the climax. This was all about him, not her.

"I think it's time to show your granddad the photos," said Chompu.

I'd considered it myself, of course, albeit briefly. Granddad Jah had earned our trust, but this was more than just sharing information. It was sharing a secret. The lieutenant and I had deliberately withheld evidence. It was a criminal offense. Granddad Jah couldn't even drink a beer without Breathalyzing himself. He was a stickler. He'd made his own life miserable by being honest. I had no idea where this would fit in his moral code book. Chompu could lose everything he'd fought for on this one throw of the dice, but he'd tossed the suckers anyway.

Granddad Jah was pensive for several seconds. His head nodded in time with the bleating of the "door unfastened" buzzer. Then he looked at the policeman.

"I was wondering when you'd get around to it," he said.

"You knew I'd downloaded the pictures?" said I.

"You didn't think I'd be curious as to why a police lieutenant was going with you to your room at ten thirty in the morning?"

I should have had a snide answer to that but I was still in shock.

"Were you spying?"

"Just happened to be sitting in a bush, minding my own business. But I confess I wouldn't mind seeing those slides from closer range."

Granddad was in. We were safe. An alliance of three untrustworthy people.

"Well, if that wasn't good enough news in itself," said Chompu, "I have even more information to impart on our own modest VW inquiry. In his statement, *Tan* Sugit had mentioned being apprehended by four villains — sometimes stretching to six or eight depending on who he's talking to — driving a refrigerated Milo chocolate drink van. The Milo company reported that such a van had been stolen the previous evening. Lang Suan police found it abandoned a few hours ago behind the clay urn foundry. The print people have been all over it but it seems to have been wiped clean. It all indicates that *Tan* Sugit's abduction was not a figment of his imagination, after all."

Chompu dropped us home and promised to call as soon as the results from the Benz driver interview came to light. I put Granddad Jah in front of my computer and showed him where to click. I was on my way to find Mair in the shop when I noticed our young family of guests back on the balcony. I noticed Gogo sitting with the kids, showing them her belly. She never showed me her belly. She seemed to like everyone except me.

"Would you mind if I asked you a question?" said the father.

I hoped it wouldn't be anything difficult: the tides, the names of the islands you could vaguely see on the horizon, or the genus of the bright turquoise birds that sat regularly on our back fence. My local knowledge was remedial.

"Certainly."

He walked leisurely beside me along the path behind the beachfront tables. He was cheerful, attractive in a young-married-man kind of way, and very polite, and the question he asked was a lot simpler than I'd imagined.

"Would you be interested in selling this place?"

My first reaction was that this crowd must have escaped from some maximum security family asylum. I looked back over my shoulder at the young wife and the happy children. They seemed normal enough.

"Why?" I asked.

"We've been driving down the coast," he said, "looking for a little place to take over. My wife's father passed away last year and left us a small sum we hadn't expected. We have a modest dream to make a go of something on the coast. We aren't rolling in money but I can make you a fair offer. We like it here."

"You do? Why?"

"Haven't you looked around?"

At his bidding, I looked around. The noncommittal weather of the past week had finally got its act together and a black pudding of a storm cloud was rolling toward us, filling the entire vast sky to the east. It was a Steven Spielberg moment. I instinctively knew I should have been egging the young father on, but all I could see were the faces of his children starving to death.

"Look. Really. This is the toilet plunger of resorts. We've been here nine months and we haven't made enough money to get the truck tires pumped up."

"But that's because you don't love it."

"What?"

"None of you is really here. I've been watching you. I see you all come and go but your hearts aren't here with you. A place like this, you have to work at. You've got no food in the kitchen refrigerator, no stock in the store. The cabins are sparse and uninviting. Nobody sweeps the beach." (People sweep beaches?) "You're all just staying here. I can make you an offer to give you all the chance to be where you really want to be, wherever that is."

I walked into the shop and caught Mair darkening a white surgical mask with a black felt pen. It suddenly didn't seem important anymore. I was in a state somewhere between excited and scared legless. I knew this would be the first engagement in a long-drawn-out battle but fate had armed me.

"Mair, you know the family in room two?"

"We've got guests?" she said, tucking the mask and pen into her apron. "That's nice. Arny didn't mention it."

"That's because he probably doesn't know. He's not here. He's off romancing Granny. He's hardly been here since the family arrived. They had to drive down the coast in search of lunch. They're using their own towels. The guy fixed the cistern in the toilet. That's embarrassing."

"The cistern was broken?"

I sat beside her on the little bathroom stool and I took hold of her hand. I sighed a deep breath.

"Mair, listen. It's not working. Whatever magic you thought might happen down here, it's not. And the people in room two like it here. It's a miracle, but they want to buy the resort. I know you —"

"All right."

"All right, what?"

"I'll sell it to them."

"Really?"

"If that's what you all want. Yes, I can sell up."

I'm not sure I can actually describe the feeling that slithered through my body when she said that, but I'll try. I was ecstatic at first, elated, gold-plated. It was if a legion of warm maggots had been deployed into my veins. But, unexpectedly, their pace slowed and they grew heavy and cold and eventually froze. I had a body full of iced maggots.

"Are you sure?" I asked.

"Child, in Chiang Mai we were five people in a house. Five individuals with nothing in common but a surname. We were hemmed in by traffic and breathing soot. We floated in noise and aggression and other people's troubles. We were all so inside ourselves we stopped living for each other. I hoped coming here might pump life back into us as a family. I wanted my children and my father back while I could still recognize them, before it was too late."

"Mair, I —"

"But we gave it a good shot. Nine months is something to be proud of. I'm sure Sissi will be pleased to have us back."

It was that easy. We could all go home and be happy again. Granddad Jah to his car spotting. Arny to his asexual body shop. Me to my desk beside the head crime reporter who always promised to die, one drink at a time, but never did. And Mair to . . .

"What are you doing here, Mair?" I asked.

"Doing?"

"Yeah. And don't lie to me. It's humiliating. I don't like it. What do you do every night with your black get-up and your pest killer and your beach creeping?"

She was just about to slide into her *Titanic* smile but I suppose she realized the gig was up. She took me by the hand and massaged my knuckles with her thumb.

"We're haunting a man," she said. I held in my breath and waited. "The man who killed John. I found out who it was. The son of Auntie Summorn. He's a nasty man, a drunk, a bully. He carries a gun and threatens people. My private detective knew who'd poisoned my dog straightaway. It wasn't hard to work out how far John had walked before the poison took effect. And the man had killed countless other dogs who'd worried his precious chickens.

"I had a meeting with the owners of the other dogs he'd killed. They were all angry but the police do nothing about it. They say everyone should keep their hounds tied up. It's our fault, they say. But, child, look at this place. How can you keep a dog chained with all this beautiful nature around? Our dogs were all well fed. They didn't chase chickens because they were hungry. It was just a game to them. They played with the chicks, annoyed them a little. And his chickens weren't penned. He thought they had a right to run wherever they liked but the dogs couldn't.

"The people here were too polite or afraid to confront the thug with their suspicions. They talked to his mother but she'd long since lost control over her son. In fact she was afraid of him too. He lives in a cabin behind her house. He doesn't work. He steals. He extorts money with threats. He's a bad piece of work, Jimm. At our meeting we decided we should haunt him with the spirits of all the animals he's killed. He's a drunkard so it wasn't so difficult to invade his dreams. At night, the voices of the dogs would come to him. Their shadows would pass his window but when he ran to the door there would be nothing there. Empty bags of pest killer that he thought he'd destroyed would return every morning on his doorstep. And there would be the howls, the incessant all-night howls keeping him awake. He'd walk around the hut with his gun but there would be no dogs, yet when he went back to bed, the howls would continue. He hasn't slept for three nights.

"Last night he didn't drink any alcohol. This morning he went to Kor Kow temple to make an offering to Jao Mair Guan Im, the Chinese goddess of mercy. When he came back home he went to his mother and told her he's being haunted and asked her what he should do. She reported back to us. She told us in another day or two he should be broken completely."

Mair had a smile on her face that wasn't the old brand. It was fresh and alive and real. It was the smile I'd seen on Mayuri's face that lunchtime: young and mischievous. It was the smile another Mair had projected to us little folk to illuminate tales. It was evidence that her embers were still burning.

I walked back to room two and thanked the young father for his offer, but told him my mother had refused to sell at any price. The storm clouds had lingered briefly overhead, then labored on toward Burma without shedding a tear.

Granddad Jah was walking along the sand with his head bowed and his shoulders hunched. I caught up with him.

"Sorry we didn't show you before," I said.

"It doesn't matter."

"What do you think?"

"I think there's much more to it. I apologize to the nun. It wasn't her. This was, I don't know, psychotic. I've never seen anything like it. It wasn't a hit or a revenge killing. The photographs weren't merely a record. If you were going to document a killing like this, you'd video it. You'd film the whole thing. Then you wouldn't miss anything."

"With modern equipment you can stop at any frame and print it out," I said. "The quality's almost as good as a still camera."

"Then the expensive still camera is relevant somehow. It was as if she or he wanted individual works of art to show how clever they were. Wanted to show off."

"A sort of performance," I said.

I thought about the colors. They'd mesmerized me from the moment I'd first looked at the photos. Colors. Then the image of luminous green overalls seeped into my mind, facedown in an unfinished mosaic pool on a raft of blood. Orange hat and all. I took out my cell phone and pressed an old number.

"iFurn executive line. I'm Dr. Monique —"

"Siss, it's me. Listen, can you get back to Yoshi?"

"Toshi."

"Toshi, right. Ask him if there were any

suspects for the hotel murder in Guam, the guy who landed in the swimming pool."

"Are you suddenly taking me seriously?"

"I've always taken you seriously, *pee*. And, while you're at it, can you ask your alcoholic detective in California for more details about the weirdo who photographed road-kill? Ask him if the party hats were orange."

"I might even have another one for you."

"Another what?"

"Orange hat murder. I got a message from Taiwan. A skinny Chinese inspector. I hope he didn't doctor his profile photograph 'cause if he did his real self must be hideous. He vaguely recalled a knifing at an aviary. They didn't ever catch the killer. The peculiar thing was that she, the victim, was wearing an orange People First Party election rally hat, but she was a staunch *Kuomintang,* and their party color is blue. Originally they thought it was a political killing but nobody could see what was to be gained by it. She was an aviary worker. She cleaned up parrot shit. So, the case vanished into the dead files."

Aviary. Exotic birds. Orange hat. Color.

"OK. Include that in the sweep," I said. "I'll take anything with orange hats and colorful locations. I've got a very bad feeling this is all connected somehow."

"I could be the hottest one-legged Russian on Police Beat if we solve this one."

"You can't tell anyone anything. This is all still in the realm of the ridiculous. But let me know as soon as you get anything. There's a nun in a greasy cell in Bangkok surrounded by tomboys with tattoos and we've got to get her out."

"Will do. Over and out."

We were walking back toward the shop, me and Granddad Jah. Kow, the squid boat captain, was across the street dispensing fishballs from his side car.

"Have you heard?" he called.

"I never hear anything," I said, even though it was no longer true.

"Abbot killed up at *Wat* Feuang Fa. Some nun gutted him."

How did he do it? He fished in the empty sea at night and drove around on his motorcycle in the day. How did he one-up the world on news? So much for the media blackout. If Captain Kow knew, it wouldn't be long before every newspaper in the country heard. I was in a tough spot. I had the bulk of my story written but it didn't have an ending yet. I'd left blanks for a lot of police quotations I could harvest at the last minute, and I'd done my best to avoid accusing my nun. I knew the other rags wouldn't be so delicate. No, I wouldn't send anything yet. I hoped the blackout pressure on the newspapers was heavy enough to keep the story off the front page for at least twenty-four hours. But, by then, I had to have it all sorted out. This was my story.

The afternoon stretched out like a long, nylon net with one single tangled sprat in its snare. Boats bobbed. Palms shimmied. Clouds stuck. How long could it take to interview a suspect in a murder inquiry? All right — weeks, yes. It could take forever. But this was just a rental car driver. He couldn't have that much to say. Mair and I watched the family check out of room two and decided not to charge them. It was the least we could do for bursting their bubble. I was convinced we'd done them a favor. We thanked them for fixing the cistern and for offering us freedom. The father slipped me his name card just in case . . . I told him there was absolutely no way and put his card in my pocket.

And we waited, me and Granddad Jah. A loudspeaker van crawled by asking for old metal and bottles and tin cans and broken motors. The driver could have easily leaned out of the window and asked nicely, but he had the volume cranked up so high our windows vibrated and I almost missed the "Mamma Mia" jingle. I clicked on the phone.

"Yes?"

"Me." It was Chompu. "Lang Suan just e-mailed us the digital recording of the interview. I've sent a copy to your inbox."

Something Chiang Mai in me was shocked that Lang Suan might have the concept of digital.

"What? Why? We aren't online here," I reminded him.

"Then get somewhere that is."

We plodded along on the motorcycle, me on the back, Granddad Jah driving. I thought the excitement and urgency might prod him over sixty kph, but no. The law was the law. With such short notice we had just the one option to check my e-mail. It was three forty-five on Sunday and I knew the Internet café would be overrun with star troopers. I'd underestimated just how many there were. The line of motorcycles in front of the shop left us no choice but to park forty meters away. We pushed our way inside through a flock of young people with nowhere else to go. The owner, a young man with long hair and moon-landscape acne looked up briefly from his laptop when we entered, then looked back down again as if the door had merely been blown open by the wind. All five computers were in use, each occupied by two or three teenagers in the process of penetrating castles or massacring herds of villains.

"How long would we have to wait?" I asked the owner.

The man shrugged. It was his big profit margin period, early evenings and weekends. At twenty *baht* an hour he could clear, ooh, a hundred-and-twenty *baht* easy on an evening like this. In seventy-three years he'd have paid off the cost of the computers. It was a business that baffled me.

"All right," I shouted. "Who'd be prepared to give up a machine for . . . fifty *baht?*"

They all turned back to their games. I tried one hundred and two hundred *baht* and got the same reaction.

"All right," I said. "How much would it take?"

One group huddled and came up with a figure of five-hundred *baht.* They weren't open to haggling. It was extortion but I was desperate. I handed over the money, asked for an extra set of headphones and Granddad and I hunkered down to listen to the interview. It took fifteen minutes to download the file and, by then, Granddad was grinding his teeth. Just as well they weren't real.

In.

The recording began with several minutes of personal questions: name, address, occupation, et cetera. Then Major General Suvit, who was interviewing, got down to the nitty-gritty.

MAJOR G: Koon Wirapon, why did you come to Lang Suan last week?

DRIVER: Had a job, sir. A client wanted a Benz for eight days.

MAJOR G: Who was the client?

DRIVER: It's here. (crinkle of paper) Ming Xi Wu, from Hong Kong.

MAJOR G: Description.

DRIVER: Around fifty, short, in pretty good shape for her age, tight short perm, could have been a wig, typical Chinese face with those big old-fashioned sunglasses. Dressed in safari clothes and boots.

MAJOR G: Where did she want to go?

DRIVER: No plan really. Just look around. When she first contacted the company, the e-mail said she wanted to see temples and local birds. She was a birdwatcher. She had cameras and binoculars and stuff.

Granddad Jah and I exchanged a look. I knew his mind had gone directly to the ornithologist in our first cabana. Coincidence?

MAJOR G: So, you just drove her around?

DRIVER: Pretty much, sir. She'd ask to stop here and there and she'd hop out and take pictures or look through her binoculars.

MAJOR G: Did you take her to Wat Feuang Fa?

DRIVER: To tell the truth, sir, I'm not familiar with the names of the temples down these parts. I'm from Trat. This was my first visit to the Gulf.

MAJOR G: You might recall it. It's a small temple but it's on the crest of a hill. You can see it from the road. There's a bank of bougainvilleas to one side.

DRIVER: Oh, yes. I do recall that. My passenger was particularly interested in that one.

MAJOR G: What happened?

DRIVER: It was the second day. We're driving along and she sees this temple and it's like it's the best thing she's ever seen and she's babbling on in Chinese and I don't know what she wants. I speak English well enough but she's all single words: stop, go, slow, turn. She tells me to slow down at the temple but not stop. She directs me onto this dirt track a little bit farther on. I try to tell her we could just drive straight up to the temple but she's not having any of it. Probably didn't have a clue what I was talking about.

MAJOR G: So?

DRIVER: So she wants to take pictures of something or other, I'm guessing. Tells me to pull over on this little lane, gets her camera all set up, grabs her shoulder bag and tells me to wait. She runs off into the bushes. I turn the car round, come back and park off the track. About, I don't know, fifteen, twenty minutes later she's back and in a real state. Looks like she's been in a fight. She's all sweaty and her leg's cut. And mad, oh, is she mad. And she's going on in her language, on, on, on. I don't know what got into her but I tell you she frightened me. She says, "Go, go," so I drive her back to Pak Nam and drop her off.

MAJOR G: Where was she staying?

DRIVER: With friends, according to the e-mail. No idea where they lived. She always had me pick her up and drop her off at the hospital intersection.

MAJOR G: How did you know when to pick

her up?

DRIVER: She'd either write down a time on a bit of paper or she'd turn up at the Tiwa. That's where I was staying. She'd arranged that.

MAJOR G: And when was the next time you saw her?

DRIVER: The next night. I hadn't seen her all day. Didn't know what she wanted me to do. She turns up at the Tiwa at about eight p.m. And there I am enjoying a glass of Saeng Som and Coke on the veranda. I'm just in my shorts, aren't I? Well, it didn't occur to me she'd want the car at night. Not a lot of luminous birds out, you know? But she's all smiley and she wants to go for a drive. So I think perhaps she's in the mood for a little night life. I'm fond of the odd disco myself. But, no. She doesn't want me along. She seems to think she can just take the car off on her own. But we've got regulations, you see. If someone's renting the car to drive themselves we have to do security checks. The company hangs on to their passports and makes sure they've got international licenses. That's the law, right? But this woman booked with a driver and so there was no background check. I couldn't let her take it.

MAJOR G: So, what happened?

DRIVER: She takes out this big wad of thousand baht notes and throws it on the table in front of me. There was twenty thousand baht in there.

MAJOR G: You counted it?

DRIVER: Later, yeah. It was a lot of money but I couldn't let her just drive off. If she had an accident or drove into a brick wall, it was my arse on the line.

MAJOR G: So, you refused to let her take it?

DRIVER: At first, yes.

MAJOR G: But then?

DRIVER: I let her have it.

MAJOR G: You accepted a bribe and allowed her to break the law?

DRIVER: No. Yes, well, I took the money, but that wasn't the reason I let her have the car.

MAJOR G: And what was the reason?

DRIVER: I was afraid of her.

MAJOR G: You're a big boy. You were afraid of a little Chinese woman?

DRIVER: Yeah, I know. Saying it like that makes it sound ridiculous. But there was something about her. Something in her eyes wasn't right. And she had this shoulder bag like a military kitbag and

404

she kept reaching into it and I started imagining she had a gun in there or something.

MAJOR G: But you didn't actually see one.

DRIVER: No.

MAJOR G: Or a knife?

DRIVER: No.

MAJOR G: So you let her drive off in your car because you imagined she was dangerous.

DRIVER: (long pause) Yeah. She had her hand inside her bag when she asked me for the key.

MAJOR G: Sounds terrifying.

DRIVER: You'd have to have been there.

MAJOR G: I'm sure. And you gave her the key.

DRIVER: Yeah.

MAJOR G: And when did you drive her again?

DRIVER: I didn't.

MAJOR G: You were booked for eight days. This was day three.

DRIVER: That night I heard her arrive at about ten. I went outside but she'd gone.

MAJOR G: She'd been out alone that night with the car?

DRIVER: Yes, Major.

MAJOR G: And she returned the vehicle in one piece?

DRIVER: That's right. The Benz wasn't wrecked so I slept easier. But she kept the key with her, and the spare. Three days I don't see her at all. The Benz is parked beside my room and I had no idea what she wants me to do, so I just hang out in the cabin and watch TV and drink and eat. I mean, I was getting paid whatever happened.

MAJOR G: But you didn't mention any of this in your driving log.

DRIVER: I was afraid the boss would dock me for the days I didn't drive. I didn't tell him about the car going off without me or the money, either.

MAJOR G: So, why are you telling me?

DRIVER: They said in Phuket this is a murder inquiry. I'm not about to get myself tied up in lies if there's a murder rap at the end of it.

MAJOR G: Very wise, son. You've done time?

DRIVER: Four years in Prem. House breaking, when I was younger. I've been clean since then.

MAJOR G: So, did you see her again before you left for Phuket?

DRIVER: Yeah, it was Thursday and I was due to get the car back before Friday morning. I still didn't have a key. I was starting to think I might have to call the boss. But then she turns up. I'm on the balcony and she ignores me completely, jumps in the car and she's off. Doesn't say a word. Seems excited about some-thing.

MAJOR G: When did you get the car back?

DRIVER: I found it parked on the side of the road outside the resort later that day. The key was in the ignition so I assumed she'd finished with it. She'd put a dent in the front bumper so I imagined she was embarrassed. There was another ten thousand baht on the front seat. I tell you, a Benz with the key in the ignition and cash on the seat. In Phuket that would have survived all of forty seconds. Must be a lot of saints living down here. I left straightaway. I'd had enough of her. I stopped at a body shop on the way home and had them hammer out the dent.

There followed a good deal of back and forth establishing the times that Ming Xi Wu had the car and crosschecking the reliability of the witness. Major General Suvit wanted to know where they'd been to on the first day of the itinerary, everything the customer had said and done, and what direction she headed when she got out of the car. He was very thorough. Then he surprised me by speaking English to the driver. The policeman was pretty good, clear, easy to understand, but the driver had no idea what he was saying. The major general tried several times without success. That immediately established that it was likely the driver's communication skills that were lacking rather than the passenger's. Finally came the question I'd been waiting for.

MAJOR G: At any time, did she get you to make a telephone call to the Pak Nam police station?
DRIVER: No, sir.
MAJOR G: Nothing to do with a missing camera?
DRIVER: No.

And that was pretty much it. There were a few more questions but that was the bulk of it. We paid our forty *baht* and walked slowly back to the bike, chewing everything over.

"That major general's sharp," said Granddad.

"They've snuck one or two smart ones in since you left the force," I told him. "Were there any questions he didn't ask?"

"I would have pushed him on whether there was any chance at all of this woman being Thai, acting like a foreigner."

"You aren't still thinking about the nun?"

"Not necessarily. There's that one missing link about the phone call to Pak Nam police station reporting the lost camera. If a foreigner had made the call, they would have picked up on it."

"It could have been the friends she was staying with in Pak Nam. Accomplices. She could have had them call."

"Then there's the question of how she knew the camera had been found. How did she know it was on its way to Lang Suan with the sergeant?"

I stopped and considered the sequence of events.

"Who would have received the original call?" I asked.

"The desk sergeant."

"Sergeant Phoom himself, right. He would have passed the message upstairs. But what if nobody had bothered to tell him the original call was a fake? There was a lot going on at the station around that time. Isn't it possible he wasn't included in the loop?"

"More than likely, knowing the workings of a police station."

"And what if he'd been given a return

number to call if there was any news? He's handed the camera to take to Lang Suan but before he leaves, he calls the number and lets them know he's on his way. He's a considerate man. He thinks he's just doing the forensics department a favor. Putting the owner's mind at ease."

We were closer to Pak Nam hospital than we were to home so we detoured. Sergeant Phoom was looking a lot better but his relatives were still there around the bed making a lot of noise. I was sure he'd be grateful for his official release so he could get some peace. There was no longer a police watchman on duty. We sat with the sergeant and I asked him about the phone call. It had been placed from a cell phone and the speaker was a woman, he recalled. She was certainly a Thai and she told him she was calling on behalf of the Lang Suan police headquarters. She'd left a contact number and, as I'd suspected, Sergeant Phoom had called her back to tell her he was returning the camera. He'd inadvertently triggered his own attack. The major had ordered him to deliver the camera, but as he was a mere sergeant, nobody had bothered to explain the history or relevance of the delivery. He thought he was merely returning a lost item. He still had the number on a slip of paper in his wallet. The temptation to call it immediately filled my bladder with excitement, but I'd messed around enough with evidence. To pep the sergeant up a little, we had him phone in this revelation himself. He could blame the delay on concussion. I thought it might help him feel less like a complete loser. I told him if he was promoted on the strength of this new evidence I wanted a slap-up meal comprising anything without fish in it.

On the drive home I was thinking about the ornithologist who'd spent a week in our end room and checked out a day early. I also considered our local postman's wife, the noodle lady and forty-odd other local women who fitted or could be decorated to fit the description of the killer from Hong Kong, Ming Xi Wu. And I thought about my nun and wondered whether anyone would take the driver's statement seriously. It didn't make any sense at all to consider her a suspect. But it was only by seeing the photos that anyone else might understand. I was afraid we'd have to give them up. My thoughts were interrupted by the jaunty Swedish tone of my cell phone. It was Chompu.

"Was that your doing?" he asked.

"What's that?"

"Sergeant Phoom's amnesia with regard to the telephone number."

"Word gets around fast."

"The major had me trace it. We still had some mileage left on our old warrant with the phone company. The caller had left a return number so we didn't think they'd be directly connected to the crime. We were right. It was the number of a business service center called, uRinguist."

"What's that got to do with a missing camera?"

"Well, I haven't actually called the number yet, but I looked up their Web site. It appears they do a thriving trade in translations and interpreting. A business person arrives from overseas and needs to send a message to, say, a Thai factory owner. He calls uRinguist and leaves a message in his own language whence it's translated into Thai. A native Thai speaker then calls the factory owner ostensibly passing on the message as the visitor's personal assistant. If there's a reply, the process reverses itself and the visiting business person receives the reply in his or her own language. It gives the visitor some added status and a little class. It's one of those huge ideas everyone wishes they'd thought of."

"So, you're saying Sergeant Phoom was

called by a service?"

"Yes. They just read the message. 'Hello, I'm calling on behalf of . . .' et cetera."

"And he called back to the service."

"So it would seem. They translated the reply and probably sent a text message to the killer in her own language telling her the camera was on its way to Lang Suan. It was the moment she'd been waiting for all this time. But I'm afraid I'm going to have to make googoo eyes at the judge again to get into the uRinguist records. It's a confidential service. And all that will have to wait till the morning 'cause no self-respecting judge works on a Sunday. And I don't even have a client's name to give him."

"The Hong Kong connection was false?"

"Surprise, surprise. None of the details sent to the rental company checked out. We have no idea what her real name is, but we do know something about her."

"Shock me."

"uRinguist doesn't have Chinese interpreters. It only operates in three languages, Thai, English . . . and Japanese."

"For a century and a half now, America and Japan have formed one of the great and enduring alliances of modern times."
— GEORGE W. BUSH,
TOKYO, FEBRUARY 18, 2002

"Mika Mikata."

"That's not a really southern Californian name, is it?" I said. "Perhaps it's Mexican?"

"It's Japanese."

I could tell Sissi was stressed when she couldn't be bothered to get my jokes. Best stay serious on days such as this.

"And what was she doing in the States?"

"It was an East–West Center arts council grant. She had a year to pursue her artistic bent."

"Which was photographing roadkill?"

"Dressed roadkill. Sunglasses. Bermuda shorts. Little waistcoats."

"And hats?"

"And party hats — colored ones."

"Would have made nice postcards: *Even the roadkill parties in California.*"

"She had an exhibition of her photos."

"And that's what got your drunk detective on the case?"

"Nope. Evidently, in the States, roadkill has no rights. You can dress it up any way you like. She hadn't broken any laws. People were outraged but you know how it is in the arts; the more controversial you are, the more famous you become. One high class magazine called her 'the Caligula of on-the-edge photography.' "

"So where did the red-nosed policeman come in?"

"His name's Gerry Moore. There were complaints that some of her roadkill wasn't quite dead when she started dressing them up."

"Oh, yuck."

"One complainant specifically accused her of running over her cat on her motorcycle. When the owner ran out into the street to see what all the squealing was about, she found Mika fastening a pink tutu around dying Fluffy."

"Did she do time?"

"We're talking Los Angeles in the eighties here. Animal cruelty wasn't high on the list

415

of crime investigation. She was fined a couple of times but continued to gain notoriety from her slide show exhibitions."

"And then she vanished?"

"No. On the contrary. She blossomed. She became a celebrity. She has an enormous cult following still. She's got her own bilingual Web site and you'll never guess what she calls it."

"If it's got the word 'orange' or 'hat' in it she's mine."

"Dressed to Kill."

"You aren't serious."

"Deadly. There are quotations on there from famous artists calling her a genius and a guru. Andy Warhol said, 'She has a visual grasp of death so vivid it makes you wonder whether she's been there.' Her site gets twelve thousand hits a day."

"You've seen it?"

"It's all there; the old nostalgic roadkill period with her doing V signs behind prostrated elk, crows in tiaras splattered across windscreens, upended coyotes in pale blue baby booties. Then there's the less obviously dead roadkill pictures. Is the possum in headphones perhaps looking at the camera? Isn't that a slight blur of movement from the snake in a stocking? I have to admit it all makes spectacular yet stomach-curdling photography. But then we get to the humans."

"Oh, don't tell me."

"I don't know how. Really I don't. But she got access to morgues. Bodies laid out on their trays in bobble hats with streamers in their mouths."

"No."

"Striped football socks, boxing gloves — cross-dressing."

"That's got to be illegal."

"Unless someone recognizes a near and dear one in a Madonna cone bra she could always claim it was set up, all done with actors."

"But you think different?"

"I've seen actors die in TV dramas all the time, even ones who didn't intend to. I have a nose for bad acting. These were definitely dead bodies."

I'd read everything there was to read on criminology in Thai and English. I'd studied all the cases — the famous murders, the notorious serial killers — and one point that cropped up often was that the killers of people often began their careers by practicing on animals. Mika Mikata had started her apprenticeship in the public eye and been encouraged. She'd progressed with adoration through all the stages, and I knew there was only one more level. I knew Mika Mikata was either a potential or a practiced murderer. But there was no connection between her and our slain abbot and I could think of absolutely no reason why she'd come to our little nowhere village to do her nefarious deeds.

"Is that as far as the site goes?" I asked. "Cadavers?"

"There are three galleries. There's the free White Gallery which is all mostly weird but innocent stuff. Then there's the pay-to-view Black Gallery which wasn't that hard to get into. That's where I found the roadkill and the morgue pictures. But then there's a members-only Orange Gallery."

"Bingo. Can you get into that?"

"It's not easy."

"You're the maestro of the Net."

"Jimm, I've been a fly on the wall at a maximum secure video conference link between members of the U.S. Homeland Security. I've seen the Queen of England in her pajamas sipping Horlicks on Skype. If I say something's not easy, it's not easy. But I'm working on it."

"All right, one more question. What does she look like?"

"Mika? She's gorgeous on her Web page photo but we both know what that means.

418

Looking back at the early photos she was reasonably bland but bubbly. I imagine she's in her fifties now, still going for that cutesy manga love doll look."

"Any idea what she'd look like now without air-brushing?"

"*Nong,* the longer I spend with the Web Idol people, the more I understand that Granddad Jah could be Brad Pitt in three easy steps. Mika might be the plainest pig in the litter. I imagine she's got that every-Asian face you could do anything you want with. Look, I'm sending the glamor photo and one of the early ones to your phone."

"Thanks, Siss. Anything on the other murders?"

"You asked me about witnesses for the Guam swimming pool killing. The guy who got his hard hat painted orange. By the time Toshi had flown down, the local police had already done the interviewing. They still didn't have a suspect. There was one possible eyewitness they hadn't been able to locate. Some of the engineers said there'd been a reporter at the scene of the crime taking photographs. She had a Japanese press ID. They remarked on how quickly she'd been able to arrive there."

"Any description for her?"

"Conflicting, he said. Some remembered

her as young, others as middle-aged. Medium length hair. Toshi checked with immigration. There were no Japanese reporters registered around that time and none of the crime-scene photographs appeared in any newspapers."

"What about Taiwan? You said there might be a lead there."

"Detective Wing Shu's promised to look through his files about the aviary killing. Actually he looks a lot better in his swimming pool photos."

"Do whatever it takes, Siss."

"Yes, ma'am."

"OK. The picture's have come through."

And there she was, all cuddly and fluffed. I went through it all in my mind. Medium length hair. Young or middle-aged. That every-Asian face. It was impossible to describe to a sketch artist because the picture in the newspaper would look like everybody's mother or sister or next door neighbor. It was a face everybody would forget. With a little bit of work it could be the rouged face of a reporter in Guam or the over-mascara'd face of a Hong Kong birdwatcher. They'd remember the bad make-up and sunglasses before they remembered the person behind them. But I was certain I'd seen that face unadorned. It was drawn and blotchy and an over-generous powdering had made it look older than it was. The gray wig had completed the trick but I'd seen through it, and I could see it now. Eyes always betrayed you. I could see her in her real Lacoste sports shirt, twenty times more expensive than a Bangkok rip-off. It was tucked into tight sweatpants that gave her two bellies. She'd smiled and complimented my awful Korean even though she probably wasn't fluent herself. That's why she'd had to check out when the Korean engineers moved in to the 69 Resort. They'd know she wasn't one of them. Her cover would have been blown. I don't know why, or how, but my instincts rang loud and hearty that I'd met Mika Mikata that day.

"Are you sure?" Chompu asked.

"No. But put it all together. The 69 Resort is ten minutes' walk from the hospital intersection and another ten to the Tiwa where the driver was staying. Her room was right there beside the road so nobody would see her come or go in her disguise. She was the right age and height and I'd bet my bottom she wasn't Korean."

"Actually, I meant are you sure you really

want me to approach my volatile, uncooperative superior officer with a story like this?"

I could see his point. We were sitting on a bench in front of the four-meter white Buddha opposite the police station. Granddad Jah was pacing back and forth. I didn't really have any physical evidence to substantiate my odd suspicions. They were based on a two-minute meeting at the 69 Resort and intuition.

"You're right," I said. "One step at a time. What if you handle it like this? The police get an anonymous phone call saying that a foreign woman at the 69 Resort had been acting strangely for several days. She'd checked in a day before the killing and checked out the day of the attack on Sergeant Phoom. You trace the passport number she gave the resort, find out it doesn't exist . . ."

"What if it does?"

"Let's stay positive, shall we?"

"Right."

"We try to find witnesses who saw her disguised as Wu and then we somehow introduce Mika Mikata."

"You make it sound so simple."

It was. The opportunity presented itself sooner than we expected. We were interrupted by the ringing of Chompu's phone and he was summoned to Lang Suan for a meeting. The new direction of events had prompted the return of the Bangkok detectives. They were more than miffed when they found out the local police had taken over the inquiry when all they'd been asked to do was report on events. Bangkok already had its suspect neatly wrapped so they didn't appreciate having to come back south so soon. When they discovered that the Benz driver had already been interviewed and, upon seeing a photograph of the nun, had stated categorically that this was not the woman he'd driven, they were positively spewing stomach acid. They called an emergency meeting of everyone involved in the case, including poor wheelchair-bound Sergeant Phoom.

Nobody appreciated their condescending tone, particularly Major General Suvit, who'd been rather proud of the way he'd been handling the case since Bangkok had left it behind. Chompu informed us later that the meeting had twice erupted into a slappy, spitty shouting match. There were those present who swore the major general had reached for his pistol at one stage. The question of motive had come up from time to time. Who had a better motive than the nun? Why would a foreigner with no known connection to the victim just suddenly up and kill him? It was a question nobody could answer. Bangkok argued that murder never happened at random. Killers invariably knew their victims or had a personal stake in wanting them dead. That was the point in the proceedings when my interruption happened.

A female lieutenant entered the room with coffee, coconut biscuits and news of a tip-off. She handed the message to the major general and made the mistake of staying in the room. He told her they all had their coffee now, thank you, and asked her what she was still doing there. She'd probably asked herself the same question on a career level. She left. The major general read the note, then announced that someone had phoned in with information that there had been a woman answering the description of Ms. Wu from Hong Kong staying at the 69 Resort. She'd been seen carrying an expensive camera and, for good measure, driving a black Benz. Within seconds the room emptied, all except for Sergeant Phoom who had his elbows in forty-five-degree plaster casts and didn't have anyone to push his wheelchair. He finished his coffee and had a double helping of coconut biscuits.

The receptionist at the 69 Resort was somewhat overwhelmed when seven police vehicles sped into the parking lot. She told them she had no idea who might have called the police and it certainly wasn't her. There had been a guest, a Korean lady by the name of Do Ik. She'd paid on a day-to-day basis for her room and left unexpectedly on Wednesday. She'd tipped everyone generously and hadn't caused any trouble. Yes, she did have a camera but she was a tourist. It was only natural. Considering the economic climate, it wasn't surprising that nobody had moved into the Korean's room since her departure, especially given its proximity to the main road.

The German saluted when the police parade marched past his room, and his unexpected girlfriend ran inside the cabin. The receptionist opened the door to the Korean's room: B4.

"Has anyone been inside this room since she checked out?" one Bangkok detective asked.

"Yes, the cleaner," she replied.

"Apart from that?"

"No."

The room was a little cramped for an eighteen-man search but neither Bangkok nor Lang Suan, nor Pak Nam was prepared to yield the responsibility to the other groups. They settled on a delegation of two men from each section, a total of six. They all wore standard issue rubber gloves but they carefully lifted bedsheets and towels and opened drawers with the non-writing ends of pencils. By some incredible chance, it was an officer from the Pak Nam station who uncovered the only clue in the room. And what a clue it was. A clue so vital, in fact, that it blew the case wide open. What had, until then, been a domestic murder inquiry was suddenly of concern to the world.

Lieutenant Chompu, it was, who discovered the tiny scrap of paper that had evidently slipped down behind the cushion of one of the uncomfortable vinyl chairs. On it was a handwritten Web site address. Anyone who'd read Chompu's pep-talk notes on the Pak Nam notice board might have recognized some characteristics in the style. He'd disguised his handwriting as best he could but, as the Bangkok detectives took possession of the paper immediately, it was a connection that would never be made. Neither would anyone think to ask why the guest would write her own Internet address on a slip of paper. From the criminal point of view, there was a lot to be said for police non-cooperation.

We sat, the three of us, me, Granddad Jah and Lieutenant Chompu, at one of our beachside tables. An array of local food, bought from here and there, was covered in plates and clingfilm and untouchable in front of us. We had a bottle of 100 Pipers whiskey that Granddad Jah drank over ice, and me and Chompu drank *mizuwari*. That's Japanese for "drowned to death in water." But we still had a buzz going just from the lieutenant's telling of events.

"I zeroed in on the chair," he said. "I was able to palm the Web site address, but I thought I might be pushing my luck to slip the photo prints under the mattress. I mean, there were six of us in a room of two-by-two meters."

"Do you think it'll be enough?" I asked.

"To tie crazy Mika to Abbot Winai's murder? It's hard to say. They're very likely to find camera footage of Do Ik passing through immigration and compare it with the Web site photo and say it's a completely different person."

"She used her real passport to enter and leave the country," said Granddad.

We both looked up.

"What makes you think so?" I asked.

"She went to so much trouble to avoid

showing her ID to the rental firm. By hiring a car with a driver, she didn't need to leave her passport. And the resort didn't check either. She came to the right area. Hotels here are so desperate to get paying guests they really don't care who you are."

"The passport theory would certainly make life a lot easier if it were true," said Chompu. "But it still doesn't tie her to the murder. Unless they can get a recent photo of Mika Mikata to the Benz driver or the 69 receptionist, there'd be nothing to connect her to the killing at all. It's only your reporter's nose that ties the two women together. There's no evidence. There are no witnesses. No murder weapon's been found. And, as our Bangkok friends would hurry to point out, there's no motive."

"So, we might still be forced to give up the photographs?" I asked.

"They're not incriminating," he said. "All you can see is a hand in an oven mitt."

"Damn," I said. "It should be easy now."

"Look out! Mother at seven o'clock," said Granddad.

"Hello, you conspirators," Mair said. She'd snuck up on us from the beach side. She joined us, pushing me along the bench with her backside.

"What would we be conspiring about?" I

asked her.

"I don't know the details," she said. "But I can see secrets floating around you. You have guilty auras. Aren't you going to offer me a drink?"

"No," said Granddad Jah. "You know what you get like after half a glass."

"You see, Lieutenant?" Mair smiled at the police officer. "A girl never really grows up. Her father's always there to remind her of her morals."

A few days ago she'd thrown herself under the counter to avoid him; now she was flirting with him. Mothers! We mixed her a drink so weak the soda bubbles were beside themselves in the search for whiskey atoms. We fell into a peaceful silence, staring at the little lights out at sea, bobbing along on their polystyrene rafts. After a few months of fishing, the locals became lethargic. They put together traps of fine mesh and suspended them from small foam platforms illuminated by gas lamps. The boatmen would come back the next day to see what their indiscriminate snares had collected. They took as many immature fish as they did squid and it screwed up the ecosystem. It's illegal and irresponsible, but it's terribly pretty. The pearl tears of lamplight dotted the surface of the water all around.

"I was talking to Auntie Summorn today," Mair said.

See? A mere sip and she was about to confess to the police.

"How is she?" I asked, and elbowed her in the kidney.

"She was very well," she said. "She was telling me about her son. I'm sure you've run across Auntie Summorn's son, General . . ."

Chompu pepped up at the address.

"Mair, I —"

"His name's Daeng," she continued. "He's our local villain."

"We know him very well." Chompu nodded. "Very well."

"Then you'd probably be surprised to hear he's given up drinking and applied to enter the monkhood for a month."

"And I'm thinking of having my left leg amputated because I've lost a sock" was Chompu's response.

Mair chuckled.

"It's official," she said. "He's signed up for detox at *Wat* Ny Kow."

"Then wonders will never cease," said the policeman. "Whatever's come over him?"

"Oh, I just think a man comes to a point in his life when he gets tired of running away from his conscience. All his past deeds

430

catch up with him and . . . I mean, they're coming from different directions, obviously, the conscience and the deeds, otherwise they'd be bumping into each other and complicating things. But that's probably when his life turns around . . . because of all that jostling."

Mair had a way with idioms. Chompu looked from me to Granddad Jah and we both shrugged.

"Well, then here's to villain Daeng," said Chompu, raising his glass and downing the contents. I clinked my glass against Mair's and sniffed her cheek.

"Well done, Mair," I whispered in her ear. She threw back half her drink and smacked her lips and fluttered her eyes.

"General Chompu," she slurred, "do you know I once tied a police officer to a bamboo raft and set him off down the Kok River? It was —"

"All right, girl. You've had enough," said Granddad Jah, taking her half-empty glass. "She makes up stories when she's drunk."

"I do not. His name was Police Sergeant Major Grit Maleenon. He was naked because he —"

"Mair!"

She grabbed back her glass and laughed. We were saved the rest of the story by the arrival of our truck. In fact, hearing Mair's story might have been better. It was a moment I'd been secretly dreading, so I can't imagine how Mair felt. Arny had invited his girlfriend (and I use the term with generous caution) for dinner. The spread in front of us was all cold. Arny was half an hour late.

"Ah! Cue for the handsome and discreet officer to depart," said Chompu.

Arny and a big woman had emerged from the truck. They were half in shadow but she appeared to be wearing a parachute. Luckily it was white rather than camouflaged or we might have lost sight of her completely as they walked, arm in arm, across the car park. I leaned over the table.

"Not on your life, Lieutenant. Either you sit and eat with us or I'm telling the police ministry you lip-sync Maria Carey on duty."

"Bitch."

I felt Mair slide back on the bench and into the shadows. Granddad helped himself to a dozen or so new Pipers. The happy couple was holding hands by the time they arrived at our table. When Arny's face nosed into the table-lamp light I could see the full beam of a smile and a touching look of pride as he dipped his head in the direction of his betrothed. I'd never seen that look before. Mair obviously noticed it, too. She

432

leaned out of her shadow and smiled.

"Who do we have here?" she asked.

Arny's companion stepped up to the table and pushed her hands together into a very respectful *wai*. We all returned it, apart from Granddad Jah who grunted and took a drink instead. She was a very handsome woman, dark from the sun, with a nose that I'd seen often on carved wooden native American sculptures. Her hair was as thick as tarmac and it hung down her back like a stodgy dark cape. Yes, her head was good. I'd give it an 8.2, but I couldn't begin to score her body because of the parachute. It was somewhat worrying. It was as if she'd dropped from an airplane into a nearby field and hadn't had time to untangle herself before dinner.

"Sorry we're late," said Arny, who for some reason had decided to *wai* us also. "We were arm wrestling about what we should wear to such a high-class dinner."

He giggled. It was an Arny joke, made worse by an iron bar of nervous tension that was apparently welded to his spine. Granddad Jah didn't help.

"Well, *she* obviously lost," he said.

I turned to glare at my granddad and inadvertently kicked Chompu in the shin. He squealed. And that was the moment it

433

could have all gone wrong. Arny's face imploded, Mair's smile became a patch of Scotch tape, and I fumbled desperately through my bag of journalistic tricks to find something diplomatic to spray on the scene. But then the girlfriend laughed. It was like the grand opening of a showroom of shiny teeth. Somewhere in the back of her throat they were smashing crystal glasses and chandeliers. It was the type of laugh that left you absolutely no choice but to join in with.

"I brought some real clothes," she said. Her southern accent was musical and earthy as a saloon. "They're in the truck . . . Unless you'd prefer to put it to the vote."

Mair leaped to her feet and grabbed the woman's hand.

"I'll show you where you can change." She smiled and we all applauded. All except for Arny who stood with his lips aquiver as the two women retreated into the darkness.

"I thought she looked nice," he said.

I went over to him and hugged as much of him as I could.

"Nong," I said, "you selected that dress for your lady friend, didn't you?"

"Yes."

"You went shopping together and she let you choose a dress."

"Yes."

"Well, I've got good news for you. Any woman who'd go out in public wearing that dress, just because you were sweet enough to buy it for her, has to love you very much."

The expression on his face passed through confusion before finally alighting on joy. He laughed and I wrestled him down onto a seat. Granddad Jah fixed him a drink. By the time Mair and the girlfriend returned they were the best of friends. They probably had a lot of ancient pop songs in common; used the same brand of arthritis cream. But perhaps I'm being cruel. Arny rose to greet his lady love. She was wearing a nice shiny top that showed her toned shoulders, and huggy trousers. She certainly hadn't let herself go since the competition days. I found her rather attractive myself but I'd never admit that to Ed's sister. Her name, we learned, was Kanchana Aromdee, nickname, Gaew, and she was one of the most interesting women I'd met in a life spent meeting people. Even Granddad Jah took a shine to her. She entertained us with her anecdotes and listened attentively to ours. All the while she held Arny's hand and smiled at his profile when he spoke.

The Pipers were down to a dozen, and we'd

eaten, and the time had tumbled on by and nobody seemed in a hurry to go home. Mair told some of her most bawdy and hilarious stories, fired by the taste of whiskey on her lips. She let slip the odd curse that drew censure from Granddad and consternation from the gallery. We talked about our Gulf Bay Lovely Resort and how we could turn its fortunes around: how we'd be the Club Med of the Gulf in six months. At one stage, Chompu had received a call from Major Suvit telling him that Mika Mikata had, in fact, traveled to Thailand on her real passport to attend an international photographic symposium in Haad Yai. Our own Pak Nam fell almost to the decimal point directly between Haad Yai and Bangkok. We toasted Granddad Jah and made him an honorary Police Major General for the night. Chompu let him wear his hat. Gaew lipsticked an insignia on his coral white undervest and he didn't put up a fight.

It was almost midnight when I got the call I'd been hoping for. I staggered down to the water's edge to leave the noise of the party behind me. I sat on the sand and listened. I heard calls for my return to the table but I ignored them. Crabs were sizing me up but I didn't care. I listened and I cried and I said thank you and returned to the table where Gaew was demonstrating an unbreakable armlock on the lieutenant. Mair asked me why I'd been crying and all attention turned to me. During the meal, we'd briefly talked about the killing of the abbot and the subsequent investigation, and now I had what I hoped would be the final kill.

Sissi had found a way, via impenetrable firewalls through invisible wormholes . . . and various other jargon I'd not understood, into Mika Mikata's Web site. There, she'd found the most horrific gallery of murder masquerading as art: the step-by-step pool murder of the orange-hatted worker in Guam, an underwater assassination in the Great Barrier Reef set amid some of the most glorious colored corals and sea creatures, the aviary slaying in Taiwan, and the recently posted killing of an abbot in Thailand. In an attached blog, some arty farty pseudo-poetic nonsense about destiny. A location pinpointed on a map. A vague sense that saffron was calling to her. That her inner soul and the whim of the orange hat would finally come to select the perfect tableau to showcase her art. Mika Mikata was a dead duck. The Juree family had its first notch.

That night, as I was filling in the details of

my story, I paused to consider the victim for once. Abbot Winai would undoubtedly have seen this as his karma. He'd probably visited the moment during meditation, walking on that path beside the flowers at that particular time when Mika Mikata passed by in her rental car. He probably knew before she burst through the hedge, before she forced him to don the hat. There had been no fear in his eyes and that would have been a terrible disappointment to the crazy Japanese, the woman who crafted death.

Sissi had posted the link to the members-only Orange Gallery on the *Sangka* Council's Web site. It couldn't be traced back to her. She knew the outrage would fuel its way to the police ministry and the case would explode in the media. Everyone was looking for something exciting to nudge the yuppy rebellion off the front pages. Somehow, Mika Mikata would be punished for her cruelty.

Our resort was quiet. Everyone had gone to bed. The table was littered with bottles and plates and topped by Gogo with sauce around her mouth. The cleanup could wait. I kick-started the motorcycle and rode into Pak Nam to deliver my exclusive. It was a ghost town. The light above the 7-Eleven bathed the street in puddles of red, green and orange. As I passed, I saw the cashier yawn into a magazine. There was another light from the upstairs window of a PVC pipe and pump store, one more at the intersection. It stretched the shadow of a threadbare cat into the shape of a giraffe. But the Internet shop was as dark as Nintendo Kong's banana cellar, as quiet as Atlantis after the last of the Gorgon invaders had been destroyed. I took off my shoe and rapped against the shutter. The sound echoed around the town like a lone Pamplona bull charging through the streets, but the only reaction was a faint "What do you want?" from above the café.

"I think we need not only to eliminate the tollbooth to the middle class, I think we should knock down the tollbooth."
— GEORGE W. BUSH, NASHUA, NH,
AS QUOTED BY GAIL COLLINS IN
THE NEW YORK TIMES, FEBRUARY 1, 2000

I got an early phone call from Dtor, my friend in Chiang Mai. The urban anarchists were still occupying our Government House. They'd been there for nine days already. They had their fold-up beach chairs and had diverted their magazine subscriptions to their new temporary address. They'd even rented a bank of Portaloos. They'd set up their futons and ordered in pizza while the police stood outside wondering why they had to make do with cold fried rice and a quick wee against the back wall. Anarchy was one of the fastest-growing middle-class hobbies. It had already overtaken Pilates and tai chi. I'd seen the photos: middle-aged women in stretch trousers and sensible tops giving the finger. Let's see them try that in Burma. Anywhere else and you'd expect them to have been mowed down in a hail of machine-gun fire, beaten with batons, dragged screaming by their orthopedic shoes. This is our Government House, damn it. Our seat of power. Who do they think they are? I didn't vote for these people. But when you've got friends in high places, you know you aren't scheduled for a police massacre. You take your best iPod with you without fear it might get bumped in a skirmish. You know the authorities won't dare hurt you. You have power at your back, influence whose name dare not be spoken. So you settle down to your sudoku and send e-mails on your BlackBerry telling old schoolfriends that you're on an insurgency at the moment and the reunion might have to be put off for a week or two.

But, of course, Pak Nam cared nothing of all that. It had squid. That was the extent of its concerns. The events at *Wat* Feuang Fa had blown through my life like a monsoon and when the squall died down, I was still standing, albeit windswept and crusted in salt. After all that had happened, I imagined that the busybodies might have crept back under their rocks and left Abbot Kem and Sister Bia to whatever it was they certainly weren't doing. But a new complaint was lodged and a second IA abbot was on his way. For my own peace of mind, I needed to know what was motivating this monastic stubborn streak.

When I arrived at the temple, the nun was painting the other side of the wall and all the grass around it. She had a yarmulke of white at the back of her scalp.

"I see incarceration didn't do a thing for your painting skills," I said.

She turned to find me in very much the same position as when I'd first met her. She smiled and returned to her task.

"Some people never learn," she said.

"So I hear."

"Did Abbot Kem come back?"

"He didn't ever leave. He has a cave up there, over the crest. He goes there sometimes to consider."

That made sense. I couldn't really imagine him charging off to Bangkok to rescue his maiden. The nun put the long buffalo-tail brush in the can. It fell out, splattering her ankles before coming to rest in a white puddle at her feet. She laughed and left it there.

"It has a life of its own," she said. "How could I ever hope to tame it?"

She started off along the path, stopping briefly once to see if I was following. I hadn't arrived with a plan, no questionnaire, no tactics. If she didn't want to talk to me, I was prepared for that. I'd say goodbye and good luck and leave her alone to her secrets. But it was as if she'd been waiting for me. We sat on her porch and looked up at the sky. It was one of those days when you thought perhaps mother nature got her color ideas from looking at upmarket swimming pools.

"If only I could paint like that," she said. Unexpectedly, she looked me straight in the eye. I felt a peculiar pang of love for her. "The young policeman told me my freedom is largely due to you."

"There were a few of us, but I don't mind taking credit on their behalf."

She nodded, which I took to mean "thank you."

"There was something in his heart," she leaped in with no preview or warning. "He wasn't good looking or strong, not even a great scholar. But there was something in his heart that I could feel. I was thirteen or fourteen, passing through all those obstacle courses that teenagers have to suffer, not understanding my place on the planet. I began to ask him questions about life. Not even, 'Why are we here?' questions. Just small curiosities. 'Do you think trees feel pain?' 'Do ants wish they could be independent?' That silly level. But he always had an answer that made me think, and it always made sense to me. He cheered me up.

"And, as I grew older, I began to depend on him and his answers. We were friends, of course, by then, but he became the type of friend that is a part of you. I can't call what I felt for him 'love,' not in a physical sense. It was more like a wonderful peace to have him in my life. Perhaps my spirit was in love with his. Then he entered the monkhood. I wasn't at all surprised. I knew he needed guidance to help him make sense of all the feelings we'd discussed. When he left I felt so terribly empty, not of the person but of the message. I knew that I was ready to search for myself. I was ready to accept a life of piety and modesty.

"We remained in contact through friends. We didn't meet for many years but we were in one another's hearts. I always knew that. And then, to my surprise, I learned that I had a tumor in my brain. It was called a GBM and it was inoperable. It wasn't devastating news because we will all move along into the next life eventually, but I mentioned it in passing in a letter to Abbot Kem. To my surprise, he invited me here to spend my remaining time with an old friend. So I came. And I wait. It's started. You've already noticed my wonderful coordination. It won't be long before my mind follows my painting skill. I won't know which end of the brush to hold or what color is white.

"He and Abbot Winai spent many hours discussing me. I suppose I should have been flattered to have two such eminent men invest so much time in me. Their final decision, made on the day of the murder, was that I should stay. So, here I am."

Two? Perhaps three large chunks of wood had become embedded in my chest. I could neither breathe nor cry. I had to saw a way through them with sighs before I could speak. Nothing profound fitted at that moment.

"What was the answer to the ant question?" I asked. "Do they want to be independent? It's something I think about too."

She laughed.

"He told me to be patient. Eventually I'd be an ant and I could answer the question

445

for myself."

The tears came slow as candle wax. I'd become a regular crybaby since my move from Chiang Mai. I was embarrassed for myself and in a hurry to leave. But before I could get away she opened the door to her hut and gestured me inside.

"I was hoping you could do me one more small favor," she said.

In a cardboard box at the foot of her cot was a white bundle of fur, still as an ermine mitten. She put in her hand and lifted carefully. It was Sticky Rice, as limp as a hand puppet.

"He's not quite dead," she said. "I'm afraid he might have finally swallowed something that didn't agree with him. We lose and gain dogs daily but this tyke has found a way into my heart. I don't think I can bear to watch him die."

The dams burst as I was carrying the cardboard box to the truck. I hated crying in daylight when everyone can witness my frailties. I put the last few hours of Sticky Rice on the passenger seat and drove like an imbecile into Lang Suan to see Dr. Somboon, the cow specialist.

An hour later I pulled up in front of Mair's shop. She was in there with her haunting group. They were rearranging shelves and cleaning and throwing out ten-year-old stock. The cassette was playing something called "Spirit in the Sky." It was one of Mair's oldies but baddies, yet the local ladies were swinging their ample rears in time to the beat. They all seemed very happy. I walked around to the passenger side of the truck and collected my Leo Beer carton.

"What's in the box?" I heard.

Granddad Jah was sitting under the canopy opposite waiting for traffic to watch. I carried my patient across the road and sat beside him.

"Almost dead dog," I said.

"Planning on dressing it up, are you?"

That was as close to a joke as I'd heard from the lips of Granddad Jah in many a year and, if the taste was anything to go by, I'd be happy to wait many more for the next.

"Well, he's not guaranteed death," I said. I opened up the flaps to show him.

"You sure?"

"I took him to the vet. He didn't exactly fill me with confidence. He seemed to think ninety percent of puppies in this area die a horrid death from intestinal parasites before they're six months old. He had a sort of cocktail that worked wonders on calves, he said. He gave this little rag a shot of it, said he should really be on a saline drip but he didn't have one and, even if he did, he confessed he had trouble finding veins any smaller than a garden hose. He gave me some antibiotics just in case the mite makes it through the afternoon."

"Since when have you been a rescuer of dogs?"

"Granddad, this is Sticky Rice. He's a hero. He solved the *Wat* Feuang Fa mystery. He was the mutt that rescued the camera. He deserves a longer shot at life."

"Fair enough."

We sat for a while. It was a really bad day for traffic.

"Granddad Jah?"

"Hmm?"

"Do you see anything of Captain Waew?"

"Who?"

"The detective from Surat."

"Oh, him. No."

"You should invite him up. Hang out together."

Granddad Jah stiffened. For a man who was already eighty percent bone, that took some doing.

"Why should I do that?"

" 'Cause you make such a good team."

He half turned his head, looked at the box on my lap, then turned back.

"Don't know what you mean," he grunted.

"Stolen Milo van, wiped clean, naked gangster padlocked to a bench in a train station. 'Deserved' — *sa som* in animal blood written on his belly. Sound familiar?"

"You don't think . . . ?"

"Yes, I do. I imagine you were planning to get a confession out of him for the killing of the hippy couple. Then you found out —"

"Don't be ridiculous."

"Then, in fear of his life, he told you it was his own daughter in that VW and that she was very much alive. I imagine you were really disappointed because you both knew what a seedy character he was."

Granddad searched the horizon and the tops of the trees for traffic.

"Lucky you believed him," I forged on, " 'cause I dread to think what you might have done to him otherwise. All you were left with was humiliation. So, I think you were lucky."

A congealed blood-red pick-up truck with a black plastic fish-chest on the back plodded past at forty kilometers an hour, spitting out exhaust and causing its own force field of pollution. I stood up and waited for it to pass. The driver waved. I waved back. Everybody waved down here. I wouldn't be surprised if husbands waved at their wives when they woke up in the mornings.

"Nice touch though," I added. "Spelling my name wrong. 'Jum' indeed."

He couldn't hold back the smile.

"You're wasted as a girl, Jimm Juree," he said. "Wasted."

I took the box down to the beach and wondered whether Sticky would prefer a land or sea burial. I opened the flaps so the sun could get in and looked for evidence of breath. It was scant. I gazed up at the swimming pool sky to see if there were vultures circling overhead. Gogo had picked up on the scent of death and followed me down to the water's edge. It was true she'd eat anything but surely there were taboos, even for dogs. She stopped three meters away, turned eleven circles and lay on the hot sand with her backside pointed directly at my head.

"You're a hard bitch to love," I said.

"I hope you aren't talking to me."

Mair had followed me down to the beach. She had a tiny bottle of Yakult in her hand. I saluted a company that could convince half a country it couldn't live without weak sugared milk and germs.

"No, Mair," I said. "You're an easy bitch to love."

"What's in the box?" she asked.

450

"Sticky Rice."

"Oh, good. I bought some grilled chicken earlier."

I tipped the box on its side.

"Non-digestible," I told her.

"Oh, you poor baby," she said, reaching into the carton and lifting the limp pup onto her lap. There was evidence of very unpleasant secretions on the newspaper he'd been lying on. Despite that, Mair held Sticky to her chest and cooed at him. There was a slight movement that could have been a postmortem muscle spasm, then a definite sigh. I imagined myself as a tiny infant nestled against that same breast, almost dead, blood and vomit in my cot. Who'd have babies?

Gogo predictably walked a wide arc around me and stood close to my mother, glaring at the patient.

"The ladies and I have been talking about setting up a cooperative of home-made produce," she said. "It's something I'd been thinking about for quite some time."

"You had? Then why didn't you say anything? Why didn't you do it?"

"I was waiting."

"What for?"

"For you all to decide you liked it here."

"Wait! Who said I liked it?"

"You like it."

I pointed out to Mair that something unpleasant was leaking down the front of her shirt but she smiled and nodded knowingly.

"And Arny seems happy too," she said. "And even Father has his moments. I only wish we could convince Sissi to come down. We could be the happy family we used to be."

I wasn't sure we'd ever all been happy at the same time.

"I'm not sure Sissi would see the happy side of all this."

Mair removed the soiled newspaper and put Sticky Rice back in his box.

"The poor fellow can sleep in your room tonight."

"Inside?"

"Of course, inside. You can't leave him on the veranda with all the snakes and bats around. They sense frailty."

We stood and dusted off the sand and I picked up the box. It felt heavier, suddenly, as if Mair had donated him an organ. Perhaps she'd just pumped him full of hope.

"Did I mention Ed came by this morning?" she said. "He asked after you."

"Really?"

"Yes. He is a sweet boy."

"He didn't have his sister with him, by any chance?"

"Which one?"

"He's only got the one. The gay one."

"Don't be silly, child. Ed has three sisters, all happily married. Something like ten children between them. And I have noted that not one of them looks a bit like Ed. A little bit of extra-domestical hanky-panky in their history I wouldn't be surp— Where are you going?"

I handed her the box.

"Pump some more hope into this one, will you," I said. "I'll be back for him later."

I left her standing bemused on the beach and strode to the bicycle. Had it been physically possible, flames would have been spewing from my nostrils. I knew Ed's house. It was just off the road and impossible not to pass on the way to and from our place. In the past, I'd always turned my head away when I got close so as not to seem rude, but today I rode directly down their dirt drive and skidded in front of the open front door. His mother, a large jovial woman with sun-damaged skin, pointed me toward the southern bay.

"He'll be down with his boat," she said.

"He's got a boat? I thought he was a grass cutter."

453

"Not much my Ed can't turn his hand to," she boasted.

Although there's probably some nautical expression for it, Ed's boat was parked on a grass bank about a kilometer down the bay from our place. The craft, a typical, modest five-meter squid boat was upside down on blocks. Ed was planing, or some such woodworking venture. His top was off, and the torso that I'd imagined being ribbed like plates on a rack was, in fact, all muscle. Don't get me wrong. He wasn't steak. He was skinny but not bony. The silvery sweat clung to him like dew on a gristly vine. I threw down the bicycle and paced to the boat. He ignored me. I knocked loudly on the far side of the hull. He looked up and had the audacity to smile at me. I put my hands on my waist.

"I have come to tell you that I do not appreciate being lied to," I said.

"You don't?"

"No."

"OK."

I think he was about to return to his planing.

"And you lied to me," I said. "You told me you had a sister who didn't like the company of men."

"I know."

"But you don't."

"Nope."

"So why did you tell me you did?"

"Because you were rude."

I was stunned.

"Ha. So, how was I rude, exactly?"

"When someone comes to visit down here, you don't treat them like a servant. You don't keep them waiting or snap at them. You show manners."

"Is that right?"

"Yes."

"Well, excuse me for not knowing I was in the good manners capital of the country."

"Thank you."

"Thank . . . ? What for?"

"Your apology."

"I did not . . . I . . ." I could feel my aplomb slipping. "And, while we're on the subject, don't you think you might be considered rude in some circles for making fun of lesbians?"

"No. I don't know any lesbians."

"Really?"

"Hmm."

"Why on earth would one who wasn't one, pretend to be . . . one?"

"To keep men off."

"Is that so?"

"Hmm."

I was tangled in a net I hadn't seen myself stepping into. I suddenly wished his boat had been seaworthy and that he'd been out ahoying in the depths of the Gulf. Then I might have had more time to compose myself. I could have jousted with him with the cool head of a seasoned journalist. Instead I said, "I hate you, Ed." And he repulsed my thrust with a gorgeous smile. I retreated to my bicycle and untangled it from the tall weeds. Once it was finally upright and I was ready to ride elegantly away, I looked back at him. He was leaning against the naked wood of the boat watching me.

"One last question," I said.

"Shoot."

"Why did you really come to see me that day?"

"I was going to tell you I like the way you look. I was planning to invite you for lunch."

"Ha!" I said, pedaling frantically to get up the grass slope without having to dismount. "Little chance of that."

A victory, at last. I had swung Narsil, the sword of Aragon, one last time and wounded the beast in the heart. Yet, when I looked at the blade, the blood I saw there was all mine.

"Rarely is the question asked: Is our children learning?"
— GEORGE W. BUSH, FLORENCE, SOUTH CAROLINA, JANUARY 11, 2000

Three weeks had passed. The deckchair insurgents were repainting and decorating Government House in sunshine and mimosa tones. They'd planted rice in the ornamental ponds. They were not fooled by the subterfuge of replacing the drinking buddy of the wicked satellite dish czar with the czar's brother-in-law. So they dug themselves in and began evening classes in the art of producing Ping-Pong ball smoke bombs. The country trembled at their awesome power.

The monsoons weren't far away, but nobody knew when they'd arrive. Captain Kow said the locals could no longer predict the weather. He said there'd been a time when every fisherman could read the signs: when the crabs left the sand, how high the beetles built their nests on the trees, when the terns migrated. But now they'd all listen to the radio like the city folk. The world was messed up. And if there were storms coming, the sea wasn't giving anything away. It was almost impossible that such a vast body of water could be so polite. I could hear the hushed whispers of the embarrassed tide arriving and departing on the fine gravel. "I'm here, shhh." "No, I'm over here, shhh." Then a long empty pause before the next whispers. I admired the vastness of the scene all around me and remained in awe that I could make out the join where sea met sky. You never actually saw the horizon in Chiang Mai. You thought you did, then one day the dirty air would clear and there'd be a hulking great range of mountains looming up in front of you. But in Maprao with the Gulf stretching deceptively away from you, you knew that line — the one you had to stretch your neck to see all of, left and right — that was the edge of the world. You could sit on your back balcony and watch a hurricane pass over Cambodia, see giant cruise ships shrivel to nothing, view the creamy pink sunrise a whole continent away.

Something had changed inside me. I

began to understand why everyone within a twenty-kilometer radius was an idiot. It was for the same reason that you could live in a condominium room for years and not know that your next door neighbor was stacking body parts in his refrigerator. Ignorance breeds ignorance. If you want the world to be as narrow as your mind, you can make it so. I'd assumed I was superior to everyone in Maprao so I hadn't seen a need to confirm my status by actually talking to people. The odd thing was, once you got to know them you realized there was more common sense around you than in a whole city full of educated but suffocating people. Certainly more than in a barrel-load of monkey politicians. Living their lives wasn't desperation for the Mapraoans, it was a sensible choice for a very proud people.

I was a celebrity for a while. We had three national TV stations down here interviewing me about my role in solving the abbot's killing. The event might have slipped by unnoticed but for the bizarre demise of Mika Mikata. The self-filmed video of her suicide was on automatic feed to her Web site, and its popularity on YouTube was unprecedented. Mikata had no intention of being taken alive. With her chest-mounted cameras and her spectacular orange hat, she was dispatched by jet-propelled hangglider to the top platform of the Tokyo Tower, the world's tallest orange structure. There, she gave a heartrending but virtually incomprehensible speech and flung herself over the parapet. Viewers were able to make out the strains of "Killing Me Softly," in Japanese, as she somersaulted through the air. But, as both the still and video cameras were destroyed as she bounced off the overhanging observation deck, her actual death was not recorded, which would have been a major disappointment to her fans. However, live coverage or not, Mika Mikata's death had been as colorful as her murders.

My articles on the investigation and subsequent discovery of the killer were very well received. I even had a spread in *Matichon Weekly* magazine. I had offers of full-time positions I would have been a fool to pass up. I received personal calls from managing editors at newspapers that made the *Mail* look like a rag. Oh, I considered them. I had sleepless nights. On numerous occasions, I dialed all but the last digit of their phone numbers. But . . . well, we had a business to run. Our sleeping province, momentarily awoken with a kiss from the angel of death, had decided to press the snooze button and go back to sleep again. I spent less time scouring the newspapers and more time gutting mackerel. With the absence of intrigue, I was able to put more time and effort into our resort. The shop attendance had rocketed to an average of seven customers per day. With Gaew's help, Arny had almost doubled the room occupancy from one per five-day period to one-point-seven by the simple addition of a sign: LAST BED AND FOOD FOR 100 KMS. It wasn't exactly true, or rather it was an outright lie, but any travelers silly enough to find themselves on these back roads late at night were unlikely to sue us later. Arny had also written to Lonely Planet for inclusion in their 2010 edition. It was a bit like me writing to Mr. Pulitzer asking if I might put my name on his list, but I admired my brother's spirit.

And me? I cooked. I began what one day might be called a garden. And I fed the dogs. Yes, that was a plural. Sticky Rice pulled through. He woke up one day like a born-again canine with the kick of a small cow and has hardly dared to go back into that sleep world since. I assume my ankle was the first thing he saw when he came around because he follows it so closely I have to wipe snot off my leg after each trip through the yard. It's rather pathetic but endearing and, I confess, I might have found myself cuddling him from time to time but only while he's in rehab. Gogo continues to glare at me with disdain and maintains her orbit.

What else have I been doing? Nothing, I suppose. Oh, yes. I did come up with a solution for the mystery of the interred VW. The world would never hear of it and the story didn't even warrant a follow-up in *Thai Rat*. Readers have short attention spans and the effort of retelling the tale was beyond the editors. But my inner diva has started to write it into a screenplay for Clint. It'll be a sensation. Although the police had given up on the case, I was determined to keep it alive. I'd done all the flow charts and brainstorms and reviewed all the evidence and I found myself up against a brick wall. There was only one thing I knew for sure: that the couple in the interred VW were not the couple who had been asked to give evidence against *Tan* Sugit. There was, however, a very impressive list of things I didn't know. I didn't know where the first VW had disappeared to after its brief stay in the police parking lot, who rented the second VW and where they went, how evil Auntie Chainawat was involved and why she sold that strip of land to Old Mel, how the

VW got itself buried, or anything else. Because, to tell the truth, at that stage I knew nothing. I can't say it didn't worry me but I'd literally run out of avenues to pursue. Sissi had searched the Internet and delved into the private briefs of one or two senior policemen but she'd come up with nothing relevant. I could have left it there, I suppose, but for the memory of the driver and his girlfriend sitting calmly in their seats. There were families somewhere ever wondering what had become of their loved ones. What about their spirits? I know. It doesn't sound like me, does it? But all that hanging around in temples . . . well, something has to rub off.

One annoying phrase that kept replaying in my mind was what the old Chinese lady had said the day I asked her why she'd sold her land. Even after I edited her bad Thai in my mind, it still sounded like a second-rate martial-arts movie line: "People who connect the past and the future may know the present." I'd thought about heading back over to Ranong and beating the meaning out of her with a baseball bat, but that was on one of our very rare red meat days.

So, I began with the past. What I knew already was that, before the bridge was built across the neck of the estuary, all the land around here had been underdeveloped. Before the prawn farms there were still mangroves and much of the landscape was still covered in a thick layer of natural vegetation. Huge tracts of land were bought up by local Chinese speculators who waited for the inevitable march of time. There were no paved roads and the only settlements were to be found on the coast. The coconut and palm plantations had yet to arrive. When they did, Old Mel was one of the pioneers and I needed to imagine what the countryside was like when his family moved in.

The land office was one of a huddle of simple government buildings around the Lang Suan stadium (capacity twelve thousand — mostly standing). The office was another bruised edifice that begged not to be painted white again. Anyone could stroll up to the second floor and take a look at the square-meter plans that sketched out the allotments and their boundaries. The two plots I was searching for were clearly marked with the current borders. I could see how they fitted into the overall landgrab mosaic. If I'd so wished, I could have asked for the names of any of the neighboring owners and been given contact details. The land department did all it could to encourage the sale and resale of its dirt.

In a back room were large cardboard rolls that contained older and older versions of these plans. By digging deep, I made my way to 1980 where I found the land before its sale by the Chainawats, separated at the original border. There were two interesting differences in the surrounding plots. One was that the parcels were very much larger. The land demons hadn't yet begun to slice and dice their plots and sell them at extortionate prices. Two was the anomaly that almost all of the land divisions had remained faithful to one long continuous border, as if someone had drawn a random uneven line across the map and told everyone they were to keep to one side of it or the other. I asked the clerk why this was but she was young and more interested in her fingernails. She suggested I take a look at the geological maps of the region.

My quest led me to Professor Woot Juntasa at the department of geology of Mae Jo University. This was a pretty but minor campus of the mother Mae Jo in Chiang Mai and whenever I'd passed by, it had always seemed to be unoccupied. The day of my visit was no exception. I walked from building to building looking for somebody to guide me to the professor's study. The first human I found was the portly professor himself. His face was a shiny red mask that hinted at either too much field work in the midday sun or eczema. Either way I got the feeling he would have been happier at a campus in Scandinavia. Even under the full Finnish blast from his air-conditioning, his armpits were still forging through some tropical jungle. His eyebrows were too high on his forehead and it made all his expressions ones of surprise.

He seemed truly delighted to have something to do of more substance than teaching soil erosion to bored undergraduates. I told him about the region I was interested in and he smiled that knowing smile of an expert. He told me that not only did he have large-scale area maps of the Lang Suan river basin, he also had aerial photographs that I might find amusing. He launched off into a description of the region from the Paleolithic period and we retired to a small meeting room where he spread his maps out across the table.

"Perhaps you could point out exactly the terrain you're interested in?" he said.

It wasn't so easy without the labeled plot boundaries, but I was able to locate Old Mel's land from the bend in the river and the relief lines of the *Wat* Ny Kow cliffs.

Professor Woot laid a sheet of clear plastic over the map and I used a whiteboard pen to give an approximation of the two plots.

"Aha!" he said. It was that Sherlock Holmes moment when all becomes clear. "You know? This is a truly fascinating area. For the longest time, most of it was *nong nam,* a type of marshland. Water seeped into it from the river in the rainy season, so for three months a year it was bog. The reason the plots you mention have a regimented common border is that there was once a channel running through it known as a distributary, an offshoot of the main river."

He led me to the government survey photographs.

"These," he said, "were taken in early nineteen sixty. Here, you can clearly see the stream cutting through what was then largely wilderness. It was when this branch of the Lang Suan River overflowed that the land all around here flooded."

"Then how does an entire stream disappear?" I asked.

"Sometimes it's natural due to erosion," he said. "But in the case of the Lang Suan, it was a result of dredging. The larger fishing companies wanted to transport their catch directly to Lang Suan city so it could be shipped faster to Bangkok. The sand and silt they dug up was dumped along the banks. There was no accountability. If enough money changes hands you can get away with any amount of abuse of the environment. And matters haven't improved, I'm sad to say."

"So the silt blocked the mouth of the branch stream?"

"Exactly. It dried up."

"And suddenly all that ex-bog land increased in value."

"Right again. And I doubt that was unplanned. A little bit of pre-knowledge and the buying up of marshland for almost nothing."

This didn't make sense.

"But there is no dried stream bed between the two plots of land I'm referring to," I said.

"Of course not. Not now. Not since the storm surge of seventy-eight."

"What's a storm surge?"

"It's a sort of underwater mini tsunami that arrives with a storm. But rather than materializing as a huge wave above the water, it's actually a force that pushes up from the sea shelf as it arrives at the coast. Some surges can cause the tide to rise three meters or more. The water level rises gradually but dramatically. During the surge of seventy-eight the sea level was above that of the river for a long period. The water flowing down the river was confronted by the sea attempting to go the opposite way. There was terrible flooding and a maelstrom of mud and debris. Up in Lang Suan many people lost their homes and many were washed away in the flooding. The surge lasted for no longer than an hour but two hundred and sixty hectares were inundated.

"There was a national outcry as there always is. Once the river ran low the land barons put pressure on the authorities to conduct a new dredging and reinforce the banks. They commissioned engineers to ensure that the freak conditions of seventy-eight wouldn't affect their investments again. By the time the new levee was created and the land dried out, the old stream had disappeared completely, filled in by the mud and the silt."

So, the land Chainawat sold to Old Mel had once been the bed of a stream that had branched out from the Lang Suan River. But what advantage would there be in selling it to him? The answer to that also came from my ruddy professor.

"Every year during the monsoons Lang Suan floods," he said. "No matter what precautions they take, concrete banks, overflow tanks . . . none of it works. And the simple reason is that the river takes too long to find its way to the sea. In two thousand and two a proposal was put forward to dig a distributary to relieve the pressure on the main river and allow it to drain faster. The geological researchers discovered that there was a natural course which was the cheapest and most logical outlet: the stream running behind your *Koon* Mel's plantation. Landowners had appropriated the river land illegally. There would be no recourse for compensation."

I smiled and rolled back on my secretary chair. The cunning old witch. Granny Chainawat had somehow acquired a copy of the engineering report and knew there was every possibility she'd have a canal cut through the rear of her land. Before the announcement was made, she'd sold it. Three hectares of land from a cache of fourteen thousand. How tight-arsed can you get?

There wasn't a fleet of VW Kombis in the south of Thailand in 1978; in fact there may have been just the two. One, that driven by Sugit's hippy daughter, vanished in the south. The other? Well, as far as we know, the other was rented by the dead couple. I'd never be able to prove it but I had my theory as to what happened to those flower children. They were as happy with the Kombi as two bees in a sugared almond box. They were driving their prize north for the handover as they'd done a few times before. But this was different. This was free and easy lifestyle driving. They were young, in search of experiences, beauty, love. Looking for the wildness that they were sure lay in their souls. They'd kept to the coast road on their drive north to avoid police checkpoints on the highway. They'd missed the turnoff at La Mae and the paved roads turned into slithery clay. They should have turned back but the views were dramatic in the storms. Their hearts were thumping with exhilaration. This was excitement for two kids from the city who'd lived all their thrills through movies. The clay turned to deep mud and rock and there was no way they could cross the Lang Suan this close to the estuary. They turned back inland and decided to stop, wait it out, ride the storms.

I'd pump it up in the screenplay and put in a few gritty moments for Eastwood, but this is the way it played in my mind:

EXT. DIRT ROAD — DAY

PIP and DOOM are in the front seats of a VW Kombi driving into another deluge. The wipers can barely compete. The road is as wild as the choppy sea but they seem oblivious to the conditions. Doom has her hand on her man's thigh as he drives and they smile as the big tin beast crashes through each wall of water. She giggles nervously. The wheels spin and slither and they lurch from side to side. Then, suddenly, they arrive at the bank of a ferocious river and skid to a dramatic halt centimeters before dropping off the bank.

FADE TO EXT. MID RIVER — LATER

We focus on a colorful carved wooden rocking horse that is being buffeted along on the river current like a raft on a rapid. We think it can never stay afloat on the torrent as it bucks and dips below the surface but the horse's head returns to the surface. Then, something bewildering happens. The water in the river, once raging, first slows, and then stops flowing. For a few tense seconds, the horse floats in an impossible void as calm as a puddle. In the distance, on the bank of the river, is the VW van. The rain has stopped and the setting sun has found a crack in the clouds and is bathing the scene in a surreal orange glow. And the wooden horse, which had been slowly circling, suddenly begins to float back in the direction from which it had come. And the river water level rapidly climbs the bank like a timelapse film of tides. But the couple in the VW is oblivious to all this. All is calm now. They are smoking ganja and staring in awe at the sun's marvelous color show. Our soundtrack is Blind Faith's "Can't Find My Way Home" and it plays throughout. It plays as the riverbank crumbles and the conflicting currents begin their battle midstream. The river becomes a cauldron of threatening debris. The disaster is sudden and dramatic. The riverbank is swept away at its most vulnerable point like a sand wall. The VW lurches and drops suddenly into a deluge of water that bursts through the bank upon which they're parked. Fear on the faces of our protagonists turns to excitement as the van stays upright and is washed at speed away from the river. They struggle to attach their seat belts. Dipping and turning. Pip and Doom ride it like passengers on a funfair attraction, screaming with excitement and terror.

The ultimate trip. The van comes to a sudden, jarred halt. They're under water but the water level inside has only reached their waists. They're safe. We see their look of relief and completeness. Doom reaches to release her seat belt but there's a long groaning metallic creak all around them and the sliding door is popped off its rail by the pressure of the outside water. In under a second the van is full and we know the couple won't be seeing any more sunsets.

FADE TO EXT. MID RIVER — LATER

We are under water approaching the van from the outside. The torrent has passed and through the windscreen we see Doom and Pip still in their seats with a surprising expression of tranquility on their faces.

END

OK, we can work on the ending, but you get the point.

ACKNOWLEDGMENTS

A lot of people helped me put this story together, most without realizing it. But for their considerable patience in coaxing me through the Southern Thai dialect, I would especially like to thank Gai, Ja Dum, Jimm, Diw, Kow, Su, Gop, Dr. Bounleut, and Aung. For their cruel comments and invaluable advice I wish to acknowledge my old faithful reading disciples, especially David, Lizzie, Kye, Kay, Janet, John Cotterill, and my indispensable Jess. And, before I go, I have been asked by the officers of the Pak Nam police station to point out that there are absolutely no homosexuals, latent or practicing, employed in that establishment. I hope that's perfectly clear.